COBALT

A MAX FEND THRILLER

CHRIS BAUER

SEVERN RIVER PUBLISHING

Severn River Publishing
severnriverbooks.com

This is a work of fiction. Names, characters, businesses, places, events and incidents are either the products of the author's imagination or used in a fictitious manner. Any resemblance to actual persons, living or dead, or actual events is purely coincidental.

ISBN: 978-1-64875-496-8 (Paperback)

ALSO BY CHRIS BAUER

<u>Blessid Trauma Crime Scene Cleaners</u>

Hiding Among the Dead

Zero Island

2 Street

<u>The Maximum Risk Series</u>

Cobalt

Cradle

<u>Standalones</u>

Scars on the Face of God

Binge Killer

Jane's Baby

<u>with Andrew Watts</u>

Air Race

Never miss a new release! Sign up to receive exclusive updates from author Chris Bauer.

severnriverbooks.com

To Jennifer and Jillian:
May your children make you as proud
as you have made me

"Nature bats last."
—Robert Michael Pyle, naturalist

1

March 20
Nesquehoning, in the Pennsylvania Pocono Mountains, USA
Katanga, The Democratic Republic of the Congo, the African Continent

Wyatt Springer, age nine, bounded out the door onto the patch of worn wooden deck attached to their small prefab home. Mr. Rogers's "Won't You Be My Neighbor" slipped through his closed lips on repeat, part hum, part sing, an earworm fresh from a Saturday morning PBS session on TV. Wyatt's mother, Myrna, eyed him from inside their home, her hands in the kitchen's hot spigot water, scrubbing a frying pan. Wyatt needed a haircut, but she was reluctant to take the clippers to him. His was the straightest black hair she'd ever seen, even compared to hers, now with gathered gray streaks from her crown to her shoulders, premature for a thirty-seven-year-old. Her hair length and its color were affectations rooted in her discovery of Buffy Sainte-Marie, a Canadian Piapot Cree folksinger and activist, later in Buffy's life, early in Myrna's. A beautiful and affirming Indigenous thing. Wyatt swept his mop from his face then used his arm to sweep the melting snow off the hinged top of a molded plastic box on the deck, home to his sports equipment and outdoor toys, all protected from the cold Pocono winter.

"You need gloves," Myrna called out the open door.

"No, Momma, it's warm out here in the fog."

"They're not for the cold, honey," she said, and she appeared at the door to hand him a pair of the cheap, one-size-fits-all plastic slip-ons that were available for free when pumping gas at their local generic gas station. Free was good for people of their economic persuasion. "Here, put them on."

"Yes, Momma."

A small aircraft with an unintimidating engine putt-putted the air above them, all noise, no visual, the fog hiding it while it dopplered past. Myrna looked up on reflex, squinting as she followed the sound. Whatever it was, the Pocono skies had been busy lately, seemingly 24/7, with aircraft small and large, fixed wing and rotary.

But that putt-putting engine . . .

It stuck with her, sickened her, made her gag a little. She shook off the discomfort and went back to listening to a podcast on her phone by an Indigenous social influencer. There weren't many Indigenous podcasters. That was why she listened.

Wyatt opened the toy box and rested the heavy plastic lid against the top of his head while he looked inside. He fished through the contents: a soccer ball, a football, and a basketball, all needing air; a Frisbee with bite marks; cornhole sacks; one worn baseball; and two baseball gloves, for when Myrna played catch with him, which was what a good single mom did with her only child.

The bottom of the box gave up what he was after: a red plastic beach bucket with a square yellow face on its side, plus a matching yellow sand shovel.

"Sorry, SpongeBob," he said, admiring the cartoon, "but Little Pig's dogcrap won't pick itself up."

"Wyatt," Myrna called. "I heard that. Language, young man."

"Sorry, Momma." He pulled on the gas mitts.

On cue, their potbellied black and brown female terrier mix, Little Pig, minus one rear leg, dropped onto the deck from inside the kitchen then hopped down the steps. The fat little terrier was ancient, older than Wyatt by six years, maybe more. Little Pig took her time hopping onto the grass, sniffing at what were probably rabbit smells, then she scooted to a far corner of their fenced backyard where she relieved herself fore and aft.

"Eww, Pig. I'm gonna leave that one till last," Wyatt said. "Yuck."

————

The sun was low on the horizon. Ten-year-old Dieu-Dieu Ngoma left his family's tent and grabbed the handle of a rusty American-made children's wagon. His shovel, plus a dented aluminum bucket, trowel, and Velcro headband with a built-in forehead lamp all rattled inside the payload, the wagon bouncing next to him while he descended the hill toward the mine, or rather the hole that led into the mine. *Their* hole, an artisanal thing, which meant they were on their own without safety protocols, his family's personal entry to the copper-cobalt slags inside an existing tunnel close to the tent they called home. Dieu-Dieu mumbled a children's song in French, a popular one that all children his age sang on their way home from their digs, rarely on their way to them. Leaving work at nightfall was a joyful time; heading to work in the afternoon was not. Wishful thinking on his part, wanting today's digging to be over before it had even started.

Dieu-Dieu reached the hole and parked his wagon next to it, only a few hundred paces away from their tent. He tossed his bucket with the shovel and trowel inside it into the crevasse in the rocky hill. A tinny *clang* echoed when the tools hit bottom, a small puff of blue-gray dust rising out of the dirt from the disturbance the bucket made when it landed. Seeing the dust puff, Dieu-Dieu frowned.

"*C'est l'bordel*," he said under his breath.

French profanity. Today's shift, because of the dust, would be as messy as a bordello.

None of the artisanal digs were vented other than the holes and tunnels the families had dug for themselves. A known hazard because of the cobalt dust the digs too frequently created. He put on a dust mask from his pocket, slipped on his headband, and shimmied into the gash in the ground. He climbed down fifteen feet, where he switched on his headband light. Pock-marks surrounded him, in the walls, overhead, and on the floor, and a labyrinth of jagged gashes barely qualifying as tunnels reached into the poorly lit distance. An underground moonscape. He retrieved his tools and rose to his full height.

"*Allez au boulot,*" he told himself. *Get to work.*

He worked near the Kytoons Copper-Cobalt Mine, a surface dig located in Katanga, the Democratic Republic of the Congo, in an artisanal offshoot of the mine. The commercial tunnels and digs were run by the Chinese, but the tunnels had, as tributaries, hundreds of family artisanal entries in the general area. It was the wild, wild west of cobalt extraction. No controls, no rules, no safeguards. His parents condoned his efforts because of what they produced: copper and cobalt in whatever amount a family could extract on its own, below the radar. His father worked his hours legally for the Chinese companies seven days a week while Dieu-Dieu and the other children would dig what they could, for as long as they could, after school, in the afternoons and the evenings, often for little more than pennies a day on the black market.

"The cobalt helps the automobiles run without gas," his mother once explained to him in French. Its role in rechargeable lithium-ion batteries was to greatly increase the speed of the ions passing back and forth, which lowered battery charge time, a key to increasing the adoption of electric vehicles. Her one-sentence explanation when he was seven had short-handed the *why* for him.

Twenty minutes at a time underground was all Dieu-Dieu could handle. Oxygen was the biggest issue; there wasn't enough of it. There was also the threat of cave-ins. And sometimes, Dieu-Dieu knew, there were explosions coming from the cobalt dust, which was highly combustible. He strode a few feet, arriving at the slag of dirt and rock he'd gathered into a pile yesterday before he'd left. His first smile of the afternoon emerged. The slag pile had settled, showing tiny clumps of a sparkling turquoise-green mineral in the reflected light: cobalt flakes, hundreds of millions of years in the making, originating from salt-laden fluids carried by shallow, long ago seas containing metals that, over the ages, had mineralized the sediment.

"*Le gros lot,*" he said to himself.

The jackpot.

Paydirt.

Wyatt filled his beach bucket a third time, a winter's worth of backyard dog feces nearing resolution on this, the first day of spring. Three dollars of paydirt, that's what this task was worth to him so far, because his mom had promised him a dollar a bucket. The surface frost had gone but the poop was still frozen in spots around the backyard grass that had started to green up. It made picking up the poop easy, either by hand with the slip-on glove or with an artistic flick of the plastic shovel with his wrist. Pick or flick, he'd made a game of loading up the bucket. He'd avoided Little Pig's recent deposit, a sloppy mess he wanted nothing to do with, but he could avoid it no longer.

He approached the pile. A call from their neighbor whose property abutted theirs, side yard to side yard, distracted him, giving him a momentary reprieve. Their twenty-acre parcels ended in the forested portion of a mountain along the same property line nearly surrounded by preserved state game land. The neighbor was tending his flower garden.

"Good Saturday morning to you, young man, on this foggy spring equinox. The fog will burn off, and today will be excellent. Enjoy it, bud."

"Hi, Uncle Jesse! I sure do hope so, sir."

"Little Pig has been busy, I see. Stay the course, Wyatt. And remember to always mind your mom."

"Yes, sir. I will, sir."

Wyatt was responsible for picking up Little Pig's poo in the backyard only, not anywhere else on the property, even though the little terrier sometimes slipped through the fencing to sniff out rabbits on Uncle Jesse's land. Wyatt held his breath and leaned over, about to dig into Little Pig's great big slab o' poo. He tripped on something dark and brown poking through grass, still wet with melting snow. He crammed his shovel into dirt, found an edge to the hardened poo and leveraged it, liberating a large, dark chocolate brick with tiny flecks of green and silver-gray decorating one side of it. He raised it to his nose and sniffed.

Not poop, just a rock that smelled musty. He turned it over in his hand to look at the other side.

The fog lifted, the sun burning a hole through the sky's low ceiling, a shaft of bright, heavenly light extending earthward, illuminating Wyatt's hand. On one side of the rock, the spritzes of green glinted in the sunlight. The other side was an iridescent bluish-green that ran the full length of the brick-shaped rock, concentrated nearly as tight as a coal vein.

He skipped back to their house, his long hair framing his face, leaving the poop bucket behind. He cradled his find in his arms like a running back with a football.

His mother would think this rock was beautiful.

Dieu-Dieu lifted the shovelful of brown dirt to his face, the tiniest of green-gray specks glinting in the dust swirling around his head, the dirt rich with cobalt crystals flecked also with nickel and copper. This was good; this was very good. But the dust that filled the air around his face was bad, very bad. Farther inside the rickety tunnel, picks and shovels fell again and again like triphammers, scraping at the wall at the end of the mine. The faint whirr of gas-powered handheld grinders settled over the whole of it, both distant and close. Other children and young Congolese men were at work expanding the tunnel, working nearest their own artisanal entrances to the mine, all breathing in the dust that now had Dieu-Dieu coughing and gagging and forcing himself to spit to clear his nose and throat. It was time to return above ground to take a breathing break. He grabbed his aluminum bucket full of speckled turquoise dirt and started back toward the entry shaft when a large, dusty swirl enveloped him from behind. He quickly crabbed his way up the walls and emerged from the shaft.

He removed his mask to breathe in the clean air but it wasn't working, dust particles swirling out of the hole with him, puffing upward like a steam locomotive getting underway. He knew what this meant, knew something was wrong underground, knew he needed distance from the mine, and fast. He stumbled as he ran, coughing, weaving, then he dropped his bucket, its spilled contents glinting in the merciless evening sun.

His mother was leaving their tent, a basket of laundry balanced on her head. Her smile at him disappeared, alarm replacing it.

The grey-blue cobalt dust releasing from the hole in the ground behind him puffed again, and again—*poof, poof, poof.* He pumped his arms and legs faster.

"*Court, mon fils, court!*"

"Run, my son, run!"

"It's very pretty, Wyatt, just—really beautiful."

Myrna held the rock block with its musty smell and its large dose of mineral ore up to the light above the kitchen sink. Flecks of moist dirt flaked off, dropping into the running water.

Her house was one of two prefabs, hers and her brother-in-law Jesse's, that sat next to each other on twenty acres of property each, not far from Jim Thorpe, Pennsylvania, the "gateway to the Poconos." Both were flat properties near the road, but about five acres deep they sloped upward to become an oak forest, and they fanned out as they turned into the rocky front end of one of the mountains. The land was a blessing from her marriage, but it was also a curse. Her property had been mortgaged, then remortgaged, then remortgaged again. It was all she could do to keep up with the payments now that her husband, Jesse's brother, was gone. Most of the twenty acres were of questionable value beyond the house's backyard because of the nearby game lands, the steepness of the slope, and the deep woods portion that fronted the mountain, but Myrna liked the solitude.

"Sure is, Momma. You can have it. You can put it on the dresser in your room. Just look at it, Momma. It looks like kryptonite, doesn't it?"

It did, with a green tint and an underside metallic enough to mimic the fictional mineral from the Superman comics and movies. Her warm grin coalesced into a smooch that she planted on the top of her son's head.

"Too many superhero movies for you, sweetie. Tell you what. Thank you for giving it to me, but you should keep it. Finders keepers. It's all yours. It will look good on your desk, don't you think?"

"Okay, Momma! It'll look awesome next to my comics. I love you, Momma."

Dieu-Dieu's mother raced down the hill at her disoriented son, her face contorted knowing that this digging, this mine, the machinery underground, could make things so . . . volatile. But this was her ten-year-old son, a good, healthy, God-fearing young man, his future bright because of this new industry and what it was providing their family, the money their hard work was giving them, their hope for their country, helping them all to rise from the depths . . .

Dieu-Dieu would break the chains, would transcend the poverty, would go to university, would be a brilliant young man when he grew up, would make her so proud.

Boom.

The hillside exploded, jettisoning rock and sand and dirt and stone and bodies from the underground, the debris geysering skyward, twenty-five feet, fifty feet, a divot forming four stories deep and fifty yards wide, spreading, engulfing the hill in a pair of monstrous, earth-chewing, fire-breathing jaws. The trapdoor to hell had opened, spewing explosive dust and flames, the flailing Dieu-Dieu airborne then dropping headfirst into the crevasse that had given him up, his mother screaming to their god for mercy as the fire consumed his body.

2

Max was at the airport when the plane went down.

It could have happened anywhere in this country, and it often did. Over the last two decades, the DRC had averaged at least one or two air crashes per year. Max's infrastructure team had studied them all, the accidents, the near misses, the large-scale disasters, everything dating back as far as 1945. He'd also visited many of the country's airports. All part of the assignment.

Smoke billowed on the horizon a few miles from where they stood outside an airplane hangar. Max and his Congolese employee shielded their eyes from the sun, trying for a better look.

"I can take you there *tout de suite*, Monsieur Fend." Ex-military, ex-government, ex-commercial helicopter pilot, the contractor had been fully vetted like all other Fend Aerospace local employees.

"Thanks, but no, not now. We'll get a look at it, just not in person."

Max put his phone to his ear and spoke with urgency to someone inside the hangar.

"Manny . . . No, I didn't see it, I only see the smoke. Do this. Send out a drone. Something fast and not flashy. Stream the video output to my phone while it's recording. The crash site should be close enough to get a good transmission. I want to see—"

He swallowed hard, realizing how gruesome this video feedback would be, and how voyeuristic and detached this exchange made him sound. But they had to chase this down. Timing and proximity and opportunity all dictated it.

"Sorry, *want* is the wrong word. It's not because I want to. It's because we're able to video the crash site in real-time, so we should do it. Apologies beforehand if this ends up giving you nightmares."

While the drone became airborne, Max pulled up the flight information from the airport's private database. A Dornier 228 turboprop, capable of short takeoffs and landings, maximum weight 14,495 pounds. Takeoff weight for this flight, 14,402 pounds, close to the max. Operated by Bumble Bee Congo Airlines, a charter carrier. Pilot, copilot names. Now crashed and burning so soon after its takeoff from Goma. The pilot's mayday was immediate, the tower telling Max, "The plane failed to climb past electrical wires that crisscrossed a densely populated neighborhood."

Five minutes later, a Fend Aerospace drone hovered over the crash site and streamed its video to Max's phone.

Reminiscent of what Max had seen before. A crash in November 2019, fresh in his head because he'd just studied it. Same airport, same residential neighborhood, only a dozen or so buildings away from the first disaster. The number of casualties in this new one were pending, the fire still burning, although Max knew the aircraft type and its passenger and cargo capacity, so he could pretty much guess how bad the loss would be. The drone videoed a crowd of people on the ground trying to free whomever they could from inside the plane and the building it had struck. No audio. Those braving the flaming debris were heroes for risking their lives. There were passengers still strapped into seats, some upside-down, unconscious, semi-conscious, some flung about, some bloodied bodies and severed body parts splattered about the interior, and amid the debris . . .

All of them were burning, all were melting inside the flames.

"Anyone know what's in that building?" Max barked into his phone.

"A community center," Manny said. "It was holding religious services."

The 2019 Bumble Bee tragedy had left twenty-six dead, six of them on the ground, all from the same family, the aircraft destroying a few residences. Swap out homes, insert a community center filled with churchgoers —today's crash would be much worse in terms of the number dead.

This gig, this massive, long-term infrastructure endeavor that Fend Aerospace was spearheading here in the Congo, that of rebuilding airports and making air systems safer, gave Max great pride and great satisfaction. But it was always three steps forward, two steps back in this country, inclusive of the bribes involved. It was hard to tell if they were winning. Their perseverance was for the good of these people and for the good of the U.S., except Max needed no real prompting from his government. There was money in it, contracts worth billions, but more attractive was the feeling of major accomplishment if Fend Aerospace could pull this off. Upgrading the DRC's broken-down, sad excuse of an in-country aeronautics presence, its carriers banned from operating in the European Union because of safety and corruption concerns . . . if Fend Aerospace could turn the country into a safer, more predictable place to do air commerce, they could make the DRC an international player. After two years of planning upgrades and one year with him and Renee in-country so far, dealing with ancient fueling vehicles and jet fuel tanks, pockmarked runways, empty air traffic controller seats, and overwhelming statistics about metal fatigue in aging aircraft, Max was feeling the strain.

The drone cameras zoomed in, Max's phone capturing the livestream. Flaming aircraft parts, charred folding chairs inside the community center, and charred bodies in and around those folding chairs. Open, burning baggage pieces, duffel bags, carry-ons, a few large trunks. Then came the good news: Survivors were being dragged away from the wreckage. Two, three, five, until—

Boom. Max jumped.

Boom. BOOM.

The noise came from over the horizon a split second before the fire got a boost, visible on his phone screen, from explosions inside the blackened footprint left by the destroyed aircraft. More jet fuel on the ground? A fuel tank? Propane? The intensity of the blasts rocketed the drone skyward, almost knocking it out of the air. From inside the hangar, the drone pilot settled it back into a holding pattern above the scene, still videoing. The speck of another flying object came into camera view on the horizon: an approaching aircraft. The drone steadied, then zoomed in on it, giving the image of the aircraft more clarity.

Manny's voice on the phone. "Air ambulance, Max. Or it could be a military copter. We should probably—"

"Agreed, Manny. Reel her back in."

Max punched in a phone number and connected with a Goma International airport manager. He dispensed with the pleasantries, all business. "How many people onboard?"

The manager knew Max, knew what he and his American company meant to their airport, their air system, their infrastructure, and their country. "Fifteen passengers, two crew. Monsieur Fend, if you have a drone in the air, you must remove it. Airborne support is arriving momentarily to supplement the ground response. Please return it to the airport now."

"Will do."

Max tapped the phone video icon to return to the drone feed, still transmitting another pass over the site. This would need to be its last.

The camera stayed on the crash scene, a frenzied tableau of civilians sifting, clearing, dragging out baggage and burning bodies, and pulling at a smoking wreckage that needed no audio to grasp the horror on the screen. It panned to a corrugated wall of the single-story community center, the only section of the building still standing, the activity of the rescuers inside it frantic amid the smoke and flames and jagged metal. The drone moved to the wall's other side, the exterior, where there was no movement, no destruction, no flames, no death, only the outcome of it, pausing to capture the serenity of two long rows of bicycles in racks, waiting, Max surmised, for owners who would never return to them.

In their hotel room, the TV on in the background, Max leaned forward with his elbows on his knees. He held a beer bottle in both hands and was staring at the floor. Renee, on the sofa next to him, draped an arm around his shoulder and gripped his forearm in consolation.

"Our presence here is making a difference, Max."

"Forty-nine confirmed dead, Renee. The entire crew, all the passengers, and most of a church congregation. None of the people pulled from the wreckage lived. It almost doesn't matter what went wrong. Equipment error, pilot error, it doesn't matter. After a year here, it's still like whack-a-mole. The fires we're putting out—" He shook his head. "Poor choice of words."

"It does matter, Max, honey. Identifying each cause, wrestling it into submission. Over time—"

"We've already pumped a quarter of a billion dollars into modernizing these airports, Renee. Adding gates, rebuilding old ones, repairing the runways, updating technology. What we need to do almost immediately is help them relocate more of this airport's surrounding residential population, so when something does go down like this on takeoff or landing—"

"It's in the mix, Max. In the long-range plan. Expanding these airport footprints to create buffer zones will take a decade or more."

Too many instances like this one, in too many areas around the country. Small, fixed-wing aircraft losing two to five people, plus larger aircraft like these turboprops, plus jumbo jets with losses in the hundreds. Rotary-wing accidents as well. The per capita numbers from the Aviation Safety Network—numbers Max knew—showed that since 1945, the DRC had recorded the most passenger plane accidents in all of Africa. Primary factors were the terrain, the large size of the country, and weak regulations. Now that the DRC was experiencing unprecedented growth from its recent economic autonomy, derived from the country's coveted mineral deposits, it was like pouring gasoline on the fire.

Another fire reference. The free association was giving Max a headache. Appreciation of his beer bottle dissipated, morphing into an expectant plea to his girlfriend.

"Renee. The people in your security network, they need to be checking—"

"In due course, Max, maybe we'll go that way and put a microscope on this one. For now, the DRC agencies will go through their paces, will look at the cybersecurity aspects of it, just like the others, as part of their checklist."

No point in engaging outside help yet. Renee's clandestine network, with superlative investigative hacking skills, could wait. Too many natural causes to analyze.

"The infrastructure needs here, Renee—they're overwhelming. This is demoralizing."

Which was the reason the DRC government had cut deals with the highest bidders for building its country. A third-world nation looking to grow into a major player in the clean energy market—*the* major player— derived from one economic reality: They had access to over fifty percent of known cobalt mineral deposits the world over, which could provide seventy percent of its production, and they'd sold the extraction rights for all of it to the People's Republic of China. Exclusive access. A resource-for-infrastructure deal. Smart move, but they'd picked the wrong country as a partner.

Part of the deal was an agreement that there'd be no political interference by China in their state, no demands to better their human rights practices, no expectations for minimum working conditions. No transparency regarding corrupt government politicians. These had never been strengths for the Chinese, so from China's perspective, their demands were no problem.

Why was it, then, that Fend Aerospace was here, working in this space? Max had asked himself this more than once. The answer was that the DRC was being smart by hedging its bets. The country was spoon-feeding the world's superpowers, dangling carrots to leverage its relationships.

One relationship, completely organic and outside the country's governmental influence, stood out among the others.

"I'm having trouble living up to my father's promises to her," Max said.

The "her" in question was a London-based political activist. A British Congolese woman named Vanda Dorleac. Max's father, Charles, the aerospace pioneer and founder of Fend Aerospace, had been quite fond of her, and mourned her deeply after she died in a Congolese prison, jailed after a protest over human rights violations. Her political *cause célèbre* had been child abuse in the DRC mining industry. Thirty percent of its cobalt extraction came from artisanal mining, with the poorest of the Congolese using all labor available in their families, children included, all of them *creuseurs*, or diggers, and the government looking the other way much too often.

"Your father is still a visionary, Max. A persistent do-gooder."

"Yes. And he was in love."

Theirs had been a very private relationship, Charles Fend and Ms. Dorleac, yet it produced a public outcome: a promise from Max's American billionaire father that he would help raise the country from the depths of poverty by doing what Fend Aerospace could do within its expertise, which was to spearhead the country's airport expansion.

That promise wasn't the only impetus for Max's participation. There was too much DRC political and industrial corruption to ignore. Too much on the line economically. Too much China. Which prompted one other relationship to come calling, because work like this could not be performed in a vacuum. The CIA. Max's country needed him yet again. Needed the two of them, him and Renee LeFrancois, inclusive of her dual Canadian-American citizenship, her French language skills, her clearances, and her cybersecurity capabilities. Inclusive also of an hourglass figure above runner's legs, with high cheekbones and a dark pixie cut.

"Are we done whining, then?" Renee said. "Tomorrow's another day and all that, and maybe we just go get some dinner?"

"Look, I know there's a good Fend team in place here, working all the angles. Better training, better equipment, better technical support, with so much more on the drawing board. Our people, the locals, both governments, it's starting to come together."

"So it's a yes to the 'we're done whining' question, then?"

"Fine. Yes. I'm taking a shower."

Their work—this project—was a tangent. It was fulfilling his father's promise, sure, and it provided goodwill. But largest on the radar, the behind-the-scenes elephant in the room, was the issue of controlling the DRC cobalt markets, controlling global cobalt output, because of the importance the mineral had to the provision of climate-friendlier energy worldwide. China had the upper hand, a stranglehold on seventy-plus percent of lithium battery production around the globe, impacting the supply chain for cars, phones, and laptops. Most of the world's commercial enterprises now needed to go through the Republic of China to acquire these goods. The U.S. viewed this as dangerous to the free world. Which meant a benevolent U.S., acting wherever it could to help with infrastructure needs, might eventually cause the DRC to rethink its approach. Maybe redistribute mineral rights among other countries, and in so doing, rethink the all-hands, children-included approach, one that ignored human rights abuses, to getting the cobalt out of the ground.

"Max," Renee called to him in the bathroom. "Something in here you should see right now."

A news report on the TV by a French-speaking Congolese journalist. Max stood behind Renee in his briefs and a T-shirt, watching.

Video footage broadcasting from a remote DRC location cut into the breaking news report on the plane crash in Goma. Multiple emergency vehicles flashing red and white lights were poised at the base of a mountain ridge awaiting people on foot to descend it. Prospective injured parties, some on stretchers, some leaning against others, some walking under their own power. The banner at screen bottom scrolled past—

Renee began translating the spoken French. "In Katanga. Near one of the cobalt and copper mines . . ."

The footage was riveting in its horror, Max watching it alongside Renee now, both leaning closer to the TV in their four-room hotel suite near Goma International. The images were raw, uncensored. Men ran from an explosion in an artisanal mine, people falling, trampling one another, including children. Gruesome, horrible pictures and video, some of it coming from phone footage cued up one after another by the journalist's newsroom, and some from the shaky hands of the locals, gathered from hashtags on the social media feeds, all chronicling a massive explosion.

"*Le cobalt*," the male reporter said. "*La poudre de cobalt, provoquant l'explosion d'une mine.*"

"Cobalt powder," Renee said, translating. "It caused a mine to explode."

Aside from frequent cave-ins, the cobalt contained inside the mineral deposits in the mines was stable, not explosive. But if processed inside the tunnels after its removal from a mine, or anywhere where more primitive, abrasive machinery was used to extract it, the reporter explained, cobalt dust, a reactive element, would be created. When agitated and left exposed to the air, and any minor ignition source, the powder could catch fire and burn, even explode, making these tunnels and mining environments, if not properly vented—and not many were—extremely volatile. Max absorbed the key figures.

Number of people dead: fourteen. The number of children—

"*Dix enfants*," said the reporter. Ten.

The reporter interviewed a distraught woman, a mother, who explained in French what she had seen, the loss she'd witnessed. The camera panned below this woman's inconsolable face to what she held in her arms, Renee translating. In the most gruesome on-location news footage Max had ever seen make it to a television screen, there was her young son, or what was left of him, which was only his upper half. A TV image with staying power.

"I'm skipping dinner," he said. He'd lost his appetite.

3

Phone calls at three fifty-two a.m. were always the best.

Max dropped his hand on the nightstand, picked up his ringing phone, and squinted. He read the name and grumbled an obscenity. The phone went back on the nightstand unanswered, he might have even slammed it, the ringer now silenced.

"Who," Renee managed, eyes closed, her head buried in her pillow.

"Wilkes."

The phone wasn't done. It buzzed this time, continued buzzing, dancing like a chicken on a hot plate, then it stopped. Next up was Renee's phone, different nightstand, no ring, buzz-buzz-buzz, buzzing until it didn't. Another try at Max's phone, a tiny jolt this time. A text, which meant Wilkes had taken the hint.

Quiet in their room. All was under control. Back to sleep.

Max's eyes flashed open. He reached for his phone.

The text from Wilkes could wait. Something else had shredded his cobwebs: the drone videos from the plane crash. The giant blast.

Phone in hand, he skimmed the footage, stopped it a few times, then backed it up to watch one part again, but this time in slow motion.

He slowed it down as far as he could, slower, slower . . . and then he paused.

There—that soft-sided, barrel duffel bag lying next to a seat that contained parts of a charred human being draped across it, plus a second barrel duffel bag nearby in the debris, and a third, all similar. What was in them?

He restarted the footage. The all-consuming fire crept across one of the bags, turning its dark blue composition black. A hole in the fabric opened, exposing its contents. A spray of dust puffed out, rising toward the hovering drone's camera, spreading, flames from the burning jet fuel licking at its formless edges until—

Boom. Boom. BOOM.

A mini chain reaction. It blasted the drone skyward, the camera footage shaking, blurring, spinning, then settling into a horizontal focus before the drone pilot lowered its altitude to take it back down for another look.

These secondary explosions post-crash—unless the bags were loaded with IEDs or other bomb materials, they were out of proportion for a smaller aircraft like this. Either these bags carried explosive devices, or there was another catalyst from something on the ground, or maybe—

The slow-motion video confirmed it. Opining mumble-speak from Max soon became fully formed words. "Powder? Was that powder?"

Max keyed in a two-word search on the internet, "cobalt powder," looking for pictures.

Silvery blue, hints of green and aquamarine in some images, the Shutterstock photos validated what the drone footage showed. And if cobalt in powder form was in one gym bag, it was likely in the other two; maybe even more bags were outside the camera frame.

Max's heart began to beat faster. There was a strong likelihood now that this was cobalt, either smuggled or stolen. The duffel was flush with it, the bag able to hold maybe a hundred pounds or more.

Cobalt powder, if highly pure . . .

He downloaded pricing from a retail metal powder supplier. Confirming from more internet searches, each bag could be worth "twenty, twenty-five grand to the battery manufacturers," he said aloud.

Renee grunted something unintelligible into her pillow. Max kept thumbing his phone, kept exploring.

Destination info for the charter flight was on the airport's website. It was headed to another airport in the DRC, a short trip. But was it really going there? If the cobalt powder were being taken somewhere off-script, all bets were off on where that somewhere would have been. Maybe staying in-country, maybe not.

Another thought. The plane's weight. Max paged through his online notes. The manifest had the airplane weight below the aircraft spec maximum by something less than only a hundred pounds. If they were smuggling, they probably flirted with exceeding maximum weights all the time. Plus the Dornier 228 was a short-takeoff-and-landing model, or STOL. STOLs were expected to climb quickly, in this case a capability needed to better avoid the nearby main-branch electrical feed of the densely populated neighborhood's high-tension wires. Weight could have easily been a problem, if not the cause.

Nearing five a.m. Max hit the return-call prompt on his phone. Wherever his CIA handler Caleb Wilkes was, Max secretly hoped he was sleeping.

Five seconds, no answer, ten seconds, going on fifteen . . .

Wilkes's voice came on, groggy, with no greeting. "It could have waited, Max."

Max was feeling chipper; Renee pulled her pillow over her head. "Sure, that's what he says now that he's on the receiving end. I need to share some exclusive drone footage of what might be another smuggling operation here. A chartered plane went down yesterday. Its destination was domestic, but who knows if that was correct. Hundreds and hundreds of pounds of refined cobalt powder were onboard, in passenger carry-ons. Maybe a large operation, maybe not, maybe black market. I put a drone in the air over the crash scene, and it streamed footage until we were shooed away. I want you to have it, if for some reason someone comes looking for Renee and me. Where are you anyway?"

"Unimportant. Forward it to me. We'll add it to the library. Who has the cobalt now?"

Corruption in the DRC was rampant, approaching levels rarely seen outside the drug cartels in South America and Mexico. The CIA "library" of evidence about known, or alleged, cobalt extraction pilfering was growing.

"What I saw went up in flames, in multiple explosions."

But Max knew the civilian population had been all over the wreckage before the additional explosions. Good for them, he thought, recovering whatever precious minerals were onboard. At least good for those who hadn't been lost in the rescue effort when the cobalt powder ignited.

"Here's why I called you earlier," Wilkes said. "You'll appreciate the coincidence. The FBI is going to contact you. About a domestic U.S. opportunity we need to chase down."

"The FBI? That means there's a crime involved. So where's the opportunity?"

"In short, and without stealing the FBI's thunder, it involves potential economic espionage. We'd like you to hand over your DRC infrastructure rebuild efforts to your trusty airport management team there and return home for a while."

"To the U.S.? Look, Wilkes . . ."

Renee sat up. She exhaled, grunted her displeasure at the early hour, and left the bed for the bathroom. Max powered through. "We're making progress here. Goma International's got its struggles, and the country for sure has its share of ill-mannered bureaucrats with their hands out, but it's getting better. Whatever you've got planned—"

"Not me. The FBI."

"Whatever. Whatever they need help with, have them grab some domestic folks and work it out. I'm busy here."

"Needs to be Fend Aerospace, Max."

"Really. Why's that?'

"Let's call it an economic security mission. You and your company have deep pockets. It's necessary that it be a private and/or corporate, not a public, endeavor. Fend is a good match to the blueprint."

"They're looking for me to *spend money*? You're quite the schmoozer. You managed to make it sound even more unattractive."

"I can't say more, Max, but the money part isn't as bad as it sounds. Frankly, I think you'll want to do this. Someone will contact you. He'll make you understand better. Sorry, but I need to go."

The cornmeal porridge in a bowl made with finely ground polenta looked like cream of wheat. Three eggs, some buttered toast, coffee. Max was on his encrypted laptop eating his room service breakfast at his suite's dining area table. His phone buzzed. He pulled up a text.

Satcom call from Beast coming through on your laptop in ten, nine, eight—

The name didn't ring a bell. Max swallowed his spoonful of porridge. "Who the hell is *Beast*?"

Renee was tuned into her own laptop, eating an English muffin, paying Max no mind, her earbuds in.

A satcom image popped into a rectangle that filled the majority of Max's laptop screen. A round-faced African American man filled out the rectangle, white shirt, dark tie, his look all business, his greeting deadpan. "Hello."

Max was speechless.

2001. Division 1-AA football, Princeton vs. The University of Pennsylvania, Franklin Field, Philadelphia.

Max Fend, wide receiver, Princeton Tigers, a junior. Cornell "Beast" Oakley, senior linebacker, Penn Quakers.

It wasn't so much the large face on the screen pushing Max toward a PTSD moment, it was the voice. No, it wasn't the voice, either. It was his single word satcom greeting, *Hello*.

What Max remembered of Cornell "Beast" Oakley, number 58, was one devastating tackle. A pass play to Max over the middle, the throw too tall for him. Full extension in no man's land for lanky wide receivers was a death sentence, but Max went after it. When he regained consciousness, he was on the ground looking up. The intimidating leer on the face hanging over him featured a black mouthguard. The mouthguard had a one-word message across it in bold white letters: HELLO. Max had to be carried off the field.

"I made the catch," Max managed.

"You did," Beast said. "Then I knocked you out."

Oakley's grin on screen was slight enough to almost go unnoticed. His stern demeanor returned. Max might have gone full PTSD if that mouthguard had still been in there.

Oakley was dead serious now. "I won't ask how you are. You've had quite an impressive career, Max Fend. Kudos. As for me, I'm now Assistant Special Agent in Charge, FBI, working out of the Philly office. I'm on with you here to brief you on what the Bureau is looking for. Special Agent in Charge Flynn went to my boss, who sent me to your boss, Caleb Wilkes. You and Flynn have history, I understand. Wilkes gave us permission to contact you. We need your help. I'm guessing it won't be a hard sell."

He was setting an expectation that he'd get a yes from Max. A good negotiating skill. Dropping Agent Jake Flynn's name hadn't hurt, either. Yes, Max and Jake Flynn had history. A complicated, confrontational, yet fantastic history involving a hijacked commercial jetliner drone and how the world was struggling with the technology. Their relationship had evolved to the mutual respect stage.

So here it was, a sketchy CIA lead provided by Wilkes, followed by an FBI chaser. What new gig was so important that it trumped what he and Renee were doing in the Congo? Why so much interest in Max by his government?

"First, is anyone there with you?" Oakley said.

"Yes. Renee LeFrancois. No worries. She has full clearances."

"I know who she is. Can she hear me?"

"She's deep inside her laptop, her earbuds on, so no. But I keep no secrets from her."

"Whatever works for you. Asking only so I know if I have more than you as an audience."

"At the moment, me only."

"Fine. So I'll work in an aside here. Yes, I still have the mouthguard. Yes, I still remember that game and that tackle. It was a clean hit, but I know what it did to you."

A separated shoulder, a concussion, one broken rib. Max was gone for the rest of the season. So painful that it ruined his Thanksgiving and Christmas holidays.

With a statement like that—"I know what it did to you"—Max figured an apology was coming next.

Nope.

"What it didn't do," Oakley said, "was keep you from going on to bigger and better things."

Fine. Max would do it for him. "I accept your apology," he said.

"I didn't offer one."

"I noticed."

"Beast" had pushed his way into the Princeton locker room after the game, to check out the damage, and to wish Max a speedy recovery. It was something Max had learned only later.

A chilly stare from Max. "What do you want, Agent Oakley?"

Oakley cleared his throat and went into it. "What we'd like is for Fend Aerospace—which I assume means you, unless you need permission from your father—"

A jab at Max's inherited wealth. "He's retired, but he keeps his fingers on the pulse. This wouldn't need to involve him."

"Right. Good. What your country wants you to do is to invest some of that Fend Aerospace money in an important economic endeavor: locating a major deposit of cobalt on—under—U.S. soil, then be party to its extraction. Cobalt is the new oil, Fend. The stuff that keeps electric cars on the road and your laptop charged."

"I don't need a lesson on cobalt as a precious metal, Oakley. That's one of the reasons we're here in the DRC. The DRC controls the market."

"And China controls the DRC. We're looking to change that dynamic in a big way. Change the pecking order regarding cobalt's extraction, refinement, and distribution. Which would change the hold, globally, that China has on the products that depend on cobalt."

Renee removed her earbuds, closed her laptop, and gave Max a quizzical look. He waved her over. She poked her head on screen with Max, her short dark hair framing her face. "Agent Oakley, this is Renee LeFrancois. Renee, Agent Oakley of the FBI. Out of which office, Agent?"

"Philadelphia."

Renee grabbed a chair and joined Max in front of the laptop. She squinted, looking past Oakley's image on screen. "Palm trees in Philly?" she asked.

An azure blue background monopolized the screen's top left quadrant. Over Oakley's other shoulder were the palm trees.

He didn't turn his head, didn't flinch at the comment. "I'm on assignment in Hawaii. You'll need to visit me here, Fend. It's an integral part of the assignment. Although not the only part."

"What's in Hawaii that you want me there?" Max said.

"Volcanoes. Erupting and dormant. Where there may be volcanogenic cobalt deposits originated from a billion years ago."

The world was watching in real time as the Kīlaueavolcano on the Big Island of Hawaii, inside Hawaii Volcanoes National Park, was making a name for herself again. A vent had opened in a crater, monopolizing screentime on the webcams operated by the island's volcano observatory, the cameras providing multiple vantage points. Lava lakes were forming, spawning lava rivers. Flashy, newsworthy stuff that continued to garner worldwide attention.

"People are suddenly interested in the Hawaiian Islands as more than a tourist destination," Oakley continued. Then, refining his statement, "People, as in billionaires. And corporations, as in private and public, foreign and domestic. Plus the intelligence agencies of those foreign nations."

Max stopped him there. CIA territory. "Other nations' intel? How might you know that?"

Oakley balked at the question. "Really? You want a primer on sources and methods? The usual ways, Fend. Encrypted information ricocheting around cyberspace."

In intelligence parlance, boomerang routing. Transmissions originating in one location, say, Canada, that pinged off another nation's location, like the U.S, which the U.S. could then trace back to the originator. Tracing those pings backward and forward, and getting inside the code, enabled the U.S. cybersecurity jockeys, plus other actors, to track and examine a lot more traffic at originating sites than what the initial pings offered.

Oakley returned to his pitch. "I'm in Hawaii now, but you should also know that the Pocono Mountains in upstate Pennsylvania are under the microscope as well. We're reviewing Hawaii first. When can you get here?"

Max made facial expressions during the spiel that feigned interest he didn't have. "It all sounds so exotic, Oakley, but I think I'll pass. Fend Aerospace has no business being in the mining industry."

"Ownership rights, Fend. What's at stake here are the rights to owning a cobalt mine or two. Find a large enough deposit under U.S. soil, then put the rights for extraction out to bid among major U.S. players. The FBI, of course, would help assure that the bidding was on the up-and-up, which means we'd need to monitor the process. Which means we'd be paying very close attention to what all the players bid, to make sure no one had an unfair advantage, especially not foreign interests. Which also means we'd know what all those bids were. A look behind the curtain, so to speak."

Oakley's mouth stayed closed for a beat, letting the implication sink in.

"Sometimes the controls break down and bid information leaks. It could happen just like that here, Fend. No guarantees, of course, but it could. Deals get made, and undiversified companies like Fend Aerospace decide to diversify because there's just too damn much money in it to ignore. Mining rights get awarded, the product gets mined, and all the good guys win. Along the way, the private sector companies doing the winning get wealthy." Another pause, then came Oakley's finish, joyless and bordering on snide. "Wealth*ier*. Some people get obscenely wealthier."

The FBI and other U.S. agencies combatted economic espionage every day, domestic and foreign, wherever it reared its head. In this instance, the FBI could be the perpetrators, maybe committing economic espionage and instigating destabilization in the cobalt markets rather than preventing it, all in the name of U.S. security.

Obscenely wealthier. A comment—a circumstance—which was seemingly stuck inside Oakley's jealous craw. Two Ivy League grads. Two college football players, same era. One extremely dominant on the football field—hadn't Oakley been drafted by the NFL and washed out?—who became a government employee. The other Ivy League grad settling for domination on the global aerospace technology stage, making him a billionaire like his father.

Max Fend. More than a friend of his country's government. A super citizen, with superpowers endowed mostly by money and his company's technological developments, but also by his dedication. And his training: physical, mental, psychological. His time at the Farm. Refresher courses over the years. Hand-to-hand instruction. Firearms. If he and Oakley were to get physical now, the outcome might not be so slam-dunk a repeat of their fateful prior meeting on the football field.

"I love my country, Fend. If I could afford to go after this opportunity myself—if I were in your expensive shoes—I'd be jumping at it. And in case you're wondering," he said, breaking character, "I wear *Skechers*."

Good one, Oakley, almost clever. Sarcasm hinting that he might have a sense of humor. Max would give him credit for this attempt at closing the deal, but he recognized the negotiating tactic: acknowledge Max's wealth, stroke him about it, then call him on it. Display some self-deprecation, poor-mouth it a little, be humble, and try to shame Max into getting onboard. A good pivot, all in the interest of recruiting him.

It was, Max had to admit, almost working.

Max did the travel math in his head. Hawaii was half a world away. He could have a Fend Aerospace heavy jet in place here in the DRC in two hours, then they'd hop, skip, and jump their way across two continents and two oceans. Approximate total elapsed time from when they'd hang up the call, thirty hours.

"Where would I meet you?"

"Hilo International Airport, on the Big Island." The Island of Hawaii. "From there, we'll head out to Volcanoes National Park."

"What's out there?"

"An asteroid."

4

Aurora Jolson's black cop shoes, holdovers from the days she'd been on the job, echoed as she entered the foyer, marble everywhere, up, down, and all around. Inside, she joined a crowd of credentialed local dignitaries, citizens, and tourists, her VIP lanyard dangling. The entrance to this savings and loan in Jim Thorpe, Pennsylvania, formerly Mauch Chunk, was cavernous. Five red-bricked stories, with four tall Roman stone columns that surrounded two brushed-steel front doors, the bank abutted the old Lehigh Coal & Navigation Company, a building that dated back to the early nineteenth century. A gaudy three-dimensional gold star hung above the entrance inside the bank. The bank building's two cornerstones were to the left and right of it at ground floor level. The left stone carried a burnished copper plate bolted to its inner face, visible from inside the lobby. Line one of the plate's engraved inscription read *Erected March 21, 1873*. Line two, *History Inside—How Things Were*, suggested the stone held a time capsule. The bank's articles of incorporation confirmed the capsule's existence, but with no indications of its contents.

Wednesday, eleven a.m. Zero hour, for an event 150 years in the making.

Why liberate the time capsule's contents now, this year, 2023? It wasn't a request made by the town's forefathers, written or etched anywhere, nor was it a directive made by the bank's management at the time. No real reason for the timing other than that the local historical society had pushed for it, assuming the society would get to add the capsule's contents to its formidable stash of collectibles that occupied the town's museum, and the bank's current management had agreed. One hundred and fifty years had been long enough.

Assembled here were the mayor, one congressman, the bank's president, and two stonemasons from the local lodge, their chisels and hammers at the ready, plus a few media types and an interested town audience. But they'd need to wait a little longer. The historical society's preservation specialists were late.

Aurora sipped from her large cup of Dunkin'. The former Philadelphia police force lieutenant had retired after thirty-one years to become the police chief of this scenic, touristy, evolving, and enigmatic town soon after she left Philly, stayed on the job here for ten years, then retired again. Eligible for two pensions, plus social security, and she was collecting on all of it. Sweet. She stayed in the area after she left the job and called it home, one of only fifty or so African Americans among the town's 4,500-plus inhabitants. Divorced, no children. Aurora cut a large, imposing figure even as a senior—a little overweight, but not obese. She now administered the town watch program, the mayor installing her as lead coordinator as soon as she retired as top cop. She was an addition to the program, the current leader taking a lesser role. No power grab on her part; it had been entirely the mayor's call.

She checked her phone. The ceremony was already ten minutes late. This would be a nice, homey news story for this small town, but the assembled media—reporters, photographers, amateur archivists, and out-of-town historians—were starting to grumble. Several faces Aurora recognized from local TV news and businesses, other faces she did not.

Mauch Chunk, founded in 1818, was renamed after early twentieth-century Native American athlete and Olympic superstar Jim Thorpe. At one time—before mining coal in the region had begun a few hundred years ago—a nearby mountain ridge bore an uncanny resemblance to a sleeping bear. *Mawsch Unk*, "Bear Place" in the language of the native Munsee-Lenape peoples, became its identity. Flashing forward, present day, Jim Thorpe's mayor would soon preside over a ceremony at a savings and loan:

the opening of the building's cornerstone that was believed to possess secrets about the town's past. If only the people with the nitrile gloves and archival tweezers, the historians, would get here.

Three preservationists arrived, two men and one woman. They slipped on their unpowdered gloves and faced the front edge of the cornerstone that carried the plate, the stone's edge a different color than the rest of it. The masons took their positions on opposite sides of the cube.

A few polite hammer and chisel taps at the north-south seams on each side of the protruding block gauged its solidarity, then came the heavy-handed hammer whacks in the same spots. The three-foot-high, inches-thick fascia piece of the block moved, separating slightly from the rest of it, grout chips and dust collecting on the marble floor. Cameras snapped, TV camera video ran, and the crowd buzzed.

The hammers and chisels continued, inching the cube's fascia piece forward. After full separation, the two gloved preservationists moved in close to finish the job. They slid the heavy piece out of the way and laid it flat on a plastic floor mat, copper plate side up.

Aurora craned her neck, others in the crowd doing likewise, nudging themselves forward. It was getting close in here. Pickpockets made a living in crowds packed together like this. Maybe not in small towns like Jim Thorpe, but Aurora wasn't able to turn off the Philly cop in her, always on alert, even now looking for light-fingered hit-and-run perps. She returned her interest to the cornerstone reveal in progress.

A container was inside the hollow stone block as advertised, a copper box, dark, dingy, and discolored with a green tarnish, filling up most of the space inside the cornerstone. The artifact folks shimmied the box forward, and after nodding at each other, they slid it out the rest of the way, onto another plastic mat. They let the audience admire it before carrying it to a folding table covered by more plastic, setting the box down amid claps and whistles from the viewers.

A tall onlooker behind Aurora leaned forward for a closer look, pushing against her shoulder. She turned and scowled. "You wanna back off, mister?"

"Oh, my. Forgive me," he said, "I am sorry. This is exciting for me as a tourist. Please accept my apologies."

White male—extremely white—with straight, long white hair parted down the middle. Maybe early forties. A European accent. German, she guessed, but it could have been Russian. He pulled back to give her room, ending his crowding. He reminded her of someone, especially his lanky, strong build, yet she couldn't place him. Knowing how he'd crowded her, she checked her coat pockets. Nothing missing, nothing added. Back to the time capsule.

The contents of the box thrilled the crowd, the gloved archivists raising each item overhead as they removed it, all preserved well enough, none appearing to have any damage, water or otherwise.

A March 1873 issue of the *Carbon Democrat*, a town newspaper.

An 1872 directory of Mauch Chunk's Carbon Lodge 242 for the Free and Accepted Masons. The two stonemasons who liberated the capsule beamed, moving in for news photos.

Hardcover books, among them both volumes of *Uncle Tom's Cabin*, plus the Bible.

A hand-sized bag of coal. A sheet of postage stamps. Multiple postcards with artist-drawn pictures of the Lehigh Coal & Navigation Company building, dating back to 1840.

But what stole the show was a pocket-sized, leather-bound personal journal with entries dating from the early 1860s, authored by a first-generation German transplant by the name of—

"Günther Heintz," the mayor announced, his face quizzical, the name not something he recognized. The archivist had given him gloves before passing the journal to him, and he was gingerly paging through it, reading aloud to his audience, showing surprise and awe, and thrilling himself with each out-of-context entry that was—

"...written in ink, in English mostly, in flowing, excellent longhand. My goodness, it seems Mr. Heintz was a silver prospector! He says he settled here, in the Poconos, to dig for—"

No surprise: silver, in a silver mine. A vein he was sure was there because he'd heard the local Indigenous tribe was surviving on what they were surreptitiously mining from it. The mayor read more of Mr. Heintz's entries from the journal.

"*The Lenape know where it is* . . .

"They're friendly to me, as I am to them, but they have no intention of sharing the location. I'm unsure how many of them know its location themselves. Many bloodhound miners follow them into a stand of pine fronting a mountain near Mauch Chunk, but the red men shake loose their tails each time. I must find it!"

The ledger gave no indication if he ever found the Lenape silver source, but what Mr. Günther Heintz did *not* care about, his journal entries offered, was a discovery he'd made during his prospecting.

"Kobold. A solid vein. But I do not want kobold. It is a good mineral for smelting, for creating colors that artists cannot create elsewhere, but there is little money in it. I will have nothing to do with it. It is demonic."

The mayor read more entries from the journal, the crowd smiling, the bureaucrat feeding off their enthusiasm. Clear to the audience, he related, was how this, Mr. Heintz's story, was one that would now need to be told, with people in the crowd googling the German prospector's name, also googling "kobold" and "silver prospecting in the Poconos," and sharing the results among themselves. Aurora googled it also.

Kobold in her search bar returned "goblin" and "goblin ore," stemming from European lore that accompanied the Germans who settled in these parts of Pennsylvania. *Kobolds* could be helpful or hurtful spirits that haunted mines, households, and ships, especially ones that had sunk. But there was more to why goblin ore was considered demonic. The minerals that contained it, when smelted to produce the blue pigment used for centuries by artists for jewelry and paints, and which gave glass a distinctive blue tint, also gave off poisonous, arsenic-laced fumes.

"So it killed people," Aurora heard herself say aloud, still reading an internet entry. She looked over both shoulders, hoping she didn't have an audience. The pushy but apologetic white-haired guy was still within hearing distance, but he was on his phone, somewhat animated, speaking in what she guessed was an eastern European language, oblivious to her interest in him. But, obvious to her, he'd understood what had just been liberated from the capsule, as she heard him repeat the word *kobold*, then "silver" in English, then—

". . . tupy indziejec . . ."

His snicker and body language teed up for her that this was probably a slur, *indziejec* sounding close enough to "indigenous." When he noticed her noticing him, he lowered his voice. He headed for the building exit, but not before she'd snapped a photo of him.

Myrna Springer washed their dinner dishes by hand, Wyatt dried. No leftovers. There were never leftovers when the dinner was baked mac and cheese with sliced hotdogs, Wyatt's favorite home-cooked meal. If she was being honest with herself, it was one of Myrna's favorites, too.

"Homework done?" she asked her son. In the background, her phone droned with another Indigenous podcast, this one her most interesting, about missing, murdered, and battered women. The influencer was from the Midwest, but it had relevance everywhere. She turned it off, the topic not appropriate for Wyatt.

"Sure thing, Momma. I did it after school, before you picked me up. There wasn't much today."

The after-school program was subsidized for low-income families. Myrna Nechoha Springer, an aspiring dental technician, but for now a minimum-wage housecleaner, qualified income-wise. She and her son Wyatt were two of only a handful of Indigenous residents of Nesquehoning, according to the last census. But few in the area, or their church, or at Wyatt's elementary school, knew much about their true ethnic roots. This would be the year she would come out of hiding as a minority, when she would proudly spell out her middle name, *Nechoha*, instead of only using the middle initial on bills, accounts, and purchases, or sometimes leaving the middle name space blank, because of the stares her full name received.

The reason for her new confidence: the election of U.S. President Faye Windcolor, the first woman to hold the office, and, maybe more importantly to Myrna, the first president with Indigenous blood.

Myrna's middle name Nechoha ("nee-*CO*-ha") meant "One Who Walks Alone" in Lenape. Myrna had spent her lifetime with that name, but when her husband disappeared, the lone brother to Wyatt's Uncle Jesse, gone over three years now, she'd been forced to fully embrace the meaning. With Faye Windcolor's election as president of the United States, "President

Faye" to the world, Myrna was now unafraid to show pride in her background.

A press of a remote, and the small TV in their galley kitchen now played the evening local news. Myrna scrubbed at a baking dish but was more interested in a story about an event only five miles east of Nesquehoning, in Jim Thorpe.

The event, videotaped earlier today: the opening of a 150-year-old time capsule found in a building cornerstone.

Inside the time capsule, a silver prospector's journal. The prospector made references to precious metals and the local mining of silver, nickel, and copper, and the capsule included specimens. On camera, a local historian lifted a dark chunk of something else out of the capsule that could have easily been mistaken for a large piece of defrosting dog poo. The cameraman's closer scrutiny of the specimen rendered small specks of glittering green and blue that glinted in the camera's lens.

Myrna put aside the dish she was scrubbing.

"Here's what cobalt looks like in the wild, pre-processed. Penn State University's Geology Department let me borrow this specimen. It's what mining engineers the world over have a keen interest in.

"And somewhere here in the Poconos, some time around the Civil War, silver prospector Günther Heintz, a first-generation German, discovered a deposit of it, according to an entry in his journal." And who was not, the reporter said, interested in his discovery, so he'd walked away from it.

"Per the geologists, most cobalt worldwide is produced as a byproduct from larger scale copper and nickel mines. But my Penn State sources tell me that mines in Morocco, and arsenide ores in Canada, yield cobalt as their primary extractions, making their product highly coveted. Discovery of purer veins of cobalt, if they were part of a large enough deposit," the reporter said, "would be huge for the American economy."

The news segment ended. Myrna stood mesmerized, blinking at a TV commercial.

It would amount to nothing, she was sure, but she decided to check it out anyway. "Wyatt," she managed, "can you—Wyatt, where are you, honey? Wyatt?"

Her son had left the kitchen. He quickly reappeared. "Yes, Momma?"

"Please bring me that rock you dug up in the backyard, sweetie."

A second look at Wyatt's "kryptonite" satisfied her. Too much green, not sparkly enough, not enough blue. More a green quartz than anything.

"You still like it, don't you, Momma?"

"I love it, honey. I thought it looked like something on TV that was worth a lot of money, but it isn't the same. Oh well."

"Maybe someday it'll be worth some money, right, Momma? Like maybe a thousand bucks, or maybe more?"

She brushed his black hair off his face. "Because you love it so much, sweetie," she said, grabbing his chin for a good shake, "it's worth a million dollars to me already."

Just not today.

5

Max and Renee's Fend Aerospace jet touched down at Hilo International Airport on the Big Island of Hawaii after the final leg of their private flight. Elapsed time since their talk with Oakley, twenty-nine hours, forty minutes. It was early evening. They deplaned for a short walk on the tarmac to the terminal, gate nine.

Max reread Oakley's text, now ten minutes old. He and Renee stepped onto an escalator.

Find me at Ah Lan's Lei Stand, second floor. I'll be the one not in the Hawaiian shirt.

"Hilarious, Oakley," Max said, underwhelmed, a comment directed at Renee. "Nearly peed myself laughing. Good one. Haha."

Renee's rebuttal came without turning around. "Look, you need to cut your agent buddy some slack if this assignment is going to work."

"An acquaintance, not my buddy."

At the top of the escalator she finished with, "After a day and a half on the plane hearing you complain about him, seriously, Max, I've had it. We're all on the same side. Start acting like it."

Second floor. A grumbling Max spotted Oakley outside the entrance to the lei store. He was a tall, bulky Black man, in a charcoal gray suit, white shirt, dark gray tie, and sunglasses, notwithstanding the terminal's artificial light. The antithesis of Hawaiian attire, it screamed *I am FBI*. All except for the footwear, which were tennis shoes. *Skechers* slip-ins, Max was sure. Max grinned but forced himself to lose the smile when they reached Oakley at the lei hut.

"Fend," Oakley said, meeting Max's stare.

"Hello, Agent Oakley."

Their stares remained through a firm, muscular handshake.

Oakley greeted Renee, their handshake professional but not as vigorous. "Ms. LeFrancois, I'm Assistant Special Agent in Charge Cornell Oakley. Good to meet you in person. Aloha." He reached behind him and retrieved two fresh-cut island flower leis from a hanging display.

"For you both," he said, and placed a lei around Renee's neck first, the second one on Max, whose bow toward him was hesitant.

"Love the shoes, Agent Oakley," Max said. "New FBI dress code?"

"They're comfortable, Fend. And a bargain. Short answer is no, wiseass."

More staring, more posturing, more testosterone.

"Seriously, guys?" Renee said. "This is how it's going to go, the two of you circling each other in the schoolyard? Let's start by going with first names. I'm Renee."

The agent's smile was slight, but there was enough of it there. "I'm Cornell."

"Good to meet you, Cornell," Renee said. "Max?"

Max exhaled, disarmed by Renee's scolding. "Fine. Call me Max, Cornell. Good to see you again. For the record, I appreciate that you reached out to me back then, after that game, I hadn't known about it for a while. It was a classy move. No hard feelings. Or at least a lot less."

"*Max* it is, then. You're welcome. Let's get you two to your hotel. Early wake-up tomorrow. I'm taking you to see a volcano."

No hug or chest bump, but this was a start. Then they were off, hoofing it through the terminal, headed to the parking lot, the sun almost set. Cornell launched into the plan while they walked.

"Tomorrow morning we'll check out the park, where some of the action is, and where more could be."

"The park?" Renee asked.

"Hawaiian Volcanoes National Park. Where Kīlaueais. Eruptions and lava. You'll want to see it." As they walked, he gestured left with a head nod, where a group of people had gathered outside a bathroom, chattering in what sounded like Chinese.

"Those folks look like tourists," Cornell said, his voice low, "but things have been getting busier around here lately, and relations with China are tenuous. Inside that group are, no doubt, a few operatives. Other foreign contingents are here as well. Large groups of Russian tourists, Middle Easterners, even Pakistanis. So easy to camouflage themselves buried inside these guided tours. These foreign agencies . . . they all smell it."

Max decided to bite. "Smell what?"

"The economic independence of it. The Chinese want to maintain their advantage while everyone else is looking to chip away at it. They've all seen the geological studies, the papers done by the U.S. universities, plus their own researchers. The world is losing its mind in search of cobalt."

Four, maybe five of the people in the Chinese contingent did more than glance at them as Cornell led them past. Max paid particular attention as these alleged tourists resettled their eyeglasses or held up their phones. If Cornell was right, the three of them were being photographed.

"I know what you're thinking, Max," Cornell said, clapping Max's shoulder like they were best friends, "and you'd be right. But it's not like we could have kept your presence here quiet the whole time."

As a billionaire, Max did enjoy celebrity status. But lately it had been a bit overbearing, the notoriety in evidence outside the U.S. also. Heir to the Fend fortune; wealthy "playboy": a well-cultivated fake persona that was sometimes helpful, sometimes not. But the way these Chinese tourists looked at him, at the three of them, was different. Clinical, Max felt, like they were memorizing their features.

Cornell no doubt had it right. The game was afoot.

"I'll mention one inconvenience we'll have while you're here," he said. The liftgate to his SUV opened for their bags. "The islands are loaded with geologists this week. A convention. Good timing for them, considering there's an active volcano consuming the landscape. We'll be tripping all over them."

"How close are we, here, to the volcano?" Renee said.

"It's thirty-three miles from Hilo. It will take about an hour to reach the lava field. We'll head out there in the morning."

———

Seven a.m., outside their hotel, Agent Oakley was at the wheel of a Ford Explorer. Renee and Max climbed into the air conditioning, Renee taking shotgun, Max sitting behind her.

"About Kīlauea," Cornell said, waiting for Renee to strap herself in. "A very active volcano. Unpredictable and dangerous. It erupted again last January."

He eyed what they were wearing, Max keen to his interest. "What is it, Cornell?"

"You guys are dressed for the heat. Good. But we'll need to appreciate Kīlauea's new lava flow from a distance. The old lava fields are where we'll do some walking—"

Cornell eyed Renee's hiking boots more closely. He leaned back to check out Max's footwear. "You're wearing the same boots?" he asked Max.

"I am."

"Huh. Interesting." He started the SUV, talking while putting the volcano's destination coordinates into the GPS on his phone, synched with the vehicle display. *Beep. Beep.*

"Lalo Shadow Intruders eight-inch Black Ops boots, right?" Cornell said, still keying.

"Right," per Max.

"Took me a few days, and some sorry-ass ankle twists"—the route to Hawaii Volcanoes National Park was now onscreen—"and major, nagging foot pain, before I realized I needed better support to hike those fields." Another glance at Renee's feet, then Max's again. "You guys aren't screwing around. I'm impressed."

"I know a guy," Max said.

Trent Carpenter, to be exact. Close friend, Special Ops/Black Ops good guy, CIA asset. Max had run their new assignment past Trent on their flight, the location plus the terrain they'd be negotiating. The hiking boots were at the hotel waiting for them when they arrived.

"Three pair," Max said to Cornell.

"Three? Who's the third pair for?"

"I had a certain FBI agent in mind. As a goodwill gesture. Someone at the Agency checked your shoe size, Cornell. Just in case you came up short regarding your footwear. Glad to see you don't need them."

"I don't know whether to be happy or pissed. That was invasive, but—" Cornell put the Explorer in drive. "Hell, the pair I bought cost me more than three bills. Another twenty to get them delivered. I'll take 'em. Thanks."

"Cornell, a question," Renee said. The car left the hotel, entered a six-lane highway, and began cruising south, passing a residential section with modest single-story homes on smaller-sized lots. "We're seeing this volcano why?"

"Because I'm being a good tour guide. Because you'd be upset with me later if you made this trip and didn't see this magnificent active manifestation of how hot the core of our planet is. And because it's on the way to the main attraction."

"You're telling us," Max said, "there's been a cobalt discovery?"

"I am not. I'm saying that with this much volcanic activity, on this island, this park and what's underneath are likely candidates. Or so the geologists say." Cornell tapped the SUV computer screen and zoomed in on their travel route. "Look at these GPS points."

The closer the zoom, the more notation points appeared, with short descriptions.

Lava flow of 1959. Lava flow of 1954. Nahuku-Thurston Lava Tube.

Lava flow of 1921 . . . of 1919 . . .

Hale Ma'uma'u Volcano Crater. Halemaumau Crater. Kilauea Iki Crater...

. . . crater . . . crater . . . crater . . .

"The deal is the fluids that are on the sea floors, after millions of years of tectonic activity shifting the plates around, passed through these hydrothermal vents—volcanoes—and cobalt and other minerals precipitate. 'Volcanogenic ore deposits,' they're called. Eventually these mineral deposits, in some places, moved close enough to the surface as the volcanos emerged."

"Close enough to be mined," Renee said. "This means volcanoes are great potential sources of cobalt."

"Yes."

"Per the geologists' studies," Max said, reinforcing Renee's take. "But there are other precious rare-earth minerals that have been even more diffi-cult—more unusual—to come by in the billions and billions of years the planet's been in existence."

Signposts appeared on the highway touting exits for Walmart, the Dimple Cheek Café, and Big Island Bullies, a dog breeder. A turnoff for the Lotus Buddhist Monastery. A sign for Madame's Cathouse, not a bordello, a pet boarding service. They were halfway to the volcano park.

"It sounds like you did some homework," Cornell said, more a question.

"Renee and I both. Your 'asteroid' comment on our call, it was an eye-opener. It made me ask some questions of my team."

Fend Aerospace engineers had supplemented Renee's internet research with archived scientific papers, the Penn State geological assessments, and U.S. and foreign government investigations released to the public. Working forward from a heavenly body's origin to its abrupt end, Renee put her Rod Serling hat on—

"Picture this," she said. "An asteroid whose likely origin was the asteroid belt in the ring between the orbit of Mars and Jupiter. It left the belt, shut-tled toward Earth, and splintered from collisions with other asteroids. The splinters became meteoroids, the meteoroids entered the Earth's atmosphere and became meteors, the meteors became what we call shooting stars. When remnants of shooting stars survive the atmospheric burn, they strike the Earth as meteorites. Meteorite impact studies indicate one such strike, a large one, might have been in Hawaii, on the Big Island."

A curled lower lip accompanied a slight, appreciative head nod from Cornell. "Excellent, Renee. So you two are caught up on this," he said. "In a few minutes we'll chase down one of those alleged impacts, on foot."

"Okay. So maybe you can finish this sentence for me then, Cornell," Renee said. "We like meteorite strikes because . . . ?"

"Because asteroids are often metal rich and contain concentrations of rare-earth minerals," he said. "Harvesting a near-Earth asteroid would give us more cobalt than all the Earth's known reserves. Except they're not commercially significant unless they arrive on the planet on a silver platter. Meteorites, if we can find where they hit, do that for us. Still, it would take deep pockets to get these minerals out of the ground. Know anyone with deep pockets, Max?"

Oakley didn't wait for a response. "Sorry, silly question. Okay, we're here. As far as we can go by car." He eyed the erratic, stratified landscape in front of them. There was one other SUV in the parking area. "Good. If we got here much later, it would be super busy. Lower density now. It's why I made you guys get up early."

They exited their vehicle. Backpacks, bush hats, sunscreen, water thermoses, binoculars. A loose light shirt on Oakley, loose T-shirt tops on Max and Renee, everything long and baggy enough to conceal their handguns. As tourists, they'd be visible from a great distance on a flat surface out in the wild like this. Their weapons were precautionary.

Oakley pointed again. "See that tiny apparatus protruding from the landscape on the right, against the horizon? Not too tall? It's about a mile and a quarter away. That's where we're headed. Let's go."

Max raised his binoculars, scanning the open space. Similar apparatuses reached skyward in different places around them, all at a distance. "There's one there, and one over there, and one there ..."

"They're all operational, but the one northeast of us at two o'clock is the newest and shows the most promise. It's where they'll be working today."

"They who?" Renee asked, her binoculars also taking in the view.

"The Army Corps of Engineers."

In front of them the barren rockscape of old lava paths was filled with dipping slopes, short but steep drops, and saw-toothed, hardened lava. Here was some of the roughest terrain the Islands could throw at hikers, according to the literature Max had read. What was underfoot now was—

"The locals call it *a'ā* lava rock," Cornell said, his boots finding their purchase one careful step at a time. "A Hawaiian term. Like walking on broken glass, with some of the chunks the size of a watermelon, even larger. No real path, so it's straight ahead for us. Underneath the lava rock, there can be air pockets. They're known to roll ankles. Be careful."

"So it's '*ah-ah*,' as in the beginning of a sneeze, then," Renee said, taking one tenuous step after another.

"Indeed it is. Oh. Good," Cornell said. His binoculars focused on their destination. "Excellent. The drill is functioning. C'mon."

Two hundred yards into their trek, Cornell held them up. He raised his binoculars again. "Whoa. Check out the view dead east of us. Do it now. Oh my. Momma Kīlauea is *angry*."

Through the mist in the distance, the display turned spectacular. Max and Renee adjusted their binoculars to see that it wasn't mist, it was steam. Blasts of gas and rock and fire erupted from a crater, with orange splashes shooting skyward, then retreating, then sloshing and swirling in and out of the rim of the most active volcano on the planet. Max went from binoculars to phone, zoomed in, and began videoing. Four minutes later, Kīlauea was done showing off, and Max and Renee had captured a large sample of it.

"All right. You guys got that, right? Good," Cornell said. "We need to pick up our pace. One of the engineers texted me. He says they won't be doing a full day of drilling today because of some equipment problems."

Fifty jagged, brittle, bruising minutes later, they arrived onsite, at the lip of a crater, tired yet with no scrapes or major sprains, only shin splints. Three to four stories below grade, a group of U.S. Army types crowded the derrick-like turret that had been visible to them on the horizon, taller than it appeared from a distance because half of it was inside the crater. Pistons raised the unit's tower out of the payload of an eight-wheeled flatbed truck, the apparatus looking not unlike a mobile rocket launcher. Four-wheeled ATVs with balloon tires, their carts behind them, dotted the edge of the worksite. Up close it was easier to see what the turret housed: drill shafting that reached three stories or more and leaned away from the drilling hole that the apparatus was making in the moonscape. Similar to a well-drilling machine, except it was on a Leaning-Tower-of-Pisa angle.

"Diamond core drilling," Cornell said. "The drill bit's fortified with industrial diamonds. Expensive, but it's also the most accurate."

"I need a quick summary," Max said. "What does this thing do?"

"So you want me to put my nerd hat on," Cornell said. "Fine."

He launched into it.

"The drill, attached to hollow drill rods, can extract a continuous cylinder of rock from a few thousand feet below ground. It's the most expensive method, but it also produces the most accurate rock samples. Entire samples are brought to the surface whole, not in fragments, creating mineral rods that are broken into short lengths for analysis. Seeing the minerals in rod form better determines strength, porosity, and most importantly, the mineral composition, ripe for discovering rare earth minerals like cobalt.

"You can't appreciate this location from this vantage point. We're in what looks like just another huge volcano crater, camouflaged by all the other craters around here that filled themselves in with lava, all of it cooling over time. But from a different vantage point," Cornell pulled up some satellite photos, "it's more likely this could have been an impact site." He handed his phone to Max for a look.

"For a meteor?" Max asked, reviewing satellite pictures. They had markings on them indicating widths, measured in thousands of feet. Max gave the phone to Renee so she could see for herself.

"A meteo*rite*," she said, correcting him.

Cornell tapped his nose and pointed at her. "At least one of you has been paying attention. Those are pictures of where we're standing now."

"Agent Oakley," an engineer called from near the drill. He waved Cornell over. "A word with you, please."

Cornell joined two engineers for a discussion. When he returned, he had a small pouch with him. "They're shutting down for the day at this site. Mechanical issues with the unit's underground drilling fluid delivery. If there's no fluid, the drill can't purge the samples, which means nothing more gets coughed up today. This came from yesterday's activity."

Max and Renee crowded Cornell as he unzipped a quart-sized plastic bag. "I know, not a high-tech container. It's from a one of the engineer's lunch kits. I think it held a coupla PB&Js." He handed the bag to Max. "Check it out."

"What am I looking at?" Max said. "Do I need to touch it?"

"A borehole sample. No, just check it out from a few different angles. Some hard dirt, some speckled dirt, with metal particles in it. The brassy yellow specks are copper. There's nickel in there, too, the engineer says. Unfortunately, little to no cobalt. According to the engineers, it's been that way most of the way down, and they're almost two thousand feet deep already with this borehole."

"You're telling us this is a bust?" Max said. He held the bag up to get a better look at its contents. He handed it off to Renee.

"So far, at this spot, yes, no sign of an ancient meteorite," Cornell said, "and no indications there's a major cobalt deposit here. They'll fix the drill and get back to work on this borehole in a few days. There are other boreholes, with other diamond core drills, so the engineers will move elsewhere, but this one, because of where it was in the meteorite crater, showed more promise initially. We need to start back, guys."

"But Cornell," Max said, "if a meteor hit—"

"Meteorite," Cornell corrected. They were on the move again, retracing their trek here.

"Really? Fine, if a *meteorite* hit, and you can't find any remnants of it within one-to-two thousand feet of the surface, unless you have additional indications of significant cobalt deposits in these Hawaiian craters, unrelated to said meteor—meteorite—don't you think it's time to start barking up another tree?"

On cue, Cornell's phone began making bona fide barking noises, his ringtone the "woof, woof-woof-woof-woof" from "Who Let the Dogs Out" by the Baja Men. They shared smiles at the improbable timing.

"We're already working other trees, Max. Excuse me."

Cornell answered the call while Max and Renee smoothed out the brittle *a'ā* lava rock underfoot with their boots, then copped squats, cross-legged. Cornell paced while talking, making no effort to keep the call private. "Yes, Chief . . . Yes, I understand." He glanced at Max before finishing with, "I hope it won't be a problem, Chief. Thanks. Bye."

"Your boss?" Max asked.

"That she is. Special Agent in Charge of the Philly office. There's been another development. We need to take another trip. To another tree we should bark up."

"Before you tell me where," Max said, "you need to hear from Renee, who's been holding her tongue. We've been doing homework on cobalt mining deposits. Renee?"

Cornell put his hand up as a stop sign. "Hold on, guys, just put a pin in that. I do appreciate whatever research you and your Fend Aerospace team pulled together, but—"

"And Renee," Max said, wanting her acknowledged. "You know what Renee's consultants can do, their successes. It's all documented, some unbelievably tough Agency missions—"

"I get it Max, I really do, I know Renee's cred is stellar, and she has access to the best underground IT talent available, but I want you to hear this first. Something just fell into our laps. A strong lead, and we need to act on it fast. It means we need to go to upstate Pennsylvania. There's a 150-year-old time capsule that a bank just opened. It gave up some interesting information."

The time capsule's contents validated what the university environmental folks had been saying: There was a large concentration of cobalt under the Pennsylvania mountains, under extinct volcanoes responsible for coughing up volcanogenic minerals. Super-pure cobalt, the kind that takes less work to extract and process. A treasure-hunt dig was already in progress because while the exact location of the concentration was unknown, its deposit's size had been deemed substantial.

"A treasure hunt? Exactly who's on a treasure hunt there?" Max said.

"For one, the U.S. government. Our Army Corps friends, out of their Philly office. But word traveled fast. There have been sightings of other world beaters just like Fend Aerospace. Tesla, Amazon, Apple, and individual investors like Michael Bloomberg. Their engineers are all moving in, wanting access, looking for admittance to the party, to acquire rights to a new cobalt dig. China's Alibaba, too. There was even a Fa Xiaoling sighting."

Xiaoling was a Chinese dissident. One of the wealthiest people on the planet depending on which month it was. "Tell me this," Max said. "What convinced them there's a super pure cobalt deposit there?"

"There was a hunk of it inside the 150-year-old time capsule. My boss just sent me pictures of the sample. Have a look."

Cornell's phone photos were great. Excellent detail, with one showing a high concentration of lustrous green crystals with blue and gray specks on the underside of a rock the width of a typewriter. A pure, tight, cobalt sample.

A solid lead. It made what Max and Renee were about to tell their FBI host a much more difficult sell.

"Am I up yet, Cornell?" Renee asked. "Because I'd really like to get this off my chest."

"You have the floor," he said.

Renee sipped from her water thermos. "Super. I'm tired, so I'll cut to the chase. That's a promising lead, Cornell, seriously impressive. But you'll need to tell your boss that what she had in mind—us visiting upstate Pennsylvania—unfortunately *will* be a problem for us—at this moment, at least."

"I don't follow," Cornell said. "The Pennsylvania news is huge. If what we think is there is actually there, it's exactly what we're looking for. What makes going for a recon visit there a problem?"

"When Max and I leave here," she took another sip, "we're going to Greenland, where there might be something better."

An incredulous look from Oakley. "*What?*"

"We'll talk in the car. I can get comfortable, stretch, massage my feet a little, then fire up my laptop. I'll need it to explain."

Renee spoke from the back seat of the SUV, legs extended, feet crossed, laptop open, and mouth delivering fact after fact. Max diddled with his phone.

"All this talk about meteors and asteroids," she said. "I read up about the one that 'historians,' and I air-quote that word, say hit here on the Big Island. There's no proof, not a shred of it, unfortunately. The satellite photos talk a good game, but it's only folklore. Century after century of word of mouth. So easy for the population to deceive itself with no real science to back it up. Especially if you look at all these craters. One or more of them had to have come from meteorites, right? Except it's more like none of them did.

"So, so far, nada. That brings us to the real deal, Cornell. A meteorite that hit in Greenland.

"Might have been as far back as three million years ago or as recent as twelve thousand, or maybe during one of the Ice Ages, but the science that proves it happened is there." She was reading from her laptop. "It hit an area in the Hiawatha glacier, which is more than half a mile thick, on the northwestern side of the colony. Slammed into Earth with a force that was about—let me get this right—here it is. 'About forty-seven million times the energy released by the bomb dropped on Hiroshima during World War Two,' according to more than one scientist. It made an impact crater the size of Washington, D.C. under the glacier. Thirty-one kilometers wide. That's over nineteen miles. Ice-penetrating radar confirms it's there.

"So if we want to get up close and personal," she said, "and investigate an asteroid-sized rock full of rare-earth minerals, one that is most likely to contain a major cobalt deposit, then Greenland is the place."

"Look, Renee, listen to me." Cornell exhaled, now defensive. "I have no horse in this race. We're here in Hawaii because we're touching all the bases. They knew the info about a meteorite hitting here was only anecdotal, but all the science about cobalt forming below volcanoes is real. I want only what our country wants, which is more energy independence. Wherever it can be found, if it can be found, we will find it. I'm here to help pave the way for an American company like Fend Aerospace to get a crack at developing it. Volcanoes, and whatever it's taken to form them, make a helluva lot of sense to pursue. That's why the Army Corps is here.

"If you want to go to Greenland and freeze your ass off in major sub-zero temperatures, I can't stop you, but the Bureau has no reach there, so I also can't give you any assistance. When you're finished fighting the frostbite, I'll be in Pennsylvania, waiting for you guys."

Max reemerged from a phone texting frenzy. "I was on with Wilkes. He's making it happen in Greenland for us. We now have clearance as part of a Fed agency called the NSF."

"National Science Foundation," Renee said, her fingers dancing over her laptop.

"Exactly. Wilkes and company pushed the paperwork through. We'll need to make some connections—a *lot* of connections—and I need to get some aircraft pulled together, then we'll fly to Pituffik Air Base on Greenland's western coast. We're getting space in one of their hangars. From there it will be by helicopter, or dogsled—"

"Or windsled," Renee said, wincing, her nose buried into screenshots of extremely harsh weather conditions. "You're not going to like some of these videos, Max. Winds up to a hundred knots."

It got quiet inside the SUV, each of them taking measure of what was in store for their respective agendas over the next few weeks. Agent Oakley in upstate Pennsylvania, Max and Renee near the top of the world.

"You called it a country, Cornell." Max said. "Renee had it right. It's an island colony."

"Come again?"

"Greenland isn't its own country," Renee said. "While it is part of the North American continent, and it is self-governing, it's part of the Kingdom of Denmark, which also makes it part of the European Union. And it's the world's largest island. I've been there before in a previous life, on assignment. We'll make it work."

She'd been attached to Canada's version of the NSA, the Communications Security Establishment, or CSE. Max knew none of the details of Renee's mission there, which was pre–their relationship, only that, "What happened in Greenland," per her one-time comment, "stayed in Greenland."

Cornell watched the road, swiveling his head, the volcano national park becoming a speck in the rear view. It looked and sounded—felt—to Max like his host was disgusted with himself because of the outcome of their Hawaiian visit.

"I know one thing, Cornell," Max said.

"Enlighten me, hotshot." His crabby response sucked the air out of the SUV. "Sorry, that was uncalled for. Look, guys. I'm under a lot of pressure here, trying to move things forward. We thought it would be in Hawaii. We now think the focus will be in the Pocono Mountains, north of Philly. You're going to be half a continent north of where you need to be, and worse yet, outside the country. Greenland doesn't help us, Max. It's a tangent. If you get interested in developing a Greenland installation, it only complicates things. Again, sorry, but not sorry. Go ahead, tell me this one thing you want me to know."

"We like Denmark, and they kind of like us," Max said. "If we find something in Greenland, a Denmark colony, our chances of being the ones to get it out of the ground are almost as good as they would be if a large deposit were found in the States. But I do get it, Cornell, and it's all good. Or we'll try to make it all good, bud."

The "bud" was an attempt to make progress in their relationship, patching things up as best as possible. He hoped Cornell noticed it.

6

Feeling every bit an ex-cop from the big city now in a tightly knit small town, Aurora met her town watch crew for a two p.m. late lunch at Lorenzo's. It was a short, easy ride from her appointment with the whitewater rafting folks near Nesquehoning: eight minutes east through the middle of old Jim Thorpe, six minutes south to Lorenzo's in Lehighton. As townwatch lead, Aurora was buying them lunch. Again.

Excellent white pizza. But it was time to reveal her evil plot.

"Good afternoon, folks. Thanks for coming. Pizza good? Beer cold?"

Multiple head shakes yes, raised glasses and bottles, a few hear-hears, and affirmative grunts from full mouths.

"Good. Okay, listen up."

She ran her eyes around the long table, assessing her invitees. Eight white men, four white women. Small-business owners, shopkeepers, accountants, insurance brokers, and other cop retirees, among them Jesse Springer, a U.S. Marine who lived outside the town in Nesquehoning, and Ike Barber, former U.S. Army pilot and current fireman, the displaced head honcho for the town watch.

Aurora hadn't liked Ike's sources and methods, occasionally butting heads with him during her years as police chief. Too retributional, too off the grid. The mayor had been getting calls; he had to do something about Ike. Enter Aurora as the new leader of the team.

For her ten years as the chief in ethnically un-diverse Jim Thorpe, she'd been embraced as one of their own, and had never been made to feel unwelcome. But something changed after the mayor asked her to take over the town watch and run it like she'd run the police department. The team went along with her appointment, but their hearts weren't in it, or so her gut told her.

Don't read anything into it, was the mayor's response. *When you joined the watch, you made it a baker's dozen. Thirteen's an unlucky number. People around here can be superstitious, that's all it is. If you can win over Ike Barber, you'll do fine.*

Mass superstition was ludicrous, of course. Regardless, she planned to stay the course and wear them down over time, with praise, kindness, and efficiency. Carrots, not sticks. Provide solid law-enforcement leadership in a town watch environment. If that didn't work, she'd *buy* their respect and cooperation. She'd been a Philly cop; she knew how things worked.

"You guys are here today because, let's be honest," she flashed a big smile, "I'm bribing you by ruining your diets and contributing to your drinking problems." They returned a few smiles and chuckles. "But seriously, it's all in the name of bringing us together more as a team, and, full disclosure, to make me feel more a part of it."

Nervous looks in Ike's direction, the laughs subsiding.

"And to let you know about something I'm planning for us for this spring."

Aurora laid it out, talking over the sipping, chewing, and gulping. She'd stopped into the local rafting outfitters. All nice people, warm and enthusiastic, and more than happy to give her a good deal on the outing she was planning for the watch team.

"I want you to clear your calendars for one Saturday in June, because the Jim Thorpe Town Watch Twelve are going to put on some gear, grab a coupla rafts, and hit the Lehigh Gorge rapids for a whitewater rafting adventure, then grab some dinner afterward. No cost to you. My treat."

Good pitch, good intentions, no downside, and the nods around the table said it was a winner. At first. Then came the sideways chatter.

Is the town funding this?

"No. All me."

Is it mandatory?

"No. But hoping big time that you all decide to come."

Why are you doing this?

"More team building. Plus, deep down, I have an inferiority complex, and I need you to like me."

The table quieted, her answer bringing a few chuckles, but the questions were done. She filled the void, looking to close the deal. "Folks, what do you think? Yes or no?"

Talking among themselves supplemented furtive looks at Ike Barber, seated at one end of the table, Aurora seated at the other end.

Ike lowered his beer and searched their faces. He settled on Jesse Springer. "What do you think, Jess?"

"I'm in," he said. "It'll be fun."

Ike nodded. "I'm in, too."

After the few months she'd been onboard where she'd felt like an outcast, this felt like a vote of confidence. They were coming around.

"Outstanding," Aurora said. She raised her glass. "Cheers, team."

Aurora got to the gun shop before its six p.m. closing time, opining internally about her pizza lunch. Good midafternoon meeting with her town watch crew today. Damn good. She marched up to the glass counter to speak with the owner.

Billy-Bob's Shootin' Irons was a standalone building on Route 209. A good place for hunters' supplies, personal protection firearms, and police-issue equipment. A friend to local law enforcement. There was no Billy-Bob, though there was a Russ Kennedy.

What Billy-Bob's did not sell were assault-style rifles of any kind, or accessories for them. A person had to ask about them to learn that. It was one reason Aurora liked the place.

The other reason was Russ. Aurora and Russ were a thing. Infrequent, but frequent enough, just not lately.

"Hey Aurora. I have your order ready. Be back in a minute." Russ left the counter and went to a room in the back.

Another customer entered the store and began wandering the aisles, close to the entrance. Aurora recognized him easily: the out-of-town European from the time capsule opening a few days earlier. The white-haired dude, possibly albino, had Aurora's full attention. Russ returned to the counter with a cardboard box.

"Your order's all here. This much ammo, you must be busy at the firing range."

"Guilty. What can I tell you, guns are in my blood."

"More like the badge is still in your blood," Russ said, leaning in, the comment meant for only her.

She nodded. "I'm surprised I haven't seen you at the gun range lately." Less a surprise for her, more a disappointment. "What's up with that?"

"I'm down one employee here. I get out when I can, but not much time for it."

The other customer arrived at the counter, less interested at what the counter held, more interested in what hung on the walls behind it: rifles, shotguns, and pistols. "Hello," he said, directed at Russ.

"Be with you in a minute, sir. So, do I keep this all on the credit card, ma'am?"

Russ's gaze at her lingered a split-second, virtually imperceptible. He'd kept the question arm's-length, no names, no familiarity, she was just another customer to him, etc. No need to let a stranger know her name, in a gun shop or elsewhere, or that she was a former cop, or that they were, you know, friends with benefits. Good show, Russ.

"That is fine," the new customer said. "I can wait. Ms. Jolson deserves your attention."

Wait, what?

Aurora tossed her receipt into the box and closed her distance to this stranger. That fact that he knew her identity suddenly made the man more interesting. Russ arrived at the same time on the other side of the counter. The man's accent, his perceived foreign origin, both would be issues if he wanted to buy a gun in Pennsylvania, less so if he were interested in ammunition or accessories only.

"You know my name," she said, eyeing his face closely. Her tone was brusque, and she had to raise her chin to confront him. "How is that? Do I know you?"

"My goodness. I am sorry," he said, recoiling. "I have apparently upset you. Again. From the bank, Ms. Jolson? If you recall, I, too, was at the bank for the opening of the time capsule. That is how we know each other."

Okay, but that wasn't her only question. "A familiar face is one thing. How—why—did you track down my identity?"

"Oh. But I did not need to track you down," he said. "Your name was on the lanyard hanging around your neck."

Her VIP badge for the bank ceremony.

"And are you not also like me, very noticeable here because your coloring doesn't fit the norm in this town?" He fumbled for something in his shirt pocket. "But forgive me, I am being rude. And please know that I am not a stalker. Here."

He handed her a business card from his shirt pocket, then placed a few more onto the counter for Russ.

"I am Alex Godunov. Not the Russian ballet dancer and actor, of course. He was a Russian defector to the U.S., and he is now dead. No foul play, just alcoholism. I am a geologist with Belarusian National Technical University. It is only a coincidence that I look something like him."

Geography was not her strong suit, but because of Russia's recent invasion of Ukraine, she could now pick out Belarus on a map. She also knew where Belarusian sympathies resided—with Russia.

On the business card were his name, educational abbreviations, and his title, *Academic Department Head, Professor of Mining Engineering and Engineering Ecology*. Not a dancer's body like the celebrity Alexander Godunov; this Alex Godunov was more toned and muscular. Also on the card was a quote attributed to his namesake:

"His future remained in the past." – Engraved epitaph, Alexander Godunov, Gates Mortuary, Los Angeles.

Odd. Plus the vibes she was getting weren't good. A European mining professor in a gun shop in the Pocono Mountains. Profiling on her part for sure, but in the hood, when your cop instincts kicked in . . .

"What are you doing here?" she said.

"My. You are blunt. I am here because Penn State University released research on the prospect of finding large quantities of precious metals in this region. Their papers have enjoyed a wide audience. My visit to the region is on an advisory basis because of these studies."

"Advisor to whom?"

"Ahhh. That is information I cannot disclose. I signed a confidentiality agreement. I am sorry."

The signal the interrogation was almost over. All that was left was to understand why this white-haired, *Die Hard*–looking professor of European mine engineering was here, in a gun shop in the Poconos, scrutinizing the shop's firearms, those under glass, and those secured to the wall behind the counter.

A certain simple question required asking and answering. Thanks to Russ, Aurora wouldn't need to ask it.

"Is there something I can help you with, Mr. Godunov?" Russ said.

"Yes. Please tell me, where are your semiautomatic rifles?" Godunov asked. "I know how infatuated you Americans are with them, but I don't see any here."

"I stopped selling them. And unless you have a valid Pennsylvania ID, or some other form of U.S. identification, I can't sell you any other firearms, either."

About ten years ago is when he stopped selling assault-style rifles, Aurora wanted to add. It was soon after she'd arrived in Jim Thorpe. Soon after she'd had a talk with him about what law enforcement thought of AR-15s and other long guns in civilian hands.

"Of course. I understand. I only wanted to take a selfie with one."

"Don't sell them, don't own one."

That slammed the door on the topic. When another new customer entered the shop, the Belarusian professor paid his respects and left. Aurora now needed to do the same.

"Russ, thanks for getting that out of him. Let me pick up what I bought and head out."

"I'm sorry I've been so busy lately, Aurora." Russ placed his hand over hers, squeezed it once. "Are you busy tonight?" A smile accompanied the question. He'd just done good with the European customer, and she knew he knew it. "After I close up the store, maybe dinner and Netflix?"

"I can manage that," she said.

Myrna Springer was at work, cleaning a house, a ranch in Parryville, home to a widowed, elderly used-car salesman napping in his La-Z-Boy recliner while she worked around him. Her last of three appointments for the day. It was steady full-time work with a housecleaning company at a little more than minimum wage. It took care of her bills, but only barely. On her mind while she cleaned a mirror in the living room was her son Wyatt's block of kryptonite from their backyard.

Wyatt called it his Clark Bar, after Clark Kent. He liked the chocolate candy bar and he'd watched all the old Superman movies together with his mom, the ones with Christopher Reeve and Margot Kidder. Wyatt was a clever kid. The rock still occupied space on her son's desk. One of these days she'd have someone look at it to see if it was worth anything.

The TV was on with the local news, the late afternoon edition. Her home-owner client dozed, asleep the whole time she worked in his living room. She sprayed glass cleaner on the long mirror above the sofa, wiped it off, squirted more, wiped more off. A reflected image of what was on the TV stopped her short: a house in flames in Centralia, Pennsylvania, a reporter at the scene. The fire wasn't unusual for the town, nor was it unusual for a reporter to be there to cover it. Every house that burned in Centralia was a story, there were so few left. The flaming home was a small white two-story wood frame colonial, dated back to WWII, the reporter was saying. Myrna's heart sank. She knew the house well. At one time, it had been on her cleaning rotation. Worse yet, the man snoring quietly in his easy chair, her customer, had occupied it for decades.

It was his home, where he and his ailing wife had lived until five years ago, before the Alzheimer's killed her. Before he gave in and accepted a buyout from a governmental environmental agency and moved forty miles east to this small retirement community near Jim Thorpe.

"This house," the male reporter said, "is one of only six left in Centralia.

It is being consumed, as we speak, by a sinkhole." The camera zoomed in. "It's on fire because of the heat coming from underneath. From the legendary coal-seam fire that's been burning underground since the sixties, a fire that destroyed the town.

"There's no fire company activity here, and none is forthcoming. That's the way it's been for years with these last few buildings. The agencies in place for dealing with this disaster expect the four or five people who still call Centralia their home to leave its environs before this happens to their own residences."

Myrna moved nearer the TV and picked up the remote. She watched her sleeping client and the TV screen at the same time, the volume on but low, her finger poised near the off button should he begin stirring. The old man shouldn't see this in real time. It would break his heart to watch the house collapse in on itself, the one he and his wife had shared for all those years, him losing it yet again, this time forever, and so soon after losing his wife to her disease.

Centralia. A burning, open wound fueled by the anthracite-fired hell-hole beneath it. Thirty-five short miles west of Myrna's property in Nesque-honing. The distance between Centralia and Nesquehoning got shorter with every house that burned.

Per the EPA's latest measurements, the methane readings inside the coal fire remained high, the reporter said, and ignitable at relatively low temperatures.

"Odorless, and similar to radon, the methane migrates, and it often accumulates underground."

When pressurized, it presented a risk of explosion, even at low concentration levels.

"In Centralia," the reporter added, "they let everything burn." The cameraman panned right to show the frame house writhing inside the flames, beginning to sink below street level. With its last breath, the methane got the better of it.

Ba-boom. The home exploded, rocketing its burning debris skyward, startling Myrna, making her jump. The camera followed a trajectory of fire-works then settled on the inferno at ground level, then just as quickly, the roaring fire went out, the methane exhausted, the house gone.

"Myrna?"

Her groggy homeowner client roused himself and raised his recliner. By his bewildered look, he wasn't sure what had awakened him. "We 'bout finished yet, sweetie?"

She shut the TV off.

"Yes, Mr. Rip Van Winkle," she said, forcing a small smile, "I believe we are."

Godunov, on his hotel's Wi-Fi with a laptop, found the site, put the advertisement in, had it translated, and hit send. Off it went in search of its one-person audience. Fifteen online ads, all with the same wording, in Urdu, Pashto, Punjabi, Sindhi, others, and English, all simultaneously placed in the classified sections of Pakistan's major online newspapers.

The English version: "Meat, large amount, TBD. Great terms, negotiable. Pilot it home."

Meat, large amount, meant a substantial assignment.

TBD meant the mission was evolving.

Great terms, negotiable, meant a contract worth a minimum of $5M USD. The target and difficulty factor would impact the final amount.

Pilot was in reference to his intended audience of one, piloting airplanes among her many talents, another talent being a former intel officer, a third being a contract assassin.

Godunov took a nap.

He awakened when his phone pinged with a text. He keyed a response that began an encrypted conversation in English that authenticated their identities with each other. He awaited one texted word that would indicate they'd reached a tentative deal.

Bibi Memona Qureshi saw the posting in *The Pakistan Observer* in Punjabi from her first-class seat on a flight from Pakistan to Kuwait. After more mid-air keying at her laptop, by the time her flight had landed her itinerary had changed. She would take a different connecting flight and arrive at the Wilkes-Barre/Scranton International Airport in the United States, instead of Philadelphia, in forty-eight hours. Bibi held up her phone, puckered for the camera, and took some selfies. She picked one she liked and posted it online. Her large global audience would love it.

Alex Godunov read the response he'd been looking for.

I am en route

7

What did Max know about Greenland? What he'd read, and what he'd learned by way of a crash briefing from his Fend Aerospace think-tank execs while in the air from Hawaii to the frozen island colony, spitballing his approach. And what Renee brought to the table from her first-hand experience.

On the final leg of another long trip in another of the company's heavy jets, after two stops and more than nine hours of flight time, their plane received clearance to land. Their destination, Pituffik Air Base, was a U.S. Space Force military installation a thousand miles north of the Arctic Circle, located near Pituffik Airport in Qaanaaq, Greenland. At 15:05, their flight would be the airport's third arrival of the day on its one runway. Not a busy place.

Final approach. Max absorbed the view as they descended, the North Star Bay just beyond the runway at two o'clock, ice chunks dotting the chop. Beyond the bay, filling the width of the window and getting larger by the second, loomed the wind-whipped, panoramic Saunders Island, steep-cliffed, flat-topped, snow-covered, and uninhabited.

"Looks cold out there," Max said, unprompted. "Top-of-the-world, pro-cold." He leaned closer to the glass. The landscape below and the seascape straight ahead were other-worldly levels of intimidating. "What the hell have I done."

He retrieved his phone and checked if they had cell coverage yet. No—wait, yes. 4G. The best Greenland had to offer, which was what all the island's populated areas had. The base was close enough to the town of Qaanaaq to share the coverage.

"A balmy negative two degrees Fahrenheit out there, rookie," Renee said, her laptop open on a fold-out table. Their satcom broadband was courtesy of the Air Force Research Lab in combination with a commercial provider, new to Greenland as of 2022. "Tropical for here. And this time of year the sun's usually up for the same amount of time each day as the rest of North America. Sunlight May through August, 24/7."

Max had a few texts queued up. He was only interested in one of them. "Wilkes is here, on the ground already. But without our gear."

"You better get on that, Max. I'm not getting off this plane until my arctic pajamas show up, *mon chérie*."

"Personal needs will get here today. Everything else arrives tomorrow."

"I'll believe it when I see it. And wear it."

"Oh, ye of little faith, Renee. People owe me favors. Equipment-wise, we're getting something they were going to mothball. They got the diamond core drill running again, but the Army engineers are happy I took it off their hands. We'll go to Qaanaaq tomorrow and check all the equipment out."

"Oh look. Temperature's rising. It's now zero. A heat wave."

Quick, decisive thinking on Max's part had immediately followed the snafu in Hawaii. He'd made some calls, his people made some calls, the CIA made some calls, NASA made some calls. The Army Corps of Engineers had been on the receiving end of many of them, and voila, the diamond core drill that crapped its pants in Hawaii was repaired, then decommissioned, then acquired by Fend Aerospace. It was now on its way to the Arctic.

"The engineers, too?" Renee asked.

"Same people who were in Hawaii. The Corps of Engineers and at least one contractor. Reassigned here to a local Army Corps office."

"What? There's one in Greenland?"

"Certainly is," Max said.

"I'm sure they're thrilled with the reassignment."

"One of them is. The contractor, a Dane. She planned to retire after the Hawaiian gig wrapped. This project being where it is, with Greenland being a Denmark colony—it was a no-brainer for her. She gets to work near home."

As a name, *Greenland* was misleading. The seemingly endless flight had given Max time to brush up on it. The name had been a marketing ploy by Norse explorer Erik the Red in the year 985 to attract settlers to the frozen northern island. The entire country's vegetation was sparse, much sparser than could support its modern-day population of 58,000 people scattered along its coastline. No one lived inland. There were no trees on a land area of 836,000 square miles save for a small, forested patch on the island's southern tip. The world's second-largest ice sheet covered eighty-four percent of Greenland's landmass, the rest of it permafrost.

But the ice sheet was shrinking, Max knew, and he was aware that the shrinkage had fostered an uptick in interest from a most unlikely subset of jet-setting world travelers: the world's wealthiest billionaire entrepreneurs and industrialists. Interest that was less as tourists, far more as opportunists. And per Wilkes, they were all coming for the same reason: searching for rare-earth minerals, cobalt being of the highest interest, under the land masses newly exposed by Greenland's retreating glaciers, which had been melting a hundred times faster than estimated in the last decade. Or maybe it could be found in an asteroid-sized rock that hit the Earth three million years ago.

It was all in the drop-down data that Renee was gathering on the country.

The landing gear touched down on the icy runway. The jet shuddered when the tires skidded then grabbed, and the brakes and friction wrestled their trusty aircraft into a controlled taxi. Max and Renee clapped, and the two-man crew slapped each other's backs. Their jet made a right turn off the runway, now headed toward a hangar. Max and Renee overheard a sharp order the cockpit received from the Pituffik air traffic control tower.

"Hustle up, captain! Another arrival behind you. MAAS deployed. Copy, over."

Their captain responded, "Roger that," and their small aircraft jolted forward to move at a faster speed. MAAS, an acronym Max knew: the Mobile Aircraft Arresting System, necessary for short or compromised runways. It was usually deployed for larger, swifter aircraft. At this location, this included military jets.

"Renee—check out this next arrival."

They watched from Max's window as a military jet roared onto the icy runway they'd just vacated, braked into the arresting system, the harness and the tarmac grabbing the aircraft hard. The jet stopped a thousand or so feet after it touched down, completing an uneventful landing.

"F-16 fighter jet," Max said. "I'm impressed." Texts appeared on Max's phone. "Hold on. It's Wilkes."

Down payment on your gear is on that jet, Max. The jet is a new asset deployed for Operation Noble Defender exercises. He had room.

They had been debriefed. "Noble Defender" was part of NORAD, the North American Aerospace Defense Command. It incorporated assets from Canada and the U.S., with support from Denmark.

Max eyed the Navy jet, wondering what the pilot thought about the extra baggage hitching a ride. It taxied to a stop while their private jet found a different hangar to approach. Their aircraft rumbled forward.

"Max? I said, did Wilkes have an update on our stuff?"

"Yes. Your pajamas are in that F-16."

From the plane to Hangar 8 it would be two hundred bone-chilling paces influenced by a subzero temperature and forty miles per hour winds. A windchilled -20°F equivalent on the ground. They climbed into warm outerwear delivered to their plane's doorstep, military issue, arctic-rated, and God-sent.

Renee huddled up next to Max as they walked. His arm around her, the two of them pushed against the wind. A sergeant, part of the base's medical team, followed close behind. The hangar was visible through an ice fog that had moved in.

"My lungs, Max," she managed through a cough. "I . . . They feel like they're freezing on the inside. This is . . . this is going to make upgrading the airports in the Congo look like a playground rebuild—"

Inside the hangar they were hustled to a conference room by three of the air base's brass, led by the 821st ABG commanding officer, Colonel McTigue, and a first sergeant named Reese. Assorted Pituffik personnel plus local contractor reps for housing and dining trailed them.

"Welcome to our cold, frozen desert, Mr. Fend and Ms. LeFrancois," Colonel McTigue said. "Our military base and airport are carved into two hundred and fifty square miles of North Pole tundra. We need to go through the intake process now. I know you're tired. We'll get you out of here and into your quarters ASAP. First, the Danish liaison officer will need to check you in. Show her your passport and entry permit please."

With their papers in order, the colonel escorted them to a conference room. A long table with two folders of reading material awaited them, chairs around the table, bottled water, some granola bars, and their handler, Caleb Wilkes. His heavy duty, fluorescent yellow hoodie gave him the look of a stadium parking lot attendant.

"Max, Renee. Good to see you," Wilkes said. "Have a seat and get comfortable. Colonel McTigue is about to give you a thumbnail on life here, north of the North Pole. We'll talk after."

After they were seated, the colonel got to it. "Let me brief you on what you need to know for your stay here. In front of you is your handbook. We'll also email you a PDF copy.

"You'll quarter at the Transient Inn, where all air base personnel and out-of-town guests stay. Because you have friends in high places, we assigned you a two-room suite, and you'll have a private bath. Your pilots will stay at the inn also, in standard rooms. I understand you are here with us for this evening only, and your pilots only one night as well. You will return here for one or two nights more at some to-be-determined date in a few weeks. Is this correct?"

Wilkes's body language indicated he intended to pull rank on Max and answer the question, but Max spoke up first.

"I'll take this, Wilkes. You have some basic info on this mission, Colonel, I'm sure. I'll lend a little more detail here. Today we get settled in. Tomorrow a.m. we copter to Qaanaaq—thank you for arranging our ride—

to meet our other team members and get them settled in there. They're part of the Army Corps of Engineers, some local, some from, dare I say, Hawaii." He took a breath to give the Hawaiian reference and its tropical irony its due. Raised eyebrows, but no comments.

"Tomorrow around noon our equipment arrives Qaanaaq via Air Greenland's freight service, along with the engineers. They'll inspect it tomorrow afternoon. The next day, we'll use Air Greenland again, this time a rotary wing, to airlift it to a predetermined site on the edge of the Hiawatha Crater. We will commute back and forth to Qaanaaq daily for as many days as we need to set up the equipment and begin our dig. To sum things up, Colonel, I'm thinking three weeks or more, with two weeks or more needed to do the work, an extra week to account for weather issues. I caution you, like you might caution me, that the unpredictability of this climate could mean we're here longer. I'm confirming also that this is simply an exploratory visit. Long-term needs will be addressed pending the outcome of our search and research."

"I appreciate your clarification, Mr. Fend," the colonel said. "Do not forget that this severe arctic environment is life-threatening and ever-present, and it has the uncanny ability of finding people when they are least prepared for it. Sudden, drastic changes can and do occur daily. In winter, exposed skin can be frostbitten in less than a minute.

"The arctic gear we gave you is what all military personnel receive here, to supplement whatever you brought for yourselves. A parka, mukluks, long underwear, outdoor winter pants, mittens, a ski-like mask, goggles, and wool socks. It's not everything you'll need to survive if you get stuck out there in the elements, but it will give you a fighting chance.

"All operations on the base are self-sufficient, powered and fueled internally. Will you have access to a vehicle?" he asked Max.

Max redirected. "Wilkes?"

"Not this visit, Colonel. The return trip, maybe."

"Thank you, Mr. Wilkes. Please know that the speed limit on base is twenty-five miles per hour. That is a maximum; it's lower in some places. A twenty-four-hour taxi service is available, so do not chance a walk outside if or when your vehicles aren't available. You will notice soon enough that there are no sidewalks or paved roads on the base. Dirt and mud for four months of the year are the norm, ice and snow above the permafrost the rest of the time.

"Most of the permafrost in northern Greenland ranges from six to 1,600 feet deep. It will make your exploration efforts extremely difficult."

The colonel moved into what Pituffik Air Base had as its primary mission. "The Ballistic Missile Early Warning System, acronym BMEWS— the largest reason for our existence here—is designed to detect and track ICBMs launched against North America. There are procedures to follow in the event the base receives alerts from them. They are in your package. Are any of you armed?"

"Yes," Wilkes said. "All of us. 9mm handguns. When we do carry them, they will be concealed. The pilots and all other team members will not be armed for the duration of their stays."

"Thank you for informing us," the colonel said. "The closest town is Qaanaaq, sixty-five miles north. Be aware that there is a Danish Police Inspector and a Chief Constable assigned to this territory. Also be aware they may be concerned that you are armed. Use good sense regarding your weapons if you need to deal with these people. No international incidents please.

"I'll close your orientation with this. The Northern Lights, sadly, are not visible here at the base. It's because—and this is conveyed only to people with the highest of clearances, like yourselves—the green lights seen in the skies the world over originate right here in Qaanaaq, their hue a skyward refraction of the kryptonite that NATO keeps in storage in a fortress under the ice, where it can't hurt anybody, its location top secret for obvious reasons. Just another reason why Greenland is Greenland, right?"

Silence and curious looks around the table.

"That was a joke, friends," he said, but not cracking a smile. "If I can be of assistance in your efforts during your time here, I'm sure you or Mr. Wilkes will let me know. Sergeant, please call for a ride and have it take our guests to their quarters at the inn."

Because of the cold and their baggage, the military on-call taxi made the most sense despite the inn's proximity, a six-minute walk per Max's phone. They piled into a Chevy Tahoe, Wilkes included. Their bags went in the rear of the snow-covered, grimy SUV, which had marginally less snow and ice and grime on the inside.

They kept their chatter inside their ride to a minimum, Wilkes filling it with pleasantries and ending with, "I'm checked in already. I'll give you two some time to rest and decompress. Expect me at your room in two hours for updates on what and who we're seeing. We'll grab something to eat at the chow hall after."

"What and who we're seeing *where*?" Max asked. The cab crunched to a stop in rock star parking in front of the Transient, a three-story corrugated building in battleship gray, its embattled entrance silo needing a fresh coat of maroon.

"In and around Qaanaaq. No worries. Take some deep breaths after you check in, then we'll get this show on the road."

8

They were exhausted. Ten minutes to unpack their one bag each, and they were asleep in each other's arms five minutes after. A knock at their door, too soon after their heads hit the pillows. Max let Wilkes in. Renee pulled herself up, the two of them with cases of bedhead, each of them dragging. Wilkes handed them cups from a takeout coffee caddy.

"Sorry, no Dunkin' or Starbucks. Let's have a seat so I can update you. Things are heating up."

"I might welcome that heat right about now," Renee said, pulling herself into a hoodie to fortify her sweater. They retreated to a table.

"There have been sightings of a few extremely important 'tourists,'" Wilkes said, "and I use quotes with that word. One sighting was in this northeastern territory, but most are in the south, nearer to Nuuk, where it's slightly warmer and the glaciers are melting faster. They're not announcing themselves, staying as anonymous as possible. No entourages, only them, maybe one or two associates loosely following them, and some bodyguards. We've picked them up via facial recognition at the Greenland airports."

"And these people are . . . ?" Max asked.

Renee had her laptop fired up, ready to feed it whatever information Wilkes had. To start with, he had photos.

"See for yourself." He sent the photos to their email addresses, then spread the physical copies on the table.

Elon Musk. Jeff Bezos. Bill Gates. Tim Cook. Sir Richard Branson of Virgin Air. Some of the shots were grainy, but the zoom images helped with the clarity. Max was acquaintances with them not only because they were celebrity billionaires, but more because they were think-tank visionaries whom he and his father had shared Fend Aerospace plans and ideas with over the years. Max had one immediate question about them, and the answer needed to be no.

"These people are not here because you invited them, correct, Wilkes, as in the same capacity that you suggested I join this project?"

Wilkes smiled. "Excellent question. To answer the question I think you're asking, no, none of them are part of this project. Answering with full disclosure, however? Yes, the Agency, and the Bureau, did approach a few of them and other billionaires. I'm not naming names. They all declined."

"So we weren't your first choice," Max said.

"Correct. That doesn't mean we don't love you, Max. You know that." Wilkes picked up three of the photos and shuffled them around. "And chances are, we got them all thinking about this. But that window we opened for them closed soon after we made our pitches. If they're here, they're here on their own."

"And what is it they would be thinking about?" Max said.

"The obvious. Cobalt."

Max grabbed one of the photos for a closer look. It was an Asian woman. "Is that who I think it is?"

"Like I said, Max, I'm not naming names. But yes."

Max stared at the photo. Fa Xiaoling, early fifties, Chinese, co-founder of the Scheherazade group, the Chinese business-to-business multinational powerhouse company, was wearing a female fedora and a man's-styled suit, her image captured at Qaanaaq Airport. The most interesting aspect of the sighting, excluding the one large man by her side pulling a large dog carrier, was that she was by herself.

"So she's no longer missing, I take it?" Max said.

"She was never missing, but she wore out her welcome at home because of her criticism of China's financial regulators and banks. China's 'forced disappearance' measures account for her low profile. She's now living on a superyacht in Japan."

"It says here in Forbes," Renee read from her laptop, "that she's worth more than fifty billion dollars."

"And she's in Greenland intending to spend some of it," Wilkes said. "Her views on fossil fuels and their danger to the planet are driving her interest in promoting electric vehicles worldwide. She's read the studies about the relationship volcanos have with cobalt and with Greenland. I expect she's also very interested in the meteorite strike up north."

"Volcanos in Greenland?" Max said. "Really?"

"You put me onto this, Max, so you're getting all of it," Wilkes said. "Researchers have known for decades about a volcano corridor with thinned-out landmasses above hotspot plumes that span from Hawaii, across the Pacific to mainland U.S., then north to Greenland, then as far east as Iceland, where they're still active. When Greenland drifted westward over the Icelandic plumes sixty-plus million years ago, volcanos formed on its landmass."

Renee spoke. "Then what we have here, Wilkes, is similar to what the Bureau showed us in Hawaii."

"Yes. Simply put, just like the Army Corps on the Big Island, Fa Xiaoling is here looking for easier access to cobalt deposits, but here it could be beneath the receding glaciers. It's the newest frontier for this. And she's searching for rare-earth minerals delivered to Earth by a massive meteorite, like what we're looking for. A two-fer, potentially within hundreds of miles of each other."

"What do the Danes have to say about this?" Max said.

"That connection was already cooking. It's what got Fa here in the first place. She and the Queen of Denmark are friends. Much like the Queen is with Canada, their relationship solidified even more so because of Renee here—"

Renee raised her hand to stop Wilkes from volunteering anything else on her relationship with the Queen. She took over the topic.

"Her kingdom will do fine negotiating the development rights if things get that far," she said, "either with Fa Xiaoling representing herself, or with U.S. and Canadian companies, or with others, or in combinations. As long as the partnership financials favor her colony and the rest of Denmark. Her closeness with Canada was solidified from other reasons as well," Renee said. "I'll explain better later, Max. Are we done here, Wilkes? You promised us some food at a chow hall."

"Renee." Max stroked her arm. They were both under the bedcovers, lights out, the glow of a cold snowy night lighting up their window. Renee didn't respond.

It needed to be early to bed for them because it would be early to rise tomorrow, four-thirty a.m., for an extremely ambitious day ahead. Their light dinner at the Dundas Buffet Restaurant, one of three chow halls on the base, had been Wilkes's treat. It was then a military taxi back to the inn, the outside temperature -6°F, then to bed. But a lingering topic remained unaddressed over dinner, and since Renee seemed to be avoiding it—

Max leaned onto an elbow. "I know you're awake, Renee. Tell me what happened. With the Queen of Denmark. Tell me why she likes Canada more so because of you."

Renee didn't stir.

"We have no secrets anymore, right?" Max said. "All right, maybe some, but nothing major, right?"

She roused. "Yes, Max, there are no more major secrets."

"Then tell me what this is about."

"Except maybe for one."

She leaned over to turn on the lamp on the nightstand, illuminating Max's engrossed face. She lay her head back on her pillow and faced the ceiling, her eyes open. Max watched a pensive, faraway look emerge.

"In 2008, while I was still with the CSE in Ottawa . . ."

She'd had a cybersecurity desk job with the Communications Security Establishment, or CSE, Canada's equivalent of the U.S.'s NSA. She and Max had just attended a Princeton University reunion, separately, the last time Max would see her for years. Fast forward to 2017, when Max pulled her name up from his black-bag-job personnel file for help with a terrorist problem. Something that would utilize her hacking skills. That year, they became an espionage team. In the years that followed, they became quite a bit more.

"Canada hosted the 2008 International Ice Hockey Federation World Championships in Quebec City. Denmark's Queen Ingahild Gustavsson flew in to see her national team play 'in the country where ice hockey was born,' as she said to me. I was part of a security contingent for her delegation. I got the assignment because someone noticed the word 'hockey' on my agency bio and never checked that my sport was women's field hockey, not ice hockey. Denmark played well in the tournament, made it into the qualifying round. While we were there, there was an incident during one game. It nearly became an international disgrace for Canada."

It happened during the game's second intermission, Renee explained. Max rolled closer to her. Renee's lips pursed together then released as she recalled it.

"It was an assassination attempt, and it was so subtle, so non-confrontational, that it should have worked.

"Queen Ingahild left her suite for a trip outside. She was—is—a heavy smoker, and she needed a cigarette break. Her entourage followed, her protection details, too. Her own, plus the one assigned to her by Canada, which included me. We'd spoken a lot during the hockey game, me in a seat behind her in the suite, leaning forward to translate the stadium announcer's French into English for her. A very exciting game against Belarus that Denmark won in overtime.

"Outside the building, both security details hovered near the door. One of her staff members pulled a pack of cigarettes from a carton that had already been opened, something I noticed immediately, that the carton wasn't sealed. A Danish brand. The staffer gave the pack, also unwrapped, to her aide, who shook out a cigarette, handed it to the queen, then struck a match.

"The queen lowered her cigarette from her mouth before the aide could light it. A man on her staff had her attention. He'd lit his cigarette before helping any of the women smokers do so, an ungentlemanly thing to do, and the queen didn't like that. She said something to him in Danish that shamed him into tossing his cigarette. Her phone rang, distracting her. She answered it, turning away from him and us, her cigarette break needing to wait.

"Seconds later the staff member who she'd shamed grabbed his throat, then his chest, then dropped to his knees on the sidewalk and vomited.

"The queen ended her call and raised another cigarette to her lips, oblivious to her vomiting aide, and went looking for someone to strike a match for her.

"I threw away my unlit cigarette and slapped the queen's hand from her face, knocking her cigarette away, and I yelled to her staff to call 911. I screamed at the person holding the cigarette pack, told him to drop the pack where he stood, also the carton and the matches, do *not* toss them I said, just drop them. I pulled the queen back, out of the hands of a body-guard, away from everything that had landed on the ground, and told everyone they needed to move away from the cigarettes and the person who got sick. The guy was in pain, coughing and coiling into a ball, but they needed to move away from *all* of it, not to touch him, he'd been poisoned, and help was coming.

"Then it got crazier. I shouted at everyone to take off their outer layers of clothing, but to not do it over their heads. Slip it off, tear it or cut it off, whatever they needed to do to keep it as far as possible from their mouths or noses. The queen had on a jacket and a blouse. I looked for something sharp, scissors, a knife, found nothing nearby, so I slipped the jacket past her shoulders and then ripped off her blouse. That went over big with her protective detail, with the queen and some of her staff now exposed down to their underwear, and me too, but they soon realized why I'd done it."

Renee breathed unevenly, was suffering through the incident again, giving Max all the details.

"It was ricin, in powder form, in the cigarettes. We weren't sure at first, but we confirmed it soon enough. Inhale it, you die. Eat it, you die. Your lungs fill with fluid, your skin might turn blue, your liver, your spleen, your kidneys, they all stop working, and you die. It's a painful death that usually takes hours or days, but for some, it can happen quickly. There were a few casualties that night. Three people got severely ill, but only one person died, the early smoker. I was one of the three other casualties, either from inhaling aerosolized traces of ricin or stray tobacco. I was hospitalized for two days. The queen was not poisoned, thankfully, and she never had any of the symptoms. She still calls me on occasion, Max. She knows I saved her life."

Max stroked Renee's hair, gripped by her revealing story. He pulled himself close and leaned his head on his fisted other hand, ready to hear more. "Any resolution to the poisoning? Did they find who was responsible?"

"A Danish citizen, Iranian descent. He'd accused Denmark online of hosting members of a terrorist group responsible for attacks in Iran and in Denmark. He claimed responsibility for the poisoning, had a rambling discussion with the Danish police, then shot himself. On TikTok."

Renee heaved a large sigh, breathed deep, her eyes unfocused. Max was still in comforting mode, but he needed to know more, to understand.

"Why is this the first time I'm hearing about this? You were a hero. Why the secrecy about it?"

She composed herself. "Did you get from that what it was I was doing with the queen outside the stadium?"

A blank look from Max. "You were protecting her."

"Yes, but I was also there because I needed a cigarette. I was a smoker, Max. Did you know I smoked?"

Come to think of it, no, he hadn't known this. Huh. Wow. Renee was a field hockey player, a runner, a star triathlete. She was in prime physical condition, to this day still, even though she—they—were both in their forties.

"Cigarettes only, Max, but fessing up, I wasn't just a smoker, I was a *chain* smoker, sometimes lighting one cigarette after another. I developed the habit after becoming a shut-in cyber nerd in my windowless office at CSE. Me, super athlete, physical fitness freak, sucking in nicotine-laced smoke like it was much-needed oxygen, knowing all along what it was doing to me. Close to three packs a day, Max."

"That's . . . I agree, that's a lot, Renee, but—" Max said, grabbing her hand.

"The addiction made me feel so weak, Max. So needy. So compromised."

"When did you quit?"

"The ricin had the impact on me that it did—hospitalizing me—because my lungs were already damaged from my cigarette habit. It was then I decided that sticking things in my mouth and setting them on fire, just to breathe in additional harmful chemicals, was no longer the way to go. I quit cold turkey, from more than two packs a day to zero. No lapses."

Heavy snow gusted against the hotel window casement, in the dark, reminding them where they were, where they were going tomorrow, and how early they needed to get up to get ready for a very ambitious day.

They fell asleep in each other's arms. Max's overnight was filled with vivid, noir-ish dreams that had him seeing a dark-haired, action-hero female in a sultry cobalt-blue dress on a pulpy book cover, a lit cigarette between her full, crimson lips, her hand slapping a similarly dressed woman in the face, both of them knowing the slap was for her own good.

9

Aurora took a bite of what was left of her second Arby's sandwich, a cheddar cheese roast beef, and looked past her steering wheel. In front of her, Jim Thorpe's Memorial Park. On her passenger seat was a large order of curly fries, her fully charged phone, and her Maglite. Her Diet Dr Pepper occupied a cup holder and her 9mm handgun was tucked into a holster above her butt. Roast beef sandwich #1 hadn't survived the short drive up from the Lehighton restaurant.

The park's lights timed on, began earning their keep. Town watch duty for her tonight. Eight-thirty p.m. The ballfields were empty. No one was on the park's playground amusements, neither kids nor, as sometimes happened, chemically influenced adults, not that drug use was ever a major problem in Jim Thorpe. No one in the park's pavilion, no evening barbecuing. The restrooms were locked. With the sun already down and a chill in the air, there'd been only a few joggers tonight and even fewer walkers. She'd seen two cars near the park area in the past twenty minutes. She'd do this shift for as long as it took for her to consume her late dinner, then take a short, cop-beat walk, then she'd head home.

A difference in philosophy. That was what separated her from Ike Barber, the watch's former leader. He preferred patrolling the borough's busier sections on a random schedule that covered sixteen or so hours a day. Not Aurora's approach, who knew to coordinate their watch efforts with police department resources, so citizens weren't out at all times of the day and night doing law enforcement's job and getting in the way. Looser, less strict, less military. This wasn't inner-city Philly—it was a much smaller town with a low crime rate. Something the police department was proud of, and, she knew now, made the town watch folks even prouder.

She left her car, discarded her dinner in a trash bin, and began her walk. The night was clear, the chill enough that she could see her breath, but it wasn't cold, not really. March was leaving like a lamb. Through the trees, on the other side of the park, the traffic signal at the end of a one-way side street turned red with no traffic impacted by it. Another cycle through green, yellow, red, the street still empty, then another one. Yawn. Aurora would call it a night.

Four cars entered the periphery, moving up the side street in tandem, right to left. Two SUVs, two sedans, driving slow enough to obey the posted speed limit of fifteen MPH. The red traffic light stopped them, no other traffic at the intersection. The twenty seconds it took for the light to change felt more like minutes.

Aurora asked herself, a little ashamed for thinking this: *Who obeys a 15 mph speed limit, really?*

The vehicles were different makes, the streetlights revealing their colors: one maroon, one brown, two black. They seemed to be traveling together. The traffic light turned green, they all signaled for a right turn, they all made it through. All good, law-abiding drivers. No other traffic behind them. Aurora quick-stepped her way to the corner, needing to burp through the heartburn the Arby's had given her as she picked up the pace, and she watched them proceed, still in tandem, around the corner, away from the park.

A sighting worthy of a note in her spiral notepad, which she made. Now she would call it a night.

She heard the helicopter but didn't look up. Airplanes and copters around the Poconos were like white noise lately, not like the screaming engines from larger commercial jets landing at or leaving Philly International as they gained altitude or descended, all of it white noise in its own right, but louder.

The copter dropped in altitude, its flashing running lights keeping it from being ignored. It followed the same direction as the four cars. To Aurora, the copter was unmistakably military, and was unmistakably hauling a tall and wide—massive, at least thirty-by-twenty—wooden crate at the end of metal cabling, low enough that it wasn't just passing through.

Myrna tossed Little Pig's misshapen Frisbee into the Rubbermaid storage bin on the deck next to her house. She held the lid to the bin up, lingering over its contents, pondering whether she should dig through the toy pile. It was the beginning of baseball season, the time of year when Wyatt would start asking about his dad. Myrna decided she'd confront it tomorrow morning, to try to overwhelm his despair, subdue it, not give it a chance to stake a claim.

The large baseball glove was visible under a yellow wiffleball bat and lawn darts. She pulled the glove out, admired it, then brought it to her nose for a whiff of the neatsfoot oil massaged into the dark leather.

Spring. This is what spring smells like.

And looked like. Her backyard had emerged from the snow. Wild-flowers filled the perimeter, and the daffodil bulbs she'd planted pushed through the moist earth, the yellow blooms lovely, invigorating.

She shoved her left hand inside the glove and pounded the pocket with a fist, like she'd seen real ballplayers do on TV. Like her husband did when he was a teenager, with this very glove. Worn, flexible, comfortable, it was fully "broken in," baseball talk, but not by her. Ken had been a ballplayer in high school. A legend in his own mind; the personification of Springsteen's "Glory Days." For Myrna, however, it conjured mixed feelings whenever she picked it up and placed her hand inside it. Ken's hand belonged there, and not instead of hers—she loved playing catch with Wyatt—but in addition to, as the primary user. The glove was old, but it was in good condition, and she could ill-afford to buy another one for herself to use. She'd instead spent the money on a new baseball glove for Wyatt last year.

Ken Springer, her husband of eight years, father to Wyatt: a lover, then a hater, of his own wife.

After a hard swallow, she removed her hand. She found Wyatt's smaller glove in the bin, plus a regulation baseball, off-white with grass stains from use in the backyard. It was the ball Ken soft-tossed to his young son back when they'd all been able to find the joy in this life of theirs, not wallow in its hardscrabble misery.

Myrna removed the ball and Wyatt's glove from the bin then closed the lid. She slipped the ball inside the smaller glove's pocket. She and Wyatt would have a catch together tomorrow.

She caught the hint of at least one new Little Pig gastrointestinal creation in the backyard. Ugh. Before they'd chance any missteps in the morning, she and Wyatt would need to spend a few minutes cleaning up after her.

10

Awake on time, dressed in layers of their military-issue outdoor wear, Max, Renee, and Wilkes took an air-base taxi with their baggage to the chow hall, then took another to the National Science Federation lab space carved out for them in the base's Hangar 4. Other than the three of them, there were no "NSF personnel" in Greenland currently—Max and crew were labeled NSF researchers for the time being, so they could have the NSF's full thirty-by-thirty space inside the hangar to themselves for the time they would need it. Temperature outside this morning, -12°F, no wind.

A sad sight greeted them in a windswept snowbank near the hangar's side door: four fur-covered legs protruded skyward, stiff as fence posts.

Sergeant Reese let them inside the hangar door. He addressed the frozen dog. "A huskie-wolf mix. Some puppies are left to run wild before getting trained for sledding." Max was the last to enter, lingering in front of the dead dog. "Inexperienced with the cold," the sergeant added, "which means some will die in it."

Behind the snowbank the sun rose as they entered the hangar, an orange-hued sky over an eastern ridge. The exterior temperature rose with it, increasing to -4°F within minutes. The difference, as minor as it was, was welcome. The forecast for the day at Pituffik: clear, little wind, and uneventful, almost pleasant, except—

"Don't let the forecast fool you," Sergeant Reese said, handing each of them a cup of coffee. "Around here, the weather decides everything. We'll stay in the hangar while the pilots make their final pass."

The copter pilots walked the perimeter of their ride, doing a visual check of the Royal Canadian Air Force CH-149 Cormorant helicopter. Acquiring the transport from the Brits had been Wilkes's doing. They climbed in and powered up the bird. Max and team watched through a hangar window as the sky began changing rapidly, the clear semi-blue giving way to a gloomy, wintery gray. The sergeant gestured casually at the horizon. "Case in point."

It moved in like a dust storm across the cloudless sky above the airport and the frosty prairie surrounding it. A snow squall from the west, rolling over the bay from flat-topped Saunders Island, picking up bluster, the sky thunderstorming until, in minutes, it went full-blotto white. Snow and ice slammed the hangar and the copter, all in the path of the cyclone of a winter storm propelled by thirty- to forty-knot winds. Their RAF ride, its blades in motion, held fast against winds that pounded the hangar and rattled its window hardware.

"Not an ideal way to start your trip," Sergeant Reese said, speaking loud enough to be heard over the freight train of snow barreling against the hangar. His hand covered one ear to better receive audio input through his earbuds. "The tower says you can still be a go if you want. The squall will ease off shortly. You should have a window to go up." His look turned expectant, awaiting feedback.

An expressionless Wilkes blew once into his clasped hands. "Max? Renee?"

Max eyed Renee. She shrugged. "I'm Canadian. I've been far enough north in my own country that I know what to expect. Let's let it die down, then we'll get it over with. Maybe it's warmer inside that helicopter than it is here in the hangar."

"It won't be," the sergeant said. "When the wind lets up, I'll board you guys."

Sixty-seven air miles from the base to Qaanaaq. The snow stayed at bay for their hop across the glaciers in the CH-149 Cormorant. The terrain beneath them, surrounding them, ahead of them on the horizon, was magnificent. Wilkes remained stoic, Renee less so but still unimpressed—glaciers looked similar, country to country—but Max was animated, snapshotting everything with his phone, the incredible views, the sun, the clouds, the snow-covered ridges, the frozen bays and inlets.

One sign, black letters on white wood, and no wider than the width of a double-hung window, identified the airport's three-story control tower as the air terminal: *Qaanaaq*.

"We're two miles northwest of the town," their pilot said on approach, "and this sign on the terminal is your only announcement that you're in Qaanaaq, population six hundred."

The helicopter touched down on the airport's lone runway, snow covering the gravel. 7:15 a.m. They offloaded their bags and hustled inside the small terminal to warm up. Bio breaks and coffee refills for them all, the pilots included, before the pilots returned outside for reinspection of their bird, then back inside for chats with Max and Renee about their planned research and where they were headed. Max heard words from the pilots like *ambitious, formidable, impressive,* but he translated them all to mean "you guys are crazy." A half-hour after they'd arrived, the Cormorant helicopter was back in the air.

Their ride to the hotel was arranged for the afternoon. Hours ahead of them until then, here at the airport, waiting for equipment and their team to arrive, hoping the weather and the travel connections would cooperate.

The Inuit airport manager spoke to them in English, mindful of his computer terminal screen. "Air Greenland cargo flight arriving."

This was it. All seven members of his team on this flight, an Airbus, the only one in the Air Greenland fleet. It was on time to their destination in Greenland via a connection in Reykjavik, Iceland. Outstanding. Max had met each of them only briefly while they worked the Hawaiian volcanoes, near the active Kīlauea. But it was more important that they all knew each other, knew all the equipment, and had all been part of the Army Corps' Hawaiian project, the Pentagon onboard with it. Fend Aerospace needed to hit the ground running. By engaging an experienced team familiar with the equipment and each other, Max gave himself the best chance of exploration success in the shortest amount of time.

One non-Corps team member exception: a Danish consultant, female.

The passengers offloaded from the huge crimson jet, their personal gear in hand and on their backs. They spread out, two and three abreast, looking smart and confident on their approach to the terminal. Max raised his phone and zoomed the lens, recording them for posterity, stride for stride, from his vantage point inside the building. Maybe a seminal moment for this ambitious endeavor, and playing it back in slow motion would be legendary, the stuff of action movie trailers. Damn, they looked good, so in control, so professional—

"Bear-dar," the airport manager said, almost to himself. The manager's gaze moved to a small audio speaker the size of a toaster, resting on a side desk. The bulb atop the speaker was flashing red. Then came the speaker's automated voice.

"*Status alert, status alert.*"

The manager moved quickly to a different desktop. Renee was close enough that she could see the screen, but Max and Wilkes were across the lobby. Multiple security camera feeds were coming through from different angles, showing different stretches around the airport, with one angle suddenly overwhelming the others, consuming the entire screen. The manager's quick clicks zoomed the camera in for a closer look. It showed an area behind the red Air Greenland jet, between the jet and the bay, not visible in this line of sight from inside the terminal but visible from the terminal building's tower, where large ice chunks could be seen gliding though frigid water past the airport, and where the fence around the airport had been trampled.

"*Bear-dar!*" the airport manager yelled, now in panic mode. He picked up a satellite phone, punched in some numbers, and began speaking rapidly, not in English.

"Uh, Max," Renee called, her look concerned, the manager's inflection making all the difference. "I think he said 'bear.' Max?"

The manager slammed the phone down. When he got up from his seat behind the counter, he had a rifle with a scope.

Wilkes and Max moved quickly outside, beckoning the passengers toward them, raising their voices, imploring them then screaming at them to move, move, *move.*

"Behind you! Hustle up! Polar bear!"

The animal emerged from around the Airbus and stood on its hind legs. At this distance, Max guessed its height at seven feet plus. It dropped down and started its run, increasing its speed by a gear or two to a near gallop, its destination obvious, Max's team, who finally got the message, dropped their baggage, and began sprinting, or attempted to. The snowy, iced runway was winning, their footing compromised, each person trying to stay upright while speed-walking or jogging their way to safety, until one of them fell. When she tried to stand, she couldn't. Two of her passenger friends gathered her up and began dragging her forward, but the sure-footed bear was gaining.

Inside the terminal a second automated voice alert came through the speaker, with Renee alone now, the only person to hear it. She checked the security camera feed. Moving through the hole in the fence, having climbed out of the ice-pocked bay, was another large polar bear.

Looks passed between Max and Wilkes bookending the building's double-door entry.

Wilkes slipped his handgun from the holster inside his jacket, Max did likewise from one behind his right hip. They split up, Wilkes moving left, Max right, to get better angles, to get the drop by shooting around the desperate people scrambling closer to them. Max wondered if the two of them would have enough bullets.

The charging bear snarled then roared, sensing a kill, now only a few strides behind her prey. His gun raised, Max took aim, would go for multiple head shots, his finger on the trigger—

Crack! Crack! Shots came from overhead, from the airport manager on the control tower's catwalk. The bear staggered. Four more shots, same origin, with the bear taking one more step, one more stagger, then dropping. It stopped writhing only a moment before the trailing bear moved in, confused, sniffing, mewling, then pushing at the motionless body, nudging it.

Max and Wilkes lowered their guns and eyed the catwalk railing above them. The airport manager leaned over it, his rifle still trained on the bear reunion in progress. He lowered his gun, the seven passengers still stampeding toward the terminal.

"A momma and her cub?" Max said to Wilkes. The bear reunion was depressing.

"My guess, yes," Wilkes said. Then his eyes got larger. "Oh-oh."

The second bear was charging. Max hazarded a look at the catwalk while shoving the passengers past him, gun raised, ready to engage. The Inuit manager exhaled deeply, his expression resigned, pained. He raised his rifle again. This next part, Max knew, would be tough on this man. He sighted his target.

Three more shots followed. The second bear was now down, writhing on the ice. Another rifle shot. When its echo expired, so had the younger bear. With both animals gone, their commingled blood created crimson flowers on the snow-covered tarmac.

The wind picked up, devastatingly cold and determined to make itself relevant again, its bone-chilling gusts battling Max's adrenaline rush. Once the adrenaline was gone, the remorse moved in. That, plus the weather, was all Max could handle. He felt it now in his fingers—the tingle. Frostbite, making a claim. Best to get back inside the terminal before it gained a footing. Wilkes joined him.

The hugs among the seven passengers were tear-filled, all relieved to be inside but devastated by what it had taken to secure their safety. Max ushered the new arrivals back, away from the window. There was no need for them to relive what might have been a disaster. But it was also out of respect for the innocent parties who were only doing what came naturally to them.

The airport manager descended a back stairway to rejoin the group in the lobby, his face serious, bordering on apologetic. The room erupted in appreciation, clapping, whistling, thanking him for his sharpshooting efforts. He moved behind the counter, raised his hands to quiet everyone, then spoke.

"The polar bear has nothing to fear in its environment," the airport manager said, "except for humans. Pray for the spirits of these glorious animals. Local hunters will arrive soon. They will make sure these wonderful beings have not died in vain."

He pasted on a smile, tapped at his desktop keyboard, and asked the new arrivals, all officially U.S. Army soldiers save one, to get in line and provide their identification and other local Qaanaaq clearance info. Once they were all cleared, Max asked them all to gather in a corner and chill, the pun intended, while he spoke with the airport manager a moment. He had a few questions.

"What caliber was that rifle you used?"

A ten-shot .308 cartridge Ruger Predator, he said. It needed to be that caliber or higher because there was too much fur, skin, and fat on the animal to use anything less. The manager retrieved a 9mm handgun from under the counter, like the one Max carried. "If this is the only gun you have, the only way to avoid a painful death by a *nanuq*," he said, "is to use it on yourself."

"*Nanuq*, meaning polar bear?"

"Yes. And do not take the time to do any aiming for body parts on a charging bear if your life depends on taking it down. Stick as many bullets in it as possible, everywhere possible. If it is a hundred yards away, aim for the bear. If it gets within twenty feet of you, your best option is to aim for your own head."

Gallows humor. Last question for the guy. "What the hell is 'bear-dar'?"

"Motion-tracking radar for polar bears," he said. "Do not laugh. We are a test site for it. It is a security alert system based on radar principles enhanced by artificial intelligence. It is learning to alert on bears only, and we here in Qaanaaq are happy to have it. It saves human lives," he said, looking around the room. "Today, we just added to the total."

"Developed in Canada," Renee volunteered, eavesdropping. "As soon as I heard the word, I checked it out online. Very slick, Max. Maybe Fend Aerospace could have a use for it."

All eyes inside the building turned, keen to the noise of ATVs arriving out front on the tarmac, five of them, each pulling a wagon, one Inuit hunter per vehicle. They slowed as they approached the bears, surrounded them, then came to a stop. No one dismounted. They each instead removed items from around their persons—needles, knives, scrapers, other hunting tools—and they offered them to the bears.

"Their offerings are out of respect to Nanuq, the deity of polar bears," the manager explained to Max. "Please, we must let them work now to harvest the animals. I will send someone out to retrieve the passengers' belongings from the runway."

11

"I am Hannah Taat," the Danish consultant said to Renee, extending her hand. "Call me Hannah."

They were inside the terminal's baggage delivery door, Renee and Hannah Taat at the end of a belt emptying onto a small baggage carousel. The other passengers gave Hannah space because a) they were gentlemen and b) she was the passenger who fell on the tarmac in the path of a polar bear, which made her the one passenger among them the least likely to still be alive, something she'd need to process on her own. Renee felt Hannah was handling that aspect well. She returned Hannah's greeting.

"I met Max in Hawaii," Hannah said. "I did not meet you."

Hannah had been hired by the Army Corps for help with their exploratory stint in the Islands. Light-skinned, light-haired, very Nordic. Hers was another in a long line of double-A, Greenlandic-Scandinavian names, this one also a palindrome. With her head covering off, Hannah's blonde hair showed its short spikes. The convenience of her national origin had been greatly welcomed by one person at least, that being Ms. Taat herself, something that she mentioned to Renee, with her being "extremely happy to be returning home to close out my career."

The pilots busied themselves unloading the Air Greenland plane. Still on the runway as well were the five Inuit men, laboring on and around the two bear carcasses. 10:15 a.m., temperature outside, 3°F. Temperature inside the hangar, a sultry 60°F.

"Pardon me, Renee, but I must sit." Hannah slowly lowered herself and her bruised hip and tailbone onto a folding chair close by. Renee remained standing near the tiny carousel, awaiting Hannah's instruction. "That one," Hannah said, pointing.

Renee grabbed the wheeled duffel and rolled it over. Bag delivered, Renee found a window and peeked out. Hannah stayed seated with her baggage. Her engineer associates left the carousel and returned to the lobby with their bags.

"Now for the main event," Renee said, watching and listening to a diesel truck's approach.

"Sorry, but I'm not getting up," Hannah said, rubbing her hip. "I know what it looks like."

The terminal's two-story door opened. The eight-wheeled truck rumbled inside, bringing with it a ferocious wind gust that forced Renee back a step. The burly driver, an Army engineer, powered the truck off and jumped from the cab to the floor.

This was the diamond core drill from Hawaii, winterized to an insane level. Not an intimidating piece of equipment, Renee realized, now that she was standing next to it, because the shafting was folded down, into the payload. With the shafting raised, it could dominate a countryside's horizon. Standard heavy-duty truck tires. Construction-yellow body, with silver and black rods for the mineral extractions tucked into the shaft. The cargo glistened from the frosty precipitation it had collected.

"So Max now owns this thing," Renee said. She commenced a walk around the drill truck's perimeter, admiring its gleaming silver, black, and white against the backdrop of the yellow body.

"Yes," Hannah said. "She's a beautiful machine, Renee, and I am determined to make her Greenland debut a worthwhile one. We hope she handles the drilling quickly and easily, either through rock or through glacier."

The building's second cargo-receiving door raised, allowing more breath-stealing gusts of wind to swirl into the hangar. A forklift rumbled inside.

"The fuel," Hannah said, admiring a six-pack of barrels bundled together. "Diesel. A few thousand gallons of it. Tomorrow's flight will have materials to build a platform for the drill truck. It needs to be elevated one meter off the ground. It generates too much energy to rest on the permafrost without defrosting it."

Renee managed some "uh-huhs" that kept Hannah talking while Renee circled the drill again.

"We'll use spread footings that go down about ten feet. The prefabbed concrete columns that support the platform system need to be strong enough to support the truck and the drill. We have other prefabbed materials . . . we must keep the construction moving . . . "

If the thing did what it was supposed to do, and found what they hoped it would find, they'd be kneeling in front of it when the exploration was over, Hannah said, praising it like a goddess, probably a lot like the first oil drillers did. But discovery was one thing. Mining production would be a whole different animal—if they even got that far here, or wherever else in Greenland that might be.

"Building an operation here will have its challenges," Renee said, "and making it functional even more so. But this isn't sustainable. Not with this power source. Not without adding a fuel pipeline. And certainly not here, at the top of the world. The logistics for a mining operation will be a nightmare."

"Goodness, Renee, you are certainly direct," Hannah said, smiling. "But you are correct. We're not even sure we'll get the equipment to work in these conditions, let alone the issue of finding what we're after. But mining it will be a future problem, with hopefully a favorable resolution. I won't be party to any mining operation, but I do hope to benefit from it while I spend some of my retirement in the Mediterranean, as much of it as my finances will afford me."

Renee was a lot less skeptical than she was letting on, aware of what Max and Wilkes had planned. What would greatly help sustainability of working mining operations in this abominable environment would be a better energy source. Wilkes was already working on acquiring one: a small module nuclear reactor, or SMR.

The language about SMRs that Max had been hearing from nuclear science nerds: small stature, compact, passive safety features, less redundancy needed. Underground placement possible, for protection from natural or man-made hazards. Modular design. Suitable for remote regions like here, and for specific applications such as mining.

And there was a good chance Wilkes could shake one SMR loose from a decommissioned nuclear submarine or aircraft carrier somewhere. More than one if necessary, because there were apparently many, many decommed nuclear subs and warships awaiting dismantling.

"So the drill functioned at full capacity again before you packed it up in Hawaii?" Renee asked. She peered more closely at something tucked under the collapsed shaft, something odd in there that got her attention. She leaned in to check it out.

"Yes. The Corps restarted her quickly enough with the FBI looking over their shoulders. They replaced a few parts and brought it back to spec. She was behaving quite well just before the trip here. Max got himself a bargain. Renee? . . . Hello?"

Renee reached inside the drill's guts, under a piston, and touched something round and hard and brown and bark-like, something incongruous for this environment.

"Oh. You found them. Not hidden well enough, I suppose."

"Coconuts?" Renee said. "You smuggled *coconuts*?"

"And pineapples. Yes, indeed we did. No idea what the fruit import laws are for Greenland, but we went for it. The team loves their Hawaiian pineapples, coconuts, and coconut milk."

Max, Wilkes, and the engineers entered the hangar area and took their turns wandering the perimeters of the equipment like Renee had. One engineer threaded his hand through the interior of the drill shaft, also like Renee, loosened the stowaway fruit, and removed it before the airport manager could notice it, the engineer's associates giving him cover. Four coconuts, four pineapples. Smiles reverberated from the team members. Max and Wilkes rolled their eyes.

"ETA for our rides to Hotel Qaanaaq is a few minutes," Max

announced. "Our badass diamond core drill will keep in here until tomorrow, according to the airport manager. Let's get back inside the lobby."

A 4x4 Chevy Tahoe awaited them at the front door, its engine running and exhaust swirling in the cold. Two p.m. Two spry seniors exited, rosy-cheeked and cheerful, one male, one female, both Inuit. Max recognized them from their Facebook pages and the hotel's low-key website as hotel owners Hans and Birthe, a husband-and-wife team. Their internet presence was minimal, but it was loaded with charm, much like they seemed in person. Distance to the hotel was under three miles. "Three trips," Max said to Wilkes, "to get everyone moved over. You, me, and Renee are first."

Hotel Qaanaaq had no sign to identify it, and *hotel* as a descriptor wasn't exactly accurate, *lodge* making more sense. A red, single-story, rectangular building best described as utilitarian, it was etched into the side of a glacial drift hill, with a view from its doorstep of a fjord that cut a distant iceberg in half, the crease exposing its magnificent glacial blue interior.

Only five guest rooms in the hotel, all doubles, but the owners had arrangements with local Qaanaaq residents for overflow when needed. This was one of those times. There was a separate dining room, which served family-style meals, and a lounge, both richly decorated with Inuit art and culture. Max and his team were about to overrun the place. The owners' daughter took them to their rooms while her parents made a second run back to the airport. She walked them down a corridor displaying more Qaanaaq history, a memorial to the expeditions that had passed through their doors, including people who wanted to pilot kites to the North Pole or drive sledges, larger and heavier than typical dog sleds, around it. The daughter's smile was sweet, but she was all business.

"Three stores in Qaanaaq. They sell clothing, hardware, small appliances, groceries, alcohol. They're replenished twice yearly, in the summer months, when the supply ships can make it through. You can rent warm outer clothing if you need it. Polar bear pants, wool-lined hooded anorak jackets, *kamik* boots made from sealskin with lamb fur inside. Sealskin mittens. The key is to keep the water on the outside, meaning always stay dry.

"There's also a hospital. And yes, those were outboard motors you just saw out there, left with those small boats on the frozen sea. The air here is very dry, so the outboards do fine when left outside, waiting for the thaw. Here we are, Mr. Wilkes. Your room."

He would double up with one of the Army engineers for their Qaanaaq stay. With Wilkes left to unpack, the daughter led Max and Renee to their quarters. Inside it were two single beds.

"Just like my dorm room," Renee said once the daughter had gone.

"We got quite busy in that dorm room, if I recall," Max said, and he dropped his backpack onto the hardwood flooring. He fit an arm under Renee's coat and pulled her close, leaning in to place a gentle kiss on her cheek. Her return kiss on his lips said it was all good, Max, this arrangement was fine, they'd make each other warm, but that sort of oneness would need to keep for now.

They returned to the dining room as the next wave of his team arrived, Hannah Taat among the four of them. She hobbled inside and quickly teared up, speaking Danish to the daughter of the owners, the two women now with ear-to-ear smiles. It had been a long time, years, and their hug was joyful and animated.

Max worked his way around the dining room, absorbing the details of Qaanaaq life as chronicled by the hotel owners, photographs and trinkets on the walls and on display tables. He moved to the lounge for more of the same, including a collage of photographs arranged on a cork bulletin board with a note at bottom that labeled the display as "Visitors 2023." Faces of happy people, no names attached, many ethnicities but mostly Inuit, and all dressed for warmth. On the table beneath it, one photo was apparently awaiting display: a Polaroid of a handsome brindle bull terrier hamming it up for the camera with a big pittie smile.

"That, apparently, is 'Xī Pí,'" Wilkes said, enunciating the *shee-pee*. His comment announced he'd entered the lounge. "The owners' daughter gave me the spelling and the pronunciation. She also told me there's no picture of the dog's owner out there. Per the owner's request."

"Is the owner Chinese?" Max asked, examining the dog's picture more closely.

"Yes, a woman, the daughter said," Wilkes added.

On Max's mind, and on Wilkes's mind because he nodded at Max's guess, with neither of them speaking their conclusion: this was billionaire

Fa Xiaoling's dog, meaning Xiaoling was in the neighborhood. When passing through this area of the country, one needed to pass through here.

"A recent guest, if the photo's not on the wall yet," Max said.

"And maybe still in the area," per Wilkes. "I'll be asking the owners some pointed questions, none of which I expect to generate any real information, but it all fits."

"What all fits?" Renee said, now with them.

"This dog." Max made room in front of the picture for Renee to see it. "Wilkes, tell Renee the dog's name."

Renee wrote it down, then took a photo of the photo. "Translated," she read from her phone, "it stands for *Chinese opera music*. It can also mean *hippie*. What a beautiful dog."

All caught up, they welcomed the last two carloads of team members, the spillover to be redistributed to nearby personal residences. Max stood at the hotel windows, plain and functional with homemade curtains, enjoying the vibrant exteriors of the small Qaanaaq homes that peppered the slope where the hotel was perched. The setting reminded him of northern New England fishing towns full of tall tales of adventure and raging seas and joyful sea-going explorations, but a place that was also party to painful losses coming from unforgiving environments.

Laughter from the dining room. Hotel owner Birthe held up, for her husband and daughter to see, what a guest had just gifted them: a coconut and a pineapple. She hugged the Army Corps engineer. Her husband took their picture together, the engineer having earned a spot on the wall in the lounge.

"Supper at five-thirty p.m.," Birthe announced, "and coconut and oatmeal cookies for dessert. Our new engineer friend has also given me the recipe."

After dinner—a mix of game meats like polar bear and reindeer, locally harvested fish, and canned vegetables more recognizable to the hotel guests than the meats were—it was early retirement to their sleeping quarters for the team, here and around town.

"Max."

Renee's back was against the headboard of her bunk, their two bunks pushed together, the light of her laptop illuminating her face. They'd kissed and warmed and cuddled themselves but were too tired for much else. Max was drifting off, his arm draped across her stomach. He stirred.

Renee's laptop was tapped into communication systems powered by polar orbiting satellites. Most of it was weather-related equipment, but never exclusively so. Wilkes was also online, and they were trading messages.

"Wilkes says radar shows there are blips out there on the ice. One man-made location showing multiple pieces of equipment. We'll make it a point to see them tomorrow when we copter over them to coordinates on the edge of Hiawatha."

The plan for tomorrow morning was to bucket-brigade themselves back to the airport to meet up with a Sikorsky CH-53K King Stallion. The massive military helicopter would fly them seventy miles to an edge of the Hiawatha impact crater, carrying their diamond core drill truck payload plus ten passengers. From this point forward, their daily commute would be between these two locations.

"Net that out for me, Renee. What is Wilkes saying?"

"That she's already there. She's been here, at this hotel, and now she's already operational out there. Maybe not her, personally, right now on the ice at that location, but her people."

"She being Fa Xiaoling?" Max said.

"Yes. It will be her site."

Max was now fully awake and irritated. "Damn it. Just how could she pull something like that off? Who does she know? She can't have connections like we have—"

"Do you hear yourself?" Renee said. "She's got forty-plus billion dollars to play with, plus she's close friends with the Danish monarchy. She's got more pull than *we* have, Max, and my guess, probably more money, right?"

A grumpy Max agreed. Fa Xiaoling was a billionaire's billionaire. And she'd put her climate change stake in the ground already. She couldn't even be considered a competitor. If anything, Fa had an axe to grind with her own government, who expected her to stay out of China's way—as their enemy, the enemy of my enemy, etc.—when it came to the worldwide economic dominance the Chinese Communist Party enjoyed regarding the production and distribution of cobalt.

Max grumbled himself to sleep. The wind whipped against their window, the seals on nearby ice floes howled like dogs at the moon, and just outside the hotel the wandering, part-wolf huskies ignored their seaworthy neighbors and huddled together to keep warm.

12

Their ride, the Sikorsky King Stallion, was a monster, the largest and heaviest helicopter in the U.S. military, a Marine Corps bird that was a hauler, not a fighter, but was also equipped with three .50 caliber machine guns. Its key stat was it could airlift a load of 35,000 pounds plus thirty passengers. The diamond drill had been loaded and secured onboard the helicopter, plus a Marine forklift, plus thousands of gallons of diesel, plus subsistence supplies. The copter's crew of five had been very busy getting this done overnight.

Max spoke to Wilkes as they strode toward the copter's rear cargo-load door, crossing the tarmac with eight other warmly dressed passengers. Renee accompanied the hobbling Hannah. They leaned under the uplift created by the bird's spinning rotors. "How the hell did you manage this, Wilkes?"

"Because of Operation Noble Defender exercises out of Pituffik. This bird was in the vicinity. Plus we know people, right? After you, Max."

They climbed up the loading ramp and slipped past their payload items to the folding canvas seats lining the cabin bulkhead. The team had bunched themselves into the seats behind the cockpit, the first few seats left open for Max and Wilkes. A crew member handed them headphones; they put them on.

"Do you copy, Mr. Wilkes?" the Marine pilot said, his voice coming through the phones.

"Yes, I copy," Wilkes said.

"We'll first cruise those new coordinates, sir. Strap in, please."

"Roger that, Lieutenant Colonel," Wilkes said. "Thank you."

With that, they were in the air. ETA for the touchdown coordinates, sixty minutes. ETA for the additional coordinates, a flyby, was earlier, only twenty-two minutes, their pilot said. Twenty minutes into the ride, the pilot spoke to Wilkes through the headphones: "Sir, we're nearing the flyover. We will photograph it, but would you like to see it real-time?"

Wilkes and Max unbuckled themselves and moved to the bulkhead as directed, to peer out a window. The copter dropped from a swollen, snow-engorged gray sky that was considerably better at a lower ceiling, and settled in at an "altitude of one thousand feet," according to the co-pilot. Around them, drifting clouds and no precipitation. The bird hovered, giving them a clean view of the site that had interested Wilkes.

"Equipment, but no people," Wilkes said, the pilot and Max hearing his observation. "A derrick. Make that two derricks. I can't tell what's inside them, can you, Lieutenant Colonel? Max?"

The pilot said no. Max, with the aid of binoculars, said yes. "It looks like drilling equipment, partly below grade. Snow piled up around the platform footings. I can't tell if anything's operating. The snow could be gathered there because that's what this environment will do, even if the equipment is running. Lieutenant Colonel, are you taking photos? Do you see anything generating heat?"

"We're on it, sir," the co-pilot said through the earphones. "Video and stills. The images will determine if the equipment is operating. Right now, we're not picking anything up, sir. The site looks cold."

Snaking toward one of the derricks were covered rectangular boxes with black hosing sticking out of the snow. Diesel generators, Max decided. And there was a tiny building close by that he decided was a shelter, not unlike what his team intended to build for themselves at their site. The arrangement was similar to the footprint the Army Corps had in mind for them for Max's site.

"Seen enough, gentlemen?" the pilot said.

Wilkes answered in the affirmative. The King Stallion moved out again, heading farther north and east, their intended destination more removed from the receding glacier than this site was, at least on paper.

The sky cleared. Max and Wilkes were at the window again, watching below as the copter navigated over a terrain that went from all white to all brown. They'd crossed over, moving away from the glacier, and they were now above terra firma that was covered only in permafrost, not meters-deep glacial ice. These were newly exposed parts of the Greenland landscape, not visible since the last ice age and previously not explorable; accessible now because of changes in the climate. The promised land for entrepreneurs in search of habitats untapped of their rare-earth mineral content. But these areas were less attractive because this land was more prohibitively north, making it more difficult to stay here long enough to coax the frozen tundra into giving up its secrets, compared to the receding glaciers that Greenland's southern tip boasted.

Except this area had the Hiawatha Glacier, a spot ten times more attractive from Max's perspective, because—

"Mr. Wilkes, I'm going to take her up, so we can get a better view of the crater," the lieutenant colonel said.

—because beneath this ice sheet was bedrock, anywhere from 1.7 to 2 billion years old, and it was also where there'd been a meteorite strike anywhere between half a million to fifty-eight million years ago, the diameter of the divot from the impact almost a mile wide. With radar-imaging discoveries made as recently as 2022, these were now considered facts. It was the reason they were here, at the top of the world, chasing cobalt in the bedrock, natural or asteroid-injected or both.

"When we bank at the higher altitude," the pilot said, "make sure to watch outside the window. You'll get the full visual impact of the western edge of the crater."

A sweeping bank took them along the edge. Like the pilot promised, it gave them a good view of where they'd be setting up shop.

"Passengers," the pilot said, moving into his best GPS voice imitation, "you have arrived at your destination. We're going in, Mr. Wilkes."

The landing was smooth on the rough but flat terrain. The co-pilot announced the outside temperature as 0°F; with windchill, -9°F. Warm by Greenland standards.

Max addressed his team, now suited up in fluorescent yellow head-to-toe and looking like Ralphie's younger brother Randy dressed for his walk to school in *A Christmas Story*. "Can you hear me through the transmitters? Please raise your hands to answer yes." Affirmative responses, all.

"When that cargo ramp drops, we need to be all business," Max said. "When you leave the copter, you carry something. When you return, if there's trash or other detritus, you carry something back inside. We'll have only a few minutes at a time to work with each trip outside, then we'll need to hustle back inside here. If your extremities feel the least bit tingly, head back inside. Keep your headgear on at all times, including your helmets. And should anything come rumbling out of the sea or over land at us, know that all our fine Marine gentlemen here are equipped with the same rifle firepower, or better, as we saw at the airport. We'll spend as much time as we can today offloading our payload and the prefab cabin building materials, then we build. Any questions?"

There were none.

"Good. Let's go."

Getting set up to survive in this harsh environment would take days. Today's trip was courtesy of the U.S. Marines. Tomorrow's trip would be the same, but in a different, smaller aircraft. It paid to have friends in high places. It also paid to have a government that wanted helpful, benevolent, generous citizens with high clearances to succeed.

The shelter they were erecting was stop-gap, to be replaced by something more substantial as the days wore on. By midmorning it was under roof, by midafternoon it had diesel-powered heat. The drill and its fixings and the rest of the diesel fuel had been offloaded but remained under camouflage wrapping, the start of their installations days away.

"Attention! Attention!" came through their headsets, the co-pilot speaking, his message blasting their ears. "We have company! Get back onboard immediately!"

It was too late. They couldn't see or hear what the co-pilot was able to see, but they saw the outcome of it. An unidentified object dropped within thirty yards of the drill, an oblong cage that crashed onto the rocky landscape and split open. Then objects number two, three, and four dropped in quick succession, thudding farther away from their encampment, jettisoned from an unseen aircraft, and startling the team members into paralysis, everyone mesmerized, no one responding to the co-pilot's directions. Max screamed at his team members via his headset, they needed to get back onboard the aircraft *now*, it was a life and death situation, but even with that, he hesitated obeying his own orders.

The oblong cage, the one item that split open closest to where they all stood—he had to trot past it on his path to the helicopter. It stopped him short, its blood-smeared contents devastating, heartbreaking...

It was an animal crate, and what crept into his head were the words from Wilkes last night, "*Shee-pee*," describing how to pronounce a certain pet dog's name. Here was that dog, Xī Pí, his bull terrier body bloody and broken from the impact, or bloody from an event prior to the impact, Max couldn't tell, the dog's mangled carcass in one piece but barely, hanging together by its rib cage.

The other three objects dotting their site all took form in his head now without needing to see them close-up. These would all be bodies, the other three human-looking in shape and size.

They clambered inside the copter and Max did a headcount, his team all onboard, then he leaned into the cockpit and spoke to the pilot.

"Close the rear door, Captain, *now*. Let's get this tin can airborne."

The pilot took them up, his eyes steeled on the radar. Max and Wilkes were told to sit their asses back down, to stay away from the cockpit and the windows, and remain strapped in while the crew assessed the danger from the air, their ride about to test the upper limits of its cruise speed of 170 knots, or 200 miles per hour.

They were seventy miles out of Qaanaaq and 150 miles from Pituffik, where their small Marine unit was based. There were other airports in Greenland, although none in this territory, which made commercial flyovers possible but improbable. Regardless, the Marine crew had sniffed out something that could possibly have had bad intentions, and they'd been proven right. The best place for them to be, was airborne.

Communication with Pituffik Air Base was direct and immediate, their pilot getting instructions from their tower and reading them back. The five-man crew got busy, the three non-pilots taking their positions behind the copter's three .50 caliber guns.

Wilkes barked info at Max, on their own radio frequency, Max's team no longer able to hear the pilots and crew. "I know what's happening, Max," he said. "Initial reaction was to chase, but that lasted about three seconds. We're considered part of the National Science Foundation research team, which makes us non-combatant, which makes us precious cargo. This copter will head southwest toward Qaanaaq, away from a potential flashpoint, to protect us from whatever just befell these other explorers. F-35s from Pituffik have already been scrambled."

"It's a drone, Max. They are chasing a large drone. In a minute the rogue aircraft will be out of commission. If they can force it down without destroying it, they will, but it will likely end up scattered in fragments around the eastern part of the Hiawatha Glacier."

Max got animated. "We need to go back *now*, Wilkes, you copy? Get that across to the pilot. We need to see what the hell else—*who* the hell else—they dropped from that drone."

Because, Max was thinking, *if they killed her dog...*

It was either a warning to the dog's owner—the worst kind of intimidation—or the owner herself was also one of the other victims. Which would mean these deaths were warnings for Max's team.

The moments ticked by with no info from their pilots, their ride on a rapidly increasing beeline away from their new encampment. A thundering roar interrupted the airflow above them, zapping the surrounding airspace like a bolt of lightning.

"That would be the U.S. Navy," Wilkes said in response to the deafening noise. "It won't be much longer. They're in pursuit now."

Like telepathy, their headphones crackled back into operation on cue, their pilot's voice providing an update.

"A drone has been neutralized."

That was all the pilot offered. Wilkes unstrapped himself and went forward to the cabin to speak with the pilot and his team. Soon after, the helicopter banked. Wilkes dropped back into his seat and strapped himself in again.

"We're returning to the site to gather whatever the drone dropped, Max.

They want to collect it before the elements swallow it up. Then we'll call it a day and head back."

When they landed, a crew member issued four body bags from their stores. The enemy drone had been fairly accurate, assuming its intended drop zone, their site, was chosen on purpose. In addition to the broken animal crate, the three other packages were wrapped lengthwise in blue plastic tarps and duct-taped as busy as mummies. No mistaking the shapes. All would be bodies, probably all released at the same time to thud silently onto the unforgiving terrain, peppering their exploration site, each within shouting distance of another, though none of them would do any more talking.

One was confirmed as canine, the cute pittie Xī Pí from the photo at Qaanaaq. A crew member placed the dog's mangled, splayed body into a bag and hauled it back to the copter, followed by additional trips for the pieces of the broken crate. The other crew members slid the wrapped bodies into the Navy-issue body bags and zipped them up, each grabbing an end for a trip back to the aircraft.

"These are all going to Pituffik," Wilkes said after a quick conference with the pilot. "Whatever, whoever they are, Pituffik will get first crack at identification. The medical examiner on staff there is going to be busy."

Inside the copter, all eyes were on the bags. It was all any of them could do to not unzip them, take a knife to the duct tape and the plastic tarps, and confirm what they knew. Two bags were stuffed tightly with full-bodied human beings six feet or longer in length. The third bag's contents weren't nearly as bulky, nor as long.

"My guess is two male bodyguards," Max concluded, speaking to Wilkes. "And the smaller person they were protecting."

Wilkes nodded, agreeing with the assessment. Max went to each bag as the crew members secured it to the floor, his phone snapping away, same as Wilkes and Renee. The smaller body, in all likelihood, would be Chinese billionaire Fa Xiaoling.

Max's mind wandered. Did she have children? Were there other causes she championed? Charities? Who might now share in her vast wealth, economic, altruistic, and empowering? An outgrowth of this remarkable woman's life, one filled with so benevolent and entrepreneurial a spirit.

Had she made a difference? Was the world a better place for her having been in it?

The maudlin subsided, practicality rushing in to claim the territory: These were executions. Who might benefit from them?

Other billionaires, entrepreneurs? But was this really a competition? No, at least not to Max. More like survival against overtly dominant economic repression, with the prospect of recasting a global monopoly, and the redistribution of natural resources controlled by—held hostage by—a foreign power, hanging in the balance.

Fa Xiaoling, a large thorn in the side of the People's Republic of China: dead now, most likely, because of her crusade for a cleaner Earth and the reallocation of its mineral wealth in the process. Something that, had she been successful, would have directly conflicted with her country's preeminence in the world markets.

The gloves were off. This was the first salvo, an overt attempt to suggest that Max and his team, and the U.S., should get the hell outta Dodge.

"Ready to take us back up," the pilot announced. "All passengers, please secure yourselves. ETA Qaanaaq Airport, forty minutes."

The bird lifted, Max's team speaking quietly with their neighbors, Hannah in conversation with Renee and the engineers in conversation with one another.

Max settled his gaze on Renee until she caught him doing it. She returned his stare with a caring, calming smile. Max managed a thankful smile in return, but the exchange couldn't deflect the grim sense of foreboding he felt.

Another glance at the smaller body bag, next to the one with the dog.

What might *he*, Max Fend, leave behind that would make a difference?

On the ground in Qaanaaq, in the early evening hours, they warmed themselves inside the terminal building while awaiting the first decision. It came quickly. Permission from Langley, through Wilkes, to view the bodies.

"We can open the body bags for a peek before they're transported to Pituffik. The copter crew gets to see, plus you, me, and Renee only, Max.

We'll do it after your engineering team leaves for the hotel. We look, we take some pictures, we don't touch. We leave the forensics to the medical examiner at the base."

They climbed into the helicopter, its rotors spinning, the interior warm, the big bird preparing for its return to the air base. The co-pilot remained at the controls, leaving the pilot and the rest of the crew with Wilkes, Max, and Renee. When they were finished here, this ride would leave. Wilkes moved to the smaller body bag first.

"I see no reason to prolong the drama, Max. Let's get at this one first, to satisfy our curiosity. Lieutenant Colonel, please have at it."

"Go ahead, Corporal," the pilot said.

Max and Renee had their phone cameras rolling. Wilkes found his laptop, secured a line, and got into a chat with Langley.

The pilot directed his Marine to begin, nitrile gloves from naval stores on the corporal's hands. He unzipped the bag as far south as what they assumed to be the chest. A nod from the pilot, and the corporal removed his Ka-Bar knife from its sheath and began cutting through the gray duct-tape surrounding the head first. He finished the cut from the crown to below the shoulders, peeled the tape back, a second Marine carefully holding up the head. With the tape gone, the blue tarp was visible underneath. Another nod from his boss, and he sliced carefully through the tarp, a skillful job at keeping the knife's blade away from the face. The face was now fully exposed.

Female. Chinese. Renee turned off her camera and retrieved a full facial photo of Fa Xiaoling from a CIA dossier on her phone. She held it next to this woman's lifeless face. Despite the hole in the victim's forehead and the powder burn from a shot at close range, Renee's declaration, "It's her," seemed accurate.

No surprises delivered with victims two and three. Large Chinese males, thirties, short haircuts, but their faces showed no signs of trauma. "Let's see more," Wilkes said.

Another nod from the pilot. *Zip, zip.* Exposing the neck and chest as far south as their waists, this was where the action was. Blood covered the fluorescent orange outerwear, the smears from multiple bullet entry wounds, with frozen blood pooled under their torsos, attaching the clothed bodies to the inside of the tarp.

"Is anyone interested in looking at the dog?" Renee asked, looking from face to face. "I expect he saw the whole thing go down, too."

The corporal waited on an order from his superior. The lieutenant colonel nodded again, and the corporal unzipped the bag for the dog. Inside it, no plastic tarp, no duct tape, just a mangled, bloodied bull terrier whose brindle body was nearly halved by its impact with the ground.

The corporal looked more closely. "There's a bullet entry wound in his head," he offered. "At least the tough little dude didn't suffer."

He more than didn't suffer, Max realized. "Look there. On his tooth. A hunk of fabric." They all leaned in. "He took a bite out of someone. Part of a coat, or maybe a glove."

The material in the dog's mouth was bloody, but one thing it wasn't, was fluorescent. Not orange, not yellow.

"That shredded material looks white," Max said. "Fa's people were all on the edge of the glacier, on snow and ice. They were dressed to be seen out here, a safety thing, in orange, with reflective striping. Then along comes someone in a snowy environment all dressed in white. In a snow squall, or in a blizzard, there's a chance no one saw them coming."

"Dressed not to be seen," Renee said.

"Too many James Bond movies," Wilkes said to them both. "But yes, that fits. Forensics will examine it." He paused and took a deep breath. "Okay, we're done here. Lieutenant Colonel, please zip them back up and get them ready for their ride back to the base. Max, more input is on its way from the States. Let's get inside to wait for our ride back to the hotel."

13

"Let me buy you a beer, Max."

A long, crazy day behind them. Wilkes came back from the hotel kitchen with two bottles, no glasses. The lounge off the dining room was empty, the research team decompressing in their spaces here at the hotel or in residences around town. Renee was back in their room.

"Qajaq. A Greenlandic brew," Wilkes said and raised his bottle. "Made from icebergs thousands of years old. Cheers."

Max didn't trust Wilkes's taste in beers. Back at Pituffik, a microbrew Wilkes had suggested he try smelled like sneaker feet. Max did the smell test on this one. Much better. He raised his bottle. "Cheers."

"So, we have orders from Langley," Wilkes said. "The short of it is, we need to go back."

"Back where? To the impact crater? Of course we're going back."

"No. Not the site you staked out. We need to go back to the States. Go home. For now. Fa Xiaoling's death was a warning. Our protection here can't be guaranteed. We can't risk an international incident. The Danes know about Fa now. Her murder is going to be a nightmare for them. They want us out, the Agency wants us out—"

Max got hot. "This is BS, Wilkes. I've got major time, effort, and resources invested here. We're doing a good thing, for our country, the global climate crisis, the energy crisis. You pulled me into this, and now someone says, 'Thanks, but no thanks, you're going home'? No."

"There is no 'no' here, Max. You saw the assets they had to deploy today. Our copter, then the F-35 after the fact. They blew that drone out of the sky, and now they need to find all the pieces to analyze whose aircraft it was. Too costly, and it could get even costlier, in human and weaponry losses, especially if it turns ugly."

"Wilkes—no, damn it—"

"Hold on, Max, calm down. there's a 'however'—"

Wilkes held up his hand before Max could respond further. "It's not a done deal. Someone's calling an emergency meeting. They're looking for approvals and some additional funding at a higher level. They're looking to tap into some double-secret military and Agency budget money."

"For what?"

"To set up protection for the operation, at least until the exploration is complete."

"So we're good then?" Max said. "We don't need to leave?"

"Yes and no. The Army Corps can stay, because you're funding them, and because they're the U.S. Army. The Army won't concede to intimidation, and they can handle themselves. Renee, you, and I, however, because of our affiliation, we need to go home."

Langley wanted its assets back in the States. That's what Max was hearing.

"How long before we know about additional approvals?" Max asked.

"Days, a few weeks maybe."

"If nothing happens in a few days, we'll need to send them all home," Max said. "I'll decide after we get back. I expect Hannah will want to stay, too, for now, and that might work out best, for her and for us. So in the meantime it'll be business as usual for them."

Discussion over. They drained their beers, Max making a mental note of the microbrewery name. *Qajaq.* Excellent beer; probably even better from a tap. And yet another palindromic Nordic name. Which brought him back to Hannah Taat, his Danish engineer. Hopefully she'd see the good in this plan as well.

He would address his team in the morning.

A quick discussion with Renee before bed, a few early morning comms, then a gathering of Max's team in the hotel lounge after breakfast. Max gave them an update, stemming from yesterday's developments.

"There's been a significant change in our approach," he announced. "For the Army Corps engineer folks, you will hear this directly from your superiors, but I'll give you the overview: You are to remain on task, but you must proceed with the utmost caution. Transportation to the exploration site going forward will be by civilian contractor aircraft, the providers to be vetted within a few days. Our benefactors in the States are looking for additional avenues—read that as 'more Congressional funding'—to provide for your protection. I'm sorry to announce that Renee, Wilkes, and I have been summoned back home," he said. "The Feds want the civilians out of Greenland because they can't guarantee our safety."

A small lie. It was because they were covert CIA, not ordinary citizens.

"But Hannah has decided to stay with the team. We trust you'll protect her. Keep yourselves armed, always. Stay in communication with Pituffik. In the short run, you should sit tight and wait on the air transport contractor approvals. When they come through, it will be back to the site to continue the assembly. More to come. My transport out of Qaanaaq, with Renee and Mr. Wilkes, will be here in twenty minutes, but I'll be back."

Handshakes all around. When the lounge cleared, Max found himself alone in front of the photos on the corkboard wall. The Polaroid of Xī Pí, the smiling pit bull, was now tacked to it. Hans and Birthe materialized next to him, Birthe with a black Sharpie in her hand. She patted Max's back, but no words were exchanged. She leaned past him to pen a message at the bottom of pittie Xī Pí's pinned picture.

Hvil i fred, unge mand.

"It is Danish," she said. "It means 'Rest in peace, young fellow.'"

A few too many things were dying in this brutal environment, Max opined internally. Husky puppies, bull terriers, Chinese billionaires. And that wasn't even including the polar bears. If inexperience didn't get you, a bad-news foreign operative might.

Birthe wiped a tear from her eye, as did Hans and Max from theirs. Hans removed a rifle and cartridges from the gun cabinet in the lounge. "For my car," he said.

14

Myrna sat upright on the sofa in her living room, ignoring the TV. What had her attention was her coffee table, papered over in bills. Some were current, with near-future expectations, others were past due. Which should she pay? Her mortgage? Something toward her home equity loan? The used car loan for her ten-year-old Toyota 4Runner? What about her dental tech school tuition payment? Plus, Wyatt needed braces. She also needed a grocery store run.

Thank goodness for the state's food assistance program. She unzippered a pouch, pulled out her assistance card, checked her coupons on it. She'd do fine tomorrow at the local IGA if she stayed with the specials.

She got online, found a creditor's website, and was about to contribute something toward a past-due amount when a popup ad distracted her. New social influencer Eva Biswas, indigenous to India, beautiful, fluent in many languages, and a charismatic small-business owner, was scheduled to appear as a presenter at a symposium in Wilkes-Barre. Tickets were only twenty dollars.

Could she swing it?

No, not in the budget this month. She paid off the propane bill instead.

A daguerreotype image filled her TV screen on the ten o'clock news: Günther Heintz, the silver prospector whose nineteenth-century story had monopolized the local news cycle for days. Another segment on him, with more on the time capsule, the daguerreotype's photographer, and the photographer's process. Plus Heintz's time in the mountains in a coal miner's village in nearby Eckley, the village preserved. WNEP, based in Wilkes-Barre, was living off the notoriety, the local population fascinated by it, and fascinated also that the time capsule had become a national story.

"Momma."

Wyatt appeared alongside the sofa, his night clothes disheveled and drenched from a fever, his cheeks red. "I just threw up in the toilet, Momma. A lot."

She felt his burning forehead then located a thermometer. A 102° temperature. Manageable. A bug of some sort, making the rounds at school. The fever might have broken already. A change of pajamas. No need for a trip to urgent care. She was still paying off the last late-night visit. But if he needed to go, he'd go. This time it would be a wait and see.

She dosed him with children's cold and flu medicine and had him crawl under a blanket and rest on the living room sofa with her. Little Pig, their crazy three-legged terrier who was now missing her human brother in bed, appeared in the doorway, got a running start, and was able to join them after two failed attempts at bettering the sofa cushions. Ten minutes later Wyatt was asleep on the sofa, his arm around his dog.

Even with all their money problems, she loved their life, and she could never understand why her husband hadn't. Why it had never been enough for him. Why he'd taken it out on her. Verbal abuse that had become physical, this after he'd been fired for drinking and doing drugs on the job, that job being a local cop. The drinking got worse, the drugs got worse, her beatings got worse. The despair finally got the better of him. He disappeared soon after giving her a beating that had severely damaged her hearing in one ear.

She let the TV ramble on, the volume low. More on Heintz, another station carrying the story about the newly discovered daguerreotype, the prospector's search for silver, his good relationship with the Indigenous population, his disinterest in "goblin *kobold*." And how the mineral brought vibrancy to other colored metals ". . . with cobalt green resulting from its combination with zinc in the rarest of instances on ocean floors, before the Earth's oceans receded."

The cobalt buzz was frenzied and furious and viral, but she'd still managed to miss that bit of info before. *Green* cobalt? Extremely rare.

Myrna carried Wyatt to his bedroom, Little Pig underfoot all the way. The fat terrier preceded him under the bedcovers. She tucked them both in and turned off the bed lamp. His Sock Monkey nightlight came alive in the darkness.

Wyatt's musty kryptonite brick, his Clark Bar, sat green side up on his desk, illuminated by the nightlight. She picked it up for another look at it.

Max and Renee's connecting flight touched down at Wilkes-Barre/Scranton International. No fanfare, no special transportation, just an airport limo service to Jim Thorpe forty-five minutes away, to meet with Assistant Special Agent Cornell Oakley and get right back into it. Wilkes flew through to DC.

"Nice idea, meeting here, Cornell," Max said. His eyes wandered the walls of the café. Canaries was a busy little specialty coffee shop on a busy little Jim Thorpe street. It was Cornell's choice for them to meet here to exchange debriefings.

"I like the coal-mining aspect," Cornell said. "For my money, miners are some of the toughest blue collar workers in the U.S." Themed drinks, trinkets that included antique mining canary cages, plus there was a small shrine to America's Native American Olympic hero Jim Thorpe, the town's namesake. A large screen played clips from movies and documentaries that highlighted the importance of the carbon dioxide–sensing canaries for miners, interspersed with Jim Thorpe archival film footage.

"You're drinking a Liquid Carbon Latte," Cornell said. "Non-alcoholic. Butterscotch, caramel, a hint of anise, and edible charcoal for color. Where are you staying?"

"About that. Renee, heard anything yet?" Max said.

"The motorhome is en route. ETA by nightfall. We'll be staying at an RV campground on the other side of the borough."

"Great, you can grill up some steaks when you invite me to dinner," Cornell said, "which needs to be soon. Look, I heard what happened to you guys up there, Max. A tough break. It was a smart choice to abort. The Bureau's picked up similar chatter around here, too. I need to fill you in."

"The North Pole isn't rid of us yet, Cornell. As soon as some things get buttoned down, we'll be going back. Wilkes is working out the details."

Cornell nodded, indicating he knew what those details were. "Not a similar issue here, Max. The approvals are already ironed out for that additional piece you—we—will need."

For the protection. Safety from unknown bad actors, foreign, maybe even domestic. The Bureau had it handled. Bureau assets, other government agency assets, military assets. Ducks in a row. Cornell spoke cryptically, but Max and Renee understood: the pump was primed, all systems were go, things had advanced to a "let's-get'r-done" attitude. All that was left to do was decide where to dig, then get the permits.

There were meteorites in Greenland, and radar able to see underground had provided ample probability that they'd eventually find something of value. Here in the Poconos, they had a German prospector's nineteenth-century journal discovered in a bank cornerstone that mentioned a *kobold* ore treasure, but with no map.

"So the idea is, Max, we get some media coverage," Cornell said. "We, as in you."

"Excuse me?"

"You have the name recognition. 'Billionaire Max Fend to invest in a mining operation in the Poconos' is a good headline," he said in a low voice. "No need to announce where, just a few interviews saying Fend Aerospace is here, in coal country, and you'll be mining for precious minerals on a very large scale, willing to pump millions into the operation."

Max shook his head no. "That will create a feeding frenzy, Cornell. It will be like throwing chum in the water, for the sharks as well as for the flounder."

Then it hit him: That was the whole idea.

"All right, all right, I get it," Max said. "If the sharks bite here in the States—foreign actors like Russia, or China, or other countries feeling threatened, like the oil giants in the Middle East—no issue, they will be neutralized, thanks to the 'protection,'" his fingers air quoted. "But the flounder . . . you *want* the local flounder to bite."

"Exactly," Cornell said. "You will have deputized a region of people to do the search for you. It might already be happening, we just don't know where. The time capsule reporting could have stimulated it. People looking to strike it rich with a cobalt mine claim. They don't need to know you're flying as blind as they are."

Renee finished the last of her Liquid Carbon and swiped away a black frothy mustache with her sleeve like an English pub veteran. She picked up a black cookie from a plate, another Cornell treat, dark chocolate speckled with chocolate chips. Carbon County Coal Cracker, the cellophane called it. She ripped open the packaging, leaned into the conversation, and chewed. "Max. Why don't you tell him how much money Fend Aerospace is putting into the exploration here."

"Renee, is that really necessary—?"

"Just tell him."

"Close to fifty million. For the exploration. If the digs are successful and a contract comes out of it, the next budget will be at least two hundred million, but not all Fend Aerospace money. One correction, Renee: *I'm* guaranteeing the Fend portion personally, not Fend Aerospace."

Just like in Greenland, Max finished in his head. These numbers were starting to sound crazy, even to him.

Cornell stayed silent, in full absorption mode. Max now realized Cornell hadn't known he was worth anywhere near that amount, let alone that it was actually many multiples of those numbers.

"And *that* reaction, right here," Renee said, reveling in Cornell's slack-jawed silence, "is the same 'wow' you will see from the general population when a public relations campaign begins. Which will generate leads. It's a good plan. "

Cornell found his tongue again. "I'll get the ball rolling tomorrow. Two other things. One, there's a boogeyman here. The Centralia coal-seam fire."

"We're aware of it," Max said.

"We need to stay away from it. Too volatile. No drilling anywhere near it. Otherwise, we maybe see an event of cataclysmic proportions. Number two, about this town—"

The café table they shared suddenly rattled, the glass front door, the entire space that was the interior of the store, everything shook at once, a tremor that was enough to make glasses and coffee cups on the counter dance, and cookies in the bakery display case slide flat. Probably not an earthquake, but it felt like one. Max and Renee saw the cause: A U.S. Army cargo hauler rumbled past the storefront and down main street, pulling an enclosed trailer, putting all the touristy pedestrians on notice as it ambled by.

"Really, Cornell?" Max said. "Already?"

"The Army Corps of Engineers are getting in front of some things. It's a —" Cornell picked up his iPhone, checked his notes.

"A medium tactical vehicle," Renee finished for him, her laptop open. "All five tons of it."

"Yes. An overland arrival. Some equipment's being airlifted by copter. And that brings me to the second potential obstacle. Jim Thorpe has a very active town watch group. They stick their civilian noses into everything around here. Local law enforcement, the mayor, they're all onboard with us being here, but the neighborhood watch folks? They're nosy little SOBs, and they feel entitled. Just be aware they're out there, and know that we'll need to make nice with them."

"Gremlins," Renee volunteered, breaking off more of the Coal Cracker. "We'll be making nice with the local gremlins while we search for *kobold*, a.k.a. gremlin ore. Ironic.

"I like this cookie," she added.

Cornell drove them to the RV park at dusk. They stopped at the campsite office to sign some paperwork and pick up keys that had been left for them, then Cornell dropped them off at their campsite. Their home-sweet-class-A-motorhome, all forty-plus feet of it, was parked and connected and looking fully operational, its patio awning and slide-outs open, interior lights on. In a parking space next to it was a Ford Bronco rental SUV, their local transportation.

They hauled their bags to the RV door, Max pausing for a look at the neighboring campsite. He was treated to a feeble vision, a flickering camp-fire that illuminated an antique camper in full camping mode, its bed-wing sleeping quarters folded out. The small truck was not in good condition. Two flat tires, a rusted-out rear bumper, and the white body was full of rust. Wildflowers sprouted from what looked like its spare tire lying on the grass close by. Max guessed the camper hadn't moved from this campsite next to this lake in decades. Leaning against the camper was a Vespa scooter.

A woman in a lawn chair acknowledged their arrival with a tip of her black hat, flat-brimmed with a hand-beaded band, then she returned to poking at whatever was cooking in the iron skillet in the campfire. Rising, floating embers illuminated her worn, leathery face, wrinkled and tan and framed by gray braids, a Willie Nelson look. Behind her, on a clothesline, was a row of hanging fish, probably trout, clipped there by spring-loaded clothespins. A canoe lay alongside the camper. Max nodded to her, but then decided that a simple nod wasn't a good enough acknowledgment.

"International Harvester Scout," he called to her from the front step of the motorhome. "1964. Not many of those campers were made."

"1963," she said, correcting him. "One of the first eighty-eight off the line. Not for sale."

Max heard Renee calling him from inside the motorhome. He nodded to their neighbor again and went inside the Winnebago with Renee.

"This motorhome is beautiful," she said. She passed the living area, found the refrigerator, checked inside, nodded at its contents. "Stocked, too. Excellent. This is the way to travel, Max."

She popped open a beer bottle, wandered past the kitchen space, and opened the sliding door to the bedroom in the rear. The king bed had been made up, was already turned down, and mints were on the pillows. Nice touch.

Max, trailing her, moved closer and wrapped his arms around her for a hug from behind, burying his nose in her short, dark hair. "The local RV people were very accommodating. Let's turn the heat up a little, get a shower, and call it a night, shall we?"

A few hours later, lights off, showered, and tucked into bed, Max was roused by sounds coming from the campsite next door. Slamming doors, loud knocking, and muffled voices, one of them a male sounding not especially quiet and not especially patient. Max checked the time on his phone. A little after midnight. He climbed out of bed and peeked through the blinds. His neighbor was now outside, pulling her hanging fish from the line and placing them in a cooler. A man followed in her footsteps, scowling at her. Max was unable to hear the exchange, but got the gist of it: According to her guest, she was slow, she was old, she was not cooperating. Max slipped out of bed and pulled on jeans and a tee. He left his 9mm on the shelf.

He zipped himself into a windbreaker, and stepped outside to see the younger man reaching around the back of the woman's head and pulling her to him. Then came the slap to the face in the moonlight, the defiant woman striking the impatient guy with enough of her open hand to make him take a sideways step. After that came the retaliation, a fist to her face that sent the old woman tumbling backward onto the grass. The man descended on her, both fists pummeling her head while she tried to cover herself, then a right foot to her side. She grunted in pain. He lifted her up by the shoulder, loaded up for another punch—

Max didn't announce himself before commencing the beating, unaware just how upset this had made him. His brain locked into fight mode.

Incapacitate him quickly.

Fists to the solar plexus and the throat. Knee to the groin, knee to the chin. Sleeper hold, choke him out.

Call the police. See if the woman needs medical attention.

Max was up to the "call the police part," and he was having trouble with it.

You attacked a defenseless older woman—let's make it so you don't do that again—

"Max. Max!"

Renee was screaming in his ear, Max further disfiguring the man's face with his fists.

"Stop! He's unconscious. I called 911—Someone's here already—Stop! *Max!*"

A spotlight from a Ford Explorer hit Max in the face while he leaned back over the guy he'd pummeled. He now saw the damage he'd done, a bloody, disfigured mess, but it was a bloody mess that was still breathing, a condition Max was tempted to remedy—

"Hold it right there!" came the order. A female voice, the beam from her Maglite now in his face. The spotlight from her Explorer remained on the stationary male on the ground. Max relented, shifting his attention to the victimized senior to help her sit up in the grass, then stand, her face blood-ied, but also full of tears.

"It's the drugs," she whimpered. "My grandson Peter—it's the drugs . . ."

Two emergency vehicles appeared, Ford Explorers number two and three, both advertising themselves as Jim Thorpe Police Department, plus an EMS vehicle. The police made quick work of cuffing and stuffing the complaining grandson into a patrol car perp seat after getting the grandmother's statement.

Max held his neighbor's hand while an emergency tech checked the woman's vitals and listened to her complain about being on a stretcher. He stayed by her side but remained quiet, letting the process work itself out. She acquiesced, soon placing her hand over Max's, asking the EMT to wait before loading her into the ambulance. She addressed him.

"Would you be a dear and put the cooler inside my camper please, and close the door? The raccoons—"

"We'll take care of it," Max said. "I'm so sorry this happened to you, ma'am. I'm Max. This is Renee."

"Eunice. And I know who you are, Mr. Fend. I'm sorry, too. Thank you again for helping me."

He handed her a business card. "Call me Max. And do call me if you need a ride back."

The ambulance gone, the police took statements from Max, Renee, and other RV guests, then settled back in their police vehicle. Max checked the time. 1:10 a.m. The patrol car left the campground with their prisoner, headed to the hospital. Medical attention first, then jail.

"Mr. Fend."

The first person on the scene was circling back to him. She was a stocky African American woman, the one who had shone the Maglite on him. The floodlight on her older Ford Explorer revealed it had once been a cop car.

"Aurora Jolson," she announced. "Retired police chief, living a quiet life here in the Poconos. Sad to say the quiet part's been hit and miss. I'm now a town watch volunteer, and I'm here in that capacity. Hearing other campground guests tell it, it seems you've had some training."

Max dusted himself off and looked for Renee. She was at the back door of his neighbor's camper, shoving the ice cooler inside. She pulled the door shut.

Max went into his cover spiel, a rote response. "I've had one-on-one training in hand-to-hand. My company's risk management folks demanded it. I've had elusive and at-risk driving skills courses, the whole Key Man insurance gamut. Protects me, protects my company."

Max assessed his questioner, her inquisitive disposition, her vehicle, and the large Maglite she was so quick on the draw with. He didn't see a gun, but if she was former law enforcement, she had one for sure. He had a question. "You got here before the police did. How'd that happen?"

Another vehicle pulled in behind Ms. Jolson's. Another Ford Explorer, with yet another floodlight. She gave it a thumbs-up, then gestured at campsites along the trail before and after Max's. The SUV backed out, put on its floodlight, then cruised the area.

"Short answer, I was in the neighborhood," she said, "and I have a police scanner in the car. All the town watch folks do. My friend will look for her grandson's car. He probably didn't walk here. We know him, the police know him. He's harassed her before, but far as we know, he never attacked her. And after what you did to him, he might never harass her again. Then again, he could go a completely different way. I would watch your back, Mr. Fend."

"Call me Max."

"I know who you are. I also know why you're here. The region's residents have been getting a little nervous, all because of that damn time capsule. The FBI sneaking around, the U.S. Army stashing its assets in and around town—if there's something worth digging up, they want Big Business to get the hell on top of it, maybe bring some industry back to the region. If not, you're all welcome to just go the hell home."

Renee arrived at the conversation, complained she was tired, a pointed approach, Max knew, because she'd sensed he needed saving from more pontification from this ex-cop. But the truth was, he was on the same page with Ms. Jolson.

Max threw her a bone. "Let's meet some other time when we can talk more. Today closed out a long trip for us, and we're a few time zones out of whack, so right about now—"

"Fine. Take my card. But know this, Max Fend—" Aurora Jolson's voice was more pointed and effective than any finger she could have poked into his chest.

"These coal cracker families have been looking for reasons to be proud of themselves again. They're pissed the climate change experts painted a big target on their backs and ripped out their hearts and their livelihood by crippling the anthracite coal industry in favor of cleaner energy. But deep down, they get it. We all get it. They don't want to be the problem anymore. They want someone to help them become part of the solution. They want to go back to work, and finding a major cobalt deposit would make that happen. Have a good rest of your night."

15

No press conferences, Max told Cornell. He'd do a few interviews with local news stations, choose some podcasts he could join, and Fend Aerospace would blast a prepared message out to social media outlets.

Today would be the last of three scripted days of public relations, with Fend Aerospace's media group driving it. The message was simple: We're going after the cobalt researchers say is here. And you can help.

Other U.S. players were now visible, buying time on radio, TV, and invading peoples' website experiences with popups. Searches online for cobalt rendered cookie-prompted responses from Tesla, Microsoft, and Apple—"Got cobalt? Tell us, Carbon County!"—plus U.S. lithium-ion battery makers and others. All now had presences in the Poconos, criss-crossing the area. They could smell the supply chain wins that a major cobalt discovery might provide them after standing in line for so long with their hands out, waiting on the benevolence of the Chinese.

Max, Renee, and Cornell were back at Canaries, the coffee shop, for a mid-morning discussion and another of the surprisingly good Liquid Carbon Lattes.

"Your motorhome comfy?" Cornell asked.

"It's great," Max said. "RV park with campsites on a lake. Some drama there the first night, but it all worked out. Get us up to speed, please."

"Only domestic players so far," Cornell shared. "No foreign interests visible yet. Unless someone's shilling for them, which could happen."

"I have a list of trigger-happy hackers willing to check out internet presences and reverse engineer them," Renee said. "Say the word."

"Not there yet, Renee. Max, the Army engineers set up their operation north of here, near the Eckley Miners' Village. Ever heard of it?"

Max hadn't. Renee keyed at her laptop. "Learning about it right now."

She read aloud from a web presence. Another Pocono tourist attraction. Irish, Germans, and other Europeans had called it home while working the coal mines in the nineteenth century.

"Heintz, the German silver prospector with the journal," she said. "Online comments say he stayed there in the 1850s and '60s, in one of the rooming houses. The houses are still standing."

"Good to know," Max said, then turned to Cornell. "Did the engineers bring my new diamond core drills?"

"All three. I'm forever learning how deep your pockets are, Max. And the reach of your connections. Show-off."

"Hey. Not the right attitude. I'm just looking to move things along. Two will be deployed as soon as it makes the most sense. The third is a spare."

At the table behind Cornell, a woman closed her laptop. Dark hair, long and sleek; excellent shampoo commercial material. She checked her face in her phone camera, or maybe she was taking a selfie, Max wasn't sure, but her phone was held eye-level. From the way it was angled, its photos would include the back of Cornell's head plus full facials of Max and Renee if the woman got the zoom and depth perception correct, and it looked like this was what she was doing. Max leaned around Cornell, went right at the issue.

"Hey. Miss. You're not very good at this, are you? Sneaking photos of people? Care to explain yourself?"

She turned around, not trying to hide a flashy smile full of perfect teeth. A photogenic media or celebrity type, she wouldn't have looked out of place starring in a Bollywood feature. A face made for the screen, whether here, or in India, or elsewhere.

"Busted," she said. "You're Max Fend. I'm Eva Biswas. Freelance social media influencer, writer, reporter, and photographer. I do on-location work for *The Arab News* out of Saudi Arabia, but you won't see my byline anywhere. I ghostwrite for people whose names I can't reveal to you—or you, or you," she said, her eyes smiling at Cornell and Renee in succession. She handed Cornell enough business cards for the entire coffee shop and flashed her teeth at Max again. "What might happen here in the States, Mr. Fend, is of great interest to the Middle East. To China and Russia too, of course. Something that could approach biblical proportions economically, correct?"

Clever, mentioning the Bible, certainly a scene-stealer in woodsy evangelical environments across Pennsylvania, as in everywhere in the state outside of Pittsburgh and Philadelphia. Yes, cobalt was topical. And anything labeled "the new oil" would get the Middle East's attention also.

Her English was flawless. A middle America voice made for radio, a face made for TV. Her age, if Max had to guess, was mid-thirties. "Is there something you want, Miss Biswas?" Max asked.

"You've invested in this treasure hunt, as I understand it," she said. "The whole world is watching. Any insights on what the plan is? How to make something happen?"

"When there's news, everyone will know, I'm sure, but we're still in exploratory mode," Max said. "Until then—"

"Max." Renee leaned forward. She gripped his arm, a cue for him to shut up. She drilled a stare at the woman, interested in what was still in the woman's hand: her phone.

"Turn it off," Renee demanded of her. "Now. *Off*, or I take it away from you, and you won't like what I do to it."

Max and Cornell caught on. Ms. Biswas was recording them—audio, video as well. The images probably weren't steady, but the audio would assuredly be good enough to know who was speaking.

"Oops. Sorry," Ms. Biswas said. "An occupational misstep. I didn't intend—"

"Yes, you did," Cornell said. "That's it, we're done here." Cornell puffed up his torso enough to fill the space between their café table and the eavesdropper's. "That was not cool, Miss. Max, Renee, we're leaving."

On the sidewalk outside the café, Cornell looked right then left then over his shoulder, the nosy reporter still inside, visible in the window, her hands now at a laptop keyboard. "That's the last time I buy you guys a Liquid Carbon Latte."

"No worries. I don't think any trade secrets were spilled," Max said, "because there aren't any yet."

"Yeah, well, now she knows that," Renee said. "Probably also heard 'drills,' 'only domestic players,' 'Army,' and I don't remember what else." She keyed at her phone. "I'm looking her up online, right—now."

Cornell shook Max's hand, their conversation finished, except for a parting comment.

"Go have your meeting in Eckley with the Army engineers and let them update you, then you update them. After that, dinner tonight, your place. You can cook me some ribeye on your barbecue. I'll be there at seven-thirty."

Renee stared at her phone, then refocused on Ms. Biswas, still sitting at the picture window fronting the coffee shop. When the woman returned her stare, Renee didn't flinch, but instead glared back until Ms. Biswas smiled then returned her focus to her laptop.

Renee read from her phone search. "Ah, Max? Cornell?"

They answered in unison. "What?"

"She has over two million TikTok followers here in the States, five million across India, the Middle East, and China. And her TikTok account is only eighteen months old. I found some pre-TikTok info on her. Fuzzy photos, before she became famous. Her resume says she was formerly an elementary school teacher in Mumbai. It says also she was a battered housewife. She reinvented herself as an influencer with a gonzo journalism bend. Probably by pulling rude crap on unsuspecting newsmakers like she just did with us. Her account mentions she's here for an influencer symposium at the Mohegan Sun Pocono Casino."

Renee scowled at the café picture window. Ms. Biswas stayed focused at her laptop screen, ignoring Renee's stare.

"Perfect face, smug attitude, trained voice," Renee said. "Fake, fake, and fake. I don't like her."

Wyatt hurried to his mother's idling car in their stone driveway. He hopped into the back seat, put the shoebox on the seat next to him, then belted himself in.

"Ready, young man?" his mom said.

"Ready, Momma!"

Myrna left their driveway in her aging Toyota 4Runner with her son and his rocky half-block of kryptonite, their destination a gemologist's shop in Jim Thorpe. They waved to Uncle Jesse draining a cold one on his porch as they passed his house.

The coal industry, as far as Myrna could remember from word-of-mouth anecdotes over the years, had also yielded crystals, non-precious gemstones, nickel, and other rocks of real or faux merit for over a hundred years now, and had even burped up a hunk of gold the size and shape of an adult thumb back in the 1920s, but no substantial precious metal deposits were found after the initial excitement. In Jim Thorpe and the surrounding Pocono towns and villages, the anecdotes created a robust trade in rare-earth trinket tourism. Nothing that had ever interested Myrna, never a party to a precious-metals frenzy because she could never afford to be. She'd always been focused on trading her unskilled labor for an hourly paycheck, necessary for her family's survival even before her husband went missing, but much more so afterward.

But Wyatt had pleaded with her to do this, to sell his kryptonite, and she knew why. Her birthday was soon, and he wanted to buy his mother a present. She'd heard him talk to Little Pig about it on the deck, him stroking her snout to elicit Pig's licks and kisses after a short game of fetch with the Frisbee. Her heart melted, and she'd cried herself to sleep that night, she was so proud of him.

"Here we are, Wyatt," Myrna said. They were in a small parking lot off Main Street, six spaces. No parking meters, Myrna thankful for small favors. "You ready, honey?"

"Sure, Momma, ready!" Wyatt grabbed his shoebox and tucked it under his arm. They walked under the store sign reading *N. Hughes, Jeweler, Appraiser, Gemologist*, which ran the length of the shop's porch overhang. They entered the store.

The inside was not what Myrna was expecting. Glass jewelry cases on both sides, and one against the back wall also, the shop well lit, with security cameras in all the corners—that was all expected. The unexpected part was the proprietor, a small Asian woman standing beside the glass counter at the deep end of the shop, her arms at her sides. She was older, with a wizened, worn face and drooping eyelids behind her eyeglasses, in a black dress with multiple strings of pearls around her neck. She managed a smile, but it looked like it took a lot out of her. Myrna held Wyatt's hand as they approached her, Myrna fully aware she was being evaluated. They were the only customers in the shop. Mounted television monitors bookended the front counter, one displaying financial news, the other tuned to an entertainment news program, with other wall mounts surrounding them, some of them playing security camera footage of the shop.

"Is the proprietor here?" Myrna asked the Asian woman. A second smartly dressed woman had entered from a side doorway, younger, also Asian, and Myrna noticed how her question to the older woman had frozen the younger one. It was apparently the wrong thing to ask.

"I am the proprietor. I am Sophie Ming Hughes," she said in accented English, her chin raised. "Norman Hughes was my husband. He is gone now." So, too, was her smile.

"Oh. I am so sorry, ma'am," Myrna said. "For your loss, and for my mistake. Please accept my apology. I was wondering if—"

"What is your name?"

"Oh. Right. Myrna. I see you do appraisals. I have—"

"Last name."

Myrna stiffened, wondering why the questions regarding her identity, until she understood. Myrna didn't look like a jewelry store customer. She looked much poorer, looked like she couldn't possibly have anything of value that would interest a gemologist, unless she was trying to pawn stolen goods. Her heart fell.

This was a mistake. To think an appraiser might have an interest in buying something from her or Wyatt now seemed laughable. The woman wanted her full name, Myrna was sure, in case she tried to steal something.

"I'm sorry, ma'am, this was a bad idea. Wyatt, honey, we need to go."

"Wait. No, it is I who should be sorry." The proprietor's face softened. "I apologize. I do not need your full name unless we decide there is something I can do for you. Come, let me see what it is that you have in the box. Some jewelry? Old coins?"

Wyatt held the shoebox up and carefully handed it to Myrna. She placed it on the counter and removed the lid. "My son found this rock, and he's quite proud of it. I've searched the internet, probably not asking the right search questions, so I need an expert's opinion. We, um, would like to see what it's worth. He's saving up to buy something special for me that he won't tell me about, aren't you, honey?

"Yes, Momma," he said, beaming.

"I understand," Ms. Hughes said. The gemologist hovered, scrutinizing the top of the rock in the box, flat, almost like a brick. She examined it closely but by sight only, her hands remaining at her sides. "I see flecks of nickel, a hint of copper, some zinc, plus purple quartz." She eyed Wyatt, whose face stayed bright, cheerful, and anxious. "It is certainly a cornucopia of minerals you have found here, young man. Do you know what *cornucopia* means? It means there's plenty of good things inside it." She nodded at Myrna, who now knew where this was going, which was nowhere all that good.

"And I know someone who might be very interested in it. The quartz is most interesting. I will give that person's name and address to your mother, and she can take you to that shop. It is nearby. I think it will be useful to them. Good luck."

Myrna looked at the card. She knew the store. *Gem Thorpe*, a touristy gift shop for amethyst and other quartzes, non-precious minerals, metals and gems, and carved fantastical figures like purple unicorns. If Ms. Hughes had it right, whatever *Gem Thorpe* would give her for the rock would come mostly from charity, an appeasement to reward her son for his eagerness to please his mother, something Myrna might even need to surreptitiously supplement for any money to change hands.

But a skeptical Myrna knew that certified gemologist Sophie Ming Hughes had this wrong.

"Turn the rock over, ma'am. Please."

Ms. Hughes's jaw tightened at hearing the request. She glared at Myrna, then pulled on a pair of gloves, picked up the square-shaped rock, and flipped it over.

Her eyes widened, staring at a jagged concentration of minerals in a speckled iridescent green vein that ran the full length of the rock. "Remarkable." She eyed Myrna with new interest. "Do you know what this is?"

Myrna did now. "Well, that's why I came here, hoping you might help identify it for me."

"I am an appraiser. I evaluate precious gems, gold, jewelry, other valuables. I am not a geologist, so I am not absolutely sure, but . . ."

Yes, you are sure, Myrna thought, *I could tell by your look.*

". . . there is a possibility this underside green strip is cobalt, mixed with zinc. A very fine concentration of it, which would render a beautiful turquoise-green powder when it is refined."

"I see," Myrna said. She waited for whatever else Ms. Hughes might have to say, as in what she might offer for it, except now, based on her reaction, Myrna knew that much more could be involved in this potential transaction, its beauty providing the least of its value.

Ms. Hughes blinked first. "May I scrape off a pinch, to analyze it better?" She gestured to her helper, the younger counter person across the room, most likely her daughter, for her to join them. The daughter brought a pouch with her, which Ms. Hughes unfolded to reveal a set of scraping instruments and a small, square piece of porcelain.

"No, I am not also a dentist," she said, her smile tight—humorless, Myrna thought—"but we often get a mined stone and other gems in here that need cleaning up." She raised a stainless-steel needle above one end of the green vein, then placed the porcelain square underneath to catch whatever flakes or powder her scraping would loosen. "This is called a streak plate," she said, tapping the porcelain. "I can check the color of this specimen to validate it, after I make a few scrapes. May I?"

Myrna nodded.

"Momma, look," Wyatt said, pointing at a mounted TV. Myrna shushed him but did as he asked, for one glance at least, to satisfy him. "That man is at the Miner's Village. Can we go back there sometime? I went there for a school trip, remember?"

The label at the bottom of the TV screen was in all caps:

BILLIONAIRE MAX FEND IN JIM THORPE, PA. He was being interviewed by a financial news correspondent. The TV provided video only.

Interesting. But the next part of the description at bottom stopped her cold: *WHERE'S THE COBALT?*

Other hanging TVs were broadcasting the Financial Times with multiple stock indices, domestic and foreign, including the Mexican, the Nikkei, and the Shanghai Stock exchanges.

Scrape, scrape, scrape.

Flecks of potential cobalt dust dropped onto the streak plate, awaiting pronouncement. Ms. Hughes and her daughter remained focused on the specimen, the mother now with her eyeglasses off and a magnifier between her eye and the mineral smear, gazing intently at it. "Where did you say you found this rock?"

Myrna's voice stuck in her throat, keeping her from responding, but her better judgment soon closed her down completely.

Ms. Hughes kept talking, oblivious to the TV report. "I will give you two hundred dollars for this brick, cash. How does that sound? My daughter will take your name and address, fill out a receipt, and your son will be rewarded for his work. Young man, where did you find this?"

Her second attempt at pinpointing the rock's origin. Myrna kept Wyatt from speaking with a hand on his shoulder. As shocking to her as the financial news segment about Max Fend, what was on the second screen was crazier, where a viral social media post showed Mr. Fend being filmed at the coalminers–themed café in town, one block up, one block over from where she and Wyatt were now.

Myrna tensed, but she kept herself from glancing at any of the TV screens behind the proprietor.

"I'm sorry, Ms. Hughes, but we've changed our minds. We're going to keep it. Thank you."

She scooped up the rock, returned it to the shoebox, and was careless enough on purpose to knock the porcelain plate off the glass counter onto the floor, scattering the scraped cobalt.

Ms. Hughes and daughter barely noticed her clumsiness, engrossed in the additional TV screens Myrna wasn't even aware were there, the ones mounted on the wall at the front of the store, behind Myrna. She and Wyatt hurried out the door and into her silver 4Runner, Ms. Hughes now at the front window of her store, her phone camera raised.

"Momma, where are we going?" Wyatt said from the back seat. The shoebox with Wyatt's "Clark Bar" was on the floor in front of the passenger seat, next to Myrna.

"To get a hot cocoa for you and a latte for me at Canaries, sweetie. Both larges. How does that sound?"

"Great!"

She would call the news station, would look up that social media video —TikTok?—would speak to the baristas at Canaries, would check to see if any of these people knew where Mr. Fend, billionaire cobalt hunter, was staying locally. She needed to pay him a visit.

Sophie Ming Hughes and her daughter finished cleaning up the speckled green cobalt dust on the glass counter with a soft gemologist's brush, sliding the stray powder into a plastic bag. The blue-green smear left by the flecked cobalt pieces on the streak plate was still visible. She packaged the porcelain plate in a larger plastic bag, added the smaller bag with the powder, and ziplocked the two together.

"Put it in the safe," she said to her daughter in Chinese.

Sophie Ming Hughes thumbed through the photos on her phone to find the video she'd taken of the woman with the cobalt brick that she recorded after the woman's hasty exit. Her walk to her parking space, her son's hand in hers, the truck leaving the parking lot. A slim woman, taller than the tiny Ms. Hughes, her hair long and straight and black with streaks of gray. Her age maybe late thirties, the gray the giveaway. Her son's hair was also black, a deep, beautiful onyx, long for a boy, almost to his shoulders. Ten years old she guessed, maybe younger. They both looked Caucasian, but their beautiful black, straight hair was a troublesome fit for that ethnicity. Easily identifiable, especially if they were together. The end of the video gave up the truck's Pennsylvania license plate, all seven digits.

Not lost on Ms. Hughes was the significance of what had just happened. The customer was savvy, not short-sighted, had initially been looking to make some money quickly, but she pivoted when her son mentioned a touristy miner's village up north, something he'd seen on the TV. The customer soon excused her way out the door of the shop, no personal information exchanged.

Her name. What was her first name?

Her daughter remembered, said *Mirna*, spelling it out in the English alphabet amid their discussion in Chinese, although she couldn't really be sure of the spelling, only the phonetics of it. Ms. Hughes wrote the letters down, saying them aloud while doing it.

She stiffened her posture to face one of the TVs, the screen showing facts and figures for global stock indices broadcast by the Financial Times. She held her phone to her ear, waiting for it to connect. Her eyeglasses reflected the financial data traveling across the lenses, all of it in Chinese.

Her call went through, then played the automated response in Chinese, then English.

"Consulate General of the People's Republic of China in New York. If you know your party's extension, please enter it or say it now."

Sophie Ming knew the extension. She spoke it into the phone.

16

Protein shake, then cereal and milk. Max needed a shower after his morning run through the downtown area, but he would eat something first. Down the steps of the motorhome, his bowl steady, he munched his blueberry cereal. The picnic table assigned to his campsite, a brown composite, looked freshly power washed and probably was, knowing how his Fend Aerospace chief of staff had taken care of getting them set up here. He climbed onto the seat and continued eating his breakfast while checking his phone for news, messages, and calls, thumbing, keying, chewing, and not paying attention otherwise. It was not quite seven a.m., and Renee was sleeping in.

"Hello? Max Fend?"

Her voice surprised him, snapping his focus away from his phone. His first reaction, sadly, was to question if he had his 9mm with him. He did not. Not that she looked like a threat. Still, Max put his hand up, signifying she should stop her advance. She obliged.

"Who's asking?" he said, wary partially of her, partially of the small shoebox she carried under her arm. He extricated himself from the picnic table, stood, and squared his feet.

"My name is Myrna Springer. Myrna, with a 'y.' I saw you on the news. Can I speak with you a moment?"

Warm face, maybe a bit skittish. Thin, lanky body buried in a hooded sweatshirt, the hood off her head, the name of a cleaning service with a logo above the left breast pocket. Long black hair tucked inside the sweatshirt. Behind her, on the access road, a truck that hadn't been there before, an older model, silver. It was empty of anyone else, as far as he could tell.

Her eyes looked as wary as he felt. They each kept their respective distances.

"Yes, I'm Max Fend. Don't take this the wrong way, but tell me what's in the shoebox before coming any closer, please."

"Well, it's a rock with a lot of different minerals in it, and it's why I'm here."

A faint smile emerged on her face, but it was there, and it made her dimples pop.

"Looks plain on top, but the underside has, ah, what looks like cobalt in it." She confirmed her assertion with a few nods, agreeing with herself. "A large concentration of it, I think."

Max relaxed and gestured at the picnic table. "Would you like to have a seat while I look at it?"

She sat, he sat, the shoebox between them. She lifted the rock out, a brick-like thing with nothing remarkable on the topside, like she said, but when she turned it over and placed it on the shoebox lid—

"My son calls this his kryptonite."

Max was tempted to agree, purely out of excitement building inside him, ignoring that the green minerals had some blue in them, making it maybe as valuable as any piece of all-green kryptonite might be, if kryptonite could be found anywhere. He paused to look into her eyes, to gauge her sincerity. This rock, and its purveyor, could be the leads they'd been looking for.

"May I?" he said, still not reaching for it.

She nodded and slid the box top over.

He picked up the rock in both hands. Lighter than he expected. The streak of blue-green mineral was dense except for a spot that was flakier than the rest, near one of the corners, where he was tempted to insert his finger but didn't.

"I had someone chip a few crystals off where you can see it's flaking," she said, "just before I came looking for you."

He remained calm, wanting to not scare her away, and he searched for something to say that would make her feel comfortable in sharing information without him having to ask the one question he wanted answered.

Best to generalize, he decided. "Tell me more about your rock."

Ms. Springer evaluated the request while further evaluating him. A look at his top-of-the-line motorhome, a glance at his shiny new Ford Bronco. Then came her study of his photogenic face with its early morning stubble. Her study ended with her contemplating his empty blue cereal bowl and the spoon sitting in it: still life on the picnic table. The bowl and spoon and the spilled milk next to it was apparently what did it, an incongruous grouping in front of a luxurious motorhome. This was Max Fend in a nutshell nowadays, a billionaire, but unpretentious as hell.

"My son dug it up," she said. "It was such a special, one-of-a-kind find for him that we didn't go looking for more of it."

Max rested the rock back on the box top, upside down, the bluish-green streak visible. "I'm far from an expert, Ms. Springer, but it looks like the real deal."

"Cobalt, then."

"To me, yes, cobalt. A high concentration of it. It's what we're looking for."

But he wasn't going to ask what he wanted to ask. If she was comfortable enough, if he'd earned enough of her trust, she'd volunteer the next part herself.

"My son found it picking up after our dog. I'm hoping there's a lot more." Then, finally, "I live on twenty acres in Nesquehoning, Mr. Fend. Next to a state game land parcel. My address and phone number are on the back of this card."

She handed her cleaning service employer's card to him. "Where do we go from here?"

Max exhaled a breath he didn't know he was holding. Renee exited the motorhome with a busy serving tray, balancing mugs, carafes, plastic utensils, plus other coffee-break fixings on her way to the table. The motorhome's tension door closed slowly behind her.

"Renee LeFrancois, my girlfriend," Max announced, "showered, fresh," —he welcomed her to the table, kissing her cheek after she sat down— "and smelling a whole lot better than I do. This is Myrna Springer, Renee. She tracked me down, and we've been talking. We've had an interesting development."

"Hi. Coffee and tea for you both here. Help yourself. Catch me up later, Max. Don't let me slow you down."

Myrna finished discussing what had brought her here: yesterday's visit to the gemologist, Max's interview on TV, her visit to Canaries, and a TikTok post from a social media influencer. She was now on her way to work, and her son was on his way to school. "I'll finish my last job today around three. Can you be at my place by four?"

"We can. But fill me in first. The gemologist—can we have a name? What happened there?"

Myrna obliged, saying where she'd gone for the appraisal. The appraiser saw what she had and knew enough about minerals to officially pronounce it cobalt. Myrna said she reneged on selling it to the gemologist when Myrna saw Max on TV at the store.

"Does she know your name?" Max asked. "Your address? Anything that could trace what you showed her back to you?"

"No. Hell, I don't know. My first name only, no address. Her daughter took pictures of the rock with her phone. And she has scrapings from it, although I was clumsy on the way out and ruined the specimen. Or at least I hope I did."

Still worrisome, Max thought. Something was no doubt left behind. And if a phone camera was in play, Myrna for sure left more of a trail than she realized. He didn't want to scare her, but this was now a major concern. The appraiser might be looking for her, and if the appraiser had the right resources . . .

"Renee."

"I know, Max," Renee said, keying the jewelry store name into her phone. They would now need to know all they could about the place. "I'll work on it."

"Myrna," Max said. "I can call you Myrna, right?"

"Yes."

"Great. Max and Renee here. Look. We'll catch up to you today at your place, but be aware that, going forward, things around here—around you—might get very busy. Pay attention to your surroundings. Is there anyone else at home, a husband, a boyfriend, dogs?"

"My husband's gone, and our guard dog is a three-legged terrier who's more like a pig. My son Wyatt, he's only nine." She now showed the concern that she hadn't shown earlier, a lot less flippant. "This can't affect him . . ."

"Understood, Myrna. Not to alarm you, but depending on where we go with this, we'll work on getting some protection for you if necessary."

Calls to Cornell and Wilkes were in order. Things had changed, for Myrna, for them, for everyone. Even if this wasn't what they thought it was, it made no difference. Perception was reality. And if anyone so much as thought Myrna was sitting on something potentially this valuable, the reality was, things could get dicey for her going forward.

"Go to work today and we'll meet you later at your place. In the meantime, we'll make some calls."

"Cornell?"

Max and Renee called their FBI contact from the Ford Bronco while heading to downtown Jim Thorpe. Max dished on the potential breakthrough, giving him the good news first, about what they expected to learn from a visit to Myrna Springer's home later today. Kudos from Cornell echoed around their SUV. So where were they headed now?

"Someone else might know about Myrna's special rock," Max said. He looked at the GPS navigation, had an address cued up. The N. Hughes jewelry store. "Her first stop wasn't to see me, it was to see an appraiser in Jim Thorpe."

"How'd that work out? Does the appraiser know where—"

"We don't know what she knows," Renee said, reading from her phone. "The gemologist she saw was an older woman. The store's been in business over thirty years. Her American husband died and left it to her. She's

Chinese, Shui Ming Hughes. She goes by 'Sophie.' My research shows she came to the U.S. thirty-plus years ago and was married within a week."

"A marriage green card," Cornell said. "She ever become a naturalized citizen?"

"From what we can find, no. If she had, she'd lose her Chinese citizenship." More thumbing on her phone. "I see seven jewelry stores in the Jim Thorpe area that Myrna could have picked at random. She walked into this one."

"The appraiser being Chinese is a coincidence," Cornell said. "Means nothing."

"Probably," Max said. "But it doesn't matter. Someone else locally now knows what she found. That's not good. It also doesn't matter if Myrna's got something significant happening with cobalt on her property or not. The problem is, other people might think she does. She'll need protection. She has a nine-year-old son. What can you do for her?"

"We're the FBI, Max. Protection isn't something we do."

"Whatever happened to 'protect and serve'?"

"A local police thing, not us. Look, I'll get you names of some former FBI personnel doing protection work as soon as I get off the phone. It might take a few days—"

"Yeah, well, no, not fast enough," Max said. "I'll get someone in place by tonight, tomorrow at worst, right after Renee and I meet with Myrna this afternoon. And I just got through with the Army engineers. One of my drills will be functioning on her property by tomorrow afternoon, if Myrna agrees. I'm hanging up now. Our mystery jewelry store is in my sights. Recon on it begins right—now."

They parked across the street, not in the store's lot. Renee fed a parking meter, they watched, they took pictures. A few customers entered and left the shop. No red flags. From their vantage point, Renee could take no decent photos of any employees inside the shop, Chinese or otherwise.

"How about I go in," Renee said, "and take a look around, get some pictures?"

Not something Max, billionaire celebrity aerospace guy, could do. He'd become too visible lately.

"Good idea, yes, do that." Max retrieved a business card from his wallet. "I'll make a few more calls."

On the card he fished out was maybe a short-term solution for Myrna's protection. He'd hire this woman, this retired cop. He'd hire the whole damn town watch if he had to. His phone to his ear, the call went through.

"Aurora Jolson? This is Max Fend."

17

ETA ten minutes to Nesquehoning, where Myrna Springer lived. A pleasant drive out of Jim Thorpe, Max at the wheel, even during the p.m. rush hour. Their SUV windows were down in the spring-like weather, the sunroof open, the late afternoon sunshine spilling inside.

"Far cry from Greenland, Max," Renee said, her chin raised to better breathe in the comfortably cool, but not cold, air. "Have you heard from Wilkes?"

"Nothing from him, but an email from Hannah Taat this morning. The helicopter contractors have been vetted, and she and the other engineers are back at work on the Hiawatha impact site. The weather's been letting up a little, so that's good. The diamond core drill is on its platform, the derrick around it is up. The shelter shack is in place. They're ready to start drilling."

"How about funding for their protection? Anything approved yet?" Her cheeks were flushed from the chilly air, rosy in the breeze that blew her dark pixie cut off her face. Max could tell she was enjoying this ride.

"Any day now, Wilkes told me. They found budget money, so it will happen. No other warning shots or incidents to suggest we should leave Qaanaaq. On the ground or in the air."

"He's going to want you back over there, Max, and soon."

Max grimaced at that truth. It was friggin' crazy-wild up there in Green-land, weather-wise, nature-wise, espionage-wise, but the potential reward, for the U.S. as a country and for Max Fend, new cobalt mining guru, would be worth it. And now, at this moment, right here in upstate Pennsylvania, they might be sitting on an even larger breakthrough.

Life was good. Sensational, actually. He reached across the console and squeezed Renee's shoulder. "We'll cross that bridge when we need to. In the meantime, you should get as comfortable as you can with Myrna Springer. We might all be partners soon.

"And tell me more about the jewelry appraiser. We now have photos of —what's her name again?"

"Shui Ming Hughes, the store's proprietor," Renee said. "'Sophie.' Great photos of her and her daughter both. The play when I went in the store was, I had them model diamond earrings for me. I also had Sophie bring out other diamonds as well. I took photos of them and her together. Multiple carats, in case you're wondering. Big ones. Just because I could. You'll see them later, assuming you want to."

"I know my answer needs to be yes." A smile crept across his face. "I mean, they're diamonds, right?"

"There's no message here, Max, sweetie. You'll see the proprietor up close in the photos, you'll also see some gorgeous diamonds, that's all. The diamonds, they're just beautiful."

The Bronco GPS announced they'd arrived at the address. A two-lane road. A prefab ranch home, tan siding, colonial blue shutters in need of painting, a front lawn starting to green up. A single working mom doing the best she could. All in all, a fine place. He drove up the stone driveway, shut the SUV down. He found sunglasses and a wide-brimmed Australian outback hat and donned them both; minor camouflage from nosy neigh-bors. He grabbed a backpack from the back seat. They met Myrna on her front step. She waved at a neighbor at his mailbox. He waved back but lingered to get a look at Max and Renee. Myrna hustled the two of them to her backyard, talking as she walked.

"That's Wyatt's Uncle Jesse. My husband's brother. A great person to have as a neighbor after I lost my husband. He adores Wyatt, and he loves me, too—as my brother-in-law," she added, looking over her shoulder at them to make that clear. "Okay. Let's get started."

She gestured at the fenced-in section. "First, there could be landmines back here from Little Pig, our dog. We try to stay ahead of them, but Pig's gotten worse in her old age, eating more—Wyatt hands her scraps on the sly—and giving herself some digestive problems that manifest themselves out here."

Behind them the back door to her house sprang open and slapped against the siding, then slapped back closed against the frame. In between the slaps her son jettisoned off the deck onto the grass to catch up with his mother and her guests.

Good-looking kid with long, straight, beautiful black hair, and a face with a natural, covetous tan.

"Wyatt, say hello to Ms. LeFrancois and Mr. Fend."

"Hello."

It took until this moment, her with her son, for Max to realize something that was for sure best left unacknowledged regardless of the revelation: Myrna and her son were Native American, or appeared to be. Wyatt had the hair and the pigmentation, and on Max's closer inspection of his mother, she fit the description, too.

"Wyatt, show Mr. Fend where you dug up your kryptonite brick, please."

"Yes, Momma."

He pointed as he walked—"landmine . . . landmine . . ."—until they reached the fence at the farthest edge of the backyard grass. Beyond the fence, the slope of the property, the remaining nineteen acres, began its rise, disappearing into the woods. "Right about here. I had a plastic shovel. I stuck the edge of it in the dirt and wiggled it. I pulled the brick out, then I ran inside with it to show Momma."

Max got into a crouch, moved some twigs out of the way, and touched the ground where Wyatt pointed. It was moist, even at this late hour in the afternoon. "Wet from melting snow?"

"I dunno," Wyatt said. "Maybe." He looked at his mom. "Little Pig coulda just peed there, too."

Max smiled at that, didn't do a smell test, found a paper towel in his backpack, and wiped his fingers just in case. "Is there a shovel? Where's the shovel you used, son?"

"Hold on," Myrna said, and went to the shed. She returned with a spade. "Sturdier than the sand shovel he uses to clean up after our dog. Use this instead."

Max went to work, digging down a foot, the ground frozen the farther he went, finding no rocks with similar markings in them. He decided not to widen or attempt to deepen the search here. He shoveled the dirt back in the hole and asked Myrna if he could dig elsewhere.

"Of course. Let me get another shovel. I'll help."

Before long they'd opened multiple holes in different spots around the fenced backyard, producing no rocks with any promising content. Wyatt's kryptonite rock was clearly a real find, not fake, but how it got onto—into—their property, rising to where it became visible to Wyatt, was at this point a mystery. Max wiped his face and hands with a towel Myrna brought him. She did the same with another towel.

"I suggest this, Myrna. Finding something just now, today, would be wonderful, but I knew it would be a stretch. If you'll permit me, I'll bring some heavy-duty drilling equipment in here tomorrow and a few engineers from the U.S. Army who know how to use it. They'll need a few days to get set up, but this is the direction we'd need to go anyway to see what's underneath here. And as a temporary incentive—"

Max held his thought. He eyed her backyard, gauged her house's footprint on the property, and decided how the engineers would need to go about getting the equipment back here. Not too much of a problem, but the side and rear of her lawn would be destroyed.

"Okay, to minimize your inconvenience, and to legitimize, and maximize, my intentions, I want you to have something. But first, do you have any water in the house that your son could get me? I'm really thirsty."

Myrna understood and played along. "Wyatt, please get Mr. Fend and Ms. LeFrancois bottles of water from the fridge, honey."

Wyatt scampered off. Max resettled his bush cap and surreptitiously eyed their surroundings. No audience, far as he could tell. He fumbled in his backpack and pulled out two thick manila envelopes. He handed them to her, her look at them quizzical. She unclasped one and peeked inside.

Cash.

"I place no restrictions on what you do with this. Me giving you this is not a binding contract for either of us. I know that when the engineers come back here, the machinery they bring with them will chew up your property. I expect this money will cover the damage. If nothing comes of this effort, use it to make your lawn and property right again and keep the rest. And if it doesn't cover the damage, I will make up the difference the same way. But I think this will be enough."

She stole another look inside the yellow envelope. It held hundreds and hundreds of hundred-dollar bills. Myrna was speechless, her eyes unblinking, now searching Max's and Renee's faces.

"Where . . . how . . . ? This isn't dirty money, is it?"

Max remained serious, although a part of him wished he could produce a CIA card or secret-agent-spy-superhero ID with a presidential seal on it to let her know he was a good guy, not a mobster or a drug dealer.

"It's—no, of course not, Myrna. It's from your government by way of me and Fend Aerospace. It's a hundred thousand dollars. Don't pull any of it out while we're out here. Wait until you're inside your house. You might need to be creative about how you get it into the bank, but I see that as a fun problem to have. And know that it's yours, Myrna. For you, if you give us your permission to dig. To show our sincerity. To make you whole, after we dig up a chunk of your property. You would do good not to, ah, call attention to yourself by spending it all in one place, as they say, but I know you won't."

She closed the clasp. Her eyes teared up, and in them Max could see that she wanted to hug him, but she was restraining herself. A simple, sincere smile emerged, and it caught the tears rolling down her cheeks. She swiped at them, regained her composure, a nervous chuckle slipping out.

"Okay. I, ah, sure, that's fine. You have my permission. I suppose I'll need to call out sick tomorrow," she said.

The trucks arrived at Myrna's after the bus picked up Wyatt for school in the morning. A large backhoe on a flatbed, a 4x4 four-door pickup, and five additional men in coveralls in the pickup. A five-ton delivery truck, an eight-wheeler, with a canvas-covered payload. No advertising on any of it.

A new septic system. That was what she needed. Max suggested this to her as their cover for her neighbors, but only one of them had a significant view of her property, her brother-in-law.

"I don't feel comfortable telling Jesse that," Myrna said. "I don't lie to him. He's a cop, he's my friend, and he's Wyatt's uncle."

She hadn't brought Wyatt into confidence about why these people were coming back today. No additional kryptonite had been found yesterday. A bummer, she'd told him, but she'd also learned they needed a new septic system, which meant the backyard would need to be dug up. Not totally a lie. She might need a new soil field and septic system after this heavy equipment had its way. If things went a certain way, she might also need a new place to live.

"It's only until we know, Myrna," Max said. He pulled the brim of his hat down to further shield his eyes from an early sun, absorbing the panorama that ran parallel to Myrna's, a similar twenty acres next door, the brother-in-law's place, which also abutted the wooded mountain and the state's public game lands. "There's no reason to think that whatever might be under your property here would stop at your property line. Your brother-in-law can and will be brought into this as soon as it makes sense, but it shouldn't be earlier."

"How long before that can happen?" she said. The offloaded backhoe appeared from around the side of the house, snorting and chugging, its tires churning up the grass and leaving behind a small, rutty-muddy mess.

"It could be weeks, could be longer, could be tomorrow. In the meantime, we need to take care of something important." He read a text on his phone. "Renee will be here in fifteen minutes. The person bringing her is someone I hope you'll embrace as a resource. While we wait, let me show you the nifty apparatus on the back of that truck sitting out front of your house."

Max had one of the engineers loosen the tie-down on the canvas covering the rear of the large delivery truck. He and Myrna moved in close as the engineer lifted the canvas up.

"The monstrosity under here is a diamond core drill. If there's a significant cobalt deposit out back of your house, or in the hills behind it, or under them, this machine will show it to us."

Myrna walked the perimeter of the truck's contents with wide-eyed wonder, not touching anything, Max trailing her, giving her room.

"Should I be seeing sparkles here somewhere from the diamonds?" she asked, a coy smile emerging.

"Well, no, the industrial diamonds are affixed to black metal rotary drill bits, each bit the size of a large fist, several of them packed away in there somewhere. All business, minimal sparkle."

She examined what was about to lay waste to parts of her property while Max found himself in an odd place, examining her. A gem of a woman, her silky black, Indigenous hair seamed with gray-white strands akin to veins of precious silver running through the darkest, purest coal regions of Pennsylvania. Her scent—what was it she was wearing?

"What about it? Max?"

Wildflowers. Her wildflower scent . . . it was fascinating. "Sorry. What about what again?"

"Is it noisy, I asked."

"Sad to say, yes, enough to be annoying."

Her beauty—her persona, and her vulnerability—caught him off guard, his reaction to her more a concern than an appreciation. He suddenly felt uncomfortable.

His phone dinged. Saved by a text.

"They'll be here in a minute," he said.

Aurora Jolson's repurposed police SUV arrived, Renee riding shotgun and out of the vehicle first. A peck on Max's cheek.

Untucked camouflage khaki tee, dark slacks, sunglasses, police issue boots: Ms. Jolson looked ready for a SWAT event.

"Myrna, I know you and Ms. Jolson have history—"

Max had gathered their story from his discussion with Aurora: When Myrna's husband Ken went missing, Aurora had been Jim Thorpe's police chief, Ken Springer a cop on her force. She'd fired him. What happened afterward hadn't gone the way any of them had wanted. Some bad blood remained.

"We've hired Ms. Jolson to hang out with you, for, you know—"

"Protection," Myrna said, finishing for him. "What will the neighbors say," came out as sarcasm, but it had an edge. "Overkill in my opinion. Whatever."

"Better safe than sorry," Max said. "She and Jim Thorpe's watch group will keep an eye on things, and you, and your son, even though you don't live inside their jurisdiction. Tell me if this will be a problem for you."

She focused intently on the former police chief. Myrna's life was a struggle with her husband gone, Aurora had told Max. Regardless, Myrna had only wanted closure on the case.

"Ms. Jolson and I have some things we can talk about. We'll make it work."

18

Cornell arrived at Myrna's property the same time as the Mexican-American food truck. The road outside Myrna's house was suddenly busier, with the food truck parked on the shoulder ahead of a cargo van and a trailer. In case there were doubts about what was underway in the back-yard, the cargo van carried a stenciled description, a few of the stenciled letters weather-beaten because of age, or at least mimicking it. Myrna didn't have a swimming pool, so the truck was there, ostensibly, for one reason.

Tiny's Discount Allied Septic Service and Pool Water. Below the business name: *Septics Pumped, Pools Filled, Not Same Truck.* Below that, a phone number without an area code.

"The van's a nice touch," Cornell said. He and Max crunched on gorditas and cheesy nachos, dinner provided for the entire group, Max's treat. They'd squeezed into folding chairs like the engineers had, the chairs dotting the backyard. After the dinner break it was back to work setting up. The engineers needed to work well beyond the rear fence, which was there to keep the dog from roaming. It was Myrna's property back there, but it cut into the slope where heavy woods and State Game lands parcel No. 141, adjacent to a few private parcels, began.

"I feel good about this, Cornell," Max said. "I don't know how far down they'll need to dig, but it doesn't matter. This equipment is a monster. We'll keep it under wraps until the derrick can be built over it, then the derrick gets a camouflage cover."

"Overkill in my opinion, but you're the guy with the deep pockets," Cornell said.

"Overwhelm this effort, solution it ASAP, and be the change we're advocating. That's the approach. You seeing similar activity anywhere else around here?"

"Other players have showed up," Cornell said. "After other entrepreneurs heard of your interest, they started queuing up. Their approach to attacking the search has been to buy up what they can. Old coal mines, strip mines. Property with sinkholes. Anywhere they can get access to abandoned tunnels without too much effort."

The aluminum storm door to the rear of Myrna's home pushed open then slapped shut, too quickly in Max's estimation. The door's tension was off, and at some point it might jar the window glass out of the frame, with dangerous implications. Someone should do something about it.

Otherwise—

"You need to meet someone else, Cornell." Max chin-pointed at the deck. "Myrna's kid. He's nine. He adores sports. Hey Wyatt," Max called. He tossed a questioning look at Myrna, who was chatting with Renee. Aurora Jolson was at a picnic table, her face buried in a burrito. The message of his look was, would meeting Cornell Oakley be okay?

Myrna nodded. Max waved Wyatt over.

"Follow my lead," Max said to Cornell.

"Wyatt Springer, I would like you to meet the toughest linebacker to ever play college football in the city of Philadelphia. It was many, many years ago, as I'm sure you can tell with him getting old and all"—that last part earning a condemning look from Cornell that Max didn't dare acknowledge—"but when he played, he was known as Beast. Mr. Cornell 'Beast' Oakley, meet young Mr. Wyatt Springer. Wyatt, meet Beast. Wyatt loves to watch and play football and baseball, Cornell. College, the pros, all of it."

"Wow. Mr. Beast, what number did you wear? Who did you play for? Did you play for the Eagles? How about the Giants?"

Max piled it on. "Wyatt, you'll need to give Mr. Oakley some space here. He's old and he works for me now. He's part of the group who's going to fix this mess with your toilets as soon as possible."

Cornell narrowed his eyes, his pained headshake nearly imperceptible. If looks could kill . . .

They planned to also work nights back here, on Myrna's property, for this exploratory effort, but not starting tonight. Max and Renee paid their respects, Max confirming he'd be back tomorrow, Renee maybe, maybe not. Renee waited for him back at the SUV while everyone packed up.

"Back to work again tomorrow, Myrna?" Max asked.

"Afraid so. You won't need me here. You've brought yourself a water truck and a porta-potty, and you have access to food trucks."

"Yes, you're off the hook for tomorrow, but I do have a favor. Can you get Wyatt to bring his kryptonite brick out here? I have a proposition for him."

She called through the back door of the house. Wyatt came out with the shoe box under his arm.

"Okay. Now, here's the deal, Wyatt," Max said. "But first, let me see the rock again."

Max picked it out of the box and made a production of examining it from multiple angles, nodding at its appeal. "If it's all right with your mother, I'd like to buy this from you, Wyatt. For five hundred dollars. But there's one condition." Max's conspiratorial wink connected with Myrna. "I'll come back to that. Can you use five hundred dollars, Wyatt?"

"Sure can! Momma, did you hear that? Wow. Sure, Mr. Fend, if Momma says okay, then okay!" Wyatt went to his momma and gave her a hug around her waist while seeking her permission with his eyes. "Momma?"

"Well, I think you should hear what his condition is, right, young man?"

Her face radiated at his display of manners, his deference to asking her permission, and this shared moment of theirs. It made her heart swell with pride. Max didn't miss it, their smiles infectious.

"Can you tell Wyatt what your one condition is, Mr. Fend, so I can send him off to bed to contemplate your deal?"

"My condition, Wyatt, is that I don't want to be responsible for keeping an eye on it. So if we make this deal, I want you to do that for me. Put it in your room, check on it every day, then when the time comes, when we're finished with this work out there on your property, we'll talk about me taking it with me. Can you do that for me?"

"Uh," Wyatt looked at his mother, "um, sure, Mr. Fend, I think that's okay. Right, Momma? It's okay, right, Momma? Momma?"

Her look at Max needed help from an emotional swallow and a swipe of her finger at a tear. She nodded and answered a whispered "yes," followed by a stronger one, that Max could tell was meant for them both, him and her son.

He'd had the cash in his pockets. All twenties, ready to make this gesture happen, so her son could better experience the feel of more cash in his hands while Max did this young man a solid. Wyatt accepted the money, put it in the shoebox, kissed his momma, and ran inside the house, the money and the kryptonite in the box together.

"You didn't need to do that," she said. "That was wonderful. Thank you."

A light squeeze, her hand on his forearm, punctuated her message.

New day, different roach coach at Myrna's home, this time serving breakfast burritos. No, there wasn't a theme here, people gonna work, people gonna need a good breakfast, and these foodies were available. Starting time, seven a.m. Tomorrow it would be a crepes truck.

"Fend," Max said, answering the phone before looking. "Good morning, Wilkes. Where are you?" He and Renee sat on a step next to Myrna's back deck, chowing down.

"Wherever the phone shows me, Max. It's accurate."

Pituffik Air Base, Greenland.

"What's on your mind, Caleb?" Max asked the question with little enthusiasm.

"Sounds like you're not excited to hear from me, Max. Give me your update first."

Off the top of Max's head. Equipment had been delivered to a large residential property in Nesquehoning, Pennsylvania, abutting a mountain. The home of a nice single parent who had sought Max out. An excellent cobalt sample and a great lead. It would be life-changing for the woman if it worked out. She'd be a good partner for whoever got her business. The Army Corps of Engineers was here. The FBI was here. They'd added a geologist from Penn State. They'd be ready to drill tomorrow, or the next day at the latest, expecting to soon sample whatever the shaft coughed up as it manhandled the woman's backyard. It would all be legendary.

"Sounds promising," Wilkes said. "On this end, things are about to change in a big way, too."

Government approval for the funding for full-on protection was due shortly. Max's operation out of Pituffik was about to become part of the Noble Defender program, the U.S.-Canada based Arctic initiative, in about the time it would take for Max to arrive there if he could find the right flight connections tomorrow. The protection included fixed and rotary wing flyovers. Supply drops. Not Wilkes's style, Max knew, to label it "epic" or "legendary," but they would have been appropriate labels.

"Yeah, well, I won't be there that soon, Wilkes. I want to see some output from this unit here first. I owe it to these guys and to the FBI. I owe it to the property owner. Plus, let's face it, it's warmer here."

Wilkes stayed quiet.

"A little sarcasm, Wilkes, okay? As soon as I can, after this Pennsylvania unit pulls up something we can look at, I'll head up north to meet with everyone."

Still no commentary from Wilkes. The "warmer" comment got a thumbs-up from Renee. She hadn't moved from her seat next to Max on the deck steps. She was still eating.

"Wilkes?" Max prompted. "What's happening on your end, Wilkes? Did we lose you?"

"Here's what I'm doing, Max. I see Nesquehoning as a dot of a town online. I see your potential new partner's property. I see it being in *very* close proximity to that coal mine fire. You don't see that as an issue?"

"Renee," Max said, "can you check the Centralia coal-seam fire, again, to see how far east it reaches?"

"Nowhere close to her property, Max. Don't know exactly where it is, but the Pennsy geologists have a handle on its general perimeter. The engineers and the geologists said it's still expanding, but provisions can be made. They said we'll be fine."

"Someone needs to put the fire out," Max said under his breath.

"What was that?" Wilkes said.

"Renee says we'll be fine. At some point, though, it'll make sense to put real federal money into extinguishing that fire, annoying as it is."

"Taken under advisement," Wilkes said. "But know this. Decades ago, there was much talk about dirty bombs; there still is, so don't lose sight of that. Everyone knows how to make them in all their primitive glory. They're easy to build because they use conventional explosives. Place them alongside radioactive material, detonate them, and watch the radioactive dust disperse. If you find some cobalt-60, which is radioactive and only one little isotope hardier than cobalt-59, the stable mineral we're after, and salt an explosion with it, you've got a dirty bomb. Far-reaching, long-lasting, deadly implications."

"There's no easy way to get cobalt-60, Wilkes," Max said. "It's a synthetic. It doesn't occur naturally."

"And it's not manufactured in the U.S., but sadly, it's all over the place. In medical equipment, in medical waste, as a byproduct of nuclear power plants. Sure, not easy to get, not easily transportable, not easily kept under wraps, but it's doable. There's probably already some of it out there, unaccounted for. The only thing good about it is, it's not always lethal. But do know this.

"I'm reading online material from the Federation of American Scientists. 'If a bomb containing five pounds of TNT was salted with point-zero-three ounces of cobalt-60, with a half-life exceeding five years, and exploded at the tip of Manhattan, it would make that area of the city uninhabitable for decades.'"

"So let me get this straight, Wilkes. You're suggesting we walk away from this property, and this region, the best U.S. lead we have, to avoid that as a hypothetical? Is this what I'm hearing? No one's successfully detonated a dirty bomb anywhere *ever*."

Max stood, was riled up. Renee kept at her laptop on the deck steps, sipping orange juice.

"Look. The cobalt needs to be found," Max said. "Hopefully a large enough deposit that it changes the world's economic dynamics. Sure, it's not ideal that it's near this coal fire. So, here's one for you: a brainstorm. Make every financial bid for cobalt mining rights *anywhere* in this region contingent on also sharing the cost of putting out the Centralia coal fire. We've already heard putting out the fire is doable; it just needs to be funded. I have no idea how the bidding process will work, especially being this close to public game lands, but however these properties need to be handled to get at this natural resource, this needs to be included. You getting all this, Wilkes? You writing this down?"

Silence on Wilkes's end said he was noting it somewhere. Then, "That would mean Fend Aerospace, too," Wilkes said.

"Yes. Of course. Draw from the commercial wealth of all the bidders for whatever properties are deemed viable. Find one company to propose the solution and have all the bidders being awarded cobalt mining contracts pay their fair share for the fire fix. Wilkes, I believe I just solved a huge problem here. I suggest you get the word out, that each bidder will need to share in this cost. If bidders want in, they'll need to pitch in."

"Fine. Taken under—"

"I know, 'advisement.' Okay then. My work is done here, for tonight at least. You'll hear from me in a coupla days. I'm closing out the call. Bye."

Wow. Max was feeling extra proud of himself. "Renee—"

"I heard, Max. You look like the Cheshire Cat, and I know it's not from anything you ate. Those breakfast burritos were terrible. But Wilkes has a point. Add one isotope to common cobalt, the stable element becomes highly radioactive. Include that in the dust dispersed from any of those cobalt explosions we're seeing overseas, this becomes an environmental catastrophe."

"I get it. That's why the fire needs to be extinguished. If a bidder comes up with a good plan for that, they pretty much will also have a lock on getting a mining contract. But it won't be Fend Aerospace. We're only doing this for the exploration, then we'll be there as a financial partner, not as the sole backer. Someone else can spearhead the fire cleanup."

"So what I'm hearing is," Renee rubbed his arm, acknowledging that he did good, "you're still here in the States for the short run."

"Indeed I am."

19

Midafternoon at the Myrna Springer property. The "septic system cleanup" for the family home was going swimmingly, as far as Max could tell. The derrick covering the diamond core drill was up, with drill and derrick both sitting on space carved into the foothill about 150 yards from the back of Myrna's house. The drill was on a leveled-off, low-rise section of the slope, just before the forest pine took over the property. Max took another bite from an apple.

Myrna's neighbor, hanging over the split rails, waved hello at Max then followed it with upturned fingers suggesting he join him at the property line. A resigned Max found space for the apple core in a Little Pig poop bucket on his way to the fence. He pretty much already knew everything he needed to know about Myrna's neighbor Jesse Springer. Renee and their mutual associates had made sure of that. Renee would be a late show here today.

Jesse Randolph Springer. Local citizen. Two tours in the Marine Corps, an air pilot, fixed and rotary wing, where he'd excelled. Served in Iraq, came back, became a local cop, in the force for fourteen years, now flew only for fun, and with family and friends only. Close to his older brother Ken, Myrna's missing husband, junior to Ken by four years. Double wedding for the brothers. Ken entered the Jim Thorpe police department

first, after some college, was never in the military, his li'l brother Jesse
heading overseas with his new wife. Jesse came back and joined the same
department. The brothers bought properties next to each other. They knew
everything there was to know about each other as siblings, as kids, and as
adults. Jesse divorced, had no children, hadn't remarried. Devoted uncle to
Wyatt and brother-in-law to Myrna, helping them out with bills and
babysitting and anything else when he could, and when Myrna would
let him.

Per Cornell Oakley, the FBI had no file on him. His military records,
coming through Wilkes, showed exemplary performance. So what Max
had to figure out was how to stay clandestine about what might be going
down on Myrna's property without playing this guy for a fool, because
chances were, he wasn't.

That had all been a waste of time.

"Jesse Springer."

"Max Fend."

"What I'm about to say might come off as a little rude, Mr. Fend, but
hear me out." He cleared his throat.

"There is no septic system problem. There is no water problem. There
is no soil field problem. There is one problem, and it's that big magilla out
there calling the shots for his crew," he said, pointing. "He's an Army Corps
engineer I met during the Iraq War. I flew him and his team all over the
desert. Small world, right? Truth be told, I thought he'd never handle doing
his twenty in the military. He liked giving orders, not taking them. So tell
me this: Is he going to make it? Will he get his twenty? Because as of now,
he should be closing in on it. And please don't insult me by saying these
people are bona fide residential septic workers, not part of the Army Corps.
If you do, I'll need to spend a whole lot more time making sure you're not
taking advantage of my sister-in-law."

Only a few homes on this road, and the only neighbor they'd needed to
buy into the septic system charade hadn't bought into any of it.

"Okay then," Max said, pivoting. "So let's start over. There's a strong
possibility Ms. Springer has a precious metal deposit on her property. She
sought me out, came to me with a high-grade sample of it—cobalt—that
she says her son found in her backyard. Me being here means we intend to

find out if what the geological studies say might be under the Pocono Mountains, in large quantities, is accurate, and mineable, and on her property."

"Who's 'we'?"

"You know who I am. It's not something I'm able to hide, although I was going for 'Man of Intrigue,'" he said with a tip of his bush hat, "while on her property. The world thinks 'Billionaire' is my first name. My company wants to find this high-grade cobalt, wants to make the U.S. a major player in it, and wants to unseat China as the world's premier supplier, who's currently got a stranglehold on its availability." A subtle, sarcastic shrug. "That's all. And we know how much this region could use the industry. No ulterior motives here, Mr. Springer, you have my word on that. Cobalt is, right now, one of the most highly coveted cogs in fighting climate change . . ."

Mr. Jesse Springer let Max ramble. When Max finished his pitch, Jesse put his hand across the fence a second time, initiating a reintroduction.

"Jesse Springer. Jim Thorpe Police Department. Also part of the Jim Thorpe town watch. Brother-in-law to Myrna, uncle to Wyatt, guardians of both, my two dearest relatives. Call me Jesse."

"Max." Their handshake was firmer now. "I guess that means you know Aurora Jolson?"

"Chief Jolson. Of course. My boss in the department, until she retired."

"She's with the town watch now."

"She is at that. Running the show there, too. Still learning the watch ropes," Jesse said, "but she's doing fine."

"Well, add to her resume that she's also now providing personal protection for Myrna and Wyatt. Not something Myrna asked for, but I suggested it, and Myrna said okay."

A nod from Jesse, and Max saw in his face a genuine appreciation. Something that said Uncle Jesse would give him, capital-B Billionaire Max Fend, big-pockets stranger, the benefit of the doubt. This had been an interview; a vetting. Max had passed.

"If Myrna's good with it," Jesse said, "I'm good with it."

True only because of that vetting, Max knew, but no splitting hairs here. Due diligence was now complete on both sides.

"Good. Excellent. A favor, then. We need to keep all this quiet, this work we're doing back here, until there's some news. Does that work?"

"I can do that," Jesse said.

Curious to Max was, there'd been no mention of Jesse's missing brother, Myrna's husband. Max guessed it wasn't an oversight. A topic for another time.

On Max's phone, some news by way of a text from one of the engineers at the derrick, a hundred yards away.

On my way, he texted back.

Renee and Aurora on foot, takeout coffees in hand, left Acorn Court and entered tree-lined Broadway in downtown Jim Thorpe. A few horns beeped as cars trickled by them in the slow-moving traffic. Aurora acknowledged the horns with a wave, then acknowledged to Renee that, "As adorable as you are, honey," Aurora's wave would handle things for them both. She caught Renee up on Myrna's husband: what Aurora knew, what she didn't.

"Ken Springer was a cop on the force for many years here. The only job he ever had. We don't know where he is after he surprised his brother by grabbing a parachute and jumping from a small plane they were in, somewhere in upstate New York."

"You're saying he parachuted from a small plane, an unannounced, unplanned jump, the aircraft not in distress?"

"Yes. I got along well with Ken Springer. Until I didn't, which was three, almost four years ago. I'm an old bird, Renee, but I can still bust heads when needed, and that's what happened with Ken Springer. His drug use, his drinking on the job, it got worse, and when I pulled him into a conference room at the station for a come-to-Jesus personal intervention, it got physical. Truth be told, child, he beat me up pretty good, with other cops needing to pull him off me, but do understand that the boy did suffer. Lord, did he suffer. Still, there were no hospital visits for either of us, just ice packs and Advil. We jailed him that day and we gave him some choices, all related to counseling. He declined all of it. So I fired him. Kicked his ass to the curb. But I didn't charge him, and that was a huge mistake, because I know better. A judge would have forced him to get the help he needed. Things might have turned out different."

Renee volunteered what she knew about Myrna's husband because, after all, as Renee was now telling it, "I'm a research freak, Aurora. Big things will happen to Myrna going forward if her property has what we think it has buried underneath. We checked some of her background."

Renee had known nothing about Ken Springer's assault on Aurora, but what she did know about was "That plane ride he took with his brother. That stuck out. Was that the last time he was seen alive?"

"Yes."

"Who else was in the plane?"

"Ike Barber. He was the pilot. The three of them were going on a hunting trip up north, that's how they'd pitched it to Ken. But their plan was to do an intervention, not hunt. Get him to enter a rehab program facility in upstate New York that the police HR folks said they'd pay for, including the small aircraft rental. Springer saw through the ruse, apparently before they'd boarded. He decided not to be in the plane when they landed."

"Who's Ike Barber?"

"A town fireman. Old enough like me that he should retire. A town watch volunteer. Also a former military pilot, U.S. Army."

"Any money missing from anywhere? I mean, did it look like he was trying to disappear and start over, and he grabbed what he could, D. B. Cooper style?"

"Plenty of money was missing, honey, but it was all from beforehand. Massive credit card debt, all his doing, from the drinking and the drugging, which he left Myrna to handle. Additional cash taken? No. Their meager bank account was intact. The police and the town watch teams kicked in and bailed her out of most of the debt when it looked like he wasn't coming back. Myrna is a sweetheart, and her son Wyatt is a charmer. She's a real fighter, Renee. If this cobalt mining thing works out for her, ain't no one gonna be upset about it." Aurora checked her phone for the time.

"Oops. Oh my. I lost track. Myrna's shift is ending. We need to head back. I drive her to and from work each day. We meet Wyatt when the school bus drops him off. And Renee? Honey?"

"Yes?"

Aurora looked down her nose at her, some in disgust, but most in admonishment. Renee knew what was coming.

"Stop interrogating me. You want to see the missing person's case file on Ken Springer, I'll show it to you, but this little grilling-me thing you're doing here, don't you never try it again. We on the same page, honey?"

We're down 88 feet. We found something.

The text brought Max out to the drill. He stood over the output from the first few drilling attempts, minerals and dirt and unidentified rock tightly packed into tube-shaped rods as wide as a man's calf. When more minerals entered the tubes from below the earlier scoops were extruded out the top, into a bin with the other core rod output. The engineer pointed.

"That one, that one, and that one. When they come up from the borehole, we label the approximate depths of the pull. Those were at sixty-one feet, sixty-six feet, seventy feet. Feast your eyes, Mr. Fend."

All three samples had nothing that looked like cobalt in them. Also no obvious nickel, zinc, or copper. None of the samples did. But what they did have was—

"Oh, my," Max said.

Silver veins in each, an inch thick.

"What we see here, sir, is high-grade silver ore. If we find nothing else of value, there's at least this."

Max turned one borehole sample around in his hand, admiring it from different angles. One thing was certain: if silver ore this rich was underneath Myrna Springer's property, and it could be extracted, she was finished cleaning houses for a living.

He texted Renee, would text Myrna next, then Cornell.

News. We'll want to verify this against the time capsule info from Günther Heintz. Short version is, no cobalt yet on Myrna's property, but...

There was silver on it. Maybe a lot. Maybe it was the silver vein Günther Heintz was after, the one the Indigenous people were mining when Heintz found the *kobold* in the 1860s and dismissed it.

I'm texting Myrna now.

———————

Myrna had finished her last housecleaning job of the day and was sitting on the house's porch, her phone in hand, waiting for Aurora.

Multiple texts came through from the same number.

Myrna. Max Fend. A surprise.

Better if I told you in person, but I can't wait, so here it is...

20

"Dinner on me," Myrna said. "Pizza. Wyatt's favorite. It arrives in ten minutes. But we'll need to move those things out of the way before we can serve it."

The three borehole samples, six cylindrical inches across, four inches high, and thickly veined with silver ore, occupied her small kitchen table. Max, Renee, and Aurora crowded the rancher's small dining area, admiring them. Cornell brought the refreshments—soft drinks, beer, wine, water— and plastic drinkware, then he talked young Wyatt into tossing a football with him in the backyard. Outside, Little Pig barked, more at Cornell's tight yet soft-toss spirals, less at Wyatt's best efforts at strong-arming his tosses in return.

Myrna dropped the paper plates and napkins onto the table. She was blunt with Max. "These silver samples—what are they worth? Enough to pay for braces for Wyatt?"

Max had no experience here, neither on the precious minerals side nor on the childhood braces side. His guess was there was maybe five pounds of silver ore in all the samples combined. "Maybe it's enough. But I'd wait. A few more samples like this, maybe you can upgrade from the metal kind like I had as a kid to plastic aligners. But don't lose sight of the bigger picture here, Myrna. There's a lot more silver where this came from. It's even money that this is part of the silver vein the Lenape knew about. The one that Günther Heintz, our time capsule buddy, was searching for.

"I don't know if you've gotten your arms around this yet, Myrna, but there is one sure thing here. You won't need to clean houses for a living after this."

Myrna blinked hard then reached for him with an impromptu, tear-filled hug. Max played through, getting caught up in it, too, Renee's eyes tearing up also.

"We can talk more about how to get the silver out of the ground. But if there's cobalt down there, too, this will all become a blur to you shortly, and to us as well."

With dinner finished, Myrna got busy removing pizza boxes and wrapping the few cold leftover slices. She found room in her refrigerator; dinner for them tomorrow. Max stayed at the table, sipping beer with Cornell. It was getting close to last call for everyone. Renee and Aurora were out back on the deck, leaning over the railing, night descending on them.

A text hit Max's phone. From Renee.

Join me out back. Mum's the word.

The storm door slapped shut and Max appeared outside. It slapped shut a second time, Cornell joining them. Aurora had Renee's phone in her hand, studying the screen. Renee nodded in her direction.

"I showed her the photos I took of that jewelry store. Aurora is super interested in one of the customers."

"This guy," Aurora said, pointing. "He was at the time capsule event at the bank. I also saw him at a gun store in Jim Thorpe. His name is Alex. I've got his business cards on me somewhere. Here." She handed one to Renee.

Odd guy, and cocky, Aurora said. "Extremely Caucasian. He said he's a European mine engineering professor in Belarus. In the States because the university's cobalt research is everywhere, he said. He visited the gun shop as a tourist—at least this was what he told the gun shop owner—to see some assault-style weapons. Just so you know, the shop doesn't carry them anymore."

"Renee, honey," Max said, "you getting all this?"

"Duly noted. 'Eastern European professor cases Pennsylvania gun shop. Very white. Likes weapons he can't buy. News at eleven.'"

It sounded sarcastic, but Max knew it wasn't. Renee would ferret out more on this guy later.

Aurora analyzed the photos again. "Nothing's off with him in particular, other than he's real visible. But college teachers are weird, know what I'm saying? They don't blend in. He's like that."

Cornell nodded. "That dude is the whitest dude I have ever seen."

"A pigmentation issue," Aurora said. Then she heard herself. "Someone tell me I didn't just say that."

"Albinism," Renee said. "For him, it means he never goes unnoticed. For us it means we have a mine engineering professor from a Russia-sympathetic country who stopped into a gemologist business that had a Chinese woman as proprietor."

"Then the store had a beautiful French-Canadian tourist with a sudden interest in expensive diamonds," Max said. "Who thought the Poconos would be such a melting pot?" He paused at Renee's eye roll. "What? You did hear me say 'beautiful,' right, Renee?"

Was there anything to this? Even with no major cobalt find yet, the region was already drawing close international scrutiny.

"We're neglecting our hostess," Max said, watching Myrna through the window, scurrying around her kitchen. "I'm heading back inside to thank her, then I think we should call it a night. She's got a lot to think about, and we'll be overwhelming her with a helluva lot more if we're lucky."

The bowling ball was secured tightly inside the lead-lined trunk of a Volvo sedan, tucked inside a gorgeous bowling ball bag, a nifty colorful number in cobalt blue leather. The bag's interior was lined with lead inserts, including the padded bottom. Additional protective padding fattened up the bag's walls to eliminate concerns, of which there were many, about jostling. Upstate Pennsylvania liked its bowlers—adored its bowlers, their research had told them—so neither the bag nor the ball would look out of place.

He entered off-street parking for the historic Henry Packer Mansion Inn hotel and parked the Volvo. Six hours round trip to the Russian Consulate-

General building in NYC and back. He found a small baggage cart, placed his overnight bag onto it, and did likewise with the bowling ball bag, a two-handed effort, carefully guiding the cart to an elevator. He unloaded everything in his room.

No one would miss this sample because no one in the U.S. other than Russian consulate personnel knew of its existence, aside from the top-secret Russian approvals needed from the highest levels.

He wanted another look at it. Just a peek.

Zip, zip, and the bag was open. He moved the top padding out of the way and peered inside.

A magnificent creation. The ball's turquoise-green exterior was made from cobalt and zinc pigments ground into a resin that gave the ball its bright, unique, blue-green color. Underneath the smooth, polished metallic resin was, according to the specs, a 100% protective lead core, which ballooned the weight of the ball to 132 pounds. All lead, except for what was sealed inside it, deposited there through the thumb hole: a polished metal capsule the size of a C battery. Etched onto the capsule in large letters was a caution: "Danger – Radiation – Co-60 – *Drop & Run* – 7-1-63."

His Russian accomplices had indulged themselves with an inscription that mimicked one attributed to the Manhattan Project. Radiation humor. Clever. And part of a stunt that would come at the expense of the American people if the logistics could be worked out, which they would be.

If anyone had been close enough to read the admonition for the original Los Alamos, New Mexico sample back then, it would have already been too late for them; they'd be dead inside of five days. The same would be true with this one, buried inside the ball's lead core, if it were mishandled.

Alex Godunov had seen the *Drop & Run* caution message on this new vessel in photos because he was, among other things, the mule—the person who would deliver it to where it needed to go. He had no other instructions yet. What he did know was the 132-pound bowling ball that contained a highly radioactive cobalt-60 sample would never see the inside of a bowling alley.

21

Day two at Myrna Springer's property, a Saturday. An early start, everyone buoyed by the silver ore discovery the day before.

Max and Cornell trekked to the drill site to meet with the team and bring them coffee and bagels. Wyatt was at Little League baseball practice with Myrna, and Aurora had accompanied them. The diamond core drill engineers had set up thirty yards to the right of the first hole. If the silver vein ran in this direction, so be it, but the new borehole was not placed there with that expectation. The silver discovery was fun, and glorious, and for one person it would be life-changing, but it was yesterday's news.

There were twenty acres to explore. The property had given up a dirt-and-mineral brick laced with "kryptonite" to young Wyatt long after she'd given up a chunk of *kobold* to Mr. Günther Heintz a century and a half earlier.

How much more cobalt did she have, and how pure was it?

Max sipped his coffee, Cornell chewed his bagel, and the drill broke ground for the new bore. It was time to find out.

Cornell tended to Bureau business in his sedan in front of Max's vehicle, both parked outside Myrna's house. Max conducted business from his SUV passenger seat, his laptop locked onto two different satcom meetings. Wilkes ran one of the video calls from the Pituffik Air Base in Greenland, pulling in Hannah Taat from Qaanaaq, plus Max, plus Renee, who was multitasking with her hacker contacts from the comfort of their offsite RV. Wilkes's update: Air support protection at the Hiawatha impact site was now fully approved, but they would be on their own at tundra level for the time being, monitored by flyovers.

Max's other video call was with the DRC airport manager, getting an update on the Dornier 228 turboprop air crash at Goma International. He concentrated on the Goma call.

"Very bad news, Monsieur Fend," his DRC airport partner said. The man's face was haggard, looking exhausted and frustrated. "My government, it, ah, found some of the people who looted the crash site."

Max wanted to correct him; they were rescuers, not looters. Max's drone had recorded the video footage. These people had been looking for survivors. If they took things from the plane, it had been a crime of opportunity perpetrated by people who were destitute, which was most of the DRC population.

But their poverty wouldn't matter. He pretty much had figured out what the airport manager was about to tell him.

"The Army retrieved what they stole from the plane, I am told. I am ashamed to tell you that the rescuers who were found with the stolen goods were executed. Not by my countrymen, Monsieur Fend. But my countrymen did not try to stop it."

"Who killed them?"

"Not at liberty to say, Monsieur."

"What was stolen?" Max knew that answer, but was looking for confirmation that the airport manager knew.

"I cannot say."

Max shouldn't have asked; it put the man in a bad position. The benevolent DRC residents had paid an ultimate price for stealing cobalt powder that had already been stolen.

"... but I am so ashamed because of it, Monsieur Fend."

Max ended the call with his DRC airport counterpart. Later today he'd speak with his Fend Aerospace project manager about the airport's infrastructure progress and pass along the tragic update on the rescuers. He rejoined the other call with Wilkes, Renee, and Hannah. Time to wrap things up.

"Other than the aerial protection," Max said, "it sounds like nothing else has changed in Greenland, Wilkes. I'll head back to see you guys after we have more news about what we have or don't have here in the States. We're close. We need to see it get farther along."

Wilkes's face stayed blank, which meant a one-on-one with him was sure to follow Max's update, to tell Max to get his ass in gear, that he needed to get back to big, bad, frigid Greenland to help shore up the exploration effort there. Hannah stayed the obedient Fend Aerospace contractor, smiling through her boss's declaration. They were drilling now, yes, she said, it was still extremely cold, but the days were getting longer, and there was more sun.

Myrna's old 4Runner entered the stone driveway, the crunch of the tires distracting him. She and Wyatt, with Aurora riding shotgun, were back from Wyatt's baseball practice. Plus he'd received a text he needed to read...

He glanced at it. From the lead Army engineer at the new borehole.

147 feet. You need to see this.

"We'll talk later, Wilkes. I'll catch up with you, Renee, too. Gotta go."

Max trotted past Myrna and her passengers, offering a hand wave and smile through his breathy message, "New samples," while remaining cautiously calm. The drill was still operating on his approach to the site, continuing to pound at inner earth, compressing more minerals into the metal rod insertion now in operation at a great depth. The new samples pushed the old samples out the end of the rod protruding above the surface. Another engineer broke off cylindrical chunks of it to fit inside a box side-by-side, marking the penetration depths on each chunk, each pending later analysis. But this output . . . it wasn't similar to what had come before it—

"Thar she blows," the university geologist said, pointing at one of the extrusions held up by an engineer. It was three feet in length and a foot around; the engineer balanced it on its end. A cylindrical mineral stick.

"What we have here is another volcanogenic ore deposit," the geologist said, "but this one contains the rarest of rare earth minerals."

Max's eyes grew large as he circled the sample, examining its exposed circumference. Silver-gray veins, but with major blue-green concentrations.

"Winner winner chicken dinner?" Max asked the geologist.

"Steak night, Mr. Fend. The primary product of this sample is cobalt. We have it marked as coming up from 147 feet, but I'm sure it runs deeper, too."

Wyatt's kryptonite. It was glorious.

"It could also run shallower than that, though, right?" Max said. "In other boreholes, it might not be as deep? Myrna's son found it poking through the grass."

"Correct. Other boreholes might find it closer to the surface."

The bagels and coffee breakfast soon became a bagel and champagne brunch. After yesterday's silver-ore find, Max had purchased a case of champagne in anticipation. No one had ever called him a pessimist.

"Paydirt," he said to himself.

A frenzy of texts followed, to Renee at the RV—*I'll uber over,* she said —to Cornell, and to Myrna inside her house.

We did it Myrna. We have arrived. Welcome to Kryptonite City. Champagne on me.

No text to Wilkes. Not yet.

Myrna, young Wyatt, Aurora, Cornell, the engineers, the university geologist—Max snapped picture after phone picture of their celebration and the reason for it, the mineral samples from the dig, their fingers pointing at the cobalt, the diamond core drill, the derrick. Backslapping, handshakes, hugging, and massive smiles. Max took a panoramic photo of the site, the lens rolling past Myrna's house and the ranch home next to it. In addition to Renee's pending arrival, he realized someone else he was forgetting.

Myrna's neighbor, her brother-in-law. Jesse Springer needed to know. Max had promised him.

He pulled Myrna aside. "Text your brother-in-law, Myrna. The news should come from you. Have him join us."

Her eyes said *Thank you for letting it come from me, thank you for all of this.*

She smiled as she typed into her phone, called Wyatt over, took some selfies of mother and son, then sent the texts off, asking Jesse to stop over after his police shift.

This, Max internalized, was how she must have looked before life had gotten so hard for her. Happy, buoyant, fulfilled. Warm. Beautiful. A new beginning for little Wyatt, too. Wide smiles from them both that filled the screen as they posed, Max imagining Wyatt with straight white teeth after a few years of braces, to go with his straight black hair. Max's heart filled with that image, and with Myrna beaming, so proud of her son—

He caught himself beaming at her beaming.

She waved him over. "Can we take one with you?" she asked.

Max begged off, then complied. Max, Myrna, Wyatt in between, their arms around Wyatt's shoulder.

Done. Myrna sent the photo to Max. He pulled it up. His smile in it—

My goodness, when was the last time he smiled that large in a photo? All of this, the celebration, the champagne, him experiencing so much joy—

—with a woman other than Renee.

Where was Renee? Was she here already?

Yes, she was, on the periphery, there long enough for her champagne cup to be half empty. Her face gave no indication she'd witnessed anything out of the ordinary, no indication she'd seen Max beaming as gloriously as he had, but he still felt awkward. Worse yet, he felt guilty.

Renee was on her way over to see them. A good time for him to turn his exchange with Myrna into a business conversation.

"I know it's still early, but you're going to need lots of legal help, Myrna. A mountain of it." He shook his head. "Sorry, poor pun. But you *will* need it, and so will my company, and so will whoever excavates this deposit. So will the federal government, considering where this discovery is, depending on the direction the dig needs to go."

It abutted SGL parcel No. 141, possessed of many unique natural habitats. One of a few preserved hunters' and fishermen's state game land parcels in the state of Pennsylvania. Seventeen thousand acres in this one, home to black bear, white-tailed deer, ruffed grouse, coyote, bobcat, gray fox, and mink, plus other woodsy creatures. State bureaucratic miracles would be needed, shepherded by federal intervention, to get permission to open the game lands for mineral excavation. No easy task considering how much damage the coal industry had done to the area in the last few centuries.

But not true regarding private property, where the discovery was. The rights to drill and mine were up for grabs by the highest bidder, with fewer strings attached. It had all been scoped out ahead of time by the Bureau, per Cornell, and by the Agency per Wilkes, and by private industry folks like Fend Aerospace's corporate geniuses, and contractors à la Renee LeFrancois, who was ahead of the curve on most of it, too. She just wasn't ahead of the curve on what had made Max's heart flutter a moment ago, and the guilt that came with it.

Renee listened as Max spewed facts and figures to Myrna. He dragged her over to a table and asked Renee to fire up her laptop. "The crash course on mineral rights ownership begins now," Max said to Myrna. "Ready?"

Scrolling down the laptop screen was a search of mineral rights auctioneers, brokers, and attorneys. Then came the running list of mining companies whose specialties were precious metals and rare-earth minerals. Last came a short list of environmentally conscious land trauma experts. Companies that the state of Pennsylvania would need to pick from if Max were going to shame every excavator with a new Pocono cobalt stake into including the cost of eliminating the Centralia coal-seam fire as part of their bids. Finally, a spreadsheet summarizing all of it, with Max's choices of contractors from a curated list of recommendations.

He clarified. "These need to be *your* choices here, Myrna, all of them, including the approach about handling the underground fire. I'm hoping you see the merit in that. Renee, can you help her navigate these listings here? Maybe help her cull the list down and get ready to reach out to some of them?"

"Sure. But I need to talk with you."

More texts, to Wilkes and Hannah, to make sure they understood about the discovery. In Max's estimation—the intuition of an optimist—Nesquehoning and Jim Thorpe were about to become the center of America's cobalt existence, maybe the world's.

Wilkes called him.

"Excellent," Wilkes said. "Incredible news. But we're still also interested in Greenland. When can you get here?"

"I'm not going to abandon Myrna, Wilkes. This is huge, and a lot of people will come at her, telling her how she should spend her lottery winnings. Her property will become an unrecognizable mess, so I see her needing to relocate. The same for her brother-in-law. I'll head north to see you guys in a few weeks. Gotta go, Wilkes, bye."

The glad-handing around him continued, the champagne flowed. Myrna, Wyatt, now Uncle Jesse. Aurora, Cornell, the engineers.

Time for his tête-à-tête with Renee.

Away from the crowd, Max let Renee lead.

"I was late, Max, because of our campsite neighbor Eunice. She's a mess."

"Eunice with the drugged-out grandson."

"That one. She can't find him. None of his friends, Eunice's daughter, no one has seen him since he was released from jail. Eunice is super worried something happened to him."

"Maybe some other neighbor living next door to some other grand-mother beat the crap out of him, too," Max said. "With a guy like that, it's sometimes just a question of finding the body. Are the police on it?"

"She says yes, but she thinks they're putting in less than a full effort looking for him."

Max couldn't blame them. "We can't do much more than put a pin in that, Renee. You told her I'm not in any way responsible, right?"

"The first words out of my mouth."

"Did she believe you?"

"Seventy-thirty yes."

"I can live with that. Okay then. We'll move forward with what we have going on here, which will keep us extremely busy."

"I have a question for you, Max."

Her posture was unreadable, facing him with her arms at her sides, her beautiful eyes steadied on his. This big news about the cobalt find didn't seem to do for her what it did for everyone else.

"Should I be worried," she said, "about Myrna?"

How does a guy talk to a girlfriend about experiencing heart flutters for a person who isn't her?

"What about Myrna, honey?"

The awkward "honey" did him in, showing he *did* have an idea what this was about. But it didn't matter, he was sure now she already knew something was off, and he needed to acknowledge it. Renee was the woman he loved—he wouldn't embarrass himself by making her spell out what she'd already noticed.

He waved off his flippant response. "No, you shouldn't be worried," he said and reached for her hand. She let him take and hold it.

"I don't know what I was feeling. It was a moment where I glimpsed a calmer, saner life than what I've had so far. Where I saw a wonderful family dealt a really bad hand and in desperate need of a breadwinner, and I'm a pretty good breadwinner. It's the part of me that tries to be all things to all people."

"A wonderful, attractive family," Renee said. "She's beautiful, and her son is adorable."

"Wonderful and attractive family, yes, but that's too basic, and it's not fair."

"I think you're not seeing the other side of this, Max. How she looks at you."

Incorrect. He had seen it. It was part of what fueled his reaction to Myrna's fangirl behavior. "It's an infatuation thing going on there, Renee. No worries, she knows you and I are a couple."

"That carries no weight, Max. My divorce proved that."

He hadn't forgotten her debrief to him on that. An experience made more painful because her husband's infidelity had involved a close friend of hers.

Max moved closer, initiating a hug, and Renee let it happen. It became a full-faced, open-eyed kiss started by Max and finished by Renee, and it gave Max a wonderful feeling, like things were going to be okay. They remained in each other's arms. "I hope this hug carries the weight it needs to, Renee," Max said.

"Me, too."

Their noisy, clapping audience of associates approved of it, with Max noticing young Wyatt first, him in a Superman pose, hands on hips and legs spread, with hair just as black as actor Christopher Reeve's but longer. Myrna draped her arm over her son's shoulder, her smile at Wyatt prompting a mother-son hug. More wonderfulness for Max to absorb.

Back to business. "Tomorrow is going to be monstrous, Renee. Wilkes will debrief the Agency and Cornell will update his superiors. Cornell has it on good authority that President Windcolor has been following our progress, receiving reports daily. This discovery is in her backyard."

President Faye Windcolor. As a descendant of Munsee Lenape Native Americans, she was a former Pocono area resident.

"The digging will start as soon as Myrna gives a verbal agreement. The heavy contract language will get hammered out after she decides who she'll accept bids from. Digging, sampling, gauging the size of the deposit, deciding on which company will go after putting out the Centralia coal fire —it all starts now."

Renee pressed her thumb into his palm and gave his hand a squeeze, grounding his excitement, replacing it with cautious enthusiasm. "Hopefully, Max, it lives up to the predictive modeling. The expectations of the university geologists, the mineral industry, the energy and economic markets . . . " she trailed off.

He closed his hand around hers. This was the start of an excellent new adventure, for him, for her, for these property owners, for their country, and for the world.

"We're about to see Nesquehoning, Pennsylvania, become the center of America's cobalt existence," he said, "and you and I are in the thick of it."

Another kiss from him, this one gentle and appreciative.

"I'm so glad I'm getting to share this with you, Renee."

22

Two Weeks Later, Mid-May

"I found more on them," Renee said. Her laptop screen glowed, lighting up her face while she rested against the bed's backboard. Eleven-thirty p.m. in the motorhome at the RV campsite. Max and Renee lay amid scattered bedsheets.

"I'm exhausted," Max said. "Can that be tomorrow's business?"

There'd been other news outside of the cobalt vein discoveries on the two side-by-side Nesquehoning properties, Myrna's and her brother-in-law Jesse's. A defunct Pocono mining company had accepted a qualifying bid for the purchase of an old coal mine to the west of the Springer properties, between Nesquehoning and Centralia. Rare Earth Metallurgical, Inc., bought the rights to reopen the mine, another strategic purchase hustled through the process to get the most out of whatever cobalt deposits lay beneath Pocono mountain country as soon as possible. Rare Earth had also signed on to obliterate the sixty-year-old hellfire buried beneath the Keystone state's still coal-engorged underbelly, with its hot release points and open fire pits venting themselves throughout the region. Their approach would be to excavate the entire multiple-mile perimeter of it, going as wide and as deep as necessary.

"Listen to me a moment, Max. Tracing them back," she said, still keying, "Rare Earth is the U.S. arm of a reconfigured Canadian company. They have an excellent reputation for eliminating underground mine fires in the U.S. and Canada. They're huge, and it looks like they'll be up to the task."

Max made a noise in his pillow. "Good. It means Wilkes paid attention to me. If they're here, the Agency and the Bureau must like them. We'll all need to pay for the coal fire cleanup, but at least it'll get done. Maybe northeastern Pennsylvania gets to finally turn a corner here. In the meantime"—he groped at her laptop—"turn it off, we need to get some sleep."

She leaned her laptop away from his reach. What now filled the screen made her open her eyes wider.

Peoples names. The list was long. Rare Earth Metallurgical's current and prior board of directors, its company officers, its other senior and upper management team. The top officer spots were held by scientists heavy on doctorates and other academic credentials. But buried among the upper management team—

"Huh," she said.

Max roused. "*Huh* meaning what?"

"Some of the principles of one of the Rare Earth acquisitions are eastern European, and some are Russian. Geologists, academics from the Baltics, a lot of mining experts. They get high marks as a progressive company because the team is multinational. On the surface, they look like they'll be an excellent coalition."

"On the surface means there's a 'but' in there somewhere."

"Not sure. The trail . . . it might reach farther out, connections beyond the Baltics, maybe Asian. Tell me this. How often have we heard the word 'academics' and 'mining' in the same sentence lately?"

Max was up on his elbow now. "Once."

"Exactly."

It was when they'd talked with Aurora Jolson about the ultra-white-haired mining professor who showed up at the gem appraisal store. A very visible person. "A long shot," Max said, "but is his name there?"

Renee fumbled around inside a laptop bag. "I got this business card from Aurora. His name is Alex Godunov." She perused the corporation's list. "No, he's not here. But that just means he's not overt."

"Look. Renee. We're not looking for any odd connections here. Hanging around Wilkes too much has warped our thinking. I mean, why can't we appreciate an average, everyday, massive U.S. cobalt discovery, one that's destined to change world economics overnight, without also thinking there's a covert aspect to all of it?"

"We can't, because that's who we are, Max. And here,"—*tap, tap, tap*— "wow. Here's the first estimate on the size of the Pocono deposits. These Rare Earth Metallurgical people pulled it together. You and Wilkes and Cornell Oakley were copied on this. And other top Fed folks up the line."

"What? Someone sized it already?"

"Rare Earth says it's around the same size as the DRC deposit. Three-point-five million metric tons."

"You're reading this where?"

"It was part of their bid for the old mine they want. Add to that, Elon Musk's people are using some voodoo underground electron imaging equipment that says the deposit may be even larger. I don't know how any of these groups size these things, so don't ask me. But either way, two independent scientific groups say these Pennsylvania deposits are enormous."

Max dropped his head back onto his pillow, his wide-eyed awareness now fueled by new mental gymnastics. *No sleep for you, Mr. Fend*, he thought. "Does that estimate include looking at the state game lands?"

"Doesn't say," Renee said.

The state hunting territories that the Pocono Mountain ranges sat on. Access to them would be prohibited, except—

Always easier to ask for forgiveness than to ask for permission.

"They'll drill down," Max said, thinking aloud, "then they'll drill sideways. Wherever the cobalt veins lead."

But state game lands were, after all, owned by the Commonwealth of Pennsylvania. Someone eventually would realize the need, and the proper protocols would be followed, permits issued, environmental studies performed, and decisions made about the greater good. All that would happen, just not at first.

Maybe now he and Renee could get some sleep. He reached up for a tug at her shoulder, to give her a peck on the cheek—

She was listing starboard, already asleep. He closed her laptop, moved it off the bed, and pulled the sheet up over her shoulders. Lights out, finally, at twelve-thirty.

Maybe not. At Eunice's campsite, next to his, the fire was still crackling, tossing embers skyward. Max pulled on a sweatshirt and gym pants and headed outside.

"Eunice. Hi." He sat in a lawn chair next to her.

"Hi." She was wrapped in a light throw blanket with Tex-Mex patterns on it. Her look into her dying fire was fixed, emotionless, staring past what to Max was the wonder of a microcosmic flame as it suffered through its demise like a star collapsing on itself, about to flicker out. Something beyond the fire held her interest, dancing in her unblinking eyes. Or maybe her mind was on overload. The two of them sat next to each other steeped in non-conversation, with no engagement, until there was.

"Where do you call home, Mr. Fend?"

"Please, call me Max. Home? Most recently the DC area, but I'm on the move a lot. I have a sailboat, and that lets me hang around wherever there's a large enough body of water, whenever and wherever I feel like it. So home is usually somewhere other than where I am at that moment."

She poked at the fire. "Your sailboat is a yacht, isn't it?"

"That's fair. Sure."

"No matter. You're no better, no worse than the rest of us when it comes to our wanderings. Everyone is always from somewhere else. I'm from somewhere else, too. Plenty of somewhere elses. One of them was Centralia, home of the coal fire. But I don't talk about it. Too painful."

The next few moments stayed empty, contemplative. Then, "Any news on your grandson?" Until that was resolved, it had to be topmost in her thoughts.

It took nearly ten seconds for her to answer. "No." Five seconds more. "No one's seen anything, no one knows anything. How does someone just disappear?"

A rhetorical question. Max let her respond to it.

"Peter could be in the Lehigh River. He could be in a Scranton drug house with a needle in his arm. He could be beaten and left defenseless somewhere. I've prepared myself for all that. His ma and I, we're both prepared. We just need to know."

Max heard a vehicle turn onto the short trail leading to their adjacent campsites. He strained to surveil it; it was creeping along with the headlights off. It stopped, the ignition turned off, and one door opened and closed.

He felt under his sweatshirt for his 9mm, lay his hand atop it, and stood. He wanted to be visible. The campground's ambient light validated there were no other occupants sitting up in the vehicle's seats.

Eunice was on her feet and eager, ready to receive her company, her flashlight piercing the darkness. It exposed the man on his approach, no weapon evident.

"Hey, Eunice." A friendly male voice. It preceded its owner, who clicked on a penlight and shuffled forward in hiking boots, toward Eunice's camper. He shifted the light's beam as he got closer. "Oh. Fend. Hi."

"Ike! Oh, Ike!" Eunice said. Max heard relief in her response, but also desperation.

Ike Barber, part of Jim Thorpe town watch, delivered a huge bear hug to her while cooing greetings into her ear during their embrace.

The intensity of the hug said this was a friendship that spanned years, maybe decades. Mr. Ike Barber, however, looked pained, delivering his hug without a smile. He and Eunice separated, still holding each other by elbows and arms. Eunice searched Ike's face.

"Two reasons for me stopping by, Eunice. A town watch wellness check for one, just because you know I love you, and two, to give you an update if you were awake. Sorry to say your grandson's car was found by police in a drug-infested section of Philadelphia. No damage to it, but there was drug paraphernalia inside, recently used. Some clothes, a little cash, but not your grandson. He might have been—sorry, might *be*—living out of it, panhandling his way from fix to fix on the streets, the Philly cops told our locals."

"His car, but no Peter," she said, sizing up the news.

"No Peter. I also updated your daughter. I figured I'd stop by here, guessing you might still be up, contemplating your campfire. I guessed right."

"Thank you, Ike," Eunice said, and she gave him a peck on the cheek. She politely pulled away, her eyes tearing up. She found a small jug of water nearby and emptied it onto her dying, earthbound star. An un-majestic end to yet another glorious, seemingly perpetual fire, one that Max and Renee had also come to appreciate. She contemplated the rising smoke from the embers, and Ike Barber moved closer to grip her elbow for support as she said a quiet prayer. This news was not unexpected, Max realized, and it supplied what he surmised Eunice had been waiting for, the closest thing to closure she could hope for, her grandson swallowed up by his addiction and most likely not returning. Eunice climbed the steps to her old camper and entered it without another word.

"Will she be all right?" Max asked Ike, the two men staring at the door as she locked herself in.

Ike Barber lit a cigarette, sucked at it, and blew out the smoke. "She won't hurt herself, if that's what you're asking, but she knows this was it. The last straw. No more searching locally, no more searching, period. Once they get to Philly or New York, or to Florida, or California, they're off the grid, and barring a miracle, they don't ever come back. For Eunice and her daughter, this should have happened long ago. A painful existence for them, living day-to-day not knowing when the next shakedown or beating from him was coming."

Ike studied the red-tipped cigarette cupped in his hand, its smoke rising. "Aurora shared with us what you did to him after his last attack on Eunice, Fend. That, my friend, was long overdue." He gulped in another draw of smoke then squinted at Max as he released it. "Just like this update I gave her tonight. The man had to go."

He tossed his dead cigarette into the dead fire.

"Here's to hoping Eunice can have a restful night. Good rest of the night to you, too, Fend. Things should be a little quieter for her from here on in."

_____

An early wake-up for them with three unanswered phone calls in succession from Wilkes, to Max and Renee both. Then came the texts, all to Max. He relented and pulled them up, sensing a controlled boil behind Wilkes's keyed entries.

You need to be here yesterday Max

"Here" was the Hiawatha impact crater, Greenland.

I applaud your work, the find, the great news, all of it, but get your ass up here now

Your Greenland team just made its first significant find

Major deposit 1800 feet copper nickel but it mostly looks like veins of high cobalt content

Geologists say good chance this is on the lip of the meteorite strike

Reports on no similar successes to the south, Musk & Bezos & others, nothing happening there

You'll hear from Hannah Taat

She says the Queen of Denmark is onboard ready to make it all happen here for us, a deal, resources, all of it

This is great news Max. We're in a good place.

I want you here. Now.

Ingahild Gustavsson, Queen of Denmark, Renee's ex-smoking buddy, was ready to cozy up to an extraction deal with the U.S. as a partner. Max read the entire string to Renee while they lay in each other's arms, each still exhausted and needing much more than the five hours of sleep they'd gotten.

"This is not bad news, Max," Renee said. "This is outstanding. Why aren't you excited?"

"I am, but the timing is the issue. They've just started digging here. I want to see this dig, this mother-of-all-deposits in the Poconos, up close and personal. I want to go into the mine, I want to see it being extracted. After I do, I'll head up north to see this new meteorite phenomenon that, from the way Wilkes describes it, could give the U.S. another slam-dunk edge in the clean energy markets."

"Max, honey?"

"What?"

"You just moved the goalposts—on Wilkes, on the Agency. You're keeping the Bureau happy, and that's good, how could they not be, but are you sure that's all you're dealing with here by delaying this?"

"Yes. I'm sure." A sincere answer. Fend Aerospace wasn't the only principal investor involved in the Myrna and Jesse Springer digs; there were others. Sharing the wealth and the risk, Max's original story, original approach—he was sticking with all of it. But his company was supplying some of the manpower here. Fend project managers were arriving daily, teaming with the other partners. He had to see this thing in action.

"We'll wrestle this into some semblance of production," he said. "They're already digging, already identifying the best ways to enter each of these twenty-acre parcels. And we can't forget the state game lands adjacent to the properties on two sides, either. I'll do Greenland as soon as I can see some bona fide product come out of the ground here. That's a promise, Renee. And I'm making that promise"—he keyed at his phone—"to Wilkes right . . . now."

He would soon speak with Hannah Taat, his Greenland contractor, would applaud her for her outstanding efforts at keeping the team focused, and would promise her additional financial rewards on the heels of their triumph. Max and Fend Aerospace were two for two in the mineral markets. Beginner's luck? More like beginner's brute force belligerence.

He would also speak with Wilkes, would confirm this as a plan, would give him a timetable, would stick to it, cross his heart. The heavy extraction equipment was moving into Nesquehoning today, all day; it wouldn't be long now. He texted Wilkes.

How is protection going for the Greenland team?

Air support in place?

Check, per Wilkes.

Ground support?

Nothing military, but the personnel at the Hiawatha crater site now had substantial personal firepower: Stinger shoulder-fired missile launchers, a stash of long guns and handguns, neck-to-toe Kevlar, combat helmets, even their own "bear-dar," all designed to keep them safe.

He finished communicating with Wilkes and Hannah Taat and segued into a late morning breakfast of cereal, yogurt, juice, and more coffee. Max's internal monologue filled the swatches of air between the bites and the sips and the small talk. One niggling itch reared itself.

Myrna and Wyatt also needed to be safe. Needed to be protected, cared for, and shepherded into this new life of theirs.

But neither Wilkes nor Renee nor Myrna would hear any of that. It would only complicate things.

23

Close of business for the day, eight p.m., the sun dropping below the pine forest to their backs. Nods and beer bottle salutes circled the tiny deck in back of Myrna's house, Agent Cornell Oakley back in the mix to close out his Bureau assignment. Three days after contact with Wilkes, Max was almost packed for his return trip to Qaanaaq, Greenland.

"I gave my two-week notice to my employer," Myrna told Max and Renee. "I thought I'd be working the rest of my life cleaning houses. Today is a day," she sniffled, holding back tears, "I thought would never come. I have you all to thank for this."

The mining operation, not yet officially dedicated, had already produced significant quantities of the highest-grade cobalt ever seen in the U.S., and was poised to move to a higher level, a much larger operation. Sections of her twenty acres and Jesse's adjacent property had been bull-dozed and large pine trees had been felled; these land parcels in Nesque-honing were fast becoming mini industrial complexes. Silos, massive industrial underground augers, conveyor belts, other processing equipment, much of it was either in place and functioning or close to it, occupying more than half of their properties. It came from the full-court press from the Feds and private industry combined. Everyone knew the stakes. They were witnessing a beautiful thing.

Myrna had found a ten-acre, Wyatt-approved homestead north of Jim Thorpe for them. But the clincher for her—the highlight of her struggling single-mother existence, the bluest of blue collars—had just been announced: there would be a ribbon-cutting ceremony to officially open their cobalt mines, conducted on her property by U.S. President Faye Windcolor.

Beer for the new crew, beer for everybody. The Army Corps had moved on; they came, they saw, they'd conquered, and the Poconos would never be the same. New geologists and mining engineers were in place, supplied by Allied Super Auger, a mining engineering company that also served a smaller U.S. cobalt extraction installation in Idaho. Fend Aerospace became their silent 25% partner for this site in Pennsylvania.

They sipped, they pondered the burgeoning industry spreading east inside these two private properties. Pockmarks were scattered throughout, starter holes boring deep, lots of yellow caution tape, the larger strip digs taking hold closer to the house. The black holes in the distance were getting more shadowy and blacker as the sun lowered in the sky behind them.

Something was off, however. These digs on the eastern horizon—maybe they weren't getting darker and blacker as the sun set. Max squinted to see better.

Was the cloudless nighttime sky with stars and a bright halfmoon playing tricks? Max wondered aloud if the mining team was finished working on the sections farthest from Myrna's house, closest to the state game lands. Not much of it was visible from here because of a dip in the acreage before it turned upward, into the mountain. Myrna finished her beer and was quick to respond.

"I was promised no more digging back there for now. They're focusing closer in." She stepped off the deck to surveil her backyard, now a mother in search of her precocious son.

"Wyatt!" she called. "Let's go, Superman. Off to bed, young man." The call was stronger the second time. "Wyatt! You and Little Pig—inside —now."

They all listened, heard no response. Myrna returned to the deck, poked her head inside her kitchen door and called again, then she went inside the house to check. She returned quickly.

"No leash. He's out there somewhere with Little Pig."

She found a flashlight and marched off the deck, the rest of them equipping themselves with penlights, camera phones, and more flashlights, a group of nine people there to close out the day, all now looking for her son. Myrna strode the most quickly, staying in the lead as her flashlight swept the trail in front of her, scanning an area full of tree stumps, overturned dirt, and ruts from heavy machinery.

"Max, need to have a word with you," Myrna called over her shoulder, more breathless than a moment ago.

He hustled up next to her.

"There's something I should have told you earlier," she said.

Renee, Cornell, and the other team members were spreading out. The comment kept Max close. "I'm listening."

"These areas farthest in the back—the spots where the mining company doesn't want to work—"

Their lights picked up the eerie green-eyed reflections of critters on the flat edge of the pine forest anxious about this search party's advance. The animals skittered about, the chatter of this disruption alerting the local ecosystem that human drama was queueing up. Max quickly reminded himself there were other predators out here in the Pocono Mountains—foxes, owls, hawks, mountain lions, bears . . .

He patted the 9mm tucked in the holster in his waistband, a reflex. He and Myrna sidestepped more pockmarks.

"Finish your sentence, Myrna—what about these areas back here?"

"I'm, ah, letting some close friends dig back here. The husbands of my housecleaner co-workers. They've been out of work for too long. Whatever they can dig up, I told them they can keep. I mean, there's no harm in that, right?"

In his head, major worry now.

Artisanal digs, here in the Poconos, just like the Congo. These things are dangerous. This can't be happening.

"We'll talk later," Max said. "After we find Wy—"

They heard a loud hiss, like air releasing from a massive tire, or a soaring bottle rocket, a short burst of it, then one, two, and more of them, each a release of pressure, *pfttt, pfttt, pfttt* . . .

A large spritz of dust jettisoned skyward in the low light seventy or so yards ahead, a geyser of smoke and debris, the sparkling dirt glistening in the starlight like fireworks. The ground beneath them jumped, burped, and rumbled, all manifesting itself for the second it took for the noise of a single, large explosion to reach them.

Ba-boom.

Cornell outran Myrna, Max outran Cornell, each entering a gray-white ground-level shroud with the beams from their flashlights reflecting off crystals of descending soil fragments settling on a deep forest green carpet. A dizzy adult zigzagged toward them, his hands covering his ears, his head covered in dust and dirt. He fell onto his knees coughing, gasping, gulping in whatever clean air he could.

"Others?" Max screamed at him. "Are there others out there with you—?"

"Unnhh—others—no, they are all out of the holes—*aghhh* . . ."

Max saw clearly now where the blast had originated, a horizontal dig into the mountainside starting on Myrna's property, the tiny tunnel directed toward game land territory. The smoking gun hole continued its long exhale, spewing cloudy particles into his face as he approached. He covered his nose and mouth with his shirt, his squinting eyes filtering out whatever irritants it could. He was facing the artisanal tunnel now and the impact of the explosion seemed more foreboding because the orifice was so small. Crawlspace only, leading into a dark abyss, augers from local hardware stores askew of it. No better than the artisanal digs he'd seen in the DRC. He coughed and sneezed into his hand then looked at what the tunnel was releasing: airborne specks of dirt, some of it glittering. Cobalt dust.

Max's flashlight penetrated the darkness, but the beam couldn't reach far enough.

"Hand augers," Max said aloud, Cornell behind him now. "How long have they been at this—has to have been days for them to get that far in—"

Cornell agreed. "There'll be hell to pay because of this, Max. You know this will have repercussions—"

But there was still no Wyatt. There was, however, suddenly Little Pig, who sprang into Max's arms and squirmed as they stood outside the tunnel, sinking her teeth into his forearm. She snarled, repositioned her mouth grip onto his wrist and jumped out of his arms, pulling Max away from the tunnel.

"Owww, stop, *owww*," Max said, but he'd gotten her message. Little Pig beckoned him, hobbling ten, fifteen, twenty feet in front of him, bouncing up and down to make sure Max was following her to a different rock pile outside a different small tunnel that looked smaller in circumference than the other one. Smoke wafted from between the pile of rocks at the entrance, chilling Max. Something under there was on the verge of igniting. And now, visible through the haze seeping from the pile, he saw a child's hand. In the hand was a pocket-sized piece of what was surely kryptonite, regardless of its speckled blue-green consistency. Clutched among the blandness of the stones, Max could have been convinced the cobalt glowed green.

"He's here!" Max screamed and began throwing rocks and debris wildly everywhere, clawing furiously at the pile and an unmoving Wyatt, a dog leash in Wyatt's one hand, a rare-earth rocky mineral treasure in the other. Max pulled and shoved and scraped and bore down, freeing the arms, then the chest, then the legs, then focusing on Wyatt's dust-covered head. Brushing his face clean, he patted him down checking for misshapen limbs before pulling out his body. He moved him to the grass, lay him there, and he started CPR.

"Renee! Myrna! Call 911!"

Two minutes later they coaxed the first cough from Wyatt's lungs, followed by more coughs with choking in between, then a few full breaths, then some deeper breathing. Max patted young Wyatt's arms and legs, looked over his neck, checked his head, then scanned his body for bleeding. No broken skin, no blood, just a small child felled by flying, exploding mine fragments, fighting for his life.

Wyatt's eyes remained closed, his one hand gripping a blue-green rock, the other now empty of the dog leash and groping to connect with his savior. Max wrapped his hand in his and watched Wyatt's eyes open a sliver. His grip was tight, even after his eyes closed again.

"Does anything hurt, Wyatt?"

"My foot."

The EMTs got to work, gently lifting him onto a gurney. Wyatt cried when his mother hugged him, Myrna wiping away his tears, a mother's caring smile emerging through her own sobbing.

Oxygen, an IV, pain meds, checks of his extremities, sips of water. Probable broken ankle, other injuries unknown. Wyatt was ready to go. Two more ambulances arrived.

"Little Pig," Wyatt said in not much more than a whisper.

"She's fine, Wyatt," Myrna said, her voice as soft as his. "She brought Max to you."

Max kissed Renee then followed alongside Wyatt's battered body to the emergency vehicle, Myrna cooing into her son's ear. The EMTs told Max he couldn't ride along, but Wyatt would not let go of his hand, which got Max a seat next to him.

Myrna promised Wyatt he wasn't in trouble. She also promised she wouldn't lose the new piece of kryptonite he'd dug out of the mine for her.

Dusk. Godunov was on a fat-tired ATV, helmeted because he knew what terrain like this did to unsuspecting riders. Headlights on, it was a slow ride, moving across the forest floor as gingerly as he could, negotiating his way around deadfalls and rocks and past full, healthy pine trees, using a compass, the ATV odometer, and his instincts. No GPS to speak of. The Pocono Mountains were notorious for dead spots. But what he was looking for had been visible to the cartographers, out here somewhere per satellite images, just not on the beaten path, and he'd mapped out the route himself, deciding that a straight line starting from the defunct coal mine property his employer had just acquired was the best approach. On paper, the ride looked to be eight miles. He was into mile number seven. The woods were darkening with every foot the ATV traveled.

He'd worked many digs during this clandestine career of his, in many countries—Europe, Africa, Russia—chasing the newest clean-energy prize, cobalt, in search of the rare pure discoveries, not derivatives of copper and nickel digs. The equivalent of what had been found in the Bou-Azzer mine in Morocco, plus in some smaller, less viable locations in Canada. The news that had startled the world mineral markets of late was the discovery in Nesquehoning, Pennsylvania, deemed as large as the estimated tonnage in the DRC, but as pure as Morocco. It was the reason he was here, in the U.S. It was of major interest to his employer, and of major interest, and threat, to many national economies in the cobalt-producing and utilization pecking order.

He was fluorescent, his vest, his footwear, and his helmet all colored in caution-tape yellow. Whatever game animals were in season out here, he didn't want hunters to mistake him for them. Even though by all rights no one should be out in the woods hunting or being hunted this late at night, that wouldn't stop poachers. Godunov was armed with a powerful semiautomatic handgun. The Pennsylvania forests had mountain lion and black bear populations. If they mistook him for prey, he'd be able to defend himself. At least that was the plan.

Godunov stopped for a swig of water and to check his notes. The "pothole," called as such by a Google Maps cartographer, had to be close. It was one of only two known large potholes in northeast Pennsylvania, the other one celebrated as a tourist attraction north and east of here, in Archbald, Lackawanna County, with a state park built around it. The one he was looking for had no name, was on the map only as "Carbon County pothole," small "p." Another geological masterpiece, per the myriad of internet notes on it, much like the one in Archbald, and at 127 feet it was more than triple the other's depth, though both potholes had resulted from the same millions of years of glacial melting that bore tornado-shaped funnels into the earth.

Its coordinates were compelling. It was due east of Centralia, and due farther east of the abandoned coal mine now owned by his employer, which meant the order, moving east, was Centralia, then the distant abandoned coal mine, then the pothole, then Nesquehoning, then Jim Thorpe. A stretch of thirty-five miles. On paper, at least, the pothole was positioned nicely, where it was needed for it to be of use to him.

He stopped the ATV and took off his helmet. In front of him, in the vehicle's headlights, was the Carbon County pothole, small "p."

Not impressive. It was easy to understand why there was little tourist interest. There were no barriers to keep people from entering it for most of its amoebic-shaped perimeter, because nine-tenths of it wasn't steep and had only a casual incline, gentle enough that someone could drop a blanket on it and relax for a nap. A wide hole, but not intimidating, except for the last tenth of it, visible across from his vantage point. He illuminated that section by flashlight, and could tell it was a steep drop. The cyclone fencing protecting it was ten to twelve feet high and ran forty or so feet wide, curling around its edges. The fencing was sufficient warning for passersby to stay away.

He snapped flash photos of the fenced section, angle after angle, before walking down the incline to get close to it. The next stream of pictures came from an infrared handheld telephoto lens. He zoomed in on the steep drop, a poor angle, checking on thermal imaging as well as measuring the depth as best he could. The hotspots began at a depth of at least ninety feet. Was that deep enough? He didn't know.

He trudged back up the incline, his photo shoot over. He'd seen what he'd come to see. He'd analyze the data later.

At the ATV, its lights off, he checked his phone. No service. He walked the perimeter of the pothole, his flashlight guiding him. Connectivity at last, halfway around. He thumbed through some messages, expecting the important one, its timing predetermined, that was supposed to come tonight. He found it.

Bibi Memona Qureshi's text: Anything new? I'm bored

Yes, there was, finally. He typed back.

Additional clarity, he texted. Subject has been identified. Date location time still TBD

He waited for another of her texts, then had to wait longer.

The ground beneath him rumbled, a *ba-boom* that shook the pine trees, putting the woods surrounding him on notice.

From where? In front of him? Yes, it was from the east. It animated the forest, night birds taking flight, pine needles rustling, critters scurrying. One boom only, distant, but discernable as an explosion, then quiet again.

Just before he put his phone away, Bibi texted a response.

What do we do next

He was feeling benevolent, or maybe impatient. He would offer her some rapid-fire info rather wait for her to ask for it piecemeal.

A difficult assignment. Our benefactors are evaluating it. The fee will be triple.

This is because they want you to be the one to do it, they want absolute cooperation, they want you to be satisfied, and they want to make sure it happens. All supplies will come from the benefactors.

You will understand when there is more info. Are we good for now?

Movement to his right, outside the perimeter of the clearing that was the pothole, forty yards away. He raised his flashlight, saw nothing, but he heard the growl and tree branches snapping. Whatever it was, it was on the move, headed in his direction and taking the long way around the hole.

He drew the gun from a side holster without hesitation. Flashlight in one hand, handgun in the other, he sprinted the short distance to the ATV and keyed the ignition, the predator charging behind him. He could see it now: a black bear, teeth snarling, mouth contorting from bellowing a deafening, spit-drenched roar, a gallop about to be a sprint, towards its target. Outrunning the bear in the ATV was no longer an option. Only one move Godunov could make—

He tossed his handgun and unclipped his modified, fully automatic AR-15 from the vehicle's sidesaddle, lifted it waist high, and one-armed a trigger pull that deposited thirty rounds into the face and neck of this ferocious, deep woods nightmare. The bear's paw stopped short of his face, the animal flopping off the front of the ATV and onto its side, one breath left in it before it expired.

Godunov bent over and heaved his stomach's contents onto the forest floor. He straightened up, wiped his mouth with a handkerchief, then saddled back up. He revved the engine again, turned on the headlights, and backed the ATV away from the bear carcass, a steamy haze of blood leaking from its head.

His phone beeped with a text. Bibi's delayed response.

Terms are acceptable. Awaiting instructions. Hope you are having a good night.

24

Max updated Renee with a left-handed text from the ambulance, Wyatt still gripping his other hand.

Scared and crying but breathing on his own. Drugs. His ankle might be broken

I'll be at St Luke's Miners Memorial hosp in Coaldale 10 min

The attending EMT volunteered a status to Max: Wyatt appeared to be in good shape, his vitals looked good, the ER docs would address his foot and run some tests, they would "make your son better."

Your son?

Max didn't miss the EMT's mistaken assumption but was too tired to correct him, or so he told himself. He texted Renee again.

Arrived at the ER. Love you honey

Renee keyed a *Love you* back. She lowered her phone. Aurora's face, front and center and serious, surprised her.

"I leave you guys alone for one night so I can do some community watch work—"

"The EMTs just left," Renee said. "Wyatt Springer's alive but he looked badly shaken up, his ankle is broken, maybe internal bleeding. The others walked away."

"*Others?* What others? What happened?"

Renee told her what she knew: that Myrna's friends had been digging on the property at night with Myrna's permission. Artisanal holes, just like the ones in the DRC. Wyatt climbed down one of them. No ventilation, air saturated with dust, handheld augurs, drills, liberated "kryptonite," cobalt powder, *ba-boom.*

"Come with me, girl," Aurora said and pulled Renee toward her SUV. "We're going to the hospital."

They pried Wyatt's hand from Max's before they pulled the stretcher out of the ambulance. Stadium-quality lighting illuminated the ER portico. Max watched Wyatt as they rolled him away on the gurney, Myrna hustling next to him, with Myrna leaving the gurney at the last second, the rest of it becoming a blur—

. . . and then her running over to Max, wrapping her arms around his neck, him feeling her tight hug, accepting her kiss on the cheek, accepting another one on his lips, then watching her hurry back to her son as the gurney crossed the threshold into the ER.

A blur, but it had happened. Things had taken an unforeseeable, emotional turn, and he'd been powerless to stop it.

The signals were clear now. This, here, this involvement, it was too intimate, too comfortable. He needed to pull back. The explosion had broken him down, dented his armor. It reaffirmed his mortality and the mortality of those around him, the threat of loss so severe it made him *feel* things, made him question himself. Maybe the best place for him wasn't on the outside of this small, vulnerable family, as a mentor and friend. Maybe it was on the inside, as a partner.

Max entered the ER waiting room, surprised to see it was empty of patients or family members awaiting outcomes. Wyatt's dreamy explanation of why he was in the mine surfaced: The piece he'd dug up before had gotten him $500 from Max, and he wanted to buy his momma another birthday gift, so he wanted to dig up more.

Max lasted five minutes in a waiting room chair before needing to get some air.

He paced the sidewalk, began making phone calls. He needed to finish packing, needed to confirm his itinerary out of the Poconos, needed to head north, needed to put space between himself and the cobalt frenzy in progress in Carbon County, Pennsylvania. He needed to leave all of this behind, Renee included, in favor of something less complicated, less ambiguous. A harsher environment in austere Greenland. He needed the immediacy, the in-your-face quiet, the unemotional cold of the Hiawatha impact crater dig, its cobalt discovery formidable but not as intense as what was happening here.

He needed the solitude. He needed to think things over.

<hr />

"How do you guys do it?" Renee asked. ETA for the hospital was under four minutes per Aurora, her lead foot making it happen, playing it loose with speed limits, stop signs, and traffic signals, assisted by the yellow LED strobe emergency light she'd slapped onto the roof.

"Do what?" Aurora said.

"Your 'Town Watch Twelve.' A lot of territory for twelve people to cover. Glad you stopped by when you did, but really, you folks are everywhere."

"Thirteen now. I made it a baker's dozen when the mayor asked me to run it. I'll let you in on a secret: I don't know how we do it either, and I lead the team. But if you analyze it . . ."

Which she now did for Renee. Low crime area, a dedicated, close-knit civilian watch group of people who had a good relationship with law enforcement, and a former police chief now calling the shots.

"Plus, fessin' up here, woman: we cheat. Area residents know to call a different phone number for nuisance issues—cats in trees, noise ordinances, drunk neighbors. None of the heavy lifting. That reduces the bona fide 911 activity, which makes the cops—they used to be *my* cops, when I ran the department—happy. Plus it gets a team member on the scene quicker. Win-win."

Another red traffic light came and went, Aurora bending the SUV into a right turn while leaning on the horn. Renee had a firm grip on the overhead strap handle.

"A hotline, then," Renee said on a straightaway, "like a bat signal."

"Ha. Yeah, sure. Batman's an ultra-crimefighter. He gets the extreme cases. The town watch gets the annoyance calls."

Screeech! Aurora jammed the brakes to save a squirrel from getting chewed up under her twenty-two-inch, all-season tires. She punched the gas hard again, added more horn, and barreled into another straightaway.

"A vigilante," Renee said, catching her breath.

"Excuse me?"

"Batman's a vigilante. A good guy, but he's still a vigilante."

"I guess that's one way to look at it."

At the next corner a blue street-level sign with a white H and an arrow announced their hospital destination was the next left turn. More screeching of tires, more straphanging, all the way to where the SUV stopped way short of the ER entrance in a doctors-only parking zone. Aurora shut it down.

"Question for you," Renee said, massaging her white knuckles. "Why did your mayor ask you to take over the watch?"

"Ike—Ike Barber. Too heavy-handed as the lead. Had trouble sweating the small stuff. It happens sometimes with former military who go into law enforcement."

That name again. A popular watch member.

"Small stuff?"

"The fringe. For him, there's no gray areas. Letting something go, ignoring a citizen's lapse in judgment. Situations where there's been no bad intent and no harm done. Live and let live stuff. That's not his M.O. Still, he's a major town watch asset. And Renee, honey?"

"Yes?"

"You're doing it again, girl. I stop sharing if you keep prying. Let's get inside so's we can see how Wyatt Springer's doing."

Renee was, for the most part, on the same page. There was no real concern about Ike Barber. He was a dedicated citizen still giving back, just like he had when he was in the military. Besides, as U.S. military it meant there was an abundance of info on him at her fingertips if she wanted to look for it.

Aurora pointed. "There's Max. On the phone."

"He's in the zone, I'm afraid," Renee said, watching him pace. "It might take a few minutes before we get anything out of him."

He was animated, grimacing, exasperated, barking questions, barking answers, then barking acceptances. They heard the tail end of it. Renee recognized a name. He was on with one of Fend Aerospace's secretaries. "Fine, Barney. Get one of the jets to Wilkes-Barre/Scranton International tomorrow, please. I want to leave by 2300 hours. Thanks."

25

Wilkes-Barre/Scranton International Airport, ten p.m. Renee dropped Max off at a private hangar entrance then parked the Bronco. She'd made it clear to him she was sitting this one out. It was Greenland, for God's sake, she'd done it once this year already, and she was still cold from that extended visit. Max offered only token resistance.

He slipped a breath-freshening strip into his mouth and greeted Renee as she hustled up to join him at the foot of the jet's stairs. Their goodbye kiss needed to be perfect. He wanted to leave her with as much love and passion as he could summon, wanting to make it as tender and pleasant as possible. Wanted to take with him a kiss that would last. Renee, apparently, was on the same page.

"Wow. Just, wow," he said, catching his breath. "That was wonderful."

"I like to make my goodbye kisses worth it," she said, smiling. "Come back to me in one piece, Max Fend, and with all your extremities. Pay attention to the frostbite. Stay away from the polar bears."

Her smiling eyes turned serious, tears rimming them. "And no heroics, Max, please. I beg you. Keep your head down, analyze the dig, get the hell out of there, and come back home to me. I'll work my Danish connections from here to help develop the partnership. I love you much."

"Love you much back, Renee."

Renee would handle Max's affairs at Myrna's cobalt site in partnership with the Fend Aerospace project managers who were working virtually. Wyatt had needed arthroscopic surgery on his ankle. Luckily, there had been no internal bleeding. He was still hospitalized but on the mend, Myrna there 24/7, and her brother-in-law Jesse stepping up, ecstatic to do so. Renee promised updates to Max daily. An alliance was on the horizon, needing to start now, with Renee and Myrna working together in Max's absence. A good thing? Either way, it was out of Max's control.

He boarded, settled in, and found his phone. He sent updates to Wilkes, Renee, Myrna, and Hannah Taat in Greenland. ETA Qaanaaq Airport, Greenland, 2,200 nautical miles away was seven hours, ten minutes. He lowered a mask onto his eyes, reclined his seat, and searched for an internal oasis, a happy place that could keep his worries at bay . . .

A calming image surfaced: a recovering young Wyatt in a Superman costume, sitting up in a hospital bed, holding Max's hand. Max drifted off to sleep.

Max's next leg after arriving in Qaanaaq was a Navy copter jaunt to the Hiawatha Impact Crater dig, below them now, the sun glinting off the mining site's apparatuses, the terrain still free of snow and ice. A beautiful sight. He asked the pilot to circle, to get a full appreciation of what this team of engineers had accomplished. A diamond core drill, a diesel generator, small fuel tanks, a pipeline, all visible from the air. Two warming huts for team members. Deposit boxes for the mineral output, necessary to accumulate whatever cobalt and other precious metals surfaced from the dig; also necessary to keep the environment tidy. After they landed they would load the day's mining production into the helicopter and fly to Pituffik Air Base.

The copter decreased altitude, but on the way down the co-pilot gestured overhead and to starboard. His voice came through the earphones.

"Two o'clock, Mr. Fend. Here's your site's heavenly protection."

A Navy F-16 fighter jet roared above them at three thousand feet plus, dipping a wing as a hello while staying its course due east.

"He'll go another five miles or more on patrol, watching the sky and the radar. He'll drop down to check out the terrain, maybe scare the wildlife a little, then he'll double back and return to Pituffik. The U.S. Navy has your back, Mr. Fend. I'm taking you in now."

Max bundled up, grabbed his backpack, and exited his ride. Significantly different weather here versus his last visit. Greenland, at least where they were on the edge of the receding glacier that engulfed the impact crater, was greening up. The temperature was a crisp 39°F, although the windchill made it ten degrees colder. The last weekend in May, with twenty-plus hours of daily sunlight beginning to warm the environment, this was almost comfortable.

His first text was a selfie to Renee, with no hat on, a slight smile, and only two words, one a tease: Arrived. Warm.

The helicopter powered down, two site workers port side waiting to hustle a metal trunk to the hatch Max exited. Wilkes leaned forward and met Max halfway. "You're late," he deadpanned.

"Good to see you too, Wilkes."

"A month late, Max. I've got a lot of people at the Agency pissed at me."

"I'm here now." He searched the faces of the folks near the drill. "Where's Hannah?"

"Warming up. Follow me."

Max checked the faces of the men working the drill and manning the metal storage trunks housing the borehole production. The four workers paused, trudged across the rocky terrain, and greeted Max warmly. These men were tired, Max could see it in their eyes. Weeks of hard labor in a harsh environment had exhausted them, but thankfully things had gone well, the boreholes producing proof that the site was rich with the cobalt ore the world so coveted. The exploratory phase was ending as a huge success, and the mining phase was poised to begin. Max expected an update from Renee tonight on where the Danes were in setting up production here. What had been accomplished here during his absence was amazing. He'd gladly empty more of his big corporate pockets, granting larger bonuses in appreciation of these dedicated folks, but—

His mind stopped its lofty wandering when he entered the warming hut. Hannah rose from a table, her smile warm but subdued; her body language was all wrong. A hug, then came some pleasant chatter asking about his trip, then her gesture that he have a seat at a table for some coffee. She sat across from him and wrapped her hands around a warm cup, Wilkes joining them. She exhaled a chest load of anxiety.

"This exploration—it has been a huge success," Hannah said. "You all get that. The team is very proud, and they should be. This might be a purer vein than your Pennsylvania dig; a smaller deposit, but more concentrated. But there's been a development," she said. "We need to get the hell out of here, Max. It is not safe."

With the project on the cusp of moving to the next level, mining companies would need to gear up for excavation. The approach to protecting the site would need to change.

"You will need to budget more for surveillance and for security," she said. "On the ground and in the air, the U.S. and Denmark both. We have already spoken with my government about it, and they agreed."

This was Wilkes's cue to join the conversation. "This site will stay operational for a few more days just as you see it now, armed, aware, and producing what it can in its current capacity, our air support kicking up a notch. We'll all be meeting with mining engineering experts from Denmark and the U.S. at Pituffik in the next few days to move things along in more of a private sector direction, with Fend Aerospace's help, of course."

An impatient Hannah produced her phone, reached across the table, and dropped it in front of Max. "You're taking too long to get to the point, Wilkes. Max, watch this video. It came to me two days ago from our hotel hosts in Qaanaaq."

Three minutes running time. The volume was up. The female speaker spoke in Danish, so Max couldn't understand her, but he didn't need to. Her voice was elevated and frightened enough to get the message across that they might be in great danger. Max recognized the location. She was on the roof of the Qaanaaq Hotel.

"Birthe Jenson, owner of the hotel, recorded this. I'm sure you know what that is."

He did, even in its damaged condition. "It's a wire crate for a dog. A large one," Max said. "Or it was, before it split into pieces."

The giveaway was the carnival-sized, plush, stuffed white dog sitting among the wreckage, with black eyes, a black nose, and black floppy ears. More precisely, a certain cartoon beagle that was all white and black except for red letters that had been painted on it.

"Snoopy," Max said. "What's written on it?"

"Wait for it," Hannah said.

A new camera angle showed the spray-painted message that ran down its back: SNOOPY GO HOME.

"A threat," Max said. "How credible?"

Wilkes spoke up. "Given the context, very."

"Any idea by whom?"

"It came from an aircraft," Wilkes said, "probably a drone. Ms. Jenson saw something cruising overhead before the crate's direct hit." He gave up his phone to Max. "I took pictures two nights ago when we got back from the dig. This next one, Max, stuck out. The most important aspect."

A closeup of the white tag that was stitched into the seam for the stuffed dog: *Made in Beijing, China.*

"We'll confirm that as the origin. It does fit, especially after you see what I show you next."

Wilkes thumbed from app to app on his phone until he found one Max recognized: an Agency satcom connection.

Hannah sipped at her coffee, unimpressed. Max glanced her way, wary. "Ah, Wilkes? Shouldn't we be doing this somewhere more private?"

"You mean not around Hannah? She's seen this already." Wilkes keyed in a sign-on. "These next videos went to our respective embassies in China. Ours and Denmark's. They're fresh, from yesterday. Another reason we're concerned. Here's the one the U.S. ambassador received."

Wilkes queued it up, hit play. Max leaned forward, concentrating on Wilkes's phone screen in landscape view.

A car commercial, looking very slick, very Madison Avenue, with a voiceover in Chinese and subtitles in English. Max read the subtitles as the video ran.

"The HAN EV sedan is the newest addition to BYD's luxury line of electric vehicles—"

Wilkes added context. "BYD is a Chinese carmaker. 'BYD' stands for Build Your Dreams."

The commercial's geek-level index kicked up a notch, the narrator citing, *"Acceleration to 100 kilometers per hour, or 62 mph, in 3.9 seconds. Miles per battery charge, 375, compared to Tesla at 272."* The video displayed a beautiful sedan cruising an empty highway along a panoramic countryside, the car then moving off-road to a steeper incline. It began climbing a low mountain range.

"All-wheel drive, for greater grip and better handling—"

Max noticed the logo in the right-hand corner. "Are you kidding me? This is a TikTok video?"

"Yes. They both are. Keep watching."

The commercial ended with the Han EV electric car arriving at a ski resort, blue sky overhead, the lift shuttling resort guests up the mountain, the slope busy with skiers. The message "HAN EV by BYD" occupied half of the last frame of the video, frozen on the screen.

"What do you see?" Wilkes asked Max.

Max lifted the phone closer and scrutinized all areas of the still photo. "Well, aside from the in-your-face color of the car . . . " The English caption read, *"Model shown is Cobalt Blue."*

"For one, the driver and his female passenger are Caucasian," Max said, which had been evident throughout the run time. He zoomed in on the still frame. Once he saw it, he couldn't unsee it: the car's aluminum license plate on the rear bumper had dark blue letters on reflective white, a navy-blue strip on top, a yellow strip on the bottom.

A Pennsylvania plate.

He narrowed his eyes to read the letters on it, all in caps. *UNS TABL.*

Unstable.

"What is this? Propaganda? They weaponized a car commercial?"

"The license plate was photoshopped into the frame." Wilkes tapped at his phone to pull up a second video. "The same for the one sent to the Denmark ambassador. Same message, but in Danish."

The letters for the European-style car registration plate read *USTABIL.*

Max spitballed a response. "We can read a lot into that one word, Wilkes. Any Agency insight? Are the Chinese goading us because of the cobalt powder explosion on the Springer property? Or is there another event horizon we might be looking for?"

"Working on it," Wilkes said. "Maybe threats, maybe just taunts. Langley analysts are busy unpacking both videos. What we have so far is they didn't come from a miscellaneous online TikToker. Both are connected to government-run accounts. This puts them on record that they don't like what's happening with our cobalt digs in the U.S. or in Greenland."

Hannah left her seat and crumpled her coffee cup with feeling. She tossed it overhand at the trashcan. "Today needs to be our last day here, Max. I am sorry you came all this way for nothing. Wilkes, you must call it in, and you must tell Pituffik that we are evacuating. They should send whatever is needed, a larger copter, or maybe two, for our return trip to Qaanaaq *tonight*. Maybe in a few weeks we can meet back here with whatever mining groups our respective governments select, accompanied by a military detail on the ground. But right now, we need to go."

"Hannah, please," Wilkes said, "these things take time—"

She powered through to finish her diatribe. "These are warnings, Wilkes! They change everything. We can't wait for more analysis. We are not safe here—"

Max piled on, in agreement with Hannah. "You wanted me here to see the output, Wilkes. I was good with that, and I still am. The exploration phase, for my money, has been a huge success. But this now needs to move to the next level, Caleb. Let's get everybody out of here. Tonight. Make the call, get Pituffik onboard, and we all go home in one piece."

Wilkes relented. He texted an Agency contact, then called the Pituffik Air Base commander for confirmation.

"Two helicopters have been commissioned. Hannah, get the team ready," Wilkes said. "We'll assemble at the other warming hut, away from the borehole. Max, I need a word. Follow me."

They pushed through the door to the outside. The sun greeted them low in the western sky above the ice floes in the Baffin Bay inlet. This time of year the sun wouldn't set until after midnight. To the east, the receding glacier was a football field away.

Wilkes pointed. "Let's go to the other warming hut. There are some things in there I need you to see."

Renee leaned against the doorjamb, half inside Wyatt's hospital room. Myrna sat bedside with her son.

Renee had to be honest with herself. She could see it. The connection. The warmth radiating from the face of a mother beaming at her young son and vice-versa, the two enjoying a respite from nurses poking and probing at him. Myrna held his hand, kissed it, caressed it, Wyatt smiling at the attention. She helped him out of bed and eased him onto the aluminum crutches the occupational therapist had left, the two of them giggling at their attempts to size them correctly. Wyatt negotiated a few steps for himself across the floor, into his mother's beckoning arms.

What Renee was seeing here was a family that was minus a husband and a father, but it was still a family. She could see the attraction in it—could see what Max saw in it, too. How the addition of a husband, of a father, could complete the picture for all parties involved.

She swallowed hard then smiled through a tear that rimmed her eye, quickly brushing it away. If this was what Max wanted, she could not compete. A tough realization. But she also needed to not jump to a conclusion, to not assume that her best friend and lover and partner had already made a choice, the one that would spell the end of their romantic ride, and maybe the end of their professional relationship as well.

Aurora returned from the hospital café with their drinks. She and Renee stood outside the room, sipping their beverages.

"What'd I miss?" Aurora said.

Renee's phone buzzed in the pocket of her jeans. "Only that Wyatt will be released tomorrow," she said. "He'll be on crutches because of the surgery."

Renee checked for texts. She made one pass through the list, ending with a stare at the phone display. Uncanny timing; there was something from Max. Her heart thrummed during a cursory read through each of them. Her eyes moistened again for her second pass.

Done in Greenland already. An excellent discovery. The real deal. Tell your Danish queen friend to get her checkbook ready. Exploratory phase is now officially over.

One night here, tonight, then I'm coming home.

I love you. I don't say that enough. Always have, always will. –Max

"Renee?"

Renee stayed locked onto her phone screen, oblivious to Myrna's approach. "Everything okay, Renee? Is Max okay?"

Renee shook off her starry-eyed trance. "Better than okay. Barring any aviation snafus"—her voice tripped here, ambushed by a sideways thought —"he'll be home soon."

She'd stumbled on "aviation snafus." The sidebar now resident in her head concerned Myrna's missing husband Ken. The victim of an aviation snafu of the highest order, perpetrated by himself. Despondent, he'd boarded a small plane, argued with his friends, grabbed a parachute, and jumped, disappearing into the night. After three years, presumed dead. Renee had never spoken to Myrna about it, and she wasn't about to bring it up now.

Except Myrna hadn't missed her hiccup. After a quick glance back at Wyatt, preoccupied with his phone, she engaged.

"Wyatt lost his dad because of an *aviation snafu*." A sneer came with the statement, Aurora the target.

"He jumped," Aurora said. "We've been over this, Myrna. Wasn't anything more than that."

But to Myrna, evident to Renee, there *was* more than that. It remained an open wound. "What went on in that plane, Aurora?" Myrna asked. "Did they do something to him?"

Myrna's voice was raised, her dark eyes opened wide, searching. She hazarded another peek at Wyatt, still preoccupied. Her glance turned tearful. "He loved that boy. He would have never left him. There was no note. Nothing," she said, pleading. "A man doesn't do that to his son. He doesn't make a choice to leave his child to grow up all by himself."

"I don't blame him, honey. You shouldn't either. It was the alcohol, and the drugs—"

Words squeezed through Myrna's gritted teeth. "Where's the body, Aurora? Where is it?"

"His friends said he boarded with them—"

"Who? Ike Barber? He was never friends with Ike. Ken would *not* leave Wyatt, Aurora! Something happened to Ken on that plane."

She was on her toes now, in Aurora's face, with Renee thinking she might need to get between them. Myrna spewed a few more heartbreaking, desperate, forsaken words, telling Aurora where she could stuff her protection, that she no longer wanted it. She about-faced and reentered Wyatt's room, closing the door behind her.

"You okay?" Renee said. Aurora hadn't flinched.

"He battered her. She let it happen 'cause of Wyatt. I saw enough of that in Philly," she said. "No, I'm not okay. She's still in denial about it. Let's go. She needs the space."

It had been a sad, uncomfortable, and complicated confrontation. Renee and Aurora found the elevator and exited the hospital, no words, just a brisk walk out the lobby to the SUV in the lot. The complication—implication—in Renee's newly stimulated mind came from Myrna's assertion.

Aurora fumbled with the fob. Renee spoke to her across the roof of the SUV. "Did something happen to Ken Springer on that plane?"

"What, you now? Yeah, something happened. He refused the help he needed to quit beating his wife. The help it took to keep his job. His choice to decline it, his choice to disappear," her head shook in disgust, "or maybe his choice was worse than that."

"I get it," Renee said, "but how did you guys verify any of it? Anything found during the search? Anything to show he didn't survive? Any proof of a struggle on the plane?"

"Sworn statements that he jumped. Where the plane was when he did."

"Statements from whom?"

"Ike Barber, Jesse Springer, who was one of my cops, and the pilot. End of story."

26

Wilkes opened the door to the second warming hut at the Hiawatha dig site and ushered Max inside, the wind rolling off the nearby glacier, kicking up snow behind them. Wilkes pulled the door shut against the gusts.

Max stood awestruck before the hut's interior. "Whoa."

"Warming hut" was a misnomer. There was no heat source inside, unless a person could warm up by hugging hot lead in the form of military weapons and ammunition. Surface-to-air, shoulder-fired missile launchers, a.k.a. man-portable air defense systems, a.k.a. "manpads," lined the wall. These were Stinger missiles, or bazookas on steroids, equipped with infrared homing devices capable of taking out jets, helicopters, and drones. Crates of newly issued Sig Sauer XM7 fully automated rifles, gas-operated, and magazine-fed. Kevlar. Helmets, night goggles, and 9mm handguns. Ammunition for all of it.

"Contrary to what you might think, Max, these people are not sitting ducks, ready for the slaughter. They can defend themselves."

Max scanned the small stash of munitions eye candy, impressed.

"Last time I checked," Wilkes said, "you knew how to use it all. I assume that's still true?"

"If you're asking about the Stingers, yes. If the rifles are in the M4 carbine family—"

"M27s," Wilkes said.

"I'm fine with those, too."

"We've been armed like this for weeks," Wilkes said. "And the Army Corps team members are, after all, U.S. Army, all trained as soldiers. The only non-combat-trained people here are you, me, and Hannah."

"Well, then I'd say we've got a good chance of surviving these last"—Max checked his phone—"two hours before Pituffik gets its copters here for us. It's 21:50 now. Are they on target?"

"They are."

"Then let's take a walk around the site so I can get a final look at that borehole. This mine will put the Danes on the radar for cobalt production in a big way. And it adds a cherry to the cobalt sundae the U.S. is about to cram down China's monopolistic throat."

A bulb atop a wooden box on a shelf began flashing. Max recognized the arrangement, a red bulb and a small speaker, same as in place inside the Qaanaaq Airport terminal. The speaker's automated verbal warning engaged. *"Status alert, status alert."*

Max raised his eyes, watching the flashing bulb. "You have bear-dar here? I'm impressed, Wilkes, how'd you manage—"

"No, Max, no—yes, it's bear-dar, but look at the monitor."

Next to the bear-dar speaker a screen the size of an iPad showed real-time video, its vantage point the munitions hut's roof. Its motion sensor had locked onto the Baffin Bay inlet due northeast of the crater, isolating on where the icy water lapped the stone-pocked gray beach.

"What the hell is that?" Max said.

Wilkes, on his phone, didn't reply.

If it was a polar bear, it was on its hind legs and walking, its white fur wet with bay water, with another bear walking behind it. If they were polar bears—whoa, how many were there, seven? ten? more?—they were carrying long rifles. Behind them, three military rafts on the shore. Whatever camouflage advantage these assailants thought the polar bear skins gave them, the bear-dar had eliminated it.

A rocket shell screamed overhead and exploded near the hut, shaking the ground. Max and Wilkes bolted the munitions building. The diamond core drill was in pieces, some of the drill's shrapnel airborne, raining the site with it. The borehole was now twenty-plus times its original size, wisps of smoke rising from the terrain's newest open wound. Simultaneous air and ground assaults—no, air, ground, *and sea*—were in progress. For there to be men on the beach, they had to have come from the bay, which meant—

Max pointed at a conning tower sitting stationary among the ice floes. "It's a *sub!*"

They pirouetted and reentered the munitions hut. Wilkes reemerged with a loaded XM7 assault rifle, Max with a second 9mm handgun in a pocket and a loaded Stinger, all thirty-four pure-havoc pounds of it atop his shoulder. Army Corps engineers scrambled past them into the hut to arm themselves with additional firepower.

Another shell dropped, this one hitting the diesel generator and blasting a chunk of it skyward as the diesel fuel on the ground ignited into a fireball. Max's Stinger acquired a visual on a target, a low-flying drone, two ordnances under its wing, both intact. It bore down on the exploration site, only two buildings left, the two huts. Max squared himself in front of the one with the munitions. There was no doubting the drone's target: the hut to his back.

He aimed the Stinger's infrared seeker in the drone's general direction. The seeker acquired it, emitting a long beep. Max depressed the trigger. The missile released, its propelling engine dropping away, the solid rocket igniting and screaming into the sky at 2,400 feet per second. The airborne drone was gone within seconds after the Stinger launch, its two ordnances exploding in midair, debris landing as far away as half a football field but some as close as Max's hair, which was now dusted with it. He lowered the launch tube. An Army Corpsman exiting the hut yelled into his ear. "Wanna go again, sir?"

It wasn't a question. The Corpsman lifted another loaded Stinger onto Max's shoulder. He scoured the sky but could see no other threat. The Corpsman shook his head no, not up there, how about there, pointing at the bay.

The submarine. Only its conning tower was visible, but it sat high enough that they knew the deck had to have broken the water to the right of it.

"Can't destroy it," the Corpsman said, "but if it's stationary . . ."

"No heat signature," Max shouted, "it won't track."

"Line-of-sight point and shoot, sir. If the rocket gets close enough—"

The Stinger ordnance would explode, Max finished in his head. It was worth a shot.

Max squared himself. The attacking commandos were in the way, their bearskin covers shed, the bay behind them. The Stinger beeped, found a heat signature somewhere, and Max pressed the trigger. The missile hissed while settling into its route, removed the head of one of the commandos, leaving a smoke trail before missing the conning tower but slamming into something solid and metallic to the right of it. The conning tower stuttered sideways from the impact, only the slightest of jolts, barely noticeable, but it had to have been a hit to the exposed deck. If there was damage, Max couldn't see it.

Max dropped the launch tube and unholstered his 9mm. The combat drones were there to destroy the equipment, but the soldiers advancing from the beach were there to assassinate the workers.

Wilkes, ahead of him, was firing his automatic rifle from behind a metal storage bin. Max joined him, placing a hand on his shoulder to get his attention.

"Who are these guys?" Max shouted.

"We kill them, then we find out. That might be a Sierra-class nuclear sub," Wilkes said, nearly breathless, "which means it's Russian." Their conversation broke as he fired another round.

"No more Stinger potshots at it, okay? They won't hurt it. Pituffik knows about it now, they'll deal with it. I count eight remaining commandos, Max. We can do this. Find Hannah."

Max crawled away and found cover on the ground with a vantage point. He surveilled the site.

He spotted Hannah at nine o'clock. She was behind a chunk of the twisted mess that used to be the drill derrick. She was alone, dazed, her spiked blonde head bleeding, her handgun raised but jittery. Her chest heaved—she was hyperventilating—

An assassin commando advanced on her hiding place, duck-walking his way forward. He would be there in seconds. Max watched an Army

Corpsman to the far left buckle and hit the terrain, his lower half riddled with automatic fire.

Screw it, Max had to move.

The commando was at the corner of the felled derrick, his Kalashnikov AK-12 raised to eye level, ready to slice in half whoever he found on its other side. His finger on the trigger, he took one more step before the barrel of Max's handgun slid into his ear. Max's directive to him in Russian: "*Бросайте, мудак!*" as in "Drop it, asshole!"

The assassin did as instructed. Before he could raise his hands, Max ground his gun barrel deeper into his ear and pulled the trigger. Sorry, not sorry, but there'd be no prisoners on either side. Four commandos down.

Two Navy copters arrived and began strafing the attackers with pinpoint rotary mini machine gun fire, the remaining assassins backing up then zigzagging their return to the beach, some making it, some not. When the commandos reached one of the beached rafts, the copters ceased fire, the raft motoring into the icy water toward the enemy sub.

Wilkes was on the phone with a copter pilot. He put him on speaker for Max to hear.

"*Escape hatch looks compromised. Who fired that Stinger? We're letting them go, sir. We'll watch to see if their ride back needs to be topside. The Navy will track them.*" The pilot added one word, confirming the vessel's origin. "*Russian.*"

"I don't get it," Max heard himself say, speculating. "What's their horse in this race?"

"We'll unpack it all later," Wilkes said.

The two helicopters landed. Max and Wilkes and team scoured their destroyed exploration site and found two wounded Army Corpsmen, both alive for now, Hannah the only other casualty. "There's a medic onboard," Wilkes said. "Let's get these guys and Hannah triaged, pack up a few things, and then we'll all go home."

Renee, from the comfort of the RV's king-sized bed, was deep into two databases, the Wilkes-Barre/Scranton airport database and the FAA's, her laptop helping itself to data that was over three years old. Flight plans, departures, arrivals, terminal buildings, security camera output. Cold case or not, she was looking for confirmation that Aurora's take on Ken Springer's disappearance had been better than Myrna's.

She found the flight plan she was after inside the FAA database. It cited dates, aircraft ID and type, proposed departure point and time, cruising altitude, route, pilot name (Dwight Barber), and number of passengers aboard (three). She'd filed her own flight plans when flying with Max; this one looked legit. A second flight plan was also on file, the return leg, from a small airport in the Adirondacks near Lake George, New York, the location of the rehab facility. That plan had been withdrawn, understandably so because Ken Springer had gone missing.

"After they realized what they needed to do was a search instead," she said, thinking aloud.

She'd helped herself to this info; her Agency security clearances could do wonders when she abused them. That was simple enough. But she had to go to the next level, dig deeper, run queries—get in and get out before anyone noticed. She sipped at a her latte from Canaries, a takeout, large, savoring its creamy black froth, then buckled up for a trip inside the code.

She needed airport security camera footage, wanting to look over the shoulders of each airport's security team's digitized archival material.

So much easier to ask for forgiveness than to ask for permission . . .

ACCESS DENIED—ACCESS DENIED—ACCESS DENIED

She'd need to do it the hard way. She ran one password-breaking application after another until a long string of symbols and digits provided the correct password. She populated the login with a username that was an alias matching the answer to a final security question. Someone had gotten lazy.

Welcome, Mickey Mantle.

She'd heard the name before; a famous American baseball player. As far as the Wilkes-Barre/Scranton International Airport was concerned, she was now him.

Renee lifted official Kenneth and Jesse Springer profile photos in their uniforms from the Jim Thorpe Police Department database. Ike Barber's photo was also on the town watch DB, easy to copy. She uploaded them into a facial recognition app, which compared the photos to video from the security tapes from each of the small aircraft and charter flight terminals at the airport, interior and exterior. Search date was a day in March three years prior.

"Where are you, Messrs. Springer and Barber?" she mused aloud.

Possibles for Ike Barber, one that was a 29% match, and Jesse Springer, a 24% match, from an interior camera for a small aircraft terminal a distance from the main building. Not definitive enough to confirm it was them, until one exterior camera showed with extreme clarity the aircraft that had been ID'd in the flight plan. Zooming in, she saw a clear stream of video of Ike Barber seated as the pilot, a 92% match, plus Jesse Springer at 80% in the seat next to him. But no matches better than 5% for Ken Springer in any of the archive video anywhere. Regardless, there it was. Proof that the flight existed, on the day that it was supposed to have happened, and that Ike was the pilot, and Jesse was on the plane.

On the destination side, the database at Floyd Bennett Memorial Airport, Queensbury, NY, was much easier to hack. Excellent footage. Ike Barber as pilot, taxiing to a terminal building. Ike Barber and Jesse Springer exiting the aircraft, backpacks, phones to their ears, all business, approaching the terminal. Footage she pieced together from multiple cameras followed them out of the terminal to a waiting car rental. Again, still nothing on Ken Springer better than 5%, but that validated the alleged actual account of what had happened, that he wasn't there because he'd jumped from the plane.

Everything matched the cold case file—the footage, the few interviews of the airport employees, their statements, everything.

Except there'd been no definitive Ken Springer sighting, inside the origin terminal or outside it.

That bothered her.

A text. From Max. Multiple texts. Good. A respite from her sleuthing. Plus she was so ready to tell him what she was working on. He'd be impressed by what she'd found, and more importantly, hadn't found, about Ken Springer's disappearance. She read the messages.

Before you hear it elsewhere. Hiawatha crater was attacked. I'm okay so is Wilkes

Hannah wounded but should be okay, Army engineers wounded maybe not okay

Assume Russia. Delays.

Her return texts to Max were frenzied, autocorrected but serviceable before she thought,

Screw this and tried a phone call to him, but it wouldn't go through.

Yes, she was in pain here, overly stressed, unable to do anything, worried about him, about Wilkes, too, and Hannah, so dedicated, my God, she "should be okay" per Max, but she needed to *absolutely* be okay, Hannah wanting to retire, so close to it, it shouldn't end like this for her—

Max's return texts calmed her some with hug and kiss emojis, *I am not hurt, I am fine*, then came his boasts—an enemy drone he personally destroyed with a Stinger, and a Russian nuclear sub he'd tried to sink, but that hadn't worked out. Still so full of himself, so Max. Renee was finally able to relax, knowing he was doing fine, that she'd see him soon.

She texted Aurora. Not about the Ken Springer disappearance, since that was on the back burner now, and she'd want to run it all by Max first. But Aurora did need to know about Max and what had happened in Greenland. Then she texted Special FBI Agent Cornell Oakley, who deserved the same assurances.

She took a deep breath then stared at her phone. After a pregnant moment, she tapped in a few numbers and listened as her call connected. This message deserved to be a call, not a text.

"Myrna. Hi. Renee here. Sorry to wake you. Max is fine, but something happened in Greenland."

27

. . . I am fine.

But little else was. Two Army Corpsmen were dead, and Hannah Taat had a head wound from a piece of drill shrapnel. She was on her way home to Denmark. Max, Wilkes, and the deceased Corpsmen were coptered to Nuuk, Greenland's capital, then to St. John's Airport in Newfoundland. From there the Corpsmen would be routed to Dover AFB in Delaware. Max and Wilkes were now on a private jet, Max's doing, which would be their last leg before touching down in Wilkes-Barre/Scranton International.

"I am not overreacting, I'm apoplectic," Renee said on a secure video call via her laptop. Max had his laptop open on an airline tray between him and Wilkes. "That's the word of the day, Max. Look it up if you have to. I'll wait."

Renee narrowed her eyes, scrunched her expression, then didn't wait as she'd promised, instead segueing into a status update. "Here's where we are on this end. Myrna's property is completely carved up, prefabs are going up on the lower ten acres, two of them completed. But you already knew that. What's new is three mining tunnels are underway, cutting into the side of the mountain. The artisanal tunnels are gone, the local cops and town watch folks are keeping everyone honest and away from the properties 24/7."

Wilkes interjected. "But there've been no approvals on moving onto those state game lands, Renee. If they're already there, tunneling into that space, that's not good."

"Yeah, well, here's the clincher, Wilkes: When President Windcolor gets here to cut the ribbon for these mines—"

"So that's a go?" Max said, interrupting.

"Check your communications, gentlemen. I know you've been busy trying to take out Russian nuclear subs with bazookas and all, but this is real, and it will happen soon. White House staff and the Secret Service are already here, scoping out Myrna's property. President Faye, when she gets here, date TBA, will announce a deal has been reached with state agencies to allow putting tunnel portals, properly vented, into the protected game lands, as long as the extraction companies go deep enough, and they do it the way the EPA and the Forest Service say they need to do it. That includes filling in and capping the portals when they're done harvesting the mines, whenever that might be."

Max shook his head, making major eye contact with her. "Very impressive, Renee, that's . . . that's incredible. Remind me to increase your allowance."

"Ah, I know you meant to say bonus. Something I'm sure will be in my next Fend contractor paycheck, wise guy. What's your ETA?"

"Two more hours," Max said.

"I won't be there to meet you, honey, or when you get back to the RV either. Sorry. By the way, someone else here needs to talk to you."

She turned the laptop. As the screen swiveled, Max realized where Renee was.

"Hi, Max," Myrna said, seated at her kitchen table. "I'd have Wyatt here with me to say hi, too, but he's recuperating from his surgery in his bedroom, playing video games with his Uncle Jesse."

Renee moved a chair in close to get onscreen, next to Myrna. An odd pairing, Max thought, seeing them side-by-side. He soon realized what they were doing.

"We've squared things away here, Max, Renee and me," Myrna said. Her nod at Renee came with a small smile. "Please get back here in one piece so you can continue to make some money for me. I'll need it. I found a house I'd like to bid on, and it's expensive. And I'd like to start a small business."

Renee added context. "Myrna's treating me to a trip to a casino nearby to listen to—get this—Eva Biswas, the nosey reporter from the coffee shop. She's at a symposium on Indigenous influencers, and how they can market themselves. Uncle Jesse is babysitting Wyatt. It will be a late night tonight. One last thing. Wilkes, listen up, too.

"I found a connection. Or I should say one of my former Soviet Bloc hackers did. Rare Earth Metallurgical has some interesting consultants working for them. A band of mining engineers gathered from international universities. I'm seeing finder's fee arrangements with former metallurgy professors all over the place online. Nothing wrong with that, of course, except one of those arrangements is with that Belarusian professor, Alex Godunov.

"Aurora says he's been all around town, talking to local businesspeople, collecting stories about open pit coal mining, the Centralia coal fires fiasco . . . To use a technical word, he's been snooping. He even stopped by here yesterday, all smiles, to bother Myrna, congratulating her on her good fortune. He was on top of us before we knew it, near one of the new tunnels, those ventilators so noisy, next to the game land. We should view him as a competitor, gentlemen. I'm sure his visit here was to surveil the digs on her property."

"Why do you say that?" Wilkes said, inserting himself.

"Because he got into a crouch on the ground and smelled the dirt. He picked up a handful and buried his nose in it. I swear he snorted it. Very weird. You said you'd assign additional protection for her property after the first Greenland attack. Right about now would be good, to keep the crazies away from Myrna."

28

Wilkes dropped Max off at the RV park. Max answered some emails, sent one to Hannah in Denmark, then texted his DRC project team, Oakley, and Renee, catching up everywhere he could. He slipped into the shower, deciding to stay there until the shower ran cold. He would let the sanitizing hot water clean off the stink of a long travel day. His forehead against the shower wall, the water massaging his neck and back, his mind drifted.

The rich get richer. A line that stuck with him as a university student. One of the reasons he'd agreed to give back. To help his country when his country came calling, looking for a billionaire playboy to act that part in mission after mission for the CIA. His father, Charles Fend, and Fend Aerospace, provided him with all the money he'd ever need, more than he could spend in ten lifetimes, and now he'd have even more of it from his modest shares in two cobalt mines, his involvement prompted by both the CIA and the FBI.

Would there be other missions? Probably. His handler Wilkes was young enough, bold enough, persuasive enough, and he was someone who Max now begrudgingly considered his friend. Max knew the feeling was mutual, although neither would admit it.

He toweled himself off. Texts from Renee.

Here with Myrna in the Mohegan Pocono Casino auditorium. A parade of social influencers telling/selling their stories. Audience is larger than I expected.

Myrna's got her own story to tell. I heard it on the way here.

She wants to do podcasts, connect with other abused Indigenous women, help them tell their stories too.

Nice, Max texted back, but that was the last text he would remember. Exhausted and in bed, he drifted off.

The texts kept coming.

Myrna bought backstage passes. Guess who's here.

Renee stopped texting. Her texts were landing but Max probably wasn't awake to read them now. She'd wait until morning to tell him the most interesting part, that the white-haired academic Godunov was here, in a front row seat, and he'd acknowledged them with a nod. He also greeted Eva Biswas backstage, shook her hand, and kissed it like a gentleman. When he leaned in for some words to her, he gave her his card. A pleasant exchange, smiles on both their faces, but Renee was back to where she was when she'd first met, and first confronted, Ms. Biswas: How much of her pleasing persona was fake—hair, face, attitude—and how much was real?

Renee shook off her cynicism when it was Myrna's turn to meet her. No insincerity here, just a pure fangirl gushing over a celebrity, with the celebrity's response equally spirited and appreciative. Myrna handed Ms. Biswas a program and asked her to autograph it. When the influencer turned to Renee, Renee waved off her opportunity for an audience. A snub, purely unintentional, or at best a subconscious one, but the damage had been done.

"I see," Eva Biswas said. "So you still harbor hard feelings about my coffee shop intrusion, Ms. LeFrancois?"

"Look, Ms. Biswas, this is Myrna's night." Renee grabbed Myrna's hand, a friendly gesture, Myrna good with it. "Let's stay in your social influencer lane here. Kudos on your career. Maybe for Myrna, somewhere down the road, social media influencing can be her lane, too."

"Ah. Our *lanes*," Eva Biswas repeated. "I see. My lane is, and continues to be, entirely self-actualized. Myrna's," she smiled, "if she can speak about her pain, and her truth, to other people, it will be self-actualized, too. But *your* lane, Ms. LeFrancois? I hazard it's attached to Max Fend's at the hip. How has Mr. Max Fend been lately? Still making airplanes? Still flying them? How about you? Does he let you fly any of them?"

Renee's unintended slight had hit a nerve, and she was surprised by Eva's bitter retort. How much of the retort came from knowing Max's celebrity and wealth, and knowing Renee's relationship to him, versus how much came from whoever Eva Biswas was on the inside?

An odd, obtuse comment. Did Eva know Renee flew? If so, how?

"Myrna," Renee said as they left the stage, "a favor, please. That program Ms. Biswas autographed. Can I borrow it and let Max see it?"

Professor Godunov was in his hotel. He had better info now, gleaned from the buzz around these Pocono towns, the locals willing to talk to him, willing to share their rumors about cobalt finds, cobalt digs, the cobalt explosion at a dig on Myrna Springer's property in Nesquehoning. About Centralia. About new coal fires leap-frogging underground, east from Centralia under Route 54, toward Nesquehoning. Impacting towns like Frackville, Lost Creek, Shenandoah, and one actually called Hometown. About a prospective U.S. presidential visit to the region. About a ribbon-cutting ceremony.

Godunov's Belarusian intel organization was only now just catching up. The intel officer's cryptic message to him, delivered inside the lyrics of an American railroading song, was in his email inbox. His handlers thought they were being clever. The lyrics spelled out for him things he'd already pieced together.

She'll be coming 'round the mountain when she comes
   She'll be coming 'round the mountain when she comes

. . .

She'll be driving six white horses when she comes
She'll be driving six white horses when she comes

Oh, we'll all go out to meet her when she comes
Oh, we'll all go out to meet her when she comes

We will kill the old red rooster when she comes
We will kill the old red rooster when she comes
We will kill the old red rooster we will kill the old red rooster
We will kill the old red rooster when she comes

Had they realized just how well the lyrics fit? The "mountain" was the ridge next to the two Springer cobalt digs. "She" was the half-breed Indian squaw who these moronic Americans had elected as their country's president. They would "kill the old red rooster" when she arrived, but here, the president, could be the red rooster. Wrong sex, but the right color; the words were close enough. The deliciousness of it all made his mouth water and his palms sweat.

What he knew about what had to be done, he'd already passed off to his assassin contractor: the location and the target. The specific date and time weren't available yet, but when they were determined, since the target was the U.S. president, everyone everywhere would know the particulars, his contractor needing only minimal instruction.

Tomorrow would be another big day. Another ATV tour of the nebulous perimeter of the Centralia coal-seam ignitions, the thousands of acres where hellfires had been bursting through from the underworld for over sixty years, buckling the asphalt, swallowing the terrain, destroying homes, the fire department, the last Centralia church; forming desert-like, shimmering images near and far that had been real infernos, not mirages. And it was traveling east. Rare Earth Metallurgical would conduct the ATV tour, would reinspect over seventy Department of Environmental Protection boreholes drilled in the state. These hands-on bosses would leave him to himself while they continued staking out the boundary of the original 1962 coal-seam fire. They'd determine how far out they'd need to go to completely surround it before digging down whatever depth was necessary, looking to excavate every last burning lump of it, and snuff the fire out.

But this was Rare Earth Metallurgical's plan, not the covert faction internal to Rare Earth that he was a part of, dubbed "The Professors" by their Russian handlers. A small group of Belarusian academics, recruited as Russian agents, they'd managed to infiltrate Rare Earth and other international companies.

To date, with nary a dirty bomb detonated anywhere, they'd been frustrated by security authorities in multiple countries, but it hadn't been for The Professors' lack of trying. Radioactive cesium tubes stolen from a North Carolina hospital for use in building bombs. Radioactive materials attached to an explosive device near a railway line in Kiev, Ukraine, the bomb defused. The Chicago, Illinois, arrest of an Al Qaeda operative, recruited by The Professors, who'd been building a dirty bomb that would optimize its radiological dispersion over a wide U.S. area.

And now Alex Godunov, whose handlers had secured cobalt-60 from several Russian sources, was on track to being the first to detonate a fully functional dirty bomb, and this invigorated him.

Surface sealing with clay blankets, isolation trenches, flushing the deep mine sections with sand, hydraulic cement, mixing in concrete and finely crushed rock—

Rare Earth, with the best of intentions, had found and catalogued all these failed prior attempts at eliminating the fiery underground menace, and they'd also determined that large amounts of methane had accumulated in and around it. They'd unwittingly provided a roadmap that Godunov and his Russian handlers could follow, allowing him to find underground pressure points where barriers had been installed over the years to keep the fire from advancing. It would, he expected, confirm that the one best place for making things happen would be nearest to, or maybe inside, the Carbon County pothole, small "p," itself, near Hometown, Pennsylvania. The pothole, Rare Earth had discovered, was getting hot. If someone tampered with the man-made barriers to its west, the ones that led in this direction . . .

He was not working to eliminate the fire like Rare Earth had agreed to do, he was working to exploit it. It was what The Professors wanted, their connections farther east than eastern Europe. He would help transition the coal-seam fire from a local environmental nuisance to a world-changing, no-turning-back cataclysm. How? By introducing another catalyst to the mix: less than an ounce of a mineral fortified with an additional isotope that made it highly, devastatingly volatile.

29

"Here's how we'll manage this," Cornell Oakley said to his audience. "We do nothing."

On the job again in Nesquehoning, his audience was Max, Wilkes, other FBI assets, local police, and Aurora Jolson repping the Town Watch Twelve. They were on location at the mouth of Tunnel Two, the second of three tunnels on the edges of Myrna Springer's property. Behind Cornell, the White House carpenters' hammers rose and fell, a small stage nearly complete, podium, sound, a canopy and lighting because of the threatening rain, and patriotic adornments, all in progress.

The reason for Assistant Special Agent in Charge Oakley's return: the date and time of the president's ribbon-cutting ceremony had been dropped on them with only forty-eight hours' notice, as the president had needed to be overseas for NATO meetings yesterday. The Secret Service was in all-hands-on-deck cooperation mode with other security agencies and local law enforcement. Problem was, there had been chatter. CIA assets around the globe said a serious terrorist event was imminent.

"Hold on, Cornell," Max said. "Wilkes, tell me what makes this chatter so special."

"The specificity. On U.S. soil," Wilkes said. "A terrorist attack, or an assassination attempt, something involving or influenced by the Chinese.

They won't just let the U.S. waltz in and transform the cobalt extraction and production world market overnight. The president's ceremony here is largely cosmetic. A massive photo op celebrating all the new cobalt mining activity in the region. Billions in future revenue dollars—the trade imbalance—it's all in play here because of cobalt. China's leverage as the premier, worldwide cobalt bully—their monopoly—they're now about to become one of *two* major stakeholders, Max, us and them, and they don't like sharing that distinction."

Max got all that. So much so that this would be one of his and Renee's last few days in the region. The mines were functioning. He would make an obscene amount of money from these new installations, one here, another one about to get a restart in Greenland. Time for them to ride off into the sunset. Although it wouldn't be that way today because clouds were moving in, and the president was on the way.

"So you and I will hang back and stay out of the way?" Max said.

"Yes and no," Cornell said. "We'll take up spots around the perimeter and in the crowd. Eyes and ears. But the Secret Service has this fully under control, and your boss Wilkes is on point as well."

He and Max eyed their surroundings, settling on one view, the horizon spanning west of Myrna's house, the only direction not blocked by forest.

"They're even out there," Cornell said, pointing with his chin, "on that ridge, half a mile away. The one place where someone could get off a clean shot. On the ground here, this close to the stage, we stay on task, and we watch the crowd."

Which was starting to fill in out front. With the final nail hammered, the portable podium was anchored in place, followed by a "testing, testing, one, two," sound check.

In the yard, the young, hobbling Wyatt tossed and caught a baseball with his Uncle Jesse. Renee and Myrna were inside the house together making nice. More than making nice; somehow, as far as Max could tell, they were becoming friends. Max and Renee were back on solid ground, as a couple and as partners. And Myrna was getting chummier with her brother-in-law Jesse.

"Things are working themselves out," Max said to himself, no context.

"You say something?" Cornell said.

"Nothing. Looks like rain, doesn't it?"

Renee helped Myrna put the finishing touches on a gift for VIP guest President Windcolor: Wyatt's kryptonite brick, the first one he'd dug up; the one Max had bought from him. Max offered it up, knowing its significance, and Wyatt was very excited because he was the one who would do the wrapping. The White House staff okayed it as a gift.

Renee held down the ribbon with her index finger while Myrna finished tying it and cut away the excess. Myrna centered a large pre-made bow on one of Wyatt's shoeboxes, the gift inside, the box wrapped as well as a nine-year-old could.

"Okay then," Myrna said. She placed the box on the kitchen table, admiring the red, white, and blue wrapping paper. Not all that original, but it worked.

"Renee. A question."

Myrna watched the steady stream of local, state, and federal dignitaries in business suits and dresses walk past the house and into the backyard. The road outside their homes, both hers and Jesse's next door, was blocked off to vehicles. Everyone was on foot, hoofing it from cars parked up to a hundred yards away.

"You ever see this many important people in one place like this before?" Myrna said.

Renee smiled and nodded. "Yes."

"Oh. Right. Because you and Max are, you know—"

Renee raised her index finger to her lips and shook her head. "First rule about you-know-what," Renee said, "is we don't talk about you-know-what."

Renee's phone beeped. A text. Her eyebrows raised, reinforcing her doubletake at the ID onscreen. An expat Chinese systems hacker; someone she'd thought she'd never hear from again, because—

"I thought you were dead," she murmured to herself, immediately scolding herself that this was her first reaction. Myrna hadn't heard her. Renee shook off the surprise and read the text.

Check your emails. Long string. Diagrams. You need a larger screen, use desktop or laptop.

"Excuse me," she said to Myrna. "I need to pull something up on my laptop." She moved to Myrna's living room, to the sofa and the coffee table.

She toiled inside a secure satcom link. Her eyes flicked from message to message, chart to chart, with diagrams and arrows, connecting the dots in the notes sent by this former Chinese dissident-criminal-prisoner-freelance hacker-coder from among Renee's stable of former dissident-criminal-pris-oner-freelance hacker-coder types that she'd cultivated during her fifteen-plus years working in intelligence for the U.S. and for Canada.

Work backwards, the next text said. You will see it.

Still catching up, Renee texted back.

She did as suggested and she reached the original intercept. An unencrypted email from a source in upstate Pennsylvania, sent to a university in Europe. Benign enough in content, but because it had no recognized context, the message made sense only after her Chinese dissident hacker texted that she'd matched the words in the email to a classified ad on the internet that originated from a U.S. email address over a month ago.

The next text from her hacker was a question. Do you know an Alex Godunov?

Before Renee responded, she read more texts.

An Alex Godunov posted a classified advert in 15 online newspapers in multiple Indian and Pakistani languages plus English.

Ad reads "Meat, large amount, TBD. Great terms, negotiable. Pilot it home."

These are covert contract terms, boss. Meat equals a kill. Great terms means worth $5M+. Don't know the "pilot" reference.

The email went to an academic superior at Godunov's Belarusian mining college. Or maybe it wasn't a superior, maybe it was simply an intel handler. A mistake not to encrypt? An innocent exchange? A red herring feint?

Drop-downs in the charts traced the subsequent routing for the message, the rest of the iterations encrypted, her hacker translating them. But the original unencrypted email from Godunov looked like a bona fide faux pas.

U.S. to Belarus, Belarus to Moscow, Moscow to—

"Beijing." She stiffened on the sofa. "Russia and China are working together."

Doing what, she asked herself, unable to answer the question.

Myrna poked her head into the living room, an umbrella in her hand. "For you, Renee, it's raining. A staffer said Wyatt and I need to take our seats. The president's helicopter is about two miles out. I'm so nervous."

"Okay," Renee said. "Relax, Myrna. You go, I'll catch up."

But still on Renee's mind: *pilot.*

She rang Max on her phone.

"Hey Renee. What's up?"

"That brochure you overnighted to Langley. The one with the autograph on it from Myrna's social influencer crush."

"The reporter? Eva Beeswax?"

"Eva Biswas. Did we get a response from Langley yet?"

"You would have heard if we did."

"Tell Wilkes to call them and follow up," she said. "It needs to be a rush job, like, now."

30

Mining engineer Godunov was on foot, deep inside Pocono timberland, tall oak trees and other hardwoods surrounding him. He'd driven his Volvo AWD sedan directly into the heavily forested overgrowth, off-road, his tires bobbing and weaving their way into an environment that swallowed the vehicle up, making it invisible overhead and from the road. A different approach to the pothole this time, he came in from a different direction, where the DEP's environmental reports and Rare Earth cartography said the forest canopy was heavier, except for the area around the pothole itself.

Rain assailed the trees, the canopy thick enough to capture the drizzle and gather it into larger raindrops that pelted his poncho. It was a hundred-plus yard walk to the pothole. This first trip was for the caving gear. Godunov was wearing some of it—coveralls, a helmet with a headlamp—carrying some of it, over his shoulder and in his hands—a climbing harness, thick ropes, long-armed wire snips—and had stuffed some of it into a gym bag—rope descender and ascender devices for rappelling down and climbing back up steep surfaces, plus a sheathed knife.

The smell of the clean, refreshing forest enveloped him, the drizzle rolling off the hood of his poncho and onto the bill of the helmet, then onto his face. Twenty yards ahead, with still a distance to go to the pothole, something unexpected: a wavy heat shimmer that rose from the forest floor, obscuring the pothole. There'd been a cave-in here, in the middle of the forest, the ground and the woodsy detritus around it buckling from the burgeoning hellfire beneath it. The divot was wide, maybe fifty feet, and when he moved closer it appeared to be new, based on the debris sitting two stories below the opening: smaller hardwood trees with leaves that were charred, some leaves smoking, some still green.

This excited him. It meant Rare Earth had made the headway they'd needed, digging down far enough to rediscover the Centralia coal-seam fire barriers they'd been contracted to repair throughout the system. It would allow the company to perform the next steps per the contract, excavate everything, harvest the leftover coal, and rid the area of the methane, which would extinguish the fire around its perimeter. Rare Earth could then work its way inward, as far underground as was necessary, repeat the process, create a massive, and deep, miles-wide crater that would kill the sixty-year-old fire 100% dead, complete and forever.

But he and the other clandestine Belarusian professor-agents within Rare Earth, those on the operations side, weren't going to do that.

They'd drilled through, poked holes in, and carved sections out of the original underground barriers that had kept the fire from moving east, the only direction he cared about. This created a horizontal underground chimney, a pathway that made the fires burn faster and hotter while they gulped in more oxygen, expanded more quickly, and found more coal pockets, until the expansion reached the areas close to where Godunov was standing now. He watched and listened to the sizzle, hiss, and pop inside this subterranean hole coming from rainwater cascading into it, and he thoroughly enjoyed it.

His next trip back to the car was to refill the gym bag with a gas mask, a small block of Semtex 10 plastic explosive, a wireless detonator that looked much like a cork, plus other necessities.

His final trip was for the heavy, lead-encased bowling ball with the colorful resin surface. It was nestled inside the leaded backpack inside the trunk of the Volvo, also lead-lined. Enough cushioning to protect the ball, enough lead to protect him from the ball's contents, the mother of all payloads: Russian cobalt-60, less than an ounce of it. All that was necessary. He opened the backpack, checked its contents again, and re-zippered everything. He slipped his arms into the straps and hefted the heavy pack out of the trunk.

The final forty yards. He reached the unnamed pothole and set the backpack down near the chain-link fence. A quick read of the area hadn't changed his mind: here was a highly desirable dispersal point, in a partial clearing, no tree canopy above it. He produced the wire cutters.

Snip, snip, snip, snip.

He pulled the fencing out of the way, creating an opening tall enough and wide enough for him to walk through. Fifteen more feet forward brought him to the edge of the pothole, the steep end. He leaned over to get a look, the footing wet; he fired up the Maglite. A long way down, with crevices and a sharp rock face on all sides reaching beyond the beam of the flashlight. He geared himself up with his caving equipment, tied his rope off around a tree, threaded it through the harness, slipped on a gas mask, and began to rappel down.

His prior thermal imaging readings had said there was no fire inside the pothole, but as he dropped deeper down, where it should have been getting colder, it was getting warmer.

Nearly 130 feet down was where the pothole telescoped to what felt like the bottom, and the markings on the rope confirmed the distance.

"Hot down here," he announced to himself, muffled by the mask. "Excellent."

He texted in Belarusian to his overseas handler.

Hello Professor. I am where I need to be. Methane count per mil was high all the way down. Device can stay nearer the top, the exploding methane will do the rest.

The explosion would work well, both backward and forward, because of the methane. It would strengthen the underground coal-seam fire by a hundredfold, approaching apocalyptic proportions, but also dispersing Co-60 radiation upward in all directions. Most importantly east, settling on and ruining the cobalt mines and the Pocono Mountain region for years to come.

Upward radiation, yes, but also underground, where benign cobalt-59 would be radically converted with the addition of one more isotope.

Efforts have been successful. Drilling can stop. I am a go, Professor.

A quick response Are you making it happen now, Professor Godunov?
He checked his watch. They were too early.

No. Estimate 50 min. After someone makes the phone calls.

A waiting game for them, other circumstances needing to synch up to get the sequence right and give them the cover they needed.

The detonator would handle timing the explosion. Godunov would tuck the bowling ball into a crevice two stories or less down, not visible from ground level. If all else failed, tossing it into the pothole with the Semtex and a detonator attached could do in a pinch, but he'd rather not kamikaze his way into the annals of the Belarusian espionage hall of fame.

The duffel bag was a drab army green in the trunk of a Prius parked in the empty corner of a Lowe's Home Improvement parking lot. Dawn, partly cloudy, maybe some rain on the way.

So gauche. So lower-U.S.-middle class. So not her new persona. But her old covert self was what she was channeling now. Jeans, a '60s Black Sabbath tee under a silky camo-black bowling shirt under a sleeveless forest-green vest. Boat shoes from Payless, also in camo green. Black base-ball cap, dark sunglasses.

All this green, all this black. It would blend nicely, but it was an outfit she'd rather not be caught dead in. That thought, the wording, brought her a chuckle.

Former covert Pakistani intel, former Pakistani jet pilot. Stellar military sniper ratings. A former acquaintance of Max Fend and Renee LeFrancois, not that they remembered her. Currently a premier freelance contract assassin, traveling the globe, her cover a stunning new face and body. The world was her oyster. She knew her target, knew the location, knew the timing, knew what she would earn; knew what government was paying her, didn't care. Her only alliance these days was to herself.

Another U.S. president would slide into place after this one. No big deal. She didn't know the why of it, ten million USD blinding her need to know. A quarter of a million as a down payment was in her account already, the rest to come later, after the deed.

She eyed her parking lot surroundings, two large trucks in line for early morning deliveries. Her immediate area was secure. She unzipped the bag, still in the trunk of the car.

Contents as advertised. They'd granted her requests.

Ruger tactical long-range rifle, bolt action, high precision rating, good for up to a thousand yards, or more than half a mile. A tripod. Nikon scope. Binoculars. .308 Winchester cartridge ammo. Kevlar. A small 9mm semiautomatic handgun. A camouflage rain poncho. A phone. Camo netting, camo plastic mat. A tiny OTF dagger in a sheath for hand-to-hand. A text message waiting on her phone: GPS coordinates suggesting multiple unobstructed spots on a ridge in Nesquehoning, inside State Game Land No. 141. The game land acreage wrapped around the adjacent Springer properties. Someone, not her, had done their homework.

Eva Biswas. Not who she said she was. *Try to say it fast three times—Eva Biswas was not . . .*

She chuckled. "Bibi" was a much easier name.

But as Bibi Memona Qureshi, she'd become a known entity in the international intel community, hence the reason she erased her former identity as best as she could, including altering her fingerprints.

She checked her watch. ETA to the GPS coordinates in the game lands, under twenty minutes. Find a spot, set up, and locate the target. That would take under half an hour, and she had all morning. Anticipated start for the ribbon-cutting ceremony at the new mines was ten a.m. She had time to get some breakfast.

Bibi sat cross-legged on a plastic mat on the ridge, wearing the camo poncho, the duffel bag next to her. Its contents surrounded her. She wiped the rainwater off each item, inspected it: rifle, scope, tripod, magazine. 9mm handgun. She tried out the binoculars by focusing on the stage. The numeric graphic on the lens gave the stage's distance at 847 yards. She'd had sniper kills from greater distances. Not automatic, but she knew she was good for it. Ten million dollars were riding on it. She'd get it right.

But the rain was an unwelcome complication.

It was a drizzle, not a downpour. If it remained a drizzle, it would be fine. She knew the physics of it. A bullet's supersonic speed created a shockwave, a cone that kept it from getting wet, the rain no hindrance to the sniper, letting her ability carry the day. But the shockwave cone broke down at greater distances, and at this distance from the target there could be some impact on the equipment because of the light rain. In a heavier rain, it would be worse.

These were things she'd need to adjust for, but she'd been there, done that before, so she'd do fine.

She attached the tripod to the precision rifle, inserted the magazine, and chambered a round. She lay flat under the camo netting and sighted the weapon. Per the instructions, she sent a text.

I am in position

Now came the wait for the target to arrive, and for the text command to take her out.

31

Max stood in standing-room-only space as a bystander to the right of the stage, Cornell doing the same on the other side across a small sea of folding chairs. The clouds delivered a light drizzle. Some guests huddled under umbrellas, but Max, Cornell, and the other security personnel opted for baseball caps to keep the rain off their faces. Renee, under a tiny umbrella, found Max and updated him.

" . . . a string of intel. The classified ad Godunov placed, plus leads to China . . ."

Max covered his mouth as he spoke into his mic, repeating the info to Cornell and Wilkes piecemeal.

Marine One, the president's helicopter, eased into a clearing on Jesse Springer's property, where it would be a short walk to the stage erected near Tunnel Two inside Myrna's lower acreage. All eyes were on the copter, but Max's ears, and the ears of other security personnel, awaited Wilkes's direction after they had assessed Renee's info.

"We need to find Godunov," Wilkes said. "Here's what I think we should do."

Some background talk, then Wilkes came back on their earpieces. "Cornell and his FBI team will leave the dedication ceremony to go after him. Max, you go with them. I'll stay here and assist Secret Service with their protection of the president. Renee should stick with Myrna in the audience."

Max's hot mic picked up a muffled objection.

"I know Renee's right there, Max," Wilkes said. "Don't let her give you any crap about it. Myrna and Wyatt still need their security."

"But Aurora Jolson is watching Myrna," Max said, "plus some of her town watch folks are here, too."

"That's exactly who Myrna doesn't want to hang with, remember? Renee stays here, with Myrna, to make sure she cooperates."

<hr />

A downpour. President Windcolor, under a yellow hardhat and two golf umbrellas at the tunnel's mouth, used a bullhorn to deliver comments and encouragement about the expectations aligned with these new precious-metal mines. She cut the ribbon, a brilliant cobalt blue that stretched across the entrance to the mine. She raised the arms of the Pennsylvania governor and a state senator together in celebration, the audience clapping and hollering before the rain finally forced them to scurry back to the cover of the canopy on the stage.

A White House staffer waved Myrna forward from her seat. Myrna took a deep breath, Renee next to her. Renee cupped her elbow and directed her with a chin point. "You guys are up. Go on, Myrna, you'll do fine."

Myrna and Wyatt crossed the small stage, Wyatt hobbling bravely without his crutches. Wyatt handed the president the gift in a shoebox he'd wrapped on his own, prearranged that she'd open it for the crowd to see. Not prearranged was the president's honest reaction to the brilliance, and the heft, of the greenish-blue brick. She held it above her head for a few beats, as proud as a boxer holding a championship belt.

The photographers positioned the president, Myrna, and Wyatt together for more photos; keepsakes for Myrna and Wyatt. Myrna wept happy, childlike tears, her wonderful President Faye, Indigenous like her, embracing her, the photographer snapping picture after picture.

Aurora answered her phone from her seat, her eyes on Myrna and

Wyatt still onstage. She glanced at Renee and silently mouthed who was on the phone: *Max*. Renee joined her, Max now on speaker.

Aurora caught him up, finishing with, "The ceremony's over, Max. It went great."

"Good. I'm headed west with Cornell and his agents," he said. "We've been to Godunov's hotel and the jewelry appraiser. Wilkes has Langley running down possible connections between the jeweler and the Chinese government."

Renee interrupted. "The appraiser Myrna took the cobalt brick to. Sophie Ming Hughes?"

"Her, yes. At a minimum there's some inherent old country patriotism thing going on there, but it could be worse. She and her daughter might be spies. We met with a few other shopkeepers, took statements, asked if they'd seen him today, got nowhere. Godunov's driving a white Volvo sedan. Aurora, I'll give you the plate number in a sec. We're doubling back now, heading out to the abandoned coal mine property that his employer bought. The Rare Earth folks say he could be there."

"That all sounds good, Max," Aurora said. "What do you need from me?"

"Get your town watch folks involved. Eyes and ears. Update them on Godunov's car. Tell them if they do locate him, they should *not* try to apprehend him. We want him in one piece, we don't want anyone to spook him. He needs to be interrogated."

Aurora stood, still listening, swiveling into a view of the audience. The open outdoor space was teeming with rain now, her umbrella open, Renee's, too, and the ceremony's invited guests were starting to scatter.

"Already did that, Max," Aurora said. "Ike Barber's the only watch person here outside of Jesse Springer, who just met the president." She did a slow pirouette, looking for her town watch people in the crowd. "But I don't see either Ike or Jesse now."

She checked an app on her phone, a GPS finder that tracked the movements of her town watch participants when they were on patrol. Ike Barber's app was on. Jesse Springer's was not.

"I see Ike on my town watch app. He's moving, heading west on Route

54. Wait. A few other watch folks just showed up on the app. Not sure what's going on."

Renee was next to her now, squinting at the screen and wondering why Aurora was so tense at what she was seeing.

"Max—" Aurora began.

"Yeah?"

"They're *all* on Route 54, already mobilized and heading west, Ike out front. They're converging on Hometown. Less than ten minutes from here. Where are you and Cornell?"

"Farther north and west. You need to get through to your guy ASAP. What's in Hometown?"

"Nothing special. He's not responding to me. None of them are. They must have a lead."

She froze.

Aurora looked Renee squarely in the face, her eyes suddenly wide with recognition. "Max. I know one thing it could be."

"What?" Max and Renee asked in unison.

"A deep pothole, in the middle of the woods. Deep and ornery. An old coal-seam runs through the bottom of it. DEP's been out there. Been burping smoke lately."

Max asked questions but Renee leaned in, interrupting. "Hold on, Max. Aurora—why won't your guys talk to you? What the hell is going on?"

Aurora lowered her phone, exasperated, her expression serious. Her eyes greeted Renee's, resigned, but also apologetic.

"They just heard Godunov's a bad guy. If they find him, they'll kill him."

"Talk to me, Max," Renee said. "Just you and me on the line. I told you what Aurora said about the watch team. Catch me up. Anything from Langley yet on the Eva Biswas brochure?"

"Wilkes said no. Cornell and I and his team are a little busy here, Renee, I gotta go."

"Wait—" she started, but Max was gone.

She found Wilkes's number on her phone. "Wilkes! Where are you?"

"Right here," he said, his voice simultaneously on the phone and behind her.

Their phones away, Renee went into it. "That Eva Biswas brochure. Anything on her?"

"Langley texted me. I'm reading their response now. They didn't find anything, no facial recognition, no fingerprint match. She's apparently clean. Oops—hold on."

He read another text. "A clarification. They say no print match because the brochure shows fingerprints that were surgically altered. Which means we have a problem."

The rain eased up, barely a drizzle now, the umbrellas around them closing, Renee's included.

"But they did find DNA on it," he said, "so they'll run that down."

"Yeah, well, that'll take forever."

"Agreed, but that's where they are."

"Look. Eva Biswas isn't who she says she is." A tongue twister, but she got it right. "She screwed up when she talked to me, Wilkes. She knew I could fly. How she knew I was a pilot, I have no idea. But that decoded internet ad said the advertiser wanted someone to 'pilot it home.' They wanted to hire an assassin, and they knew who they wanted.

"I've got a strong suspicion who Eva Biswas might be. If you include 'assassin' and 'pilot' in the same conversation, my money's on—"

"Bibi Memona Qureshi."

"Exactly. With a lot of work to change her face."

"And her fingerprints."

Qureshi was a Pakistani ex-military pilot who'd gone rogue and disappeared during an international air race around the Mediterranean. The race was a part of a Max and Renee mission, and a reminder that in the spy business, unless there was a dead body, vigilance needed to be forever.

"A strong maybe," Wilkes said. He began texting immediately. "I'm suggesting Langley isolate on her."

"She's hiding in plain sight as Eva Biswas, fully visible social media queen," Renee said.

"Apparently. So why is she here, in the States?"

A pinging text came through to him from Langley.

Memona Qureshi had multiple sniper kills in the Pakistan military. A dual threat, military pilot and shooter.

Wilkes went on alert, checking the stage. The president was sharing a laugh with a senator. "Secret Service needs to get her out of here, *now*."

His phone pinged, and so did Renee's, more texts arriving in rapid fashion. From Cornell, the FBI, Max, Langley, and the Secret Service.

. . . anonymous tips, FBI tip line . . .

. . . multiple calls . . .

. . . high-powered rifle . . .

. . . half a mile . . .

. . . clear shot, low ridge . . .

Additional texts arrived, each agency's personnel shocked by how specific the anonymous calls were.

. . . GPS coordinates. The callers left them.

Wilkes and Renee keyed the coordinates into their phones. The airspace above them, a no-fly zone, already had jets and copters patrolling it, but now the air support would be hearing this information. Renee shielded her eyes from the trickling rain and looked west, toward the ridge where the coordinates led. A straight view, the route a little uphill, with heavy tree cover farther up, maybe an off-road trail in there somewhere. Wilkes hustled to the stage to follow the president as the Secret Service detail ushered her toward Marine One.

Renee bolted, running hard. She passed Myrna's house, circled around front, then hit a full sprint again. She found Max's Ford Bronco, climbed in. She checked her 9mm handgun, re-seated the magazine, belted herself in, and pressed the ignition. The 4x4's transmission slammed into gear. In thirty seconds she found a trail west toward the GPS coordinates. Another thirty seconds and she was off-road, letting the four wheels grind their way up the incline, climbing, climbing . . .

She pulled up Wilkes on her phone. "The president okay?"

"Surrounded by agents but not yet inside Marine One. Where are you?"

"In a four-by-four looking to neutralize the shooter if she's out here. Closing in on the coordinates."

"You *what*? Renee, no—"

"We have the location and helicopters are circling. I'll be their Plan B. I'm just not there yet." She hung up on Wilkes's protests.

The SUV approached an incline, Renee goosing the gas for a head-on thrust at a higher speed. The 4x4 was doing great, taming the hill, in control until it wasn't. The bottom dropped out, an unseen dip that dragged her down into a cleft in the forest floor. The vehicle came out of it like it was on a ski jump, catching air then dropping hard, careening left, her control gone, and losing out to an oak tree that it broadsided.

Renee patted herself down. Bruised, but otherwise fine. She kicked open the driver's-side door and found her feet, then pushed herself up the hill toward a break in the wooded overgrowth, her weapon drawn.

Bibi lay in position on her stomach, her shoulders cramping, watching the U.S. president through the rifle scope go through her paces: cut the ribbon, accept a gift, raise it over her head like an Olympic gold medalist, hug the citizens. Ample time, less rain, easy for her to fire the weapon and stick a bullet anywhere she wanted in her target. But her phone stayed silent, and she was reduced to watching the moment slip away as the president's security detail got spooked and hustled her off stage in the direction of the presidential helicopter. Bibi needed to make it happen *now*, the window was closing, she needed the okay to pull the trigger *now*—

The phone pinged. It was the okay text.

She curled her finger around the trigger, squinted into the scope.

Target acquired.

The tripod jerked right, no shot fired, the rifle booted sideways by an out-of-breath woman in flats, Bibi's gunstock still against her shoulder. A handgun barrel ground into Bibi's temple, a two-handed effort, the camo netting caught between the gun barrel and her head.

"Relax—your grip—on the gun, Bibi. Do it. *Now!*"

She did as told.

"Stay on the ground."

It was Max Fend's girlfriend Renee, and she had the upper hand. She kicked the rifle out of reach.

Except she'd already made a huge mistake: given the chance, she should have pulled the trigger. Renee pulled her gun back, only one hand on it now, she needed room to strip the camo netting off Bibi.

A wrist sheath ejected a retractable dagger into place in Bibi's palm. Bibi shoved the dagger deep into her attacker's shoulder. Renee's handgun dropped as she howled in pain. Bibi sprang, slammed her attacker to the dirt, and drew a 9mm of her own from under her shirt. She stood over Renee and straight-armed her handgun into position, aimed it at her head, at her horrified face, she wouldn't make the same mistake, she'd point and shoot now, no warning, would execute her—

Click. No noise, no recoil, no shell ejection, no shot fired, no bullet delivered into Renee's eye socket. A second trigger pull, and a third. Nothing.

Renee blind-reached for her discarded gun in the dirt, located it, clawed at it—

Bibi tossed her 9mm to the side, retrieved her sniper rifle, nestled the stock against her shoulder and the long barrel against Renee's cheek, applying pressure. She stood on Renee's wrist until Renee could no longer hold her handgun.

Execution time. With one trigger pull, Bibi would obliterate her attacker and get the hell out of there. *Click.* Again, no blast, no bullet, no kill, a shocked Renee staring back at her, a confused Bibi breathing heavily.

Click. Again. *Click.*

The noise of the helicopter's blades preceded its appearance—*whup, whup, whup, whup, whup*—the aircraft hovering, stabilizing, almost stationary, revealing its open side door.

Bibi refocused, staring into the face of a Marine marksman in the copter, his M27 automatic rifle raised shoulder-high, trained on her. She smiled at him and returned her attention to her rifle to give it one more trigger pull, suicidal or not.

Pffft. A bullet pounded Bibi's Kevlar vest, pushing her back. *Pffft, pffft, pffft,* the second shot hit Bibi's neck, the third entered her skull through her left temple, the fourth took off the top of her head. She dropped next to Renee, her body convulsing, her mouth gagging with blood, then the convulsions and the gagging stopped.

A squad of Marines leaped out of the copter and filled the ridge, their weapons trained in all directions. The squad leader stood over the failed assassin before speaking into his headgear.

"Area secure, sir. Threat here is neutralized."

He moved to Renee, who writhed in pain while pulling herself up, the tiny dagger still in her shoulder.

"Let's get you onboard, ma'am, give you some Vitamin M, remove that knife, and triage your wound."

"Need her guns," Renee managed, grimacing, "don't forget her guns, and the ammo . . ."

"For the squad to handle, ma'am. They'll stay here. We're airlifting you to a hospital."

32

Wilkes stood over the dead female assassin on the mountain ridge, talking on the phone with Max and Cornell, who were in Cornell's FBI sedan.

"The president is safe. The Marines took out the threat. But some difficult news, Max. Renee's been wounded. She's in the ER right now. Not life-threatening. A knife wound. Her shoulder."

Max heard nothing after *Renee's been wounded*. "I want your vehicle, Cornell, now. I'm heading back—"

Wilkes became emphatic. "No, Max, no, Renee will be fine. She lost some blood, her shoulder's torn up a little, but she's fine. You guys need to find Godunov. My orders, Max, but they're Renee's orders to you, too. Something was way off about the assassination attempt. Hear me out."

He went through it. Anonymous tips, multiple agencies. How the calls pinpointed the location of the shooter. A just-in-time prevention of an assassination attempt. And, per Renee, the shooter's handgun misfiring just before the shooter shoved a precision rifle in her face, and how Renee listened to the shooter press the trigger three times.

"We have the shooter's equipment, Max, all of it, handgun, precision rifle, ammo for both, her phones. Qureshi was set up. The cartridges for the rifle and the gun—the primer for the cartridges had no propellant and no gunpowder. They weren't even blanks. We think Godunov, or whoever he's working for, set her up."

"Why?"

"For you to find out."

"Not even a guess?"

"Okay. Yes. The assassination attempt. It might have only been a distraction."

"A distraction? What the hell for?"

"Something bigger."

"What could be bigger than the assassination of the president, Wilkes?"

"To be determined, Max. *Find him.*"

<hr />

"I know where they are," Aurora said.

She was on the phone with Max who was in Cornell's FBI sedan, Cornell driving. The sedan was full, two other agents in the back seat, the car cruising Route 54 at a ridiculously high speed. Max put her on speaker.

"Who? Your town watch people?"

"Yeah. Ike and the gang. All in one place, Max, and they're still not talking to me."

"How do you know where they are if no one's talking—"

"Their phones. GPS positioning. Ike eventually turned his off, so did a few others, but not all of them. The idea that *some* of them turned them off ain't sitting well with me, and . . . Son of a—"

"What?"

"Jesse Springer just joined them, according to his phone signal. I was hoping he wasn't part of this. Hell, he was just here, meeting the president. Where are you, Max?"

"Approaching Hometown. We just crossed over the Little Schuylkill River. What's the issue, him being with your guys?"

"Not now. Here, I'm sending you their coordinates. Their GPS shows them deep in those woods, right on top of that pothole. Less than five minutes from where you said you are now."

"We're on it." Max ended the call. He texted Wilkes.

We know where he is. 5 min ETA. Here are coordinates. Going in.

33

Five minutes away by car, but getting to the pothole after exiting their vehicle in the deep woods would be a whole different story.

"Phone GPS says this way," Max announced, a few false starts behind them. They were not geared up to go trudging through the forest like this. A forest that, according to the coordinates, was on another state game land parcel. Per Max's phone, it was about two more minutes to go on foot, but the phone hadn't considered they were underdressed for navigating this terrain.

Six minutes later: "Quiet," Cornell said, one finger to his lips, one hand raised to stop their advance.

His two agents and Max held fast. Cornell's finger tapped the air, pointing in front of them, silently mouthing *There*.

Vegetation and trees still wet from the rain obscured their view, but they could see well enough. They found a thick deadfall and crouched behind it.

The entire Town Watch Twelve, not including unlucky number thirteen Aurora Jolson, surrounded him. Godunov, in a harness and other cave spelunking gear, was on his knees. Attached to the harness was a short length of rope, the rest of the rope knotted against a tree. He leaned back onto his ankles, a more comfortable position, his wrists zip-tied together behind his back, his ankles also zip-tied. Ten yards away, the site of the massive unnamed pothole created by thousands of years of dripping water from a long-ago glacier had been violated, an opening cut through the protective chain link fencing. Ike Barber was in a crouch in front of Godunov, his handgun reholstered; there were enough other handguns visible. He held the rope attached to Godunov's harness and settled into conducting an interrogation.

"I see you brought some guns," Ike said, nodding at an assault-style rifle and a handgun on the far side of the clearing, next to an empty gym bag, a backpack, and a pair of long handle fence cutters. "The guns are for what?"

"Take off these zip ties," Godunov said, scowling, "you have no right—"

"Ah, not gonna do that. Again, what are the guns for?"

"Protection from the bears. I am a mining engineer. I am doing surveillance for Rare Earth Metallurgical regarding the extent of the coal-seam fire. I'm sure you are aware of it." He searched a few of the faces of his captors, pleading his case. "I am doing nothing wrong. My government will be extremely upset about this. I have a right to be here—"

"Yeah, well, no. These are state game lands. There's no game in season, which means you can't have a hunting license, so that means you're not hunting, at least not legally. My associate here—"

Ike acknowledged another watch member with a quick glance, a chunky guy in an orange vest. The man waved his gun hand at Godunov, a casual effort.

"He lives nearby. He saw your Volvo leave the road and head into the woods right after we got some news on you that wasn't very flattering. Going after that underground fire might be the plan, at least for your company, but that's not your plan, is it? Your government doesn't matter here, Mr. Godunov. *My* government says you're working for China. Tell me, why are you here, right here, at this spot, near this pothole?"

"You are correct, I am not a hunter," Godunov said. "I am university professor contracted to do scouting, and to test the stopgap barriers that are in place to keep the coal fire from advancing. Rare Earth intends to go underneath everything and dig it all out. This pothole has shown signs that the Centralia fire has advanced this far."

"Yeah, um, some of that might be true, but again, no. Listen, you Russian bastard, according to my government, and according to what we found in your backpack, you're here to screw things up. These geological surveys, these tiny drawings on the backs of your business cards, they show distances, drill types, timeframes, the GPS points for the DEP boreholes, but with some pretty suspicious X's and the words 'breach here' next to them."

Ike Barber turned one of the business cards over and read more. "Plus this weird little quote. What the hell does this mean, '*His future remained in the past*'?"

"A quote about my namesake, Russian dancer Alexander Godunov, who is deceased. It is meaningful to me, and therapeutic."

"Okay, a little weird, but I guess I don't care," Ike said. "Not sure what you were planning, but let me tell you what *we're* planning. Screw this glacial pothole. No one bothers with it. There's another hole close by that's way more interesting. It'll give you the opportunity to study the coal-seam fire a lot more closely, on your, um, *un*tethered way down. Gentlemen, let's take him over there to that forest floor collapse so this uncooperative jackass can see for himself."

Two men lifted him under his arms and dragged him away from the fenced pothole, toward the other open pit not far in the distance ahead of them.

"You cannot do this. Stop! Please stop this . . ."

The shimmer from the forest floor collapse gave itself up at a distance, twenty, thirty yards ahead, a wide heat funnel rising from the depths.

The men stopped their march, spun Godunov around, and straightened him up to face Ike.

"Beneath this sinkhole, multiple stories deep," Ike said, pointing, "is—well, you get the idea. It's really hot down there."

"Okay. *Okay*," Godunov said. "I have some information. If I give it to you, you do not throw me in the pit. Do we have a deal?"

"Maybe."

"You will want to hear what I have to say."

"Still only a maybe."

Godunov cursed, but not in English. "First, I am not Russian, I am Belarusian."

"So what? We knew that already," Ike said.

"But I do clandestine work for Mother Russia. I—we—want to reverse our recent history. Our struggle with our identity. We want to restore the USSR to its former glory. Belarus, Russia, the old eastern European Soviet republics—we were so much stronger as part of the USSR. Our divided countries are now only shadows of ourselves. Belarus must become the Byelorussian Soviet Socialist Republic once again, and return to the USSR —become part of the proud nation that the USSR was! Our future *is* rooted in our past..."

"Not interested, Godunov. Heard enough. I'm done with this. Jesse, let's hustle this process up."

"President Putin! He is recolonizing Ukraine. He should win that war. He *will* win that war, but it will only be with the help of a very powerful ally: China."

Ike moved closer, his head adopting a sarcastic tilt. "Cut the communist crap," he said, then cuffed the side of Godunov's white-blond head, hard. "Tell me—what the hell does this have to do with exterminating the old coal mine fire?"

"This endeavor, this mining project—it is a thank-you to China from the Russians for supporting them in the Ukrainian war, delivered by way of my country, Belarus! If we shut down these new cobalt mines, China keeps its monopoly on cobalt. If China keeps its monopoly, Beijing keeps sending weapons to Russia to fight Ukraine."

Ike squinted, moving into him again. "Shut down the mines? And you would do that how?"

"Shut down the mines? And you would do that how?"

Cornell spoke in a low voice to his two agents and Max, all of them behind a thick deadfall. "Holster your weapons and keep them there. Follow my lead. On my mark. In three, two, one—"

Cornell called from behind the dead tree, showing his empty hand and waving it.

"Ike. Ike Barber!" He raised his head to make himself visible. "Agent Oakley, FBI." He raised his other hand, showing it was empty, then he stood.

"There are four of us here, Ike. We are armed, but our handguns will stay holstered. We're here to help you sort all this out. Gentlemen, show yourselves."

Max and the two agents stood, their empty hands raised in front of them, palms up. They fanned out and slow-walked their way next to Cornell, approaching Ike and his town watch team.

"Excellent work finding Godunov, Ike. You are to be commended," Cornell said, eying the cuffed prisoner. "The FBI needs to take him into custody immediately. He's a terrorist, he has information we need, and we need it now. A matter of national security. Look, we're all on the same team here, Ike. Hand him over please."

"Put your hands down, Agent Oakley, it's your lucky day," Ike said. "We put the fear of a violent death in him, at the hands of a fiery middle Earth, so he's talking now. Aren't you, Professor Godunov? You were just about to tell us how you and your beloved commie country intended to—what was it you said? Shut down the mines? To help China?"

Max was in analysis mode. Ike Barber, Jesse Springer, their watch team, they all showed weapons, a side of them he hadn't seen before. Ike held his position next to the white-haired Belarusian he'd backed up to near the lip of what looked and smelled like a burning coal sinkhole. Godunov was restrained with zip ties, his wrists twisted behind his back. The prisoner's torso had a harness around it, shoulders to waist, with a small length of rope hanging from his chest. Ike had a hold of the rope. Godunov was dressed for—what? Cave crashing? Rock climbing?

While Cornell talked, Max about-faced and retraced the path Ike's group had taken, back to the pothole, leaving Cornell to do the negotiating. Max ducked through the cut in the fence to get a closer look at the massive hole, to look directly into its mouth. Its steep, sharp-edged, conical walls reached beyond where he could see, ominous and way dark down there. Where he was at ground level he found Godunov's detritus: a helmet with the headlamp still on; a length of heavy rope; an empty gym bag; wire cutters; two guns, one a handgun, one a long gun; phones; and an over-sized, heavy backpack.

Max returned to Cornell and the team, Cornell still negotiating, the physical distance between him and Ike a little shorter. Godunov was still restrained, still the town watch's prisoner.

"Aren't you guys a little out of your jurisdiction?" Cornell asked.

"There is no jurisdiction for what we do," Ike said.

"This needs to end now, Ike," Cornell said. "You can't do this. It's the wrong approach."

"This bastard—the Russians—they're here, in our country, Oakley, pulling crap like this. I had enough of these commies in Afghanistan. I was face to face with them, up close and personal and all that, for two years. But whenever that happened, we didn't stay face to face for long."

Ike was seething, gritting his teeth. He backed Godunov up to the edge of the hellish sinkhole again, still with a hold on the rope. "Tell us what you were planning before we stopped you, damn it, or so help me God—"

"Ike," Max called, interjecting, "hold on. You said you stopped him. Before what? Before he climbed into the pothole? You sure about that?"

"He was kneeling next to it with the rope tied to his harness, Fend, looking in. He was ready to climb down—"

Max tossed the unzipped backpack, which took some effort because it was a bit heavy. It thudded on the ground a few feet from Ike. "What did you find in this backpack? You went through it, I'm sure. What was in it?"

"Papers, geology maps. Business cards with a helluva lot of damning info handwritten on them. Look, Fend—"

"It's got a lead lining, Ike. It's empty but it's still heavy, and he was only using it to *carry paper*? He wasn't on his way into the pothole. You caught him on his way out."

All eyes turned to their prisoner. A crush of rain hit the tree canopy above them, a heavy shower slipping through it, starting to leak big, heavy drops.

"What was in the backpack, Godunov?" Max said. "A lot of people here want to hurt you. Tell me what was in it, or maybe we let them."

"My country's future," he said, defiant, "inside a lead-lined bag brought here in the lead-lined trunk of a lead-lined car."

This was it. This was the other TBD event the botched assassination attempt was meant to mask.

"It's radioactive," Max decided for them. "Whatever was in that bag—it's radioactive."

Ike shoved his gun under Godunov's chin, his finger on the trigger. "What the hell was in that bag? And where the hell is it?"

"A bowling ball, with lead underneath its resin surface," Godunov said, his voice calm, "and cobalt-60 in its core. The ball is now in the pothole. Not that far down, actually, too much methane farther down. Too volatile."

Max's face splotched crimson, hot enough that the rainwater hitting his face should have sizzled. He went at Godunov, side by side with a bewildered Ike. Voices around the clearing perked up, the men looking at their phones, Max needing to get it straight from Godunov, so Max could spin it before his audience googled and figured out the severity of the situation. Otherwise, panic would settle in, and everyone might decide to bolt.

He pulled himself nose to nose with Godunov, his eyes drilling him. "You're saying there's a dirty bomb inside that pothole."

"Don't worry, there's probably enough lead to keep you from getting poisoned from the radiation if you're able to get at the sample before it goes off. But when it gets hot enough down there, with all that methane," Godunov's smile broadened, "it will destabilize underground. Above ground, too, over a wide area, including the mines, inside and out. An explosion with a small amount of cobalt-60 and high concentrations of methane . . . the chain reaction can convert unmined cobalt, if the concentrations are pure enough, into more cobalt-60. If there's as much pure cobalt underground as the geologists say there is . . . Well, do I need to continue?"

Max wanted to do what Ike wanted to do, shove this smug jackass into the fiery underworld abyss waiting in the sinkhole behind him. Rain ran down both their faces. "Listen, smart guy. I'm sure we screwed up this whole plan of yours by showing up like this. That assassination attempt happened over half an hour ago. That means *this* event, this dirty bomb here, should have happened already if the fake assassination was meant to be a distraction. And your bomb is late because *you're* late in making it happen, because Ike's people ambushed you. You have control of this. You'd never leave the detonation open-ended. Tell me how it will be detonated."

Godunov squirmed, a little less smug, but said nothing.

Max yelled to Cornell. "Go back to the pothole, find an angle where you can see what he's talking about." At Godunov: "You expected to be far away from this thing when it went off, right? Is there a timer? Something wireless?"

No response. But the sweat on Godunov's forehead and the fear in his eyes said Max was in the right ballpark. "Ike! His phones. Where are they?"

"I have the one he was carrying. Another one's back at the pothole."

Max grabbed the rope that led from Godunov's harness and pulled. "Let's take a walk, or in your case," he looked at his prisoner's ankles, "a hop. Careful, it's getting slick out here."

At the pothole, Ike handed Max both phones. He held them up in front of Godunov.

"Which one?"

"Stop this charade, Fend," Godunov said. "I can't control it. When it gets hot enough in there—could be today, could be tomorrow, could be next week—that's when it will happen. So we should all really go."

"WHICH—ONE?" Max demanded. "Tell me, or I start pushing each button on each phone, one by one."

"That means you're willing to kill everyone here including yourself."

"Nope. I'll let everyone leave except you and me. Which one, Godunov?"

Godunov's lips stayed shut.

"Max!" Cornell called across to him from the other side of the pothole, his binoculars raised. "We see it! It's not too far down, on a ledge. It's an ugly-ass cobalt bluish green. So tired of that color. Plus—I see now—there's what looks like a wad of plastic explosive on its top, and a device with a blasting cap."

Max put his hand on Godunov's harness, gritting his teeth as he one-arm lifted the man onto his toes.

"Like I said, Godunov, its detonation isn't open-ended. That means we can fix this. And we will fix it, after we get the right personnel here, with the right protection, to retrieve that thing and neutralize it. Ike, watch him, please. I need to get a closer look at what Cornell sees, and then I need to make some calls."

Ike moved in, grabbed Godunov by the collar and shoved him to the ground, the rain getting heavier. Ike's outstretched arm had his handgun at the end of it, aimed at the terrorist's face.

Max called Wilkes, speaking rapidly to him while pacing around the pothole, needing a look at what Cornell found, swiping away the bigger raindrops as they ran down his face.

"We've got Godunov, Wilkes . . . Yes, he's alive, but we have a situation here. We're going to need a bomb squad outfitted head-to-toe in gear that'll protect them from radiation. We'll need a lead-lined container and transport, also because of potential radiation. That dirty bomb hypothetical? Not hypothetical anymore. Cobalt-60, Wilkes, inside a lead-covered bowling ball with a plastic explosive slopped on its top half, then planted inside a pothole in the direct path of the coal-seam fire. We need to get someone to fish it out, then it'll need a cleared route to a radiation processing site. We'll also need—we'll also need—ah, wait, hold on . . . Oh no. Nonono—"

Max didn't see how it happened, the slanted, heavy rain distorting the view, didn't see what made their prisoner suddenly roll off the ground-level mud and grass at the top of the pothole and slip over its side. Max caught up only after Godunov was already on the way down, his head and torso and zip-tied wrists and ankles scraping the jagged ridges of the wall, bumping the sharp rock, the other abutments, loosening the dirt and the pebbles enough for them to follow him in his wake. He flipped head over butt, slamming stomach-first into a cleft in the wall where the bowling ball bomb had been firmly tucked, his compacted body curling around it for a pause in his descent. In a rain-canceling, stop motion flash of a moment, the terror on Godunov's face was so palpable it reached across the emptiness and found Max. When Godunov and the jostled bomb left their perch together, his legs pulled up to cradle it into his midsection, his horrified expression gone, replaced by a mad scientist's smile. The déjà-vu of it all surfaced when they heard him begin yelling in his best Slim Pickens *Dr. Strangelove* voice.

"*Yahooooo! Wa-HOOOOO!*"

Max resisted the urge to run; they all did. If—when—the mini dirty bomb went off, there'd be no safe distance they could reach in the time they had. The carbon-60 detonation would rip through the fiery coal seam fortified by heavy concentrations of methane, would find the unmined cobalt, would fuel and refuel a chain reaction with the help on an additional isotope created by each reaction. They stood mesmerized, watching, listening, praying . . .

The thud they heard coincided with a grunt and tiny peep of a shriek, too little breath in Godunov's lungs to do otherwise, his spirited yahoos and wahoos gone. Left behind were the sounds of rainwater dripping from tall trees onto its leaves below, into a doomed forest. They waited, collectively expecting the end: a flash, a change in air pressure, an explosion from the depths of the pothole, something. But the forest remained silent, except for the patter of the rain.

Max and Cornell sprinted to where Ike Barber and Jesse Springer stood leaning over the edge. Ike shone a military-grade super flashlight at the floor of the pothole. Still too dark to see anything down there. He fished a small pair of binoculars from a waist holster.

"They're infrared," he said to Max. "I was a Boy Scout."

Ike tested his footing on the wet ledge and leaned over. He adjusted the focus, then handed the binoculars to Max. By now a few of Ike's watch members had already left, not giving fate another chance.

The pothole had no definitive bottom, no visible floor, ending only where the telescoped, tornado-like caving funneled into a small, increasing depth of puddled rainwater. Godunov lay on his side in the puddle, gashed, bloodied, his eyes and mouth open in a dead man's silent scream with his body still cradling the bomb against his crushed chest, having cushioned the impact. From this height and distance, the bomb appeared intact.

Max adjusted the focus on the binoculars to zoom in closer. Oh-oh. Not so fast, damn it.

"Mayday, Cornell, mayday! That thing is leaking!"

The wireless detonator, stuffed into a ball's fingerhole like a cork in a wine bottle—a chunk of the detonator was intact, occupying one half of the fat hole, but the other half—

It was empty, allowing the gray-blue powdery mini-chunks inside it an easy exit, spilling onto Godunov's chest. Cobalt-60, per Godunov's admission, in powder form.

"We need to retreat *now*," Max yelled. "Go, go, go!"

The Marine helicopter landed in Jesse Springer's backyard, directly on top of the clearing vacated by the president's departed helicopter. Cornell, his FBI agents, plus Ike, Jesse, and three other town watch members were now passengers. Max sat strapped into a seat in a private Fend Aerospace copter nearby, about to lift off for the hospital where Renee was being treated. One thing Max and the other men all had in common in addition to their prospective radiation poisoning: When they exited the area near the pothole, they were all naked, having shed their clothing on the way out. Max held a Mylar emergency blanket around him while on the phone with Wilkes, who was with Renee at the hospital.

"They gave me an anti-radiation injection already, Wilkes. We all tested positive. Someone will need to track down the watch members who got spooked and left early. How's Renee?"

"She's convalescing. They kicked me out of her room. She's been updated, is asking for you, Max, but you'll need a good hazmat scrub before you get in to see her. Did the bomb squad arrive yet?"

"They came with the Marines," Max said. "Hazmatted up well enough for a walk on the moon. How about a transport vehicle for the cobalt-60?"

"A trailer with radiation containment casks arrives tonight. The roads will close for it. A large concern is moving the bomb out of the forest, from the pothole to the truck."

"Yeah, well, Godunov walked it in, in a backpack. These bomb squad guys have an ATV with balloon tires, so they should do fine getting it out. They'll also need to find our clothes; we left them in a pile back there in the woods.

"A bigger concern, Wilkes, will be cleaning it off Godunov's body. The cobalt-60 was loose, in powder form. Whatever form it was before—maybe disks inside the small lead container, inside the leaded ball, there might even still be tiny cobalt-60 disks in there, too—some of it was crushed into fairy dust and spilled all over his chest, and the rain made it a gloppy mess. They put Geiger counters on us, Wilkes. We're all dosed, we just don't know how much."

"Max, I'm sorry."

"Yeah, well, we'll deal with it. When the bomb guys get here, they're going to flip out. They'll need to seal Godunov's body inside a radiation cask at the bottom of the pothole, haul the cask out, probably with a winch, and keep the body sealed for the life of the sample. How long is that again?"

"Half-life is more than five years," Wilkes said. "They'll test it to see how old it is already. But I'm missing a big piece here, Max."

"As in what?"

"Godunov at the bottom of that hole with powdered cobalt-60 on him. How'd that happen?"

Max didn't want to talk about it, but his glance at the other copter was a tell. It carried FBI agents paid to enforce the law, plus town watch volunteers who put their lives on the line, but for free. He preferred they didn't put them under a microscope.

"I think he, ah, slipped. Heavy rain, slick grass, mud. I didn't see it happen, only saw the bomb shake loose from inside the pothole on his way down."

It was what Ike and Jesse had told him before Ike short-circuited the explanation with a shrug and an *oops*. Max hadn't pursued it. Cornell didn't intend to either.

"And Wilkes, another thing. The excavation work supposed to eliminate the coal fire? Godunov's rogue operators were there to weaken the existing underground fire barriers in place to contain it, not strengthen them..."

Exploding a bomb with radioactive cobalt in it would produce fallout and chance a chain reaction: fire, methane, unmined cobalt synthesizing into more cobalt-60 as a byproduct, then another explosion, more fire, more methane, more fallout. Worse than a dirty bomb because it could perpetuate itself until it ran out of fuel, maybe render the entire northeast corner of Pennsylvania uninhabitable.

"Rare Earth didn't stay on top of their contractors. They've got a lot of explaining to do, even after our government fires them."

"All right, all right, Max, I get it. Take a breath. Someone here wants to talk with you. I'm back in her room. You should stay away from the doomsday language while you're on with her, okay? I don't think she's feeling it. Here."

"Hi, Max honey," Renee said. "It sounds like both of us had a difficult day."

34

Two months later

The fascia for the savings and loan building's cornerstone had been resealed and the engraved metal plate re-bolted to its front. A stainless steel box with contemporary keepsakes were inside—a new time capsule—with additional markings on the plate indicating as much, and newly engraved with a "Do Not Open Until" date set 150 years from now. The original contents of the cornerstone, and the 1873 time capsule that held Günther Heintz's *kobold* journal, were on display in the Jim Thorpe Historical Society main office.

There'd been a late addition to the capsule. The White House had reached out to Myrna and the town, asking if President Windcolor could make a donation. A proclamation on Presidential stationery signed *"President Faye"* accompanied her gift.

"To the citizens of Jim Thorpe, Pennsylvania, the United States of America, and the rest of the planet:

"Be it known to all that this beautiful blue-green cobalt brick shall forever be known as Wyatt's Kryptonite in honor of nine-year-old Wyatt Springer, son of Myrna Nechoha Springer, both of Nesquehoning, Pennsylvania. Wyatt discovered it on their property on a warm March morning during my presidency, and thus

began America's successful search for, and the provision of, domestically-sourced
cobalt, greatly assisting our endeavors to clean our air."

The blue-green and brown rock-brick enjoyed no adornment, squeezed
inside a red beach bucket, going full commando with a yellow sand shovel,
all placed inside the metal box that was the capsule. Heat-sealed along with
the president's proclamation was a photograph of a three-legged dog sitting
next to her bestest buddy, both smiling for the camera, and a note hand-
printed on an index card:

"Little Pig's dogcrap wouldn't pick itself up." –Wyatt Springer

Eunice Ahoma, age eighty-two, on record as the first person to lose her
frame home to the Centralia coal fire, was at a dais in front of the savings
and loan. Max and Renee, at the rear of the crowd, knew her as their
neighbor from the RV park.

Wearing a black flat-brimmed hat with a colorful hand-beaded hat
band above her braided gray hair, and an ancient leather vest over a new
cobalt-blue bohemian dress, Eunice appeared neither nervous nor intimi-
dated. She leaned in close to the microphone. A man in a silver hardhat
held up his phone to broadcast her on FaceTime once she gave the
command. Awaiting her words were the more than twenty demolition
experts on the other end of the FaceTime call, stationed loosely around the
perimeter of an area encompassing more than five hundred square miles in
northeastern Pennsylvania.

"I am told, my dear friends, that we will feel the detonations even here,"
Eunice said into the microphone, "so brace yourselves. Are you ready?"

The crowd of a hundred-plus people responded, nearly in unison,
"Ready!"

"Wonderful. You know what to say. On my mark, everyone raise your
voices and say it with me. Three—two—one—"

"Fire in the hole!"

She was correct. The ground rumbled, the amazed crowd buzzed, and
folks held onto each other as the newest contractor in the cobalt mining
sweepstakes detonated multiple underground charges that had been strate-
gically placed, as best as could be determined, around the perimeter of the
infamous, amorphous coal fire. The beginning of the end of its sixty-year
reign of terror. Additional explosive charges lay in wait, if necessary. Then it

would be excavation and extinction by working inward toward Centralia, digging as far down as needed, and creating a crater that distant future generations might even confuse with a meteorite strike. Max and Renee embraced each other as the ground trembled, Max protecting Renee's recovering shoulder from jostling, Renee removing Max's baseball cap to tousle his full head of brown hair. A reassurance for her that the hair was still there, that he'd survived the radiation poisoning, and that he would continue to do so. He'd absorbed less than one gray of radiation from the cobalt-60, with minor vomiting and some diarrhea being the extent of his contamination. Incredibly lucky.

Max re-snugged his cap. His eyes roamed, absorbing the crowd, settling on familiar faces.

Eunice Ahoma, if she lived long enough, said she'd be one of the first to repopulate the dead town, even if that only meant relocating her '63 International Harvester to one of her "somewhere elses," her former Centralia address.

Aurora Jolson stood with her gun shop owner friend Russ. "They're more than in lust with each other," Myrna had snarked. They were fooling themselves, but no one else. Aurora reached for Russ's hand and connected.

Cornell Oakley, Assistant Special Agent in Charge, FBI, was there on his own time, as was Wilkes, both wanting to share in the celebration of the region's turnaround. They stood together on the crowd's fringe nonchalanting their interest in the festivities, sipping takeout Blue Kryptonite lattes, a new Canaries coffee shop concoction, the ingredients the same as a Liquid Carbon but with cobalt blue spirulina powder added. Supply chain issues for lithium batteries had eased once the Pennsylvania cobalt mines became operational. More parity in worldwide cobalt production meant China no longer held all the cards.

Ike Barber's baseball cap covered the small bald patches scattered around his scalp. His radiation exposure had been more serious. He kept a lower profile these days, which was true for today as well. He and Max connected across the crowd. Max tipped his hat to him, no smile, his feelings about Ike and his town watch folks still mixed. Ike reciprocated with the same lack of enthusiasm. The Town Watch Twelve would need to recruit more members, minus two since the episode at the pothole. It might soon be minus at least one more.

Myrna Springer was in the middle of the crowd, her arm around Wyatt, who had fully recovered from the artisanal mine collapse. Jesse Springer stood with them, his arm around Myrna. With the ceremony over, she excused herself from Jesse and Wyatt and made her way over to Max and Renee.

"Is today goodbye?" she said to Max.

"I'm afraid so. My Winnebago was picked up this morning. When do you move into your new home?"

"A change in plans," she said. Her glance behind her, plus a wave, acknowledged Jesse and her son chatting with other celebrants in the street, Jesse's arm around Wyatt's shoulder. A sheepish smile emerged. "Jesse and I are going to give it a shot together. We're looking for a place."

Not a shocker for Max and Renee, but still a surprise. What had surfaced during and after the national—international—crisis they'd all experienced had been some highly protected, small-town drama. Unflattering behavior that, until now, had been secret: Vigilantism hidden behind the Town Watch Twelve. When anyone who screwed with, or mistreated, someone in or around Jim Thorpe, the Town Watch Twelve screwed with them. All off the record, no police involvement, no legal system encumbrances, and no punishment too severe, including elimination.

When confronted about Godunov's "slip" at the unnamed Carbon County pothole, small "p," Ike Barber had fessed up this behavior to Max, the two of them next to one another in a Navy hospital being treated for radiation poisoning, Ike's prognosis much worse. Ike had dished first, about the Godunov *oopsie* that wasn't. Then came additional contrition. The stuff of deathbed confessions. It matched what Renee had uncovered, speculated about, and shared with Max beforehand, and she had nailed it.

Ken Springer never took that plane ride with Ike and Jesse. There'd been no rehab intervention masquerading as a hunting trip invitation, because there was no hunting trip. The last straw for Jesse had been the beating Ken delivered to Myrna that nearly deafened her in one ear. Jesse, Ken's own brother, had seen enough. He'd shot Ken in the head.

Jesse and Ike tossed his body into a steamy sinkhole right off Main

Street in Centralia in the dead of night, a hole that had previously consumed a church.

"You might say it was a Christian burial for him," Ike told Max with a straight face from his hospital bed, "even though he didn't deserve it."

The truth was, according to Ike, "There are other bodies down there, like Eunice Ahoma's worthless sack of a grandson. No one else you would know—would ever want to know—but they're down there."

Myrna leaned in, gave Max a kiss on the cheek, then did likewise with Renee. After an extended thank-you she retreated to her son, hanging with Jesse, who'd already granted Wyatt a large ice cream cone with chocolate sprinkles.

Cornell and Wilkes joined Max and Renee on the street. Their glances coalesced on Myrna at the ice cream shop, who was now assisting Wyatt in the maintenance of his dripping cone.

They all knew the score. The disaster they'd prevented, the assassination attempt that was really only a distraction. The lives that would be profoundly changed by new industry in a region that had been beaten back through no fault of its own, and was now getting another chance. Plus the gruesome ongoing truth about what the town watch did to problematic, local evil players who'd deserved to be eliminated, and had.

Myrna learned, through an intervention in Jesse's home, what had happened to her husband, and by whose hand. Learned who the people were who'd known about it, and the people who'd looked the other way. Ike summed up the intervention for Max.

"She never wanted him back. She only wanted closure. She got both. And she forgives Jesse."

The crowd was dispersing. Max and Renee led Wilkes and Cornell up the street. It would be one last latte for each of them before their departures.

Max spoke as they walked, to Cornell, but he was addressing them all. "So we're in agreement then?"

"About?" Cornell asked.

"Jim Thorpe's town watch. No additional investigations by the Bureau?" A glance at Wilkes. "Or the Agency? Aurora confirmed the local cops are on board with this."

They left the curb and entered the street, no vehicle traffic, cordoned off at this intersection because of the ceremony at the bank. It was a beautiful day in the neighborhood.

"What do you think, Wilkes?" Cornell said. "What happens in Vegas . . . ?"

"I'm good with it," Wilkes said, "there's a casino around here some-where. But tell me this, Max."

"What?"

"You still feeling lucky?"

"Don't you know it, Wilkes. Always."

"That's good, Max," Wilkes said, nodding. "That's very good."

Cradle
Maximum Risk #2

Max Fend's expertise. One girl's fury. A universe on the brink.

Max Fend's world orbits around the marvels of the stars above. As an integral cog in the imminent Artemis moon mission and the heartbeat of Fend Aerospace, he's accustomed to challenges that stretch beyond the Earth's atmosphere. Yet he's entirely unprepared for the force of nature that is Gus Gomez.

Gus isn't just a resourceful Peruvian immigrant harboring an indigenous leather pouch steeped in mystery, she's a maelstrom of history, fleeing dark shadows while simultaneously careening toward a cosmic destiny. The pouch she carries contains a crucible of secrets, and it has the potential to upend humanity's understanding of its place in the universe.

As a storm of ancient secrets and vendettas swirls, Max is thrust into the fray. But with Gus's fiery determination and enemies closing in, can Max navigate the dangers and keep the past's revelations from shattering the future?

Chris Bauer's *Cradle* crafts a tale woven in the tapestry of borderland stories and punctuated by the promise of space in the latest adrenaline-packed installment of the Maximum Risk series.

ACKNOWLEDGMENTS

Andrew Watts, who extended to me the privilege of adding to the Max Fend legacy of high-stakes thrillers.

Dave Jarret, Russ Allen, Jen Giacalone, and Kathleen Madigan. Peer writers, critiquers, and beta readers.

Don Swaim, author and moderator of the Bucks County Writers Workshop.

Daniel Dorian, author, journalist.

Randall Klein, content editor, author.

Cassie Gitkin, copyeditor, proofreader.

Unidentified Greenland blogger/author: https://www.grimble.de/Greenland2007/greenland2.html

Paula Froelich, "A Broad Abroad," in a Greenland microbrewery: "It might smell like feet, but it tastes like heaven." https://www.youtube.com/watch?v=EMJ4pdMlexE

"She'll Be Coming 'Round the Mountain," a traditional railroading folk song, lyrics by Carl Sandburg, music by Oliver Wallace, 1927.

ABOUT THE AUTHOR

"The thing I write will be the thing I write."

Chris wouldn't trade his northeast Philly upbringing of street sports played on blacktop and concrete, fistfights, brick and stone row houses, and twelve years of well-intentioned Catholic school discipline for a Philadelphia minute (think New York minute but more fickle and less forgiving). Chris has had some lengthy stops as an adult in Michigan and Connecticut, and he thinks Pittsburgh is a great city even though some of his fictional characters do not. He still does most of his own stunts, and he once passed for Chip Douglas of *My Three Sons* TV fame on a Wildwood, NJ boardwalk. He's a member of International Thriller Writers, and his work has been recognized by the National Writers Association, the Writers Room of Bucks County (PA), and the Maryland Writers Association. He likes the pie more than the turkey.

Sign up to receive exclusive updates from author Chris Bauer.

severnriverbooks.com

Printed in the United States
by Baker & Taylor Publisher Services